EZEKIEL'S SHADOW

EZEKIEL'S SHADOW

DAVID RYAN LONG

THORNDIKE PRESS
An imprint of Thomson Gale, a part of The Thomson Corporation

THOMSON
™
GALE

Detroit • New York • San Francisco • New Haven, Conn. • Waterville, Maine • London

LIBRARY OF CONGRESS CATALOGING-IN-PUBLICATION DATA

Long, David Ryan.
  Ezekiel's shadow / by David Ryan Long.
    p. cm.
  ISBN-13: 978-0-7862-9298-1 (hardcover : alk. paper)
  ISBN-10: 0-7862-9298-9 (hardcover : alk. paper)
  1. Large type books. I. Title.
PS3562.O4926E94 2007
813'.6—dc22   2006033617

Published in 2007 by arrangement with Bethany House Publishers.

Printed in the United States of America on permanent paper
10 9 8 7 6 5 4 3 2 1

For Sarah,
on whom I continue to lean.

Nothing seems so foolish as to go on
writing merely because people expect you
to write.
— Thomas Merton

PROLOGUE

Ian Merchant tried to write of death but found no words. Though the bookcases in his office sagged beneath the weight of his previous efforts — over a half dozen tomes devoted to darkness and terror — when he closed his eyes now he saw only the real thing, and it was nothing he wanted to put to paper. Howard Kepler had died in the worst possible way, and anything Ian wrote seemed cheap and simple compared to what his friend and mentor had suffered. Shutting down his computer, Ian scribbled a note for Rebecca, who was still at her evening class. Then he fled his house for a quick car ride into the bustle of downtown Titansburg, hoping the change of scenery might provide answers to the two fierce questions that dogged his days and dreams: *How will I ever write another horror novel?* And, *Who am I if I can't write anymore?*

Entering a quiet café at the end of

Gryphon Street — too far to walk for most of the summer tourists still clogging the town — Ian ordered an iced coffee and seated himself next to a window, under a chrome lobster-pot sculpture that dangled on fishing line from the ceiling. Out of habit he pulled a note pad from his jeans pocket, but he doubted that it would be filled with words by evening's end. Or at least the right words — sentences and scenes that he could send to his editor to prove he was still Ian Merchant, horror novelist. Staring at the blank square of paper before him, the same two questions whispered through his mind, and he had to look up to keep from shuddering.

Dusk was slowly gathering. With the darkness, the café window clouded with Ian's own reflection, a face journalists had described with base poeticism ever since his first nightmare had tumbled into bookstores a dozen years ago. His brown eyes were always "brooding and grim," his jaw "set," his brow "angry." They never failed to notice the thin scar that followed the curve of his chin. Ian stared at himself now, his image growing clearer as the evening's darkness swam in off the Connecticut coast. He recognized nothing of what those reporters had seen.

Instead he saw weariness and sorrow and frustration all piled on shoulders that had never been very broad in the first place. The odd thing, though, was that he didn't feel the weight of all his concerns as deeply as in years past. They affected him, to be sure — his eyes were heavy and somber, his brown curls were snarled — but beyond those feelings was something larger, something new for which he had no words and could only think of as *life.* It didn't make the questions, the worries, or the grief disappear, but it did make them manageable, as though their full weight didn't land on his narrow back. In April, when he'd visited Howard Kepler in Utah and gone on a weekend hike that ended in glory and a shallow baptism, Ian had felt all strains disappear. Upon returning, though, the same blank page stared him in the face, and the same demands flowed in from Louis, his editor. Then Howard died and the worries continued to gather. Ian didn't know how much longer he could hold them off. The questions needed answers, and so far he had found nothing that resembled a solution.

Voices roused Ian from his thoughts, and in the window's reflection he saw three men pass his table, heard them whispering his name as they settled into their chairs just to his left. If one approached he'd know they were tourists; if they let him be, they were townies, content to let their local celebrity have a few moments' peace without haranguing him for an autograph. Minutes passed without any of the men returning, so Ian allowed his eyes to move from the window to his empty note pad. He picked up his pen and tried an exercise he'd used in college, writing the first word that came to his mind. *Vacant.* He paused for a moment, pen ready, but like every other word he'd written in the past weeks, this one refused elaboration. He tried the exercise again and once more was granted a single word. After a half dozen more tries he had a neat column of words that meant nothing and could have been a laundry list for all their significance. He was about to try just once more when a voice interrupted.

"Is this where you write all your stories?"

Ian turned. One of the men who'd passed earlier, a thick-torsoed man with buzzed salt-and-pepper hair, waited for his response. Next to him a much younger fellow with a ruddy goatee grinned across the table. The third had disappeared for the moment.

"No," Ian finally answered. "Just thought a little java might prime the pumps. An old college habit."

The first man smiled. "Prime the pumps? I thought your words never stopped."

Ian shrugged; he didn't want to say his source had gone barren. Thankfully, the third of their party — a wiry fellow with a noticeable hitch in his step — returned with his drink, and the three men went back to their conversation. Ian looked to his pad, picked up his pen, and again wrote the first thing that came to him. It was easy.

Dry. Then: *I have run dry.*

Not the words he wanted to see. He tore the sheet from the pad and was balling it to be thrown out when the fellow at the table nearby spoke once more.

"Mr. Merchant," he said, "we were wondering if you could help us with something." Ian turned to look at him. "It's a writing question, and we figure since you're an author, why not go to the expert?"

Ian answered two questions about point-of-view for the men after they'd introduced themselves, and while they were thinking up a third he sat back and looked at them, wondering if a more incongruous mix could ever have gathered in the name of a writers group. In a way it pleased him, because it showed their dedication, but in another way it was just plain odd. He looked from one to the other and took each in, thankful for the break from his mute pen and barren pad of paper.

On Ian's left rocked Kevin Contrade. At first Ian thought the man had a spasm, perhaps even something medical, but soon he realized it was just a habit, a quick and constant bounce of the hips that kept the man nearly always in motion. Other than that, Ian knew little. Contrade hadn't asked a question yet, hadn't volunteered any personal information, hadn't even sustained more than a few seconds' worth of eye contact.

Next to Kevin sat Jaret Chapman, who'd needed the others at the table to back his claim of being twenty-four. Not only was his face young, but his entire demeanor struck Ian as collegiate. The incessant way he stroked his goatee, the sudden bursts of conversation, even his phrasing resembled the flock of undergrads who spent their summer breaks waiting tables and tending shops throughout Titansburg as a way to be on the coast. It didn't help that Jaret had said he was a seminary student — still mired in classes, still under the educational gun.

Finally, on Ian's right was Peter Ray, who said he was the owner of a camping outfitters store a few miles away. The man looked as though he'd spent more than a few days scaling mountains and hiking vast stretches of thick forest. He was in his upper forties and his hair was graying, but his shoulders were massive and the cut of his arms shamed Ian a little. Still, his voice was gentle and his eyes and face reminded Ian of someone he couldn't place but knew he liked. He was still trying to make the connection when Jaret asked the next question.

"How important do you think it is to have an ending in mind when you write?"

Ian nodded. It was the question that supposedly divided the artists from hacks like himself, and he'd argued it at writers conferences more than a few times. Now it seemed like a quaint idea, silly even. How could he be worried about an ending when his beginning was nowhere in sight? He blinked once or twice, pushed that thought away, and answered as best he could.

"I think there's no question that if you write toward an ending you limit your story's possibility. But that's not always a bad thing. Focus, especially at first, is good.

13

Plus, if you have a deadline looming, it helps to take the straight path rather than the long and winding one." He hoped he didn't wince as he spoke. The men seemed not to notice.

"Is that how you typically write?" asked Kevin finally.

"Typically," Ian answered, aware that nearly all his words now were tinged white with lying. He wanted the subject changed quickly, so he asked how the group had formed. Pete and Jaret both turned their heads toward Kevin, and for a fraction of a second the man stopped rocking. Just as quickly, though, he picked it up again and explained.

"On my off hours from teaching, I'm a part-time editor at the *Titan*," he said, then paused. "The weekly paper?"

Ian nodded.

"I get free classifieds — big whoop — and put in an ad about starting a writers group. These two answered, and here we are. Actually, one other guy called as well, some freak from South Joneston." He rolled his eyes a bit. "He told me over the phone that he was a vampire. I said, 'Unfortunately, the group is full.' But I suppose you've seen those folks once or twice in your life."

Ian nodded. He'd come across nearly

everything in his years of author tours — a guy who thought he was a vampire was mild compared to some of the people who showed up.

"Who was the weirdest?" Jaret asked. The young man looked as if he wanted to be shocked.

"Well," answered Ian, thinking, "there were lots of people with their teeth filed to fangs. They always scared me. And I met a woman who somehow managed to make all her clothes out of tanned ostrich skin." A thought came to him. "The weirdest, though, was probably the guy who'd been tattooed with jaguar spots all over his body." Ian shook his head and added without thinking, "Thank goodness I'm done with all that."

The others stared at him. Kevin's rocking stalled once more, and Jaret cocked his head slightly. Ian finally realized what he said as Pete leaned forward onto one of his massive forearms and fixed Ian with his steady gray eyes.

"Done?"

The way it was said, mildly yet with great weight, and the concern in the man's eyes finally triggered recognition for Ian. Something about Peter Ray reminded him greatly of Howard Kepler. Kepler had been a tiny elf of a man, skipping across the desert like a hungry jackal, while this Pete was thick and solid, but still, each had a way of looking at Ian that made him feel exposed and understood at the same time. They saw into him — transparent as could be — yet managed to like him regardless.

"You're giving up on book signings and author tours?" Pete now asked.

Ian shook his head noncommittally. He was still trying to figure out this absurd link between a man who'd led him to the very throne of God and a second man he knew not at all. Rationally there were a number of reasons to simply ignore the similarity, but Ian knew life couldn't be lived on those terms anymore. Irrationality was the reason he'd visited Howard Kepler in the first place, and the same inexplicable urging that had led him to Utah — and then to his knees — nudged him now about Peter Ray.

"Well, I'm just not sure I want to be a horror novelist for the rest of my life."

Silence followed. Jaret's mouth parted in surprise, and Kevin resumed his bouncing with even more vigor, though he kept his head down and refused to make eye contact. Ian knew the next words would have to be his own, and he suddenly felt ludicrous sitting there, opening his life to a table of strangers. Peter Ray was not Howard Kepler. He cleared his throat and gave a thin smile.

"Of course, it could be just a literary midlife crisis — Faulkner giving up novels for a chance to pen Hollywood dialogue." The others smiled with him, and the joke seemed to break the tension. He knew he needed to get out of there before he managed to say anything else ridiculous. Standing, he apologized to the men for rambling and said he needed to get home to the wife and dog. The young fellow, Jaret, was the first on his feet, offering his hand and thanking Ian with two pumps of his arm. Kevin and Pete stood next and nodded, saying it was great to get help from a real-life writer.

Ian shook his head. "You guys are as real-life as I am. Trust me." He thought for a second and added, "It's great to see, really great. This is what it's all about."

The others laughed, and Jaret told Ian to make sure to tell his editor that the next time he saw him. Either that or set up a fund himself for wannabe writers who frequent cafés in the name of art and coffee.

Ian wheeled his Jeep Cherokee out of Titansburg and finished three miles of the quarter-hour drive home before he realized he'd been thinking about the writers group the entire time. They'd reminded him of his best days in college, when chapters flowed from him as though he were a stenographer and every week he'd have a new bundle of pages to give to a cluster of friends and English majors willing to chime in with opinions. Now, especially since Howard died, he had Rebecca and Louis and that was all. The great circle of literary friends he expected after he published his first novel never appeared, and though he had his admirers, people who'd supply a blurb or two if needed, there was no queue of folks ready to twist a phrase on his behalf or his arm to make him write.

Catching himself and the small curl of self-pity, Ian snorted and asked himself aloud what exactly he would turn over to such a gathering if it existed. He had nothing. Just this drive back home and the loneliness of waiting for his wife to return from her graduate school class. The silence that stilled his fingers and cluttered his brain every time he sat at his computer was the important thing. For years he'd written and flourished without the help of others, and he needed to know why he couldn't now.

He swung the Jeep around a sharp turn, shifted in his seat, and answered the question as simply as possible. He could no longer write of death and fear because his friend and mentor had died terribly and alone in the desert. Any fiction seemed tawdry compared to the real thing. It was the reason he'd given the few people who'd asked what was wrong, because it was the most reasonable explanation that came to him. Now he wondered how true it was. A car approached with its headlights bright, and Ian flashed the driver and then sped by into the dark. Above, a broad smile of moon shone with pewter light, warming a thin cloud that drifted before it like a lampshade. Ian's Cherokee dived down a gentle hill and when it came up the backside, the trees thinned and he was high enough to catch a glimpse of the ocean's expanse spread out to the east like some great pool of ink. Just as quickly, he was back among the trees and thinking about his problem.

Others close to him had died, and he'd never stopped writing. Diseases had pared away family members until they looked slight enough to slip their skins. Hearts seized up and vessels burst, and still he could write. Even when an old college roommate's Nova was ripped in half by a tractor trailer with failed brakes, Ian continued gunning a murderous truck driver through the pages of *Semi.* So if it wasn't as simple as a paralysis from Howard's death, what else was left?

Before he could even shape the slightest of answers, he pulled up to the stop at the bottom of his development, flipped on his right-turn signal, and revved his engine to make it up the sharp incline leading to his hilltop home. The road twisted twice, but soon he crested the hill and saw the long shadow of his house. Only the porch light out front still glowed, one shining sign that Rebecca had not yet returned home. He pulled into the driveway, clicked the garage door open, was glad the temperamental thing came up without a hitch, pulled in, and killed the engine. After gathering his pad and pen, he touched the remote once more, and the door began to close. As he walked through the garage, he kept one eye on the lowering door to make sure it shut fully. About two feet before it closed, Ian heard a rustle and saw a pair of legs approach and stop outside the door. He froze and stared. He saw just a glimpse of denim and a pair of brown work boots before the garage door clanged to a stop against the cement floor.

Someone is right outside, whispered a thought, and Ian flinched as if slapped.

Startled enough to get moving, he unlocked the door into the kitchen and stepped inside without another glance back. Before he managed to shut and lock the door, however, he swore he could hear three soft scratches — as though someone were clawing at the door — from across the garage. The door shut and the lock clicked into place and Ian exhaled deeply, relieved to be secured in the safety of his home.

Those soft scrapes did not soon leave his mind, however, and as he waited for Rebecca to return home he found himself imagining any number of scenarios that might lead to such noises. Most followed the progression of the old urban legends, and though the stories were intimately familiar to him, they still managed to lift a tight patch of gooseflesh when the thoughts lingered too long in his mind.

Rebecca's return was the balm to his fevered imaginings, though she noticed immediately the flash in his eyes. "Were you writing?" she asked, the hope in her voice not masked by her controlled expression.

Ian shook his head and instead launched into the events of the evening. As he spoke he followed his wife from the hall into the living room, where she dropped her class work on top of the antique sea chest that served as their coffee table. He mentioned his frustrating day talking with the writers group and then marched behind her to the kitchen, where she pulled a glass pitcher of juice from the refrigerator. He explained how Peter Ray looked like Howard and how when the garage door lowered, a pair of legs had approached the house and stood waiting outside.

Rebecca turned, as though taken by surprise, and in a low voice he told her how he heard three hushed — almost gentle — scrapes. *Tsk-tsk-tsk.*

She stared at him, her face composed and her head tilted so that she could watch his eyes. After a few seconds, Ian realized she was waiting.

"What?" he asked.

Her hazel eyes narrowed. "You're serious about this?"

He shook his head yes, and her cheeks lost the tiniest bit of color.

"I thought you were trying it out on me."

"Trying it out?"

"Like before," she said. "When you'd come up with something a little creepy, you'd try to work it into conversation to test my reaction."

"No. No, this all really happened. The group, the feet, the three scratches."

Rebecca made a face and said, "Well, that *is* creepy."

Ian wasn't surprised that Rebecca found sleep so quickly after they'd both readied themselves for bed. A full day of work and a three-hour class would be enough to tire all but the most energetic of souls. While she lay curled in an S at his side, her body moving gently with the rhythm of rest, he stared with dogged perseverance at the whirling ceiling fan above their heads. The low hum that normally soothed him into unconsciousness tonight simply droned like some great hovering insect. He could not forget those three soft scratches at the garage door. Rebecca was right — they were creepy. They were the quick rapping of Poe's raven or the hollow tapping of Stevenson's blind pirate scuttling about on the cobblestone road. To be sure they frightened him a bit, but even more they energized him. In those three quick sounds he found himself returned to a place where blood surged faster and palms began to sweat. If he'd forgotten over the past months why he'd ever written stories, he was beginning to remember once more.

He rolled over onto his side and pushed himself close to his wife, his body tracing hers until they fit like neighboring puzzle pieces. This day, which had been filled with so much frustration, was now beginning to feel right. Confidence had seeped in from the most unlikely places — some eerie sounds and the realization that he wasn't just honoring Howard's death — and Ian felt for the first time in weeks as though he might actually roll from bed tomorrow and find words to bring with him to his computer.

He draped an arm around his wife and sighed against her neck. Instinctively, she moved a sleepy arm to sweep her hair from her neck even though it had been cut short years ago. He nuzzled against her in thanks and realized the turning of the fan above his head had lost its buzz. It was now a soothing hum, and he assumed he'd be asleep in seconds. Asleep, that is, unless someone was still waiting outside the house. Still watching from the depths of night. His eyes flickered open.

It was blessing and curse, this need to feel fear.

WEEK 1

One week later, waiting for the *Coastal Explorer* to pull from New York's Penn Station toward home, Ian could list a dozen feelings — including exhaustion and annoyance — that seemed closer at hand than the quick surge of fear that had startled him from sleep and given him a false hope that some nameless corner had been rounded. In fact, there had been no corner, no progress at all. The path was straight and downhill. Ian angled himself onto his cushioned bench, propped his feet on the oak serving table in the middle of his compartment, and stared out into the paneled corridor where a porter was explaining to a woman that this was the executive car and her seat was back this way if she would follow him.

"But these are all empty!" the woman whined before eventually turning on her heel and following the porter back to the economy section. The train lurched forward a few seconds later. Pulling closed the velvet curtain that isolated the compartment from the corridor, Ian settled back once more and sighed deeply, thankful not for the opulence of the trip, but for the solitude of which the woman had complained. He was alone. After hours of battling with Louis and others at the publishing house in an attempt to set up a final deadline, the sound of great steel wheels churning forward soothed him in a way he couldn't describe.

The train rumbled from the thin yellow light of the platform into the darkness of the tunnel. On board, Ian buried his shoulder deeper into the cushion, focused on the growl of the train as it sped under the city, and let the weight of a long day pull his eyes closed. The clack of the wheels hammered its steady rhythm. Somewhere a whistle sounded. Ian breathed deeply and felt a nearly liquid warmth spread from his feet to his waist and up toward his neck. He had just dropped off into slumber when there was a startling, metallic crash out in the hall and the sound of someone muttering to himself. Ian opened his eyes just as a small, white-haired man with enormous eyebrows peeked around the curtain into the compartment. Ian's first thought was that the man looked liked the wizard for whom Dorothy had searched so desperately.

"Get you a drink, sir?" the man asked, just the slightest hint of Irish to his voice. An engraved gold nameplate pinned to his server's jacket identified him as Lucas. "A snack, perhaps?"

Ian rubbed sleep from his eyes and requested a glass of cranberry juice. The porter pulled open the curtain and bent over his beverage cart. Ian watched how the man's hips and knees rocked and dipped with the sway, keeping perfect balance even when the train thundered around a tight corner. Did the old man even remember what it was like to be motionless? Could he remember the serenity in being still? Ian closed his eyes, felt the train rock, and wondered if the man pouring his drinks even noticed.

"Anything else?" Lucas asked, stepping into the compartment and delivering the drink. "We've got some lovely Danishes."

Ian said he'd pass and thanked him for the drink.

"Ach, no problem," said the old man with a dismissive wave of his hand. He did not leave, though, just stood in the doorway, hands in the pockets of his trim navy pants.

Most porters collected their tips at the end of the trip, so Ian wasn't sure what the man hesitated over. He was about to ask if Lucas would mind shutting the curtain once more when the old-timer spoke.

"You're the only rider up here this pass," he said and looked around the luxurious box. "Folks used to fill these trains. Now they're only worried about getting here and there quicker and quicker. When I started out on the rail, people weren't in such a rush." He looked at Ian and smiled. "It's nice to see some folks still enjoy taking their time."

Ian nodded, deciding he didn't need to mention how it had been his publisher's decision to book the train. He'd have gladly taken the local express, but Louis had insisted on "making a gesture." Ian was still their guy at the house, and they wanted to treat him that way. Help him out any way they could. As though a two-hour ride in comfort was going to solve the fact that sitting mutely before the computer dried his mouth and made his fingers tremble. The thought brought back memories from the afternoon, and Ian shifted uncomfortably in his seat, waiting for Lucas to continue on his way.

Instead the porter spoke once more. "I

started on a local line thirty-two years ago. Even made it up to conductor for a Portland-to-Boston route for a few years." He looked about once more, his liquid eyes shining beneath his thick brow. "But this . . . this car tops it all. Spent eight years here. And nobody uses it anymore!" He sighed and finished by saying, "Reminds me of something my grandfather used to tell me: 'Never live like the future was already in the past, or your past the only thing in your future.' "

Ian blinked twice and tried not to show his confusion at how the adage connected in any way to the other things the man had said. Eventually he nodded, saying it was something to think about. That seemed to please the porter, and the old man re-arranged his cart, said his good-byes, and pushed off down the aisle humming a nameless tune.

When the echoes of the clattering cart disappeared, Ian stretched out once more and tried to regain the nap that had claimed him so eagerly before. The train was now out of the city, and the late-afternoon sun blazed through his westward-facing windows. The force of heat was gone, and Ian watched the passing miles: miles of cookie-cutter townhomes, countless acres of sprawling office complexes, and the usual snarl of north-bound traffic. The thought that he'd be seeing this weekly until Labor Day knotted his stomach, and he suddenly saw how bad an idea this new deadline Louis had arranged could be. Unfortunately, it was also his last option.

His footsteps' hollow echo trailed Ian into the house, and he knew instantly that he would not be staying long. A vast emptiness was the last thing he needed to be reminded of at the moment, and with Rebecca attending her evening class until nine-thirty, his Irish setter would be his only company. Not good enough. Ian ran upstairs to change from his suit into a T-shirt, jeans, and hiking boots. Back downstairs, he put dog food in the bowl for Cain, flipped through the mail, and headed back to his Cherokee. He checked his watch and tried to remember how late the Titansburg shops were open. Most kept summer hours, leaving their doors open until nine o'clock so all the tourists could empty their wallets. Leaving now would give him only a half hour to look around, but it was better than nothing.

The back roads into town were clear once again, so it took only fifteen minutes to reach the crush of Gryphon Street. He was about to swing down Holton Avenue to a parking ramp when an Audi pulled out of a parking spot fifty feet in front of him. Ian angled the Cherokee into the spot, killed the engine, and climbed out. The air stunk of cheap pizza and high tide, and Ian could hear the screams of children demanding some new toy. Still, it was better than the thin comfort of a ticking clock. He crossed the street and headed west toward the local bookstore. He had been correct; lights glowed in all the shops. Door after door of New England knickknack stores stood open, each hawking the same collection of sweatshirts, replica lobster traps, and crockery. Ian passed the tempting window of an ice cream parlor before stopping in front of Book 'Em.

A Fort Knox of gold-foil, intrepid-young-lawyer novels filled the display case, glowing in the warm yellow light. To their left sat a memoir of a shark hunter — *Feeding Frenzy*. In another display rested a cookbook that promised enhanced spiritual communion with the dead, lower cholesterol, and firmer buns. Finally there was a historical satire positing Lindbergh as a polygamist with wives on both sides of the Pond.

There was, however, no new Ian Merchant

horror novel to keep buyers awake at night. The window contained no new paperback tie-in to an upcoming miniseries. No posters with their fierce black and red lettering. No marketing props with Ian's grim eyes and angry scar daring readers to pick up a copy of his newest nightmare. He stared at the window for a few more seconds, sighed, and walked away. His ploy for stopping by the bookstore had not worked. Instead of feeling an angry yearning to reclaim his rightful spot in the display, he felt only a dull sense of regret. It wasn't even an emptiness, a hunger waiting to be sated. Just a dreary yielding to what now seemed inevitable. Ian buried his hands in his pockets and slowly made his way down the street.

Titansburg was emptying around him. Families regrouped and bunched into SUVs to head for their hotels or shore homes. Lights began switching off in the windows of boutiques, and twice Ian heard the click of bolts locking into place. He wandered down Gryphon Street, focused on how to reconcile his determined inability to write with the newly minted deadline Louis had set for Labor Day. By the time he looked up he had reached the end of Titanburg's main strip. It was 8:56 p.m. Rebecca's class would be letting out in a few minutes, and she still would have a thirty-five-minute drive home. He looked around. The only lighted store this far down was DeCafé. Ian paused. He had no desire to be swept into another writing discussion, yet he also didn't feel like walking back and finding a booth at the pizzeria. He hesitated for a second, then laziness won out. He pushed open the door with a vague hope that the writers group had dispersed for the evening. Stepping inside, he saw that his wish was only partially fulfilled.

Peter Ray, the muscular fellow whose eyes had reminded Ian of Howard's, sat alone at a table near the back of the coffee shop. He was working on a laptop and looked up as the wind chimes above the door signaled Ian's entrance. He smiled, gave a quick wave, and returned to his writing.

Ian caught the eye of a barista, ordered a large decaf, and waited while the girl rang up his order. He handed over two dollars, got a pitifully small number of coins for change, and stepped down the counter to pick up his drink. As Ian corrected his coffee with cream and cinnamon, Peter Ray approached the counter and requested a refill. They stood in silence next to each other until Peter received his coffee and asked Ian to pass the carafe of skim milk.

Ian slid the container down and was about to retreat to a table when Pete spoke his name. Ian turned and looked at the man, expecting another writing question.

"Priming the pumps again?"

Ian smiled briefly, then saw the significance of Pete's question. The man stared at him with those same steady gray eyes, and Ian realized he wasn't just making some pleasant joke. He was returning to last week's conversation, returning to Ian's acknowledgment he might be done with horror writing. Ian took a sip of coffee and tried to think how to answer the question without lying.

"Old habits die hard," he answered finally.

Pete nodded in agreement and gave his coffee a few quick stirs. There was no follow-up question; instead, he simply invited Ian to sit down and headed toward his table. Ian paused before deciding there could be worse things than spending a few minutes sharing coffee with a man who had only acted kindly toward him. He crossed the café and took a seat to Pete's right. The man saved a spreadsheet crammed with numbers and powered down his laptop. He pinched the bridge of his nose with his fingers and then gave a great yawn, stretching as he did. Ian could see the muscles in his forearms knot in cords.

"Don't ever do your own accounting," said Pete. "Numbers are the spawn of the devil."

"And words?"

"Words," answered Pete, thinking, "are the very voice of angels."

Ian laughed. "Apparently you haven't read my books."

"Oh, I have," said Pete. "They don't let you live in Titansburg unless you've read at least one."

Ian smiled and glanced down at his watch. Nine-seventeen. Ten minutes and he would leave.

"Am I keeping you from something?" asked Pete, sincere in his concern.

"No," said Ian. "My wife has a weekly class for her master's degree. She probably won't be home for twenty minutes."

Pete raised his mug as if to take a sip of coffee but stopped, and a thin smile crossed his mouth.

Ian raised an eyebrow as if to ask what was amusing.

"Just a crazy thought," said Pete.

Ian waited.

Pete cleared his throat and said, "Well, seeing as how you're a writer who happens to be free every Wednesday . . ." His voice trailed off.

Ian understood. "I thought that one fellow didn't want any freaks in his group."

Pete laughed, a mighty laugh that seemed to come from his heart and lungs and everywhere inside. "Kevin's more of a freak than you'd imagine. We all are. What's one more?"

Ian was about to demur when Pete continued.

"I'm asking for totally selfish reasons, of course. I don't expect we'd be able to present you with anything, but I thought I'd at least make the offer."

Ian looked at Pete and saw the man's steady eyes. Pete's mouth was still curled into a small smile, and one huge hand rested on his closed laptop. Ian knew he should have declined already, but something in him wouldn't let him say the words. He thought about his self-pitying drive home from the café last week lamenting the fact that he had no literary friends. Ian looked at Pete again and found himself looking once more at Howard Kepler. He blinked, and the image vanished. The small smile and steady eyes still remained, though. Perhaps Pete was wrong about not being able to offer anything.

"We'll see," Ian said finally and drained the last of his coffee from his mug.

Pete's brow rose just slightly. "Really?" he asked.

"I need to get started on something with a pretty tight deadline, and it'll help to have some varied opinions." He was saying this aloud but it was really to himself. Justifying his otherwise irrational desire to join the group.

"Well," said Pete, flummoxed, "you know where we meet. Every Wednesday at seven."

"We'll see," said Ian again and stood. "If I'm here next week . . ."

"Good enough," said Pete.

Ian nodded, turned on his heel, and headed for the door. One hand couldn't keep from tapping anxiously at his side.

Rebecca was in her favorite chair reading *Risk Pool* by Richard Russo when Ian returned from the café. She had already changed into a T-shirt and mesh shorts for bed and had her feet tucked under the dog, who dozed in front of the chair. Rather than let Rebecca disturb the setter, Ian crossed to his wife and squeezed her hand. She lifted her face for a kiss, and after he obliged she looked at him.

"Coffee?"

Ian nodded. He backed into the wingback, wrestled his boots off, and propped his feet on the coffee table. Rebecca waited without speaking, book laid open in her lap. Once Ian had settled himself, he took a deep breath and asked if she was ready. She nodded.

He told her about his extensive meetings with Louis, the marketing team, the editorial director, and even the CFO. He tried to soften some of the things that were said, but he made sure she understood what he had understood — the company needed his novel.

"They told you that? Why?"

"Nobody said anything specific, but the underlying current was that without my book correcting the budgeted numbers, there'd be people let go."

Rebecca's lips parted, but she didn't speak. Her eyes flashed, however.

"It didn't come off as a threat," Ian told her. "More like a simple fact."

"But why would they even —"

"Hon, they're the details an agent normally hears. We skipped that route, so it's the kind of thing I need to hear." He sighed. "Anyway, we decided on a draft deadline."

Rebecca waited, one finger aimlessly tracing the spine of her book.

"Labor Day."

Ian didn't know what to expect, but he surely would not have guessed that his wife would nod in agreement at the date. Still, she sat in her chair, her head moving up and down with great deliberation.

"Maybe it's for the best," she said. "Something had to happen; we couldn't all just go on waiting and waiting for words to appear. Now they either do or they don't." As if to emphasize her point, she marked her page, closed her book, and stood. Cain groaned a bit when Rebecca's feet jostled her, but the dog demonstrated her uncanny ability to sleep through nearly anything. Soon Rebecca and Ian were taking slow steps up their winding staircase. The moon sparkled for an instant through a skylight high above the first landing before clouds gathered once more and snuffed out its platinum light.

EARLY MORNING. THURSDAY, JULY 11

Ian chose the shortest of the three walks he and Cain regularly traced through their neighborhood. He turned east out their drive and passed along the first of many old stone walls crisscrossing the land. Cain pulled some slack out on the extendible leash to sniff at signposts and saplings while

Ian watched the crumbling wall, hoping to see the fox that had appeared on earlier walks and might have a den somewhere among the litter of fallen branches and gathered leaves. Nothing stirred, however, and eventually the wall angled away back through the woods, marking a boundary long ignored and maintaining a property long forgotten.

After a gradual slope of the road north, they passed three homes and a small pond. Another quarter mile to the pond's west were a pair of baseball fields, and a few minutes after that they reached the wasted skeleton of an inn too worn even to be haunted. South of the inn stretched fifty yards of raspberry patches, still perhaps two weeks from ripe.

Ian and Cain passed them all and then turned up the final hill to their house. A lone car, the only one they'd seen that morning, passed in a rush. Cars in the morning being rarer than foxes on these walks, Ian guessed its driver was late and headed for his or her train into the city and an office at an advertising company, law firm, or investment house.

Cain and Ian rounded the last bend in the street, and as they turned down the driveway Ian saw a quick glimpse of movement through the living room window. He knew it was Rebecca, grabbing her book and stepping into the kitchen to cram in one more chapter over breakfast before leaving for work.

At the steps leading up to the porch, Cain stopped, nose to the walkway. Ian pulled at her leash twice but she refused to move, sniffing the ground and pacing in circles. Finally he gave up, figuring she'd caught the scent of a rogue squirrel, and climbed the stairs to the front door. Propped against the baseboard rested a thin beige note.

The word MERCHANT was inked in severe bold letters on the front. No signature. No message inside. No envelope even. Ian looked around the porch but saw only Cain, eyes bright, as she sniffed the ground with her eager nose.

When Ian showed Rebecca the note, she gave a shrug and said she hadn't heard anyone on the porch. They ate a quick breakfast together before Rebecca had to leave for her archiving job at the Titansburg Historical Society. She finished first, stored her plate in the dishwasher, and grabbed her bag. Ian expected a quick kiss good-bye and the sound of jingling keys, but instead she took the seat next to him and said his name. He looked up.

"I'm planning on staying late in the archives tonight."

Ian was surprised to see her eyes were excited rather than dulled by the notion. He asked what she'd be doing.

"Research," she said, and he rolled his eyes as if that were the least helpful thing he'd ever heard. "I might be changing the topic for my thesis, and I need to do a little background work before I decide."

"You can do that so late? What happened to the Civil War idea?"

"Nothing," she said, "but I may have found something I'd enjoy a little more. And I can change it at the last moment so long as my advisor approves the topic and I get twenty-five pages to her on time. It's not a done deal, but I'll probably be tied up until ten or eleven."

"More time for me to write," he said, but the words fell flat. Rebecca lowered her eyes. Ian tried again. "More time to write!" Big smile, lots of energy. Rebecca laughed, but that was the only pleasure Ian felt from the words.

Following breakfast, Ian retired to his den and pulled out his planner. All the books and his years of experience told him that a constant location and daily routine were two necessary ingredients in conjuring whatever magic was needed to fill a page with words. He sat at his desk and mapped out his schedule for the next eight weeks. Eight weeks until Labor Day; Ian counted them three times to make sure. On the plus side, he had few other commitments — the only things penciled in were a fund-raising auction at the Historical Society on August 10, Rebecca's graduation two weeks later, and their annual Labor Day party to close the summer season on September 2. With a dark pen Ian wrote one more thing in that small block of hours: *FIRST DRAFT.* Then he noted his weekly meetings downtown with Louis and snapped the planner shut. It was time to write.

Once the computer powered to life, Ian opened a file he'd been keeping over the years filled with snippets of story ideas and character traits in the hopes that something might grab hold of him. Nothing did. Ian acknowledged again that the usual steps weren't going to work to shatter this block. He pushed himself away from the desk, rolling into the middle of the office, and shut his eyes. Twice he'd felt close to breaking through and he needed to remember those moments, figure out what small thing he'd missed. He thought about returning home from the coffee shop and realizing that Howard's death — the very thing on which he'd been blaming his mute pen — could not have affected him so greatly. He also remembered his pulse racing at the thought of those three quick scratches on his garage door. That energy, that fear had been important, and it had been a long time since he'd felt that surge. He'd barely asked himself why when the answer burst upon him: it had been his hike with Howard out in the desert. That week-long journey ended in baptism, and since that point he'd thought little about the dark things that used to fill his pages. It was as though he'd stopped believing in them.

Ian opened his eyes. Was that the problem? Had kneeling before God changed his life so completely that he'd simply stopped believing in all that frightens? He thought of the three soft scratches — *tsk, tsk, tsk* — and realized it couldn't be true. There were still things that frightened him. He pushed over to his desk, pulled out a pen and pad, and started his list of the things that brought fear. If they were still out there, he could still write about them.

Blood.
Death.
Monsters.

The first words came quickly, and Ian wrote nearly anything that came to his mind, even adding fictional creations like Marley's ghost and Norman Bates because of what they represented. At the end, Ian counted forty-seven words. Many he had written about before and only one really interested him — *haunting.* He hadn't written a ghost story in a while, and it seemed the closest thing to what he felt about Howard Kepler and those three soft scratches. And himself, he realized. Sitting here in his cluttered office waiting for words to materialize, Ian realized he was troubled by the Ian Merchant who had sat here before, consumed by a voice that made his fingers dance. Howard Kepler had told him that his kneeling cry for salvation would make him a different man, and it seemed to Ian now that perhaps he was a little too different.

The decision to use a haunting as his theme did not make the writing any easier, and Ian soon found himself tackling small chores around his office instead of typing.

When noon finally arrived, Ian lingered over his lunch and was about to call Rebecca to kill time when his own line rang. He picked up, and an unrecognizable voice said his name.

"Pete said you might be joining the group."

"Group?" Ian asked, his mind occupied with placing the caller.

"The writing group."

"Kevin?" It was all Ian could manage. He had no idea why the man would be calling him.

"I'm down at the newspaper and found that we had your contact information in our database. I wanted to ask you a favor."

"Really?" replied Ian after a few seconds. He hoped it came across as incredulous as he meant it. Contrade seemed undaunted.

"It's not for me," he started and explained how one of his former English students was doing an internship at a nearby daily paper. She'd been a great student and was excelling in her sophomore classes at Northwestern, but every journalist needed a break, and Ian could be Cheryl's. He finished by saying that Ian could set the time, place, and even topics if he wanted.

"Well . . ." Ian said and Kevin interrupted.

"She's a smart young woman, Ian, and an

excellent writer. Plus she'll be appreciative; how often do you get that from a reporter?"

Ian gave a small chuckle. He had no real reason to grant this man a favor, but something in his voice made it seem like a good thing to do. He hadn't been able to decipher Kevin's standoffish front as he sat rocking across from him at the café, but listening to him praise his student and fight for her future made Ian think the man had a bit more inside than he'd imagined. He agreed and requested her number.

"Thank you," Kevin said, sincere and simple. "Someday I'll make it up to you."

Ian tried to tell the man not to worry about it, but a click sounded first, followed by the silence of a dead line. Contrade had hung up. Ian settled the receiver into its cradle and wondered if he really wanted to sit face-to-face with this odd man every week.

Rebecca called later that evening after Ian microwaved leftover stir-fry, and he enjoyed her voice as though it was dessert. She could only stay on the line for a minute and told him she'd probably be home after eleven. That hour had seemed very late to Ian, and he was frustrated not to be able to tell her anything about his day. Now, just barely after ten o'clock, he could hardly keep his eyes open as he skimmed James' *Turn of the Screw* for inspiration on the conjuring of ghosts. The book seemed bleaker but less frightening this pass, and he eventually had to put the thing aside and head upstairs lest he fall asleep on the couch and awaken to Cain's eager tongue.

As Ian readied himself for bed, he imagined his wife with him working through her nightly routine, and he phrased things in his mind that he would like to have told her. He would mention scheduling a meeting with a caterer for the Labor Day picnic. He would tell her about dinner and taking Cain for her evening walk and how the fox had been there again, under the wall. He might tell her that the Red Sox lost, but probably not. What else? He'd definitely tell her about the phone call from Kevin Contrade.

Ian rinsed his mouth, crossed the room to the windows, and stared out.

Kevin Contrade, he'd have to remind her, was one of the men in the writers group. An odd duck and not entirely friendly, Ian thought, and yet he had been the one to call.

Rebecca would ask what he called about, and Ian would say that Kevin wanted to ask a favor of Ian. Could a former student of Kevin's interview Ian? The interview would be great for her portfolio.

"What did you say?" Rebecca would ask.

"I ended up saying yes," he'd reply.

"Ian, you can't let these guys take advantage of you just because they're letting you in their little club."

"I know, I know," he'd reply. "But —"

"But what?" She'd probably shoot him a stern look.

"Nothing. I know . . . I'll be more careful. The interview will be fine, though. Short and painless. It's a week from today — next Thursday."

"Just don't tell them the my-best-friend-vanished story."

"I have to. They always ask."

Ian sighed and turned toward the bed. The room, like the night and the street alike, was quiet and dim. His vision of Rebecca vanished and he realized, in his own way and without James' help, he had managed a haunting after all — though now he wished for the Rebecca formed of flesh and bone. Wished that she might turn her car down the street at this moment, pull into the drive, and come upstairs so he could place his hands on her hips and kiss the hollow of her neck and feel her gasp.

When he turned to face the window, he saw only his own reflection. Ian pressed his face to the glass to see outside, amazed that he missed her so much. Times past, he would write for hours in the evening and barely crawl into bed before dawn, and he never missed her then. Only now, when instead of creating conversations between characters, he did so for his wife and himself.

Ian stepped away from the window once more and looked at his image again, though he didn't know what he was seeking in the reflection. Something visible, perhaps, that intimated the great turmoil he felt inside? But nothing was out of place. Or rather, everything was still out of place and therefore just right. The nose was crooked, the ears too large, and the eyelids heavy.

Ian smiled once at the glass, but it was thin and forced. He wanted Rebecca. Not having her, he decided on sleep. He paced across the room and, before shutting off the light, kicked his walking shoes under a chair, climbed into bed, and switched off the lamp.

The room was dark, and Ian stared at the ceiling for only a few seconds before his lids became heavy. Once, twice, his eyes shut and then opened wide.

A car had started outside his house.

Ian sat up in bed, wondering who could be parked in the shadow of his home, and it was only as the headlights came on — glowing through the room's thin curtains — that Ian crawled out of bed.

The three paces to the window were too far, for when he lifted the curtain, only the disappearing glow of red taillights were visible as the car coasted over the hill and out of sight.

MORNING. FRIDAY, JULY 12

"You kicked me last night," Rebecca told Ian when he finally came downstairs to join her for breakfast. He'd slept right through Rebecca's arrival home, his alarm going off, *her* alarm going off, and her slipping out of bed to start the day. She watched him now as he turned his bleary eyes from the contents of the refrigerator. He saw that she'd laid out half a grapefruit and a juice glass for him. "Did you have a nightmare?"

Ian said he couldn't remember, just that he was still quite tired, and that Cain might do without her morning walk today. Rebecca tousled his hair as she passed, kissed his unshaven jaw, and gathered her bag.

"You're going already?" he asked. His mind was now starting to remember last night, the way he'd missed her so badly.

She pointed to the clock and said, "I'm late as it is."

Before Ian could protest, she was out the door. He heard the garage door open and the sound of her car pulling away. Last night's other memory returned at the same time, and he could imagine those headlights disappearing down the road. He shook his head to clear the memory, concentrated on his grapefruit for a few seconds, and reduced it to a pinwheel of membrane and rind. Glass in hand, he took the remains and moved to the sink to drain the last trace of juice. As he squeezed, drops of juice showered everywhere, and Ian was left with only a swallow of juice.

Setting the glass aside, he grabbed some napkins to clean up the mess. Most of the juice had spritzed onto some newspapers, which he shuffled into a neat pile, but one drop landed squarely on the note he had received the other day, glistening like a bead in the middle of his name. Ian dabbed at the drop on the "A" in MERCHANT, but as he did the letter bled from deepest black to crimson. He pulled the napkin away and stared at the note. It was still legible, still his name, but where once it had been cold and chiseled, there now seemed a scarlet gash through the middle, a wound almost. Ian fanned the note with his napkin that the streak might set and bleed no further, but all the while he was very careful to keep his fingers from the swath of red.

Ian returned upstairs to ready himself for the morning. Here he found the most vivid reminders that his wife had been home at all: the shower stall was still wet, the delicate scent of her moisturizer lingered near their walk-in closet, and a square of toilet paper fresh with blotted lipstick rested on her vanity counter. Everything else, though, about the empty bedroom and bath was unchanged from the evening before. It was as if, for that one night, she really had haunted the house, floating in and through without changing a thing.

The notion stopped Ian for a second as he retrieved his running shoes from beneath the chair. He liked its subtle twist of a typical ghost story, but the only plot lines he could think through seemed maudlin and cheap. A Gothic romance of the worst sort. He slipped his shoes on, knotted the laces, and headed down the stairs. Cain lay, face on paws, at the bottom and pretended to ignore Ian until he'd stepped over her and rounded into the kitchen to grab the leash. Hearing its jingle, she sprang to her feet and padded to him, all woes forgiven. Ian scratched her neck as he fastened the nylon lead to her collar, and she responded with an obliging cock of her head. Then, after Ian pocketed his keys, the two set off into the world. The sun shone and a fair breeze snapped at them, but for the first time in weeks Ian barely noticed. He found himself turning the idea for a ghost story round and round in his mind, searching for any small hook on which to hang it.

They walked and walked and finally returned home, yet Ian still couldn't see his way through the problem. Rebecca called in the afternoon to arrange a dinner date for that night, and after hanging up, Ian retired to his den and searched through an old illustrated book of fairy tales. He was looking for a story he thought he'd seen in the volume when he came across a simple drawing of two children staring at each other through a ghost, captioned by the phrase *Transparent as could be!* It reminded him of how he had felt sitting before Howard Kepler and Peter Ray, as though they could see into the very heart of his thoughts and actions. Only the fact that each seemed to care for Ian made the situation bearable. If other people could see inside you — see the ugly thoughts and deeds you kept bottled up — most would be shocked or repulsed. The idea struck him; he had his catch.

Using this as his hook — a man, a living ghost, whose life was transparent to the world — Ian started to write for the first time in months. His fingers remembered the landscape of his keyboard, and his body still molded well into the support of his chair. He finished two pages, saved them, printed both out, and held them before him, one in each hand. A clock chimed six and Ian shut down his computer.

Changing into a navy polo and khakis, he glided from one room to another. The weight had been lifted. The lumbering force that had been gathering on his shoulders ever since he'd returned from Howard's funeral dissolved into an energy and eagerness to tell Rebecca of his breakthrough. A hunger to get back to writing. To get back to being the Ian Merchant of old.

He stopped.

The Ian Merchant of old. Hadn't he flown out to Utah in the first place to get away from that person? Hadn't Rebecca remarked that he'd been so different, so much more pleasant since his time with Howard in the desert? Hadn't he been told by Howard that kneeling outside of Zion and calling on God meant he'd been made new?

Ian tucked in his shirt, cinched his belt, and moved before the mirror. His energy was gone, but the burden had not yet returned. Instead, all he felt was a dry confusion. His image answered nothing. He'd been looking at himself more in the past weeks than ever before in his life, and never had the vision of his own face explained a thing. His physical appearance stayed the same, and yet nearly everything around him was altered. It just seemed right that somehow his own looks would be altered as well.

The door behind Ian squeaked, and when he turned he saw Cain standing in the hall. She knew she wasn't allowed in the bedroom, but she had learned to push the door open and enjoy the view. Dog and man stared at each other for a few seconds, and Ian realized she might be one of the only true constants in his life. Cain and the fact that Louis would catch one point-of-view problem in each of his manuscripts: those were two things on which he could rely.

■ ■ ■ ■

McGinnty's, as usual, was only half full and managed to be the only restaurant in town without a weekend happy-hour crush. Ian assumed it had more to do with the expensive prices of their imported pints than anything else, because the small pub was one of his and Rebecca's favorite places to eat. The half dozen booths were carved from dark, solid oak, and the owners claimed that the marble-topped bar lined with polished brass had been transported all the way from Dublin. From speakers high in the corner an Irish woman with a shatteringly clear voice sang of losing her lover, while a fife and lyre wove melodies beneath her sad tale. A waitress appeared, seated Ian, and took his order for a lemonade. As she left for the kitchen a shadow appeared over his shoulder, and when he looked up, Ian was staring into the face of his wife. He smiled wide.

"Well, there's a greeting a girl could get used to," Rebecca said and slid across from him. She had changed sometime that afternoon into denim shorts and a gray T-shirt from Ian's alma mater, Ithaca College.

"Fruitful day?" he asked.

Before she could answer the waitress

returned, dropped off Ian's lemonade, and took Rebecca's request for a tonic water and lime. The woman disappeared, and Rebecca patted the canvas bag she substituted for a briefcase. Apparently all her answers were deep within.

Ian was anxious to find out what her research uncovered, but she seemed content to rest for a moment and started conversation by asking about his day. Ian almost refused to answer on the grounds that she was the one with exciting news, but remembered that he had written. He told her about his progress. She beamed at him with the look one saw on the face of proud parents.

"I knew you would do it," she said when he finished. "What do you think made the difference?"

As Ian thought over an answer, the waitress appeared with Rebecca's drink. She noted their orders, slipped away, and left Ian once more with the question before him. Why had he been able to write today? Finally, after a few sips of lemonade, he just shook his head.

"I'm not sure. I'd been thinking a lot about the reasons I'd been giving for being blocked. I think I finally realized they weren't reasons, but excuses." It sounded good to Ian when it left his mouth, but he knew by Rebecca's expression that she wasn't as sure.

"But," she started, "those weren't just excuses, Ian. The way you talked after visiting Howard in Utah; the way you've changed even since then . . ." Her voiced trailed off and she looked perplexed. "Was that real?"

Yes! a part of Ian wanted to shout. It was the most real thing he'd experienced in years. Bowing his head and heart before God and asking to be called by his true name — it answered a life of questions and months of searching. So quickly, though, that assurance had faded. Howard died, and he was left with nothing. Talking to Rebecca like this only confused him more — it felt as though they were talking to each other in different languages. And the last thing he wanted to do was hurt her. He said nothing for the moment, just turned his glass in his hand until he found words.

"Bec, I was acting like writing my novels was at odds with what happened out in Utah. But now . . . now I'm not so sure. And if they aren't, well, I've got a first draft due in eight weeks."

"And if they are?" she asked immediately.

"If they are," he answered, entirely unsure

of himself, "then I'll trust that something will happen to end this thing once and forever."

As their meals arrived, and without another word on the subject, Ian and Rebecca forged on to new topics. He finally had a chance to tell her about the catering appointment he'd arranged and the interview to which he'd agreed, as well as the odd fact of a car waiting outside the house at all hours of the night. He got a little animated in retelling the story, even involving some of the condiment bottles in a reenactment.

Rebecca just smiled. "Maybe you are supposed to be writing," she said after he drove a mustard jar over an invisible hill. "You've gotten like this before, and it's always been before you started a novel."

"Been like what?" Ian asked, trying to figure out if he should be insulted.

"Imaginative," she answered. "Remember when you thought you found evidence of that missing child out in the woods? Or when you accused Chet the mailman of reading all our magazines before delivering them?"

"All the inserts were missing!" he cried. "Somebody had to be —"

Rebecca waved her hand to quiet him down.

"I'm not saying it's a bad thing," Rebecca replied, her voice low. "It's good. It means you're thinking. Your mind is going a million miles an hour and it's making up stories for everything. Even cars driving away from houses." She smiled and forked the last bite of shepherd's pie into her mouth.

"Well," Ian grumbled, still a little miffed at the insinuation of his being paranoid, "what do you have to show for your days in the library?"

Rebecca sighed and slumped against the booth in contentment. "A new thesis subject. But not here," she said. "I'll tell you about it at home. It feels like I've been gone forever."

That evening Ian and Rebecca settled comfortably in the upstairs library. It was her favorite room — the spot to which she would retire if they suffered through a fight or she had heard bad news from a friend. Ian had never been sure about the odd choice of mismatched bookshelves they'd purchased over three weekends of estate sales, but he'd said nothing and only entered the room when invited. He sat in an overstuffed chair they'd inherited from Rebecca's grandmother, and his wife selected the reupholstered armchair across from him. Her bag sat on one side of her feet and Cain sprawled on the other. After a second of searching through the bag she found an old black-and-white picture and handed it to him.

"Do you know who that is?"

Ian squinted at the photo in the room's dim light, but the face forged no connections in his memory. It was a woman's face. She had brown hair styled in what his mother had called a pageboy. Her eyes sparkled and she had a cleft in her chin. Ian guessed the photo was from the late fifties. Finally he handed it back to Rebecca with a shake of his head. Since she'd bothered to ask the question, Ian knew what was next.

"You've met her," Rebecca said, and Ian sighed. He'd met a lot of people.

"Who is she?" he asked. "And what does she have to do with your thesis?"

"Her name is Katherine Jacoby," answered Rebecca, holding the photo before her and staring at the woman's image. "She was an artist."

Rebecca explained that the woman had lived for years just outside town. When she died two months ago, she left her estate to the Titansburg Historical Society. She had no relatives, so all her sculptures had become the property of the museum. Rebecca had been drafted to go through her belongings and decide what might be worth keeping.

"Is she important enough to make the museum?" Ian asked.

Rebecca glared and continued.

Katherine had done a couple of sculptures displayed in Titansburg, and the museum was always thrilled to discover another local artist — especially a woman. Rebecca was excited because she'd talked with Katherine a few times at various museum functions.

"Plus," Rebecca added, her eyes heavy on Ian, "we've invited her over to the house for the Labor Day party two years in a row."

"Ah . . ." answered Ian, embarrassed.

"In fact, she was the one who carved that centerpiece last year. The one with the ghost floating out of the book?"

Ian nodded, straining to replace the image of the photo with the woman's real face. All he could say was "I remember the centerpiece."

"Do you remember her?"

"Can't say that I do," he replied and asked what had happened to the carving.

"You gave it to Louis." Rebecca's voice was now flinty, and Ian decided he'd keep his mouth shut for the next few minutes.

"Anyway," Rebecca continued, "she had no family. She didn't know her parents. She was raised by an aunt and uncle, but they were old, had no children, and died when she was at university. She never married and lived in Connecticut by herself for forty-seven years."

Ian waited for the punch line, the kicker that had gotten Rebecca to change her thesis. She handed him a second photo.

A man, his face seemingly chiseled from some cold gray stone, stood at attention in full uniform, except that instead of carrying a gun or bayonet in his arms, he held a baby. His expression and rigid posture were efficient and proper, yet his arms and hands seemed soft and comforting. Somehow, in the proper crook of his arm and the expert spreading of his fingers to support the child's rump, the soldier proved father as well.

Ian looked at his wife for explanation, and she motioned for him to flip it over.

Written on the back in the faintest pencil were the words *Katherine und sie Vater, 1927.*

"This is your Katherine?" Ian asked.

Rebecca nodded and asked if he noticed anything about the father.

Ian glanced down and said, "He's in the

army and he's not going to win the congeniality portion of any contest."

Rebecca stood, walked behind him, and pointed over Ian's shoulder at the arm the man had crooked under his daughter.

Ian looked closer. There, at the soldier's bicep just where Rebecca pointed, was a white armband with the slightest hints of crooked black markings. The child's head and thin hair covered the rest. It was impossible to be sure, but Ian knew what his wife was implying.

"Do you think she knew?" he asked. "Did she just pretend not to know who her parents were?"

Rebecca didn't answer, but her look said enough. Who wouldn't cover up the truth if they'd found this monster in their closet?

LATE MORNING. SUNDAY, JULY 14

Saturday afternoon had been clogged with yard work and the caterer's meeting, so Ian found himself with a list of errands to run when he finished reading the paper Sunday morning. Summer's glut of tourists meant that stores maintained their typical hours, so Ian knew the frame shop and pet store would both be open when he arrived in town.

The Connecticut morning was heavy as

Ian wound his way east into town, and when he heard a radio forecast of storms sweeping in from the south, he was glad he'd finished his landscaping work the day before. After his errands he could return home, retire to the porch with his wife, and watch nature's pyrotechnics over a sweating glass of iced tea. The weather report faded into a Platters tune, and Ian switched on his blinker, turned right, and found a vacant spot directly in front of the frame shop.

It was a large print of one of Howard Kepler's photos that Ian wanted framed, and he wasn't surprised when the shopkeeper, a fussy balding man with *Ed* on his nametag, asked if it was an Ansel Adams. The black-and-white image of Zion National Park's Great White Throne looked like something straight out the famous photographer's oeuvre, but Ian told the man he'd seen the photographer take this photo in the warming glow of the setting sun. He'd stood side by side with the artist as the man's camera whirred and clicked, recording a glowing image of this gargantuan wall of granite rising from the canyon floor.

"Super," said Ed without much enthusiasm, and within minutes they had chosen a pebbled charcoal matting and a black frame that the shopkeeper promised Ian would make the photo glow.

From the frame shop Ian went next door into Calhoun's Pet Emporium and purchased a box of specialty dog biscuits that Rebecca insisted made Cain's breath smell something less than canine. Ian wasn't so sure and actually was beginning to wonder if this was just a byproduct of not having kids in the house, but he thought it better not to raise that topic. He paid for the biscuits and headed back down the street toward DeCafé.

Sunburned tourist families roamed the streets searching for the ideal sweatshirt that summed up their vacation or a clever postcard to send to friends sweating it out back in the city. Flies buzzed about the streets, gathering at melting puddles of ice cream, and sea gulls could be heard squawking from dumpsters off the main street. These things, along with the gathering heat, were the things of summer Ian despised. Four amateur Rollerbladers lurched by him, and ahead stood three kids seeing who could spit the farthest. He began to swing his bag of biscuits in frustration, starting first with small, quick flicks of his wrist, then moving into long, sweeping arcs. Behind him tires squealed, and he glanced over his shoulder briefly before turning back around. Out of the corner of his eye he saw movement and couldn't stop his bag. The biscuits swept forward and knocked the visor off the head of an old woman who'd teetered from under a store awning. She'd been inches from catching the box right in the face.

"Sakes alive!" the woman cried, and Ian dropped the box with a gasp and ran to grab the white visor. A gray smudge ruined the perfect white of the cap, and rubbing it only seemed to spread the stain. Ian gave his apologies and handed the hat back to the woman.

"I am so, so sorry," he repeated, when the woman failed to reply. Perhaps he had hit her after all.

Finally she turned her head and beamed at him, a great glowing smile on her face. "You're the pool man's friend, aren't you?"

Ian stared at the woman, trying to figure out whether what he'd heard had been English. When she repeated the question Ian could only shake his head.

"I'm sorry, but I think you have me confused with someone else."

The old woman giggled a little, smoothed her hands over her gingham dress, and said, "You don't fool me. I know our pool will be done when I return. You don't fool me at all." Cocking her head to the side, she smiled again at Ian, flirting almost. Her eyes were watery and vague, and though she stood a few feet away, Ian could smell urine. He looked around, hoping to find her caregiver, but saw only families dragging unhappy dogs behind them on leashes. He turned and asked the only question that came to mind: "Where are you going, ma'am?"

The woman nodded slowly, as if thinking, and replied that this was her doll shop. She and Maddie worked in it every day after school all year long and would he like to come in. Ian nodded, but at just that moment the door to the store opened. An anxious-looking brunette came out and took the elderly woman by the hand saying, "Come, Momma." They walked into the store without another word, and Ian was about to leave when the younger woman came out again to apologize.

"My mother has Alzheimer's," she explained. "She loves the shop, but we can't keep our eyes on her all the time. Thank you for stopping."

Ian shook his head, said it was no problem, and turned to continue on his way. As he did, the woman called out from under the awning that she loved his books. Ian startled. He always did when a stranger recognized him, and when he finally turned to give his thanks, she had darted inside, leaving the door to swing shut. He gave a half wave to the storefront as his thanks and received, from the elderly woman who now stood staring out from the display window, a slender curtsy in reply. There among the half dozen porcelain dolls she stared with the same glassy expression as the miniatures about her. Their faces were smooth, though. Their cheeks were rouged. She resembled them only in the deep void of her eyes.

Driving south out of town, the sweet odor of hazelnut coffee seeping through his Cherokee, Ian saw a sign for Deep Woods Outfitters and recognized it as the store owned by Pete Ray from the writers group. Ian hadn't yet made up his mind whether to show up on Wednesday night, but he knew he was leaning in that direction and was curious to see the man in a different locale. He pulled into the gravel lot containing only a battered hatchback, got out, and walked up the three steps to the entrance. Already he could see an array of open tents, fiberglass canoes, and an entire wall of hiking shoes. Ian opened the door and stepped inside. The store was cool and silent.

Nobody else was in sight, so he busied himself about the counter for a while, checking out knives and compasses. Everything seemed to be organized by events, and Ian could make out a paddling wall, shelves of boots and sandals, cross-country ski equipment, and even some rock-climbing gear. Deep Woods was only one open floor, but it was stocked full of quality equipment — or at least expensive equipment. Any jacket that cost $350 had better be top of the line.

Four railroad-tie pillars descended from support beams throughout the room, and the one closest to the counter was covered with advertisements and photos. Ian scanned outing invitations, climbing-school applications, and sweepstakes offers before coming to an area dedicated to action snapshots of what might have been the staff, most of whom were young men with unruly hair. Pictured snowboarding, ice climbing, sea kayaking, or hauling monstrous backpacks through the desert, they looked like people who might use the word "dude." At the bottom was a single snapshot of a black-haired man Ian recognized as a younger Pete. He stood, legs crossed, on an enormous field of ice, a pick stuck in the snow in front of him. His eyes were serene, yet across his face spread the toothy grin of a child. Ian bent to get a closer look, wondering where the photo was taken.

"Can I help you?" a woman said from behind him.

Ian turned and found a young blond woman looking at him from among racks of fleece. She smiled and asked again if she could be of service. Ian said that he was looking for Peter Ray, and the woman seemed surprised. She hung up the last of the vests she had been holding and, walking toward a back office, said she would get her husband.

"Husband?" Ian mouthed silently and looked back at the photos. Indeed, there in the middle, in a snapshot he had skipped over, was gray-haired Pete standing with his arm wrapped about the waist of a woman who looked almost two decades his junior. Some snow-capped mountain towered behind them, and Ian realized Pete was a man who had seen the world.

"Ian Merchant," Pete called, walking up an aisle. "What brings you here?"

"Saw your sign, thought I'd drop in."

"Actually," said Pete with a grin, "we're not even open. I must've forgotten to lock the door."

Ian apologized and said he'd get going,

but Pete assured him that it was no problem at all. "So long as you leave with a new kayak."

They took a few minutes and toured the store, walking from the racks of polypropylene undergarments to a shelf of deeply hued climbing rope. Carabiners and belay devices were separated into bins. The store even sold dust — chalk dust for a rock climber who needed dry hands. After the tour, they poked their heads into the office and Pete introduced Christine, his wife, to Ian. On her lap sat a golden-haired girl sucking on a ring pop that looked as large as her fist. When Pete told Greta to say hello, she turned her face into her mother's chest and hid. Christine smiled for both of them, wished Ian a good day, and turned back to her computer.

As they headed back up front, Pete asked if Ian had decided on the kayak he was going to buy. "After all, Sundays are appointment only."

"Yeah, apparently I can't read," Ian laughed. "Just never even crossed my mind. All the stores downtown were open. . . ." He stopped and looked at Pete, who seemed to know what he was thinking.

"We close for two main reasons," Pete said. "First, I wanted a day that would be dedicated to my family. Second, I hold on pretty tight to the notion of a sabbath. It does a body good to rest. God knows what's best, and it isn't the extra dollars that eight more hours would get us."

Ian wasn't surprised to hear the answer. He'd seen the similarity between Howard and Pete earlier and knew it was more than just similar shades of pigment in their eyes or the way each man stared when he talked. Ian wondered if seeing into another person — that transparency — was more abundant than he'd imagined, and that thought reminded him of the two pages sitting on his desk and the offer to join the Wednesday writers group. He cleared his throat and decided to take the plunge.

"I think I'll take you up on that offer, Pete."

Pete looked perplexed. "The kayak?" he asked.

"Wednesday nights."

"How about that?" Pete said, pretty much to himself, although Ian heard it loudly enough. The man shook his head as if to rouse himself and said he'd let it be a surprise to the others. "A real writer. In our group. Wow."

"Hopefully," Ian said without explaining, turned to the door, and stepped back outside. He was surprised at the mass of thunderheads that had gathered during his time in the shop and even switched on the headlights after pulling out from the parking lot.

As he navigated the winding roads back to the safe haven of his house and Rebecca's arms, a single question rang through his mind: *Why not tell Pete about Utah?* The man talked as freely as Howard had about God and would probably be ecstatic if Ian mentioned it. He might even invite Ian to his church or some such thing. And yet, all that was shared between them was silence. Ian made a left onto Pine Cone Creek Road, and the first heavy drops of rain splashed against the windshield.

Tapping his finger on the steering wheel to the steady patter of rainfall, Ian realized that the one person he wanted with him to talk to Pete was Howard Kepler. Howard had been his witness, had dunked Ian under the churning Utah stream, and had been there to see the whole ridiculous aftermath. The baptism hadn't gone as planned, but it had still happened — as had their talk over the licking fingers of a mesquite campfire. Howard had been the one thing Ian felt he needed most: proof. And now he was gone, leaving Ian with only a pair of boots dusty with Utah dirt, three black-and-white photos, and the ever-present memory of Howard's sturdy gray eyes. Somehow, it didn't seem enough. Not enough to present to Pete Ray, and barely enough to even convince himself these days. Ian eased his Cherokee around a curve, nearly jerking it off the road when the first sharp crack of thunder split the air. A deeper echo soon followed, and as Ian aimed for home, it seemed that some nasty weather had settled in for quite a blow.

EARLY MORNING. MONDAY, JULY 15

When Ian readied himself for his morning walk, the storm had slowed to a drizzle. Outside Cain pulled the leash out taut the moment her paws hit the pavement, and Ian had to yank to slow her down. After a moment she calmed and began exploring the sitting puddles and fallen branches while Ian thought through his writing for that afternoon. Fifteen pages now were saved on his computer. His main character would soon become a walking ghost, his whole life visible to anyone who looked in his eyes.

Ian spent another ten minutes guessing at what might come next when a brown sedan whizzed by, splashing Ian and the dog with spray from its spinning tires. He turned to yell at the driver, but froze. Something in the shape of its retreating brake lights reminded him of the car that had driven off the other night. And it had just come from the direction of Ian's house.

Without a second thought, Ian broke into a jog, trying to still the thoughts that instantly came to mind.

The car had been watching their house the other night before fleeing. This time it tore away in a bigger hurry. Why was it leaving so fast? Perhaps the man had returned during the night. He'd been hidden until Ian and Cain had stepped out for their morning walk. Their daily walk.

The jog became a run.

The man knew Ian's schedule. He'd been waiting for Ian to leave. He'd been waiting for Rebecca to be alone. Rebecca was alone.

Ian burst into a full sprint and rounded the last bend. Cain stayed at his side, leash between them. As they ran toward home, rain soaked Ian and stung his face. He scrambled up the driveway and onto the front stoop.

A note, as before, was taped to the door.

Ian didn't bother with it, just opened the

door and ran inside, tearing off his rain slicker.

"Rebecca!" he called once. Hearing nothing, he shouted again, louder. Water dripped into his eyes and his chest burned. He yelled a third time. Cain barked in unison and followed as Ian passed through the foyer to the base of the stairs. Again he yelled and began running up the stairs.

After three steps he heard a door open in the upstairs hall and footsteps pad across the carpet. Rebecca poked her head over the railing of the spiral staircase and looked down. Her hair was bundled in a towel.

"What's all the yelling?" she asked, leaning over farther to look at her husband. "Goodness, you're all wet! And the dog!" Cain sat at Ian's side and they both gasped for air, chests heaving after the run.

"Are you okay?" Rebecca asked, but before Ian could begin to answer, her towel unwound from about her head and fell, drifting to Ian below. He caught it, looked up, and nodded. Rebecca stood silent, waiting for an explanation. This woman, damp and perplexed — he would sprint down a road, would run around the world for her.

Ian, watching Detective Oakley search for clues in the front yard and on the stoop, thought about how much he had gotten wrong describing police work in his novels. The facts were true enough, but the tone had been all wrong. In his books, a police appearance meant slick detective work and hot pursuits. Here, watching this Detective Oakley — a short, stocky fellow who carried only a small revolver and stood out in the slowing rain without moving much at all — Ian couldn't have said if the man was doing anything. Oakley's hands were stuffed deep in his pockets, and Ian could see that the officer was shivering. Most police deduced or solved or detected; this one just seemed to stare.

Ian walked from the window and back to the kitchen to start some coffee, glancing at the two notes the policeman had asked to see when he'd first arrived. The scarlet stain still looked like blood on the first, but it was the second that was more frightening. Ian turned back to the machine and switched the coffeemaker to brew. He didn't want to turn around, didn't want to see the notes again, so he ran some water in the sink and hoped the officer would come in shortly.

Plates and suds ran out first, though, and Ian was forced to sit at the kitchen table. He glanced at the note's black letters, each so even and final it seemed cut from a stencil.

MONSTER.

Ian looked at each letter and then the word. This note, identical in construction to the other, shallowed Ian's breathing. MER-CHANT he could handle; MONSTER warranted police.

As Ian opened the note, Oakley came through the front door and began shedding wet layers. Cain clicked her way down the hall to sniff first the officer and then his dripping clothes. Ian called out that coffee would soon be ready, and Oakley shook his hair, slicked it back with one hand, and squished his way to the kitchen, wet foot-prints in a trail behind him.

"Coffee would be super," he said, then pointed to the note. "You know what that means?"

"The note?"

"Well, more of what's inside. Where's the quote from?"

Ian looked down at the open note: *Forget there are monsters, and they will thrive.* "It's from my first novel. *Monster.* It's the open-ing line."

"Interesting," said Oakley, digging a note pad and pen from his pocket. Cain returned from the hall, sniffing once more at the stranger's feet. Oakley reached down and scratched the dog's ears. "Well, this girl's a sweetheart," he said and scratched harder. The dog sighed with pleasure.

"She's a Norman Rockwell painting in fur," Ian said. "Her name is Cain."

Oakley raised an eyebrow. "That's a mean name to give a pretty dog."

Ian stood to pour coffee and told the officer that he'd received the dog as a gift from an actor when one of his novels was made into a film. It was the character's name. Oakley said nothing more, just accepted his mug and began looking at the notes. He was careful to hold them by the edges, Ian noticed, and he stared for a long time at the words on both covers. Once, he held one of the notes close to the light, but put it back down without comment. He wrote for a minute or so in his pad while Ian waited, thinking it strange that police work was so quiet and dull. Here something unique was happening in his own house, and all he wanted to do was leave, find anything else to do.

"This one's stained," said the officer finally, pointing to the note slashed in red.

Ian nodded. "Spilled something on it." He waited for a moment and asked the question that'd been at the back of his mind: "Do you think it's blood?"

"Doubt it," answered Oakley. "Blood oxidizes to black in air. This is probably an ink of some sort. Maybe a paint."

Ian nodded, relieved, and the policeman flipped over a new page in his notebook and said that he'd like to ask Ian a few questions. It was a line Ian had written numerous times, but this time a chill went up his spine. Boring or not, *this* was real.

Ian responded to the familiar progression of queries: name, age, address, phone number, family, and the specific complaint. Next, history or reason for the complaint.

Had Ian seen anyone following him?

Did he get a look at the car? at the driver?

Did he have a schedule, some sort of routine?

Finally, Oakley began asking questions about motive — extortion, blackmail, stalking. Ian shook his head at the first two, but the third had to be admitted. Overzealous fans were known to do anything, and Ian had heard stories from other authors about harassment they'd received from those unfortunate enough to be clinically impaired. A few more possibilities were offered and noted by the officer, but they both agreed that because of the quote and because of the hide-and-seek quality, it seemed that Ian had gained some "unwanted attention," as Oakley put it.

Ian nodded. "A stalker."

"Doesn't unwanted attention sound better, though?" the officer asked, and Ian had to agree that it did.

"Mr. Merchant, I'd like you to give me names. Anyone. Any leads for someone who might be doing this."

Ian thought for a while but came up only with a rabid fan who wrote him long, graphic letters about mistakes Ian made in his novels dealing with spells or chants. He ended by saying, "Though he's in California."

"Not much of a surprise," Oakley deadpanned and jotted the name down. He ran a hand through his hair, which was now drying in stiff brown waves, and squinted at his pad as though trying to remember something. Finally he looked across the table and said, "Here's another way of looking at it: Do you have any enemies? Someone who might be mad at you for any reason?" One eyebrow twitched, but otherwise his face was still.

Ian shook his head from side to side almost reflexively, yet even as he denied it, names and faces began to come to him. His head slowed and switched to a nod.

"Anyone?" he asked, and Oakley waited.

The names, the people from his past came quickly. Every angered girlfriend, every skewered literary critic, every jealous classmate. Reporters he'd berated. A bookstore owner he had cursed out. A former agent. A television newsman named Kyle Turner whom he'd punched years back after the man insulted Rebecca. He even remembered Charles Grover, a boy from elementary school whom he would beat on Mondays for the kid's weekly lunch money. Wouldn't it be a kicker if Chuck were still angry?

Ian spoke and Oakley filled three notebook pages without comment. Finally, when the names stopped coming, the detective looked at Ian and gave a flat smile. "You should see my list."

After the evidence had been bagged up and Oakley's notebook closed, they toured the house, spending particular time on the porch doors, the garage, and other entrances. Oakley assured him that the house looked secure, so long as they locked it up every night, but advised that a house alarm might not be the worst idea. After heading back downstairs from the guestroom, the library, the master bedroom, and the small room that Rebecca called her office, the detective called the station to see if any decision had been made about a canvass. He told Ian that a patrol car had been rerouted to make irregular passes every half hour or so during the deepest hours of night. That would keep anyone from spending too much time out front.

"Captain also wanted me to ask if the Labor Day picnic was on for this year," Oakley said after he'd hung up.

Ian laughed and said of course the party was on. So long as the Titansburg Police Department could afford six men to act as security, all the others would always be welcome at his party. He stopped and stared at Oakley, realizing for the first time that he'd never met the man before. And he knew all the police from past gatherings. Old lady sculptors he'd forget, but anyone who could protect his life became an instant companion. "You're new to the force, aren't you?"

Oakley nodded. "I had to beg for this assignment just to visit your place. The others talk about your parties often. You're quite the legend."

Ian went to say something, then stopped.

The idea of a police force being in awe of him seemed absurd. They had the guns. He had only some steak knives, some blunt crystal writing awards, and a genial Irish setter.

"What brought you to Titansburg?" Ian asked.

"My wife," Oakley replied. His face became serious, coffee-colored eyes staring past Ian as if he were seeing the woman's face. "Her parents are here. Their health declined and they needed some help running their store downtown. Things had stalled for me in Pennsylvania, so it ended up being a decent time to move." He paused. "Of course our boy, Jay, might argue that with you. He doesn't see why an old doll shop was worth leaving all his friends."

Ian coughed. "A doll shop? Then —" He thought for a second. "I think I've met your wife . . . and your mother-in-law."

Oakley smiled as if he'd known all the time. "Anne told me. She was quite excited; she's a big fan of yours." The officer looked around and grinned. "We have enough of your hardcovers that I'd bet we financed at least a few of the knickknacks in this place."

Ian wasn't sure what to reply, so he smiled and said, "Your mother-in-law thought I was the pool man's friend."

"Alzheimer's," Oakley replied, and Ian thought he might explain, but the man didn't say anything more. He just rubbed his cheek for a bit and looked sad. Finally he finished, "That one comes up all the time — a pool man and his friend. No idea what it means." He smiled weakly and sighed.

Ian guessed the whole thing grieved the man greatly. He didn't know what it was like to lose someone to Alzheimer's. It must be exhausting and aggravating. Like trying to punch a shadow.

That conversation killed any chance of further discussion, so Oakley walked to a window and peered outside. He seemed relieved that it was no longer raining and didn't bother to put on any of the gear hanging from the coat tree.

Ian opened the door to see the officer out, and at the sound, Cain came jogging down from upstairs, her eyes bright and anxious. Ian caught her collar before she made it outside, and Oakley scratched her back a bit, saying that there was nothing to worry about. Everything was in order and attention was going to be paid to the house. Then he nodded, thanked Ian for the coffee, and walked to his unmarked car.

"Say hello to your wife," Ian called out for

no reason, and Oakley waved that he would. He got in his cruiser, sparked its engine to life, and pulled from the driveway. Once again Ian watched as a car topped his hill and disappeared. At least this time it was the good guys.

He stepped back inside once the car was gone and shut the door with a slam. The sound echoed through the empty halls, and Ian looked around at the quiet house. Everything was in order, just as before — even the notes were gone — yet something had changed. He felt watched and decided to go to his den, the only room in the house without windows. Originally he'd insisted on it being built that way so he wouldn't be distracted, but now it seemed to be serving a second purpose. He grabbed a sandwich and chips for lunch, called Cain, and shut the door on the rest of the world. When he switched on his computer, he noticed for the first time that he'd been stifling the smallest of trembles. Now, with the officer gone, his hand shook, quivering with the extra blood that pumped from his panicked heart. He wondered if his fingers would still once they found their place on the keys. And if he could write compelling horror nor- mally, who knew what would come out when he was frightened.

Rebecca entered Ian's office as the laser printer scrolled the final page of his first chapter into the holding tray. She had already changed for bed, and her cheeks were freshly washed pink. She leaned her hip against a cherry file cabinet, and after he'd stapled his chapter and slipped it into his briefcase, Ian turned to face his wife. Her legs were crossed at the ankle and he didn't at all mind the swell and curve of her leg disappearing into a pair of pajama shorts. He stepped forward and kissed her once on her forehead and a second time on her lips. She tasted of toothpaste.

"You have everything for tomorrow?" she asked. When Ian nodded, Rebecca said, "Do you know what you're going to tell Louis?"

He looked at her, puzzled. "About what?" he asked.

She stiffened a little, uncrossed her legs, and folded her arms across her chest. All the pleasant roundness of her body seemed to have disappeared. She was all business.

"Why you suddenly have a chapter in your briefcase," she started, "when for seven months all you showed up with were excuses. Why you have the phone number to the Titansburg police department penciled in at least four different locations in your house." She took a breath. "Why you feel an urgent need to show up at a coffee shop and talk about writing with three strangers."

Ian knew what Rebecca was looking for but answered her questions at face value instead. "I'm going to tell him that I've taken a long look at what was keeping me from writing," he said, "and that I might have been thinking too much. About the police, I'll tell Louis everything that's happened. He might have some advice." He stopped, and Rebecca stood waiting. He grinned just a bit and continued on. "About the group . . . well, I'll tell them that I was getting too lonely being left here by my wife every Wednesday night and found a place to kill some time *and* get feedback on the new chapters."

He expected Rebecca to smile, but she just blinked slowly and nodded her head.

"That's fine, Ian," she murmured. "I just want you to understand that some of us recognize how crazy things are around here. I realize it, Ian, so there's no point pretending nothing is happening." She exhaled deeply after saying this, turned, and headed out of the den for bed.

Ian had no words. He stood in silence and listened to the creak of the stairs as his wife climbed to their room. As she reached the top, Ian wondered which of the three events she was the most concerned about. Was it this sudden break from an otherwise hypochondriacal writer's block? Or the fact that he felt a sudden compulsion to meet new people? Or had she really not laid out all her fears about the stalking? They'd talked last evening, and she seemed to accept Ian's word that the police were handling the situation. She'd been so calm, in fact, that her confidence helped him put the matter aside and enjoy a decent night of sleep. Perhaps, though, things were left unsaid. And if she were really frightened, Ian knew he needed to take the situation more seriously as well. All three circumstances. He needed to make Rebecca feel reassured, make her feel that Ian Merchant could be trusted. And all that entailed, he realized as he worked his way up the stairs, was finally deciding which Ian Merchant he really was.

WEEK 2

After a morning of meetings and an afternoon of working on the manuscript with Louis, Ian and his editor headed to the train station, Louis chewing gum the entire time. He said it had been twenty-seven days since his last cigarette, and Ian was proud of the man for making the effort. They stood waiting for the *Coastal Explorer,* and by the bounce in Louis's knees, Ian guessed the man either still had issues he wanted to discuss or was trying his best to work through a craving.

"Off the record," Louis finally said, "I want to make a suggestion."

Ian waited. This was typical Louis: laying out his best idea at the last moment so that Ian couldn't reject it outright. He'd done it before, and he was usually right.

"I want you to consider doing something

that's going to sound extremely distasteful," he began. Before Ian could even raise an eyebrow in concern, the editor finished: "I want you to take notes on the stalking."

Ian blinked. His mouth opened and he tried to say something, but his voice caught and he ended up emitting just a small cough. Louis smiled a little and put his arm around Ian's shoulder. Though inches smaller than Ian and pounds lighter, he steered Ian to an empty bench against the station's tiled wall and made him sit. Louis remained standing, knees still bouncing, and looked down at Ian, a mischievous glint to his cornflower eyes.

"Not what you were expecting, was it?"

Ian admitted that it was the furthest thing from his mind.

"It'd make a good story, Ian," said Louis. "Nonfiction is hot right now, and a book on what happens will either be a quick bonus after you finish what you're working on or insurance."

"Insurance?"

A garbled message over the PA system announced the imminent arrival of Ian's train, and in seconds Ian could see the flood of engine lights as it roared around the last corner. There was a great squeal of brakes and the sigh of hydraulic systems before the porters stepped off and passengers began spilling into the station. Ian looked up at Louis and repeated his question. He knew the answer but wanted to hear his editor say it.

"Ian," Louis began, "this has been a hard year. We can't just forget what's happened. One chapter . . ." His voice faded out, and he chewed his gum slowly as if thinking very hard. When he finally found his words, he stopped chewing. "Most likely there will be no story. The whole thing will fade away or the police'll catch the guy and it'll end. I just want you to take notes." He bent down to look Ian in the face. "The company isn't asking, Ian. I'm asking. I need a book from you."

They stared at each other for a few moments until the conductor gave a yell that outbound passengers could now board. Ian moved his head in a slow nod, and Louis exhaled with great relief and began chewing his gum once more. Ian stood, not knowing quite how to say good-bye, and simply wished the man another week without a cigarette.

"Cigarettes aren't the problem anymore," Louis said with a wink. "But I think I'm addicted to this gum now."

Ian laughed, and when the conductor gave

a second call, he told Louis he'd see him again in a week. He climbed three stairs into the train, showed his ticket, and made his way down the aisle to the first-class car. All six compartments were again empty, and Ian chose the same cabin as before. He didn't feel like napping this week, just pulled a pad out and began to write down every fact he could about the mysterious notes, the police investigation, and the unknown person who was watching him, studying him, from the darkness.

Ian had just finished writing down the details of the second note — *Forget there are monsters, and they will thrive* — when he heard the beverage cart clatter down the aisle. A knock sounded on the compartment doorframe and Ian called for the porter to enter, expecting Lucas and his Irish accent. Instead, the hand that drew back the curtain belonged to a stout, older black man who greeted Ian and asked if he wanted a drink. Ian requested a ginger ale and asked if the porter had any snacks in the cart.

"Pretzels," replied the fellow. "Cashews for a dollar." He had a scratchy voice, as though he had spent too many years yelling or smoking or both. As the man placed the snack on the table, Ian saw the man's enormous hands, broad and flat as plates. Each was liver spotted and the color of fine cocoa. The porter straightened up and asked if Ian needed anything else.

"Nothing at the moment," Ian replied. "I might like some tea later, if possible."

The porter nodded. "I'll come back in maybe forty-five minutes," he said. "If you'd like it before, just push this button." He pointed to a small black call box Ian hadn't noticed before. "Ask for Trout, and I'll bring it up."

Ian nodded and the porter disappeared.

Returning to his writing, Ian jotted down the rest of the details that he could remember from Oakley's visit. When he'd finished there were several pages of notes, and it seemed odd to have the entire situation condensed so neatly — knocks, note, waiting car, scary note, police. Looking over his words, he wondered if he'd purposely left out all the frightening bits, because on paper the whole thing seemed fairly innocuous. He was about to glance through his list a second time when the porter returned. Ian glanced at his watch — the minutes had passed quickly.

Trout cleared Ian's soda and the empty pretzel wrapping and set out a small carafe of boiling water along with a mug and tea bag. He was going to step out of the compartment when Ian asked if they always had different porters each week.

"No, sir," said Trout. "We stay on the same routes for the most part. I was down in Tennessee last week for my granddaughter's wedding, but otherwise I've been on this route for the better part of eight years."

The number sounded familiar. "Same as the fellow who filled in for you."

Trout stepped into the compartment, eyebrow raised. "Nobody else has been on this train that long."

Ian paused. "I thought that's what he said. . . ."

"Was it a fellow who pretends to be Irish?"

"Pretends?"

"Yeah, skinny older guy named Lucas," said Trout, a knowing grin coming to his round face. "He's a floater we picked up from the New York subways. He was a brakeman for them for about twenty-nine years, but he never rode these trains before." Now the grin stretched into a smile. "He spins stories so that people will tip him more."

Ian opened his mouth to say something, thought better of it, and simply answered: "Well, at least I didn't tip him."

Trout found that funny and gave a solid laugh that filled the small compartment and brought tears to the man's eyes. He dabbed at them and asked if he was needed for anything else.

Ian thought a second and told Trout how Lucas had left him last week with a little piece of advice that was supposed to help him through his day. Something new might be in order since the first had come from the mouth of a liar.

Trout lowered his head in thought and when he looked up, his eyes flashed in the light spilling through the window. "This is something my daddy told me growin' up. He said, 'Trout, don't live like your future was in your past or your past was the only thing in your future.' "

"Apparently," Ian told Trout, trying hard not to laugh, "Lucas is not only a liar but a thief as well."

The train pulled into the station only a few minutes late and Ian got off, found his Cherokee, and made his way home in just under twenty minutes. Cain snoozed in a puddle of sunlight falling through the French doors on the opposite side of the kitchen and seemed unimpressed at Ian's return. A note from Rebecca on the table steered him to some leftover pasta that he microwaved while sorting through the day's mail.

Ten minutes after the microwave chimed, he'd finished his meal and was ready for the evening. He nearly headed into the den when he remembered his promise on Sunday to Peter Ray. The writers group met tonight. Hesitating only a moment, he turned back to the kitchen, picked up his keys from the counter, and headed out to the garage without another thought. Ian knew he could convince himself to stay home, but he'd been changing his mind too many times in recent days and needed to stick by a decision. He turned east out of his driveway and headed through the oncoming dusk into Titansburg.

Hitting all the lights and finding a parking spot right outside DeCafé meant an early arrival, and when Ian entered, he saw none of the others. In fact, DeCafé was empty and the owner hadn't even bothered to turn music on. Ian set his pad and pen on the counter and ordered a plain cup of coffee. The barista handed him a bone white mug and pointed to a line of carafes at the end of the counter. Each had a sign in front of it claiming the beans had been picked in some far land. Ian chose Burma, filled his mug, and took a quick tour of the café, examining the beachscapes. One striking enough might find its place on the wall next to the framed picture Howard had shot of Zion.

"New stuff at the back," said a dreadlocked man from behind the counter. "In case you're interested."

Ian waved to him in thanks and kept looking. One shot was of a wave curling over a jetty. A second image showed a gabled mansion high on a bluff, surf roiling far below. The last picture was a black-winged gull, its neck twisted so the bird could look over its own back, straight at the lens. Next to the photos were a group of pale watercolors that Ian didn't much like, so he skipped over those and made his way toward the back of the café.

Pottery — mostly latte mugs and bud vases — occupied two shelves of the far wall. Ian liked the autumnal colors the artist had chosen: forest green, deep gold, a rich brick. Behind the shelves was a tiny alcove that Ian had never even noticed. He stepped through the doorway and looked about.

Furnished as though someone had raided one too many garage sales, the nook looked like a quiet place to come read. A girl glanced up from a copy of *Spin* as Ian stood in the doorway, but just as quickly returned to her magazine. Ian almost left, but a sign over the young woman's head caught his eye and he leaned forward to make sure he'd read it correctly.

ENGAGING

Ian wondered briefly what it meant, then noticed the price tag and the custom framing and matting. This was art, and all through the room words hung like balloons in a comic strip without characters.

GROUND ZERO
FREEZING
DECISION

Ian saw little logic in either the chosen words or their arrangement on the wall, and the closest thing to a sentence still needed a few verbs as well as some creative punctuation. He shook his head, wondering who would buy something like this, and stepped to the nearest word to check the price. One hundred fifty bucks. Ian whistled, and the girl in the chair looked at him over the magazine as if he'd beckoned her.

"Expensive," he said with a shrug, and she returned to her article. Ian began reading through the words one more time, shaking his head, when he noticed one word in particular.

CHANT

The bold black letters carved into the cream canvas reminded him of something, and he stood a minute staring until it came to him.

The notes.

He had seen the dramatic lettering before — those same five letters on the note that had his last name written on it. Ian stared at the painting and slashed it with an imaginary clot of crimson. It was the same cold, thick lettering. He turned from the room and walked straight to the counter to ask about the artist. He or she had written Ian's notes.

Norman Gruitt. Ian wrote the name down on a slip of paper and made a note to call the police. He wasn't sure what connection the name might provide, but he'd always written that a bad lead was better than no lead at all. He took a sip of coffee and smiled to himself. He had found a clue. Immediately, his thoughts went to the notes Louis requested. Perhaps writing about the events might not be a bad idea. If this discovery led anywhere Ian would be the hero of his own story. Perhaps it might not make a book, but a six-page article with photos and complimentary quotes from the police on Ian's work might not be such a bad thing. Men's magazines were always looking for things like that — or maybe *Rolling Stone*.

As Ian finished his coffee, the door opened. Jaret Chapman stepped through and came to an instant stop, eyes wide. Ian waved him over, and as soon as he sat down, the door opened a second time and Peter Ray entered. He looked pleased but not surprised, and Ian was glad the man had trusted his word.

As they waited for Kevin Contrade, Pete explained how the writing group worked. Ian was happy to see things hadn't changed too much since college. Every week the group discussed a chapter written by one member and took home from a second a copy of the chapter they'd discuss the next week. Tonight was Jaret's turn for discussion and Pete would hand out his chapter for next week.

"After that I think Jaret agreed to take Kevin's place. Maybe you can hand out yours after him," said Pete. "Then we'll be in our new schedule."

Ian said however it worked out would be fine, and the conversation turned to small talk. When Pete asked Ian what had happened during the week, he burst into his story about strange words appearing on his doorstep and the police visit. Neither Pete nor Jaret spoke, and when he made them follow him to the back room to see the words, they trailed in silence. The three of them stared at the fractured sentence for twenty seconds before anyone spoke.

"Man," muttered Jaret, "you should make this into a story."

Ian laughed, said the boy had a fine career in editing ahead of him, and was about to explain what he meant when a new voice spoke.

"What are we doing back —" Kevin began to ask, then stepped into the alcove, a look of disbelief, almost disgust, on his face. His next sentence came out through clenched teeth. "What in the world are all these Norman Gruitt words doing here?"

Back at the table, Ian retold his story to Kevin. When he finished, he expected the man to supply an answer to his obvious question; instead, Kevin's rocking slowed and he seemed lost in thought. Ian couldn't say if the man had been listening at all.

Kevin looked up eventually and saw each of the men looking at him.

"I guess you want to know about Norman Gruitt," he said, voice hushed.

All three nodded, waiting.

"Are you sure you're all right?" Kevin asked Ian, and after Ian said he was fine, his wife was fine, and his dog was still dumb and happy, the teacher began his explanation.

"Norman's an old acquaintance of mine, but I can tell you that he isn't your stalker. For one thing, he's about seventy-seven." He paused. "For another, he's legally blind."

The moment Kevin said the words, Ian imagined what a fine twist it could make in the story Louis asked him to write. A second later he realized it also meant that his clue was a little less meaningful than he'd first believed. He noted both thoughts on his pad and managed to take dictation as Contrade gave a few more details about meeting Norman. He'd tutored the fellow for his high school equivalency examination and had simply remained a helping hand as Gruitt gradually lost his vision through the years.

"Are you sure the writing is the same?"

Kevin asked Ian after finishing.

Ian said he'd been convinced twenty-five minutes ago but couldn't say anymore. He was still going to pass along the information to the police, but he'd ask them to make their inquiries discreet. If that was fine with Kevin.

Kevin nodded but looked worried, and Ian noticed that his rocking had become uneven. He made no mention of it, though, and Pete broke the moment and suggested they get on with writing and critique Jaret's chapter. Most of the conversation went over Ian's head since he hadn't read the chapter, but he quickly realized that the seminary student's book, *A Genealogy of Sorts,* was a linked progression of conversion stories. This chapter, from what he could gather, focused on a young boy. Kevin and Pete agreed that the writing was improving each new chapter, agreed that narrative drive of the story was becoming clearer, and agreed that they were interested to see how the next chapter would unfold. Ian began to wonder if the group would be at all helpful when the two men reached their first disagreement. Pete felt the chapter was unique and believable, while Kevin thought it was obvious, a cliché of innocence and childlike faith.

"Like a Precious Moments figurine," explained Kevin when asked to give his reasons. "Dewy eyes, clasped hands. Who hasn't seen this before?"

Pete said he couldn't disagree more. He thought the boy was a fully developed character who had a specific and believable understanding of God. The fact that the boy's father talked to him about his thoughts, explained how to pray, made it complex.

"This chapter — more than the baseball player and more than the alcoholic — gets to the heart of genealogy," Pete said, "because it's the boy's father who is kneeling there with the kid. There's not only the spiritual family but a true blood relationship as well."

Kevin grumbled that he still thought the scene was contrived and that he had liked the earlier chapters better. Everyone nodded, and that seemed to be the final word. Jaret collected the reviewed copies of his chapter and stuffed them into a thicket of papers to be forced back into his schoolbag. Outside, a car alarm sounded, cycling twice through its repertoire of noises before being shut off. Pete handed out single chapters of his story to Kevin and Jaret and a thick stack of pages to Ian. He explained that it was all five chapters of his book and guessed the thing would make more sense if he could read it from the beginning. Ian nodded and looked at the title as he moved to the door. *Quinlin's Estate.*

Outside, a thin fog had rolled in off the water, and the evening was cooler than it had been in weeks. Jaret and Pete said goodbye and turned north. Kevin and Ian stood in front of the café. As Ian turned toward his car, Kevin cleared his throat to speak.

"I wanted to thank you for Cheryl's interview tomorrow," he said, eyes down. "I talked to her today. She's thrilled . . . nervous, but thrilled."

Ian smiled, said it was no problem. He looked at the thin man, his gaunt arms cocked so bony hands rested on what should've been hips. Every inch of him was angled and hard and yet, in his eyes, in his thanks, Ian knew he was sincere. "You look out for your students. That's a good thing."

Kevin shrugged, took a few steps, and wished Ian a safe drive home. Ian added his own farewell, wondering again about this odd man. The thought passed when he saw it was after nine-thirty. He brought the engine to life and headed toward home. Next to him lay five chapters of Pete's story and every note he'd written that day about the odd things going on around his home. He had stories to tell Rebecca when he got home and an interview with Kevin's former student tomorrow. He even had a phone call to make to Oakley and the police department about Norman Gruitt the blind artist. His Cherokee found the curves it had passed over hundreds of times with ease, and Ian tapped his fingers along to a Simon and Garfunkel song on the radio. For the first time in months, he felt that the imposing quiet had passed. His life was once more filled with language, conversation, words, and stories galore. He had things to say and things to write, and it felt as if he might never see another blank page again. He began to sing along to the music, stopping only once to laugh when he realized he had just repeated a whole chorus about the sound of silence.

EARLY MORNING. THURSDAY, JULY 18

Ian managed to get back on track for his novel and wrote sentences in his head while Cain picked her way among scattered branches and the low-hanging boughs of full evergreens. Over the creek, across mown fields heavy with broken stalks of scattered grass, up one hill and across another they walked and Ian wrote, thinking about this elusive character he'd created: a ghost of the present, living his crimes and passions and sins again and again in front of the people he met.

It would be the small things that turned people away, the hidden moments of the man's life. Strangers would meet him and see, living in his eyes, how that morning he had thought of his wife as fat rather than beautiful. See how he blamed a coworker for a lost letter. See how he pitied his own father for being old and slow. Transparent in thought and deed, the man lived on display as though without skin or edifice, and people would turn away, avoiding him until he was all alone, a ghost of the present.

Cain quickened to a trot and kept the pace for the remaining length of the walk, and by the time they rounded the mailbox she was wheezing and panting from strain. Ian wiped beading sweat from above his eyes and unleashed his dog. She scrambled up the porch and, when Ian opened the door, into a house smelling of French toast.

Rebecca leaned from behind the stove and waved to Ian, saying that she'd wanted a real breakfast this morning and that there was plenty if he was hungry. Ian hung the leash, pulled off his running shoes and socks, and walked barefoot to the kitchen, where he took a seat. Rebecca poured him a glass of orange juice and asked how many slices of French toast he'd like. Ian downed the juice and then held up three fingers.

"With strawberries?" Rebecca asked.

Ian lifted an eyebrow. "Have I missed a special occasion?"

"No, no. Just that my advisor thought my thesis change was a terrific idea and you finished a chapter and it seems like a time to celebrate with breakfast."

"Here, here," said Ian, grabbing the morning paper. A charity clambake made the front page, surrounded by an article about dangerous riptide locations on the beaches, another about a supermarket closing, and a third covering the local middle school renovation. It might feel like spring outside, but summer had reached its doldrums, a time when things moved so slowly even a local newspaper could keep up. Rebecca set a platter of powdered French toast triangles in front of him, followed by a glass bowl of sliced strawberries. Ian asked once more if there was a reason for it all. His wife laughed and shook her head no.

"But if it happens again tomorrow, I might need a favor."

■ ■ ■ ■

After breakfast, a quick phone call to the police to alert them about Norman Gruitt, and Rebecca's departure for the museum, Ian worked. Alone in his office, he put to paper all the sentences that he'd formed during the morning's walk. Three hours disappeared, and he'd just finished a chapter when he realized Cheryl Rose would appear any minute. As he walked from the den into the living room he glanced out the bay window and saw a white hatchback pull into his driveway. Kevin's student was right on time. He rushed to the kitchen to pour some juice and waited for the doorbell to ring.

One minute passed, and Ian poured himself another splash of orange juice.

A second minute passed. Ian set the juice back in the refrigerator and washed the glass.

Third minute.

Fourth.

Fifth. Ian walked to the window to look outside.

The car was stopped at the bottom of the driveway, and it didn't look like anybody was in it. He leaned over his couch to get a better view, but just as he did the doorbell chimed. He peered as hard as he could, but the angle to the front stoop was too severe, and all Ian could make out was the shadow of someone holding a notebook. The silhouette spilled down the steps and out into the yard. Ian made his way to the door, checking briefly at the peephole: it was a young African-American woman with braided hair who swayed from side to side with what Ian took to be a case of nerves. He unlatched the door and pulled it open.

The girl blinked a few times to adjust her eyes to the dim foyer light and held out her hand, introducing herself as Cheryl Rose.

Ian took her hand, said his name, and asked what in the world she'd been doing in her car for five minutes.

Cheryl inhaled quickly and looked to the floor. "Mr. Contrade taught us never to be early for an interview. He said to use the time to review questions if we have to but to never seem desperate or your subject will realize it and walk all over you." The words came out in one breath.

"Huh," said Ian, "and here I thought all journalists were just lazy roustabouts without watches or alarm clocks."

She looked up and smiled. Cheryl was tall, and when she stared at Ian he nearly looked her straight in the eye. She held his gaze.

"Can I give you a piece of advice?" Ian asked, waiting for the woman to nod. "As one who's been interviewed hundreds of times: Show up on time. You'll make a friend and you'll get better quotes."

"Gotcha," said Cheryl, then asked where Ian wanted to hold the question-and-answer session.

Ian pointed her to his den and asked if he could offer her a drink. She held up a hand to say no thanks. Ian went to the kitchen, filled a glass from the faucet, and dropped in some ice cubes. Reminding himself that this was a favor, that she was only an intern, Ian grabbed his glass and headed back to the den. Cheryl stood looking at the pictures and awards on the far wall, her hand absently stroking Cain's ears as the dog sat beside her, also looking up.

"Ready to start?" Ian asked.

The reporter nodded and took a seat, folded her notebook cover back, and waited for Ian to settle. He leaned back in his leather desk chair and told her to fire away.

The basic biographical information about Ian came first — date of birth, full name — and Ian was reminded that this was the second time in a week he'd been interviewed. Only this interviewer didn't wear a badge.

"Is this your office?" Cheryl asked when she finished her introductory questions. Ian nodded, and Cheryl said she had an idea that might make the interview a little more interesting. She stood up and pointed to his cluttered walls, a careerful of mementos in every corner of the room. She said his belongings told their own story and, if he wouldn't mind, she wanted to use his office as her door into the real Ian Merchant. The nervous girl who'd rung the doorbell was gone. Ian was staring at a confident, enthusiastic woman.

"I've done my research, Mr. Merchant," she said, again holding his gaze. "We could write the same old story about how you get your ideas and what scares you, but this is my one chance and I want to try something different."

Ian looked around his den, his eyes falling on different decorations. He nodded; it wasn't a bad idea.

"Walls do have ears," he said, and when Cheryl said that would make a great title, he asked where she'd like to start.

She pointed with her thumb over her shoulder at a framed image of a thorough-bred in full stride and said, "What's with the horse?"

"That's Katherine Shade," Ian answered.

"She's a three-year-old running on the Carolina circuit. The owners asked to name her after one of my characters, and when I said sure, they sent up the picture." He laughed and said, "The reason there's no other horses in the photo is because she came in dead last."

"How about the baseball?" Cheryl inquired, pointing to the top of a filing cabinet.

Ian turned. The bruised scuff against white horsehide still looked as black as the day he had caught it. He turned back to the reporter. "Foul ball I caught at Fenway Park. Dwight Evans hit it during a playoff game against the Angels in 1986."

She nodded and penciled some notes, looking up as she finished. She traced the clutter, and Ian watched as she passed over every plaque, decoration, and piece of art in the room. After a moment she looked back at him. "You really don't mind doing this?" she asked.

Ian said nope, so Cheryl flipped over a page in her notebook, ready to continue. Ian sipped his water, picked up a small photo across from him, and started once more.

After the third object, Cheryl stopped prompting and Ian simply spoke. Words had

116

flowed from his fingers earlier, and now they came from his mouth. It felt good not to struggle for the right thing to say, the right combination of sounds. He simply talked.

Most objects and decorations were simple. There was the original movie poster from the *Creature From the Black Lagoon,* and a shadow box that held a cape worn by Bela Lugosi in the original *Dracula.* Ian pointed out a map of the world Louis presented to him after the Portuguese translation of *Hunter* was released. Every country in which Ian sold a book was colored in, and nearly the entire globe was stained in red permanent marker.

"No royalties from Iran?" Cheryl said, looking at the map.

"Banned," said Ian and waited to see if she had anything else to add. Comments and follow-up questions were the only times she spoke; otherwise it was simply his voice.

Three cherry plaques from a booksellers association hung one under the other. Next to them was a photo a friend had sent him from Romania of a Gothic castle with severe, narrow turrets and a high drawbridge that was supposed to be part of the inspiration for the vampire mythology.

"People send me weird stuff all the time,"

Ian said, and Cheryl nodded mildly. "No," Ian stated, and she looked at him. "I mean *weird* stuff. Like a live vampire bat. Or that thing," he said, pointing to a shrunken head that had been tacked to a corkboard by its hair. "My agent, when I had one, sent me that from Zaire and told me he bartered with some tribesman to get it. Gave away a Yankees cap or something like that. Found out later it's dried Macintosh skin and he'd got it in Waynesport, New York, at an apple festival."

"That's sick."

Ian laughed. "My agent could be a character."

"No." Cheryl smiled. "I mean that people in upstate New York are making those things for a community carnival."

Ian smiled, leaned across the table, and lowered his voice to a whisper. "I've named it."

Cheryl's mouth tightened with displeasure.

Looking at the wrinkled face, Ian couldn't help but grin. "His name is Noel. Noel Buford. He used to be a psychiatrist, but you know what happens to headshrinkers with bad karma." He waited for a response.

Cheryl stopped writing and looked at Ian.

"Do you want me to use this?"

Ian sighed. "No, make that last part off the record." He leaned back in his chair. "And I'm not as odd as I sound. There was a doctor who wrote a book about the psychology behind the horror culture in America. His name was Noel Buford. Read it sometime if you have the chance. According to him I'm either a latent sociopath waiting to abuse my family or a frustrated deviant getting off on horror because the rest of me is impotent."

A worried look again crossed Cheryl's face.

Ian took a deep breath. "Pinning him to my wall and smacking him every once in a while is cathartic in a way you wouldn't believe."

The young woman finally smiled, so Ian moved on.

There was a photo of him dressed as a mummy for Halloween with two other novelists as a gypsy and a greaser at his side. Next to that was a signed photo of Jimmy Carter that Ian picked up when they worked the same book convention. He told Cheryl to read the inscription.

She stood up, approached the photo, and read: " 'You're the reason I lost to Reagan. Your Mortal Enemy, James Earl Carter,

Jr.' " She turned to Ian with a blank face.

He sighed. "My wife doesn't think it's funny either," he said. "The President and I thought it was hilarious, though. I signed a picture for him saying I used his four years of presidency as the basis of a zombie character."

Cheryl forced a smile.

"Book conventions get boring," he tried.

"They must," she replied, unconvinced, and looked around. "Anything else?"

Ian shook his head.

"What about that one?" she asked, pointing to a black-and-white photo. It was a wind-scarred rib cage half buried in drifting desert sand. "I've never seen anything like that before."

"Christmas gift," Ian said.

Cheryl blanched and said that he did get unusual gifts. Then she leaned closer. "Is there something written on it?" Before Ian answered, she got up and walked to the photo, crouching to get a closer look. She stared for a few minutes, stood, and looked at Ian.

"It's from the Bible," he answered, though she hadn't exactly asked a question.

"The poem?"

"From a psalm."

She crouched, read the words, and then

turned to Ian. "I don't get it."

"Neither did I for a long time," he replied and clapped his hands. "We gotta wrap this up. I need to work and so do you. We both need to get writing."

Cheryl looked at the photo again and shrugged. She gathered her notebook, tucked the pencil into its spiral binding, and smiled, saying again how thankful she was for the chance to speak with him. Ian opened his palms as if to say it was no problem and then walked her to the door. She said that the article was due to publish next Wednesday and that she could send him a copy if he'd like. Ian said that they got the local paper and that he'd be sure to read it right away.

"Gotta see if you quoted me right."

At the door they stopped, and Cheryl shook Ian's hand. Opening the door, she stepped outside, but instead of closing it she looked up and said there was one more thing. Ian waited.

"I spoke with Mr. Contrade last evening. He mentioned that you'd received some threatening notes."

Ian closed his eyes and breathed slowly. The girl was smart; she waited till the end to ask the tough question. After they had chatted and laughed and become acquainted.

"I was wondering if I could mention it," she continued. "Nothing too specific, just the two notes and the fact that harassment is part of your life. You said you get lots of weird things from people. It would help show the boundary between weird and dangerous."

Clever woman. Ian rubbed at his chin and tried to think of a way to keep it out of the paper but couldn't fashion anything convincing and told her she had his permission.

"Just watch the details."

"I always do."

After Cheryl let the door close, Ian headed back to his den; he had another four hours of work ahead of him before Rebecca came home. Straightening the chairs, he thought about the interview and had to admit the thing had gone far better than he could have predicted. She'd been more prepared and less intimidated than he'd expected, and she'd found an interesting hook. Cheryl had even managed not to ask why he'd become a horror writer. It was a standard question that Ian answered with a simple lie — his my-best-friend-disappeared story — because the real reasons were too complex, and explaining it would be like recounting why he was alive in the first place. The girl won points for originality; he would have to let Kevin know Cheryl had been well taught.

Ian gazed around the room and then walked to the photo that the girl had inquired about last. He looked at the image. Howard Kepler certainly had had an eye for the dramatic. How he had rigged this shot Ian had no idea, but the barren image made his mouth dry. Sand and sun and the rough texture of bone. Just the thought of that heat and wind — elements that pared ribs clean of flesh, bleached them white as teeth — made him thirsty, and he wondered what it would be like to suffer like that. Did the photographer realize, shooting this image, that one day he too would fall in the desert and face the same holocaust of hot, dry air until they'd stripped his body of its liquid strength? And even though he'd been found and flown to a hospital, that the exposure lasted too long and inside he had already become like this photo: stripped bare of life, barren, arid, and skeletal.

Ian read the words: *I am poured out like water and all my bones are out of joint. My heart has turned to wax; it has melted away within me.*

Around him was silence. His flow of words

ended for a moment and he closed his eyes. For the first time since the Utah funeral — even though the graveyard had held the ghastly reminders of heat and wind — Ian realized what it meant for his friend to die that way. Hip shattered. Fingers and arms reaching for anything stronger than sand that he might pull himself forward. Dizzying heat in a world without shadows or shade. Three days exposed to the sun. Howard died parched and cramped, his skin ablaze, his lips cracked and brittle as fired clay.

Ian slumped against the wall, and tears wet his cheeks. Such a marvelous thing was the body that it could produce water on its own — shed it in great salty drops — and yet Howard suffered so thoroughly that even his tears must have dried up. The stillness of the room was immense, and Ian sniffled. His friend's sorrow, waiting for the last painless sleep, would have been as arid and ragged as the cry of a coyote. One blasted voice crying out for water, for coolness, or if not, then for death.

Ian's chest heaved, and he imagined Howard breathing a lonely cry into the desert sky with nothing, not even an echo, for a reply. Tears tumbled from Ian's eyes, drawing together in ragged streams down his cheeks. It had come from nowhere, from a quick glance at an old photo, and yet the release felt huge.

Ian leaned with his back against the wall, unhooked the photo from its nail, and held it to his chest until his breath came back to him and the heavy pain dissolved. He straightened, walked to a filing cabinet, and slipped the image inside. There was no need, on a daily basis, to see an image of a man predicting his own death.

MORNING. FRIDAY, JULY 19

For the second day in a row the house was filled with the smells of breakfast. Bacon sizzled on a back burner while Rebecca shuffled between flipping pancakes and setting the table. Ian watched from the living room for a few minutes as his wife bounced from table to stove and wondered what the favor was that she had in mind.

She mentioned nothing while they ate, and Ian was glad for the quiet. He'd had a long night filled with dreams of desert heat and enjoyed the opportunity to bury those thoughts in a stack of pancakes, three strips of bacon, and the comfort of a shared silence. They ate and Ian didn't worry about Howard or the stalker who seemed to have disappeared or even Rebecca's request.

Pancakes disappeared, as did the bacon, and when he took the last sips of his coffee, his wife finally spoke.

"It's a good favor, I think. Or fun at least," she said, as though they'd already been on the topic. "I need your help going through Katherine Jacoby's house this Saturday. The lawyers finalized all the paper work, and the museum has full access to the estate. Her letters and papers can come home for my thesis, and the rest will go to auction."

"Breakfast for that?" Ian asked. "You're doing me a favor. I haven't ransacked a dead woman's belongings on a weekend since I was a teenager."

"Hearing what you were like as a kid, I don't doubt that."

Ian opened his mouth to say that he wasn't kidding, thought better of it, and let the moment pass. Breakfast ended, and before she left for work Rebecca looked in the refrigerator, complained there was nothing all that exciting, and suggested that Ian meet her for dinner at Patrick Henry's Diner. He agreed, and as she left she said she was taking his Cherokee so that she could haul stuff from Katherine's home. Ian blew her a kiss in response and she disappeared. As the echo of the garage door fell silent in the house, Ian loaded the dishwasher, then moved to his den. He did not let his eyes linger over the empty spot where Kepler's picture had hung, but spun his chair toward his computer and waited while it whirred to life. Words began to tumble through his mind, and when enough had gathered, he would write.

Pages flowed from Ian's fingers, and the gypsy cursed Joshua Yardley, transforming this stolid, everyday man into a ghost to the world, transparent in thought and deed. Paragraphs later, after the man returned home, his wife stared at him over the dinner table and saw a vision of her husband, his eyes following the swell of another woman's bosom as she passed him on the street. That night, Joshua's wife hugged him to her chest as they lay in bed, but she couldn't drive the ugly thought of his eager eyes from her mind. In sleep she moved to the edge of the bed, turned her back on him, and curled into a dismal ball.

Ian saved his work, stretched, and moved to the kitchen to scare up some lunch. The phone rang. Cain, drowsing in her nook near the pantry at the back corner of the kitchen, lifted her head to blink at Ian a few times before deciding sleep was her imperative today. Ian grabbed the receiver at the third ring and gave a greeting.

"You missed a note," said a voice Ian couldn't place. "There were three." The caller's inflection was small, almost birdlike.

"How do you . . ." Ian began, realized what he'd just heard, and stopped.

"See you soon," said the voice.

There was a click and then only the dull emptiness of a dead line. Without hanging up, Ian moved to the counter, found Detective Oakley's card among the numerous notes and papers piled everywhere, and dialed the police department. A receptionist transferred him to Oakley, and Ian found some comfort in the officer's assuring words that he and some men would be right over to check the grounds. Ian hung up and whistled for Cain.

The dog stood, yawned, and staggered over to Ian as he leaned against the counter. She did nothing except allow him to stroke her head, but Ian was glad not to be entirely alone. He rubbed her silky ears and scratched her neck and tried to keep from hearing the voice of the caller in his head — the chirping whisper warning him of a third note. His hand paused on the top of Cain's head, and he glanced around his home. Nothing could take away the chill of wondering whether it would be found inside or out.

For the first hour after they arrived, the police searched and Ian waited. He tried Rebecca at work a few times but was told she'd gone over to Katherine Jacoby's house. He could not write, nor was reading any help. The wasteland of afternoon television wasn't an option, so he ended up tagging along at the detective's side as they scoured the grounds. They located nothing. Two officers working in the house also failed to find even a single scrap of paper that hadn't previously been there.

Oakley ordered a second search, and the two teams switched locations. Ian and Oakley searched inside while the other pair of cops walked the grounds. A second hour passed: No third note could be found. It was now after two o'clock, and Oakley said he could no longer see the need for the other officers to remain. He exited through the French doors and crossed the lawn. Ian watched him from the kitchen and decided to try Rebecca one more time. The receptionist said she was still out of the office. Ian asked if there was any way to track her down, but the woman said the phone had been disconnected at the Jacoby place.

Ian asked for the number anyway and, just as promised, got a prerecorded message. He hung up and looked at his watch. Their date at Patrick Henry's was a little more than two hours away, and there was really nothing to tell her except that some maniac now had their phone number. Ian assumed it would sound just as bad over dinner as it might have at work.

The patio door swung open and Oakley stepped through.

"A very unproductive search."

For a few seconds Ian said nothing, trying to figure out if not finding a note was good or bad. Finally he just asked.

The detective shook his head and said he didn't know. Could mean the call was a crank. Could mean the call was legitimate but the caller was lying for some reason. Could mean they simply hadn't found the note.

Ian asked the other question that had been on his mind all afternoon. "What happens now?"

Oakley motioned for Ian to sit at the table and began to give his suggestions for stepping up security. The first was to check every window and lock on the house and make sure they all functioned. He knew it sounded simple, but it was easy to overlook the obvious in times of distress.

Ian said he'd do it the moment the police left.

"Good," the officer said. "I'd also suggest getting a security system. I can recommend some companies. A dog might not be a bad idea either."

"I have a dog."

Cain, sitting at the French door staring into the yard, turned her head a bit, caught Ian's eye, and walked over to lick his palm. He scratched her ears for a bit, and then she moved to Oakley, who also rubbed her fur. He looked at Ian and smiled.

"Oh," said Ian, "a *real* dog."

The officer nodded and gave Cain two quick slaps on her rump. He refolded the list, said there were other more drastic options — a gun, security personnel — but the situation didn't warrant extreme measures yet.

"Small favors," Ian said, trying not to sound bitter or scared. He knew he probably did a bad job of it, because Oakley did his best to assure him that all these suggestions were precautionary. Most likely the fellow would get too stupid or bold and they'd snatch him up. Then he changed the subject entirely.

"I started one of your books," he said.

"Monster."

"Really?" Ian asked, genuinely surprised.

"Scary stuff. Especially as a parent. I can't imagine seeing something grab your kid like that."

Ian nodded.

Oakley cleared his throat and said, "I don't like it."

Ian smiled because he thought the man was joking, but a glimpse of the officer's quiet eyes told him the comment was not in jest. He pursed his lips to quit the grin and asked what Oakley didn't enjoy.

The officer tried to explain.

He had seen evil. He had seen it growing up in Pittsburgh when the kid next door pushed a cat out a fifth-story window for no reason. He saw it training with the Altoona police department, tackling a bar patron who sliced someone's upper arm with a broken bottle because of an offhand comment about a jukebox song — Patsy Cline's "Fall to Pieces." He hadn't seen it yet in Titansburg but got wires every day from homicide departments in Stamford, Providence, Brooklyn, Boston, Hartford, New York, all sounding the alarm in case a killer fled from one city to another.

"It's real," he concluded. "Who needs to imagine it?"

Ian looked at the table. His standard response for the criticism was ready but he didn't use it. He just stared at the centerpiece.

"I hope I didn't offend you," said Oakley after a few seconds.

Ian shook his head. He hadn't been offended, but he did want to respond to the officer. Writing horror, no matter how much he had struggled with it lately, meant something to him and couldn't just be dismissed as overkill.

Still looking into the assortment of daisies and cattails in his table decoration, Ian said, "I don't think I'm trying to focus on the horror as much as the response it causes. The lives of people working to overcome it. I think, in a way, it's about the heroism involved. People overcoming." He looked up at Oakley and shrugged.

The officer nodded as if he understood, but narrowed his brow. "But in reality, Ian, people rarely overcome. They're victims till their dying breath, scared and scarred and worn down. Something like what you're talking about changes a person."

Ian squinted a little, trying to form an argument. Finally he stopped and simply gave his thanks.

"You were honest. I appreciate it. And I'll

think about it too."

Oakley exhaled a loud breath and smiled. "Anne, my wife, told me not to say anything."

"Smart lady," Ian answered with a wink and asked how Oakley's mother-in-law was faring.

Oakley waved so-so with his hand. "Anne could use a rest," he added. "Anything to give her a break."

Ian thought for a moment, trying to come up with an idea — a place the couple might go for a retreat — but the only suggestions that flittered through his mind involved too much cash or too long a vacation, and he wasn't sure the Oakleys had much to spare of either.

"Well . . ." said Ian, then gave up.

Oakley shifted a little in his seat. "There is one thing I think would cheer her." His eyes seemed nervous.

Ian waited.

"She'd love to meet you," Oakley said, and before Ian could even blink he rushed on. "Nothing fancy. Maybe some evening we could meet you guys for dinner. I'm sure you know some nice places. Anne would kill for a reason to dress up."

The first thing Ian understood was how difficult it had been for Oakley to make the request. The man must love his wife a great deal to place himself in such an awkward situation. The second thing he knew was that he had to respond right away or the officer would take his silence as rejection. As he opened his mouth, Ian thought of Peter Ray and how meeting new people was often a good thing. His answer was that he and Rebecca would be glad to join the Oakleys for a meal. Next week sometime.

The detective looked relieved but still uncomfortable, and only after Ian took down the man's home number did the officer gain back a little of his color. He thanked Ian twice and a third time as they reached the door. Stepping onto the front porch, Oakley assured Ian that the nightly drive-bys would continue and that some men would be speaking with Norman Gruitt tomorrow afternoon. Ian said that sounded fine but he really wanted to get back inside and lock the door until he left for dinner. Oakley headed to his car and Ian stepped into the hall, snapped the bolt shut, and moved into the living room. Through the great window he saw Oakley's unmarked car pull away. He collapsed into his leather armchair and realized for the first time how tired he was.

His hamstrings, calves, and lower back

ached as if he'd just spent hours lifting weights, and one strand of muscle in his forearm continued to pulse and quiver through some unknown phantom effort. Every ounce of Ian felt worn, and his heart would not slow. This was not the weariness of effort, but the fatigue of fear, and it would not let him find release. Instead he sat staring out the window thinking of the two soft sounds that had invaded his life — the three small scratches against his garage door and some faceless person's threat. Ian watched the boughs of an elm sway in the afternoon breeze and realized in his writing he had been wrong about one thing: Horror was not always deafening in its approach. Sometimes it was silent as death.

Thirty minutes of sitting proved long enough to calm Ian, and he began to write down everything that had happened that afternoon. He scrawled eight pages of notes, mostly focusing on Detective Michael Oakley, and realized the dinner they'd arranged might work out for his writing as well. If Oakley was about to turn into a character, it'd be good to know as much about the man as possible. When he finished recording the events of the day, he looked at the clock and saw that he'd be meeting Rebecca in forty minutes. Once more the open space of the house overwhelmed him, and he decided to head to the diner early, grabbing Pete Ray's chapters so he'd have something to read while waiting.

Driving Rebecca's gold coupe, he ended up at the diner eight minutes later. Patrick Henry's — with its ridiculous buzzing neon sign, *Give Me Great Food or Give Me Death!* — was a tattered building on a truck route and served excellent burgers and thick shakes. A waitress seated Ian in a booth and delivered water while he placed *Quinlin's Estate* in front of him. Soon he was ignoring the growl of tractor trailers rolling by, oblivious to the palsied flicker of fluorescent light above. He was absorbed in the bizarre tale of a small central Pennsylvanian town and the triangular castle that towered over it from high atop a ridge. Fifteen pages in, just when the first foreshadowing of the castle's imminent destruction was revealed, a shadow fell across the pages. Ian looked up and into Rebecca's smiling face.

"Hi there, handsome. Mind if a girl takes a seat?"

Ian closed the story and put it aside. Rebecca looked exhausted. Flushed and breathless, her hair dusty and flat, she looked to Ian liked the girl he'd first dated, and he was happy to have her sitting across from him.

"Do you know how much junk a person accumulates in a lifetime?" she asked after taking a few moments to breathe. "And this person lived alone. She was an artist, for goodness' sake, and yet the things. Things, things, things!"

Ian figured it was a rhetorical question, so he didn't respond. A waitress arrived, took their identical orders of cheeseburgers, fries, and chocolate shakes, and headed across to the kitchen window to impale their requests for the short-order cook.

Rebecca winked at Ian and drank a little of her water. Then she leaned across the table and kissed his forehead with cool, moist lips. Returning to her seat she said that he was going to enjoy working at the Jacoby house on Saturday. Ian asked why, but she wouldn't offer any more and asked how his writing had gone.

He paused. It was the wrong thing to do. Rebecca's face lost color right away, and her eyes grew wide. She leaned toward him to ask if something had happened. Ian nodded and told her about the phone call, about Oakley's visit and the officer's suggestions for securing their home. Before she could give any kind of reply, their meals arrived. Rebecca looked down at her burger as though she did not even recognize it as food. Ian managed to nibble on a French fry.

When she looked up her eyes were liquid. In them Ian saw a tiny reflection of his own face. It reminded him too clearly of the first time they'd sat across from each other in silence and sadness, paralyzed by the unfavorable answers they'd received from a fertility clinic. That time Rebecca stopped eating for two days. This time, at least, she found the strength to pick up her cheeseburger.

"I do have a little good news," Ian said at last. "Detective Oakley asked me out."

Rebecca chewed as though thinking this through and ended up responding with a simple shrug.

"Actually," said Ian, "he asked us both out. We're going to meet him and his wife for dinner next week."

"Are you sure I won't be in the way?" said Rebecca, a small grin finding its way to her face. The tension of the moment was broken, and each made a more concerted effort to eat. Twice Ian tried to get Rebecca to open up about what she'd found in Katherine's home, but had no luck. Husband and wife finished at nearly the same time, and the check was soon on the table as well. They crossed the diner together and Ian slipped his arm into hers, grabbing her hand. He said he'd drive the Cherokee home if she didn't mind, and she squeezed his fingers in reply.

The parking lot smelled of diesel fuel and seared rubber and the night had gone cold, so they parted quickly for their cars. Ian was about to shift into reverse when he heard his name being yelled. He turned and looked out the window. Rebecca stood outside her car, and Ian thought she might not have her keys after all, but then saw her bloodless face and her raised arm.

He got out of the Cherokee and walked to her. She nodded to his passenger's side door and he knew what he'd find before he even turned around.

His name, once more, in black: MER-CHANT. The third note.

He grabbed Rebecca's cell phone from her glove compartment and dialed the police, who said they'd be right over to investigate. The wind snapped through the lot, so Ian motioned to her car. They sat silent, Ian cramped into the passenger's side, and soon the windshield began to fog. When the police car arrived, its strobes shone wild and distorted through the clouded windows.

Ian squeezed his wife's hand and opened the door to step out. Turning back to tell Rebecca she could stay in the car, he saw her eyes, swollen and filled with tears. The drops caught each swirl of light, and her whole face shone blue then red then blue again as the police car's lights spun behind them.

MORNING. SATURDAY, JULY 20

Rebecca yawned three times over her cereal, and Ian wondered if she'd managed to sleep at all. She didn't complain or shuffle about with her head bowed, but he guessed that she'd seen at least a few of the witching hours. As they rinsed out their bowls and juice glasses, he asked if she still wanted to head over to Katherine Jacoby's house, and she nodded with quiet determination. Breakfast finished, they dressed for a day of packing boxes and headed to the garage. Ian's Cherokee had been surrendered to the police for a thorough examination, so they folded themselves into the coupe and made their way to the house.

Fifteen minutes of driving brought them to a small intersection of farms. Right off the road sat a tiny Cape Cod, its steep roof shingled in a kaleidoscope of painted tiles.

Rebecca pulled into the driveway and parked. A small oyster shell path led up to a front door, painted in a rich forest green. Rebecca crunched her way inside and Ian followed. The house smelled of eucalyptus and cleanser, and they combined into something akin to a cough drop. Flattened boxes lay ready to be opened, taped, and filled. Rebecca pointed Ian to the living room and asked him to start there.

Ian made a pile of old newspapers before walking to a bench covered with sewing equipment — thimbles, spools of thread, and scissors spread across its top. He turned and asked Rebecca if she wanted everything put away and she nodded. The only way they were going to sort through all Katherine Jacoby's belongings was if the place was organized.

Ian shrugged and grabbed the scissors. They wouldn't move.

He tried the thread next, but it too was stuck to the bench. He turned to say something to Rebecca but she had her hand over her mouth, trying to hold back a smile.

"It's a sculpture called *My Mother's Table*," Rebecca said, waving at the bench. "Feel the scissors."

Ian brushed his fingers along the blade carefully, so as not to nick himself, and stopped almost immediately. He tried again and turned, amazed.

"It's wood!"

Rebecca nodded, explaining that the woman's special gift was painting her wooden sculptures so they looked real. Her face was regaining its light and energy.

"We're going to play a game," she said. "There are thirty-six sculptures in the house, three more in this room. Find them."

Ian turned about in a small circle and surveyed the room. All of a sudden it seemed much larger, as though the walls had pushed back. Every corner was filled with the woman's belongings.

An umbrella stand.

Lamps: standing, table, and even a green glass hanging one.

Sofas, a television, a mantel clock, a stack of firewood, a magazine rack.

Would somebody carve out a piece of art to look precisely like a magazine rack?

He looked up. On the wall above the magazine rack hung a carved driftwood configuration, a Star of David with a cross inside its center. He pointed to it.

Rebecca nodded and said, "That's called *Megan*. It's Hebrew for something. Two more."

Ian searched. He looked at one of the

burgundy armchairs for a minute trying to determine if the light was reflecting off it correctly for something upholstered in chenille. Deciding it was, he turned to a petite stained-glass lamp. Was it really on, or simply painted to look as though it were shining? Even bending over to get a better look, he couldn't make up his mind, and it was only when he closed his eyes and the afterimage of the colored plates gleamed behind his lids that he decided it was real.

He looked to the brick fireplace along the opposite wall. The second hand on the mantel clock was moving. The iron set of tools stood in a proper brass stand. Everything looked in order there, so he examined the windowsill. Cactus and jade plants huddled in one sunny corner, while in the other corner stood a single ruby rose in a cut-glass vase.

He turned, about to give up, and then looked back at the rose. It stood supple and blooming and perfect in every respect — except there was no water in the vase.

He pointed.

"Very good," said Rebecca. "It's called *Rose*."

"Original."

She smiled, looked down at her list and back at him. "One more." Her eyes flashed with mischief.

Ian scratched at his jaw and looked around. "I'm not going to get this, am I?"

Rebecca laughed. After a few seconds she pointed to the fireplace.

"It's on the fireplace?" Ian asked.

Rebecca shook her head slowly, walked across the room, and slid her finger along the brick facing of the hearth. She turned and invited Ian to do the same.

His mouth dropped open, and the only thing he could think to say was "You gotta be kidding me."

Rebecca walked Ian through the rest of the tiny house and pointed out the sculptures. Many were obvious — a cat that blended into a dog going the other way, the clay figure of a woman stretching, a model of two arms twisting around each other in an impossible tangle — but in every room was hidden at least one "invisible" sculpture that was impossible to find without feeling. In the kitchen it was a loaf of bread on a cutting board, crumbs and knife and all. In the bathroom it was a toothbrush, carved and painted to ape nylon and plastic, a stain of toothpaste smudging its handle. In the bedroom it was a small magnifying glass that brought out the grain of wood from the case on which it sat. Just pretty illusions painted to perfect reality.

From the bedroom they crossed into what Ian had thought was going to be a guest room. Instead it turned out to be a library, lined floor to ceiling on each wall with shelves creaking under the load of books. There was a familiar smell of mildewing pages and cheap paperback ink that reminded Ian both of Rebecca's library at home and also of Louis's downtown office. Worn carpet and a faded chair suggested that Katherine Jacoby visited the room often. Ian looked to Rebecca and asked where to start.

She shrugged. "I don't know where the sculpture is in this room. I just know it's called *Book.* We're here to find it."

Ian looked back to the shelves and again his perception shifted. The room now seemed twice as large, the rows three times as long.

"We have to go through all of these books?"

"We'd have to anyway. Everything the museum decides not to keep gets auctioned."

She tossed her clipboard to the rug and walked from the room to fetch boxes, so Ian grabbed a wooden stepstool and moved to the far corner. For thirty minutes straight, Ian tumbled books into his arms from the shelves and set them in piles on the carpet. Sometimes he caught an author's name — Twain, Dickens, Greene — but most times he just filled his arms without looking and tried to make the work go as fast as he could. When he'd finished he turned and saw that Rebecca's work of listing each book and searching for anything of value was going much slower. When he asked how he could help, she told him to keep any first editions or any titles published before 1945. Ian sat down and began to sort.

It surprised him how boring the work was. He loved books and usually enjoyed looking through others' libraries, yet in this case he was simply uninterested. The majority of the books Katherine Jacoby had owned were biographies or history books, and though on occasion he found a volume he'd read, most of them he'd never seen before. Title after title, book after book, he moved through the stacks.

After about fifteen minutes Rebecca laughed and Ian looked to see what she had found. She turned the book toward him, and Ian sighed. It was one of his own: *Katherine Shade.*

"Well, her taste isn't all bad," he replied

and went back to his stack.

From the corner of his eye he saw Rebecca crack the cover. She shook her head and read, " 'To Katherine, thanks for the center-piece. It completed the table. Ian Merchant.' "

Ian leaned over and looked at the book. His writing was scrawled in black marker across the inside page and he had signed his name with the usual flourish at the *t*.

"Guess you met her after all," said Rebecca and went back to the books.

Ian stared awhile longer at the page and then shut the cover. He went back to his pile and instead of speeding through he looked at each title, checked the spines and pages to see if they had been read, and tried to recall Katherine Jacoby. Volume upon volume passed and he was about to give up when he tried to turn the cover of a book and couldn't make it budge.

He looked down and realized he was holding a carved book. He motioned for Rebecca.

"Is that Katherine?" Ian asked his wife as she slid next to him, pointing to the portrait that had been sketched on the sculpture's wooden cover.

She nodded.

"I do remember her," Ian said, looking at

Katherine's portrait and tracing over the carved letters of the title with his fingers. She'd called it *Book: The Life and Times of Katherine Jacoby* and had fashioned it to look so real that Ian had to keep touching the wooden pages with their rough edges. Katherine had learned to taunt the eye, to hide things in plain sight, and Ian shook his head as he handed Rebecca the sculpture. He realized how difficult his wife's search would be to reveal any truth about this woman's life. In uncovering one thing, she might simply cover over something more important that had been left in the open, cleverly disguised and entirely overlooked.

From the library they moved to the bedroom, boxing clothes and discarding anything common. Ian admired two quilts, one of which Rebecca said contained the entire Judaic alphabet. Folding them up, he asked how the daughter of a Nazi Stormtrooper ended up being raised Jewish.

Rebecca reached up on tiptoe to unshelve some hats stored high in the closet. When she had secured them, she said that Katherine's aunt and uncle, the couple that everyone thought were her parents, had been Jewish. Since they adopted her, it was only natural that Katherine be brought up with their customs. Rebecca had found synagogue registries that listed all three Jacobys up until the uncle's death in 1949.

"But how did she come to be with these people in the first place?" Ian asked.

"That's what I'm hoping to find out."

Her answer was short, almost annoyed. Ian watched as she boxed the remaining clothes from the closet and headed back through the door. Following her to the kitchen, Ian realized they'd been through the entire house without anything that proved Katherine Jacoby had ever been in Germany.

"Is that picture all you have?" he asked as Rebecca tossed two garbage bags of trash onto the back patio.

"There's more here, somewhere," she said.

Ian looked around the house. "But you're changing your thesis . . ." he prompted.

Rebecca turned, color rising to her cheeks. "Things don't add up," she said. "Katherine looked nothing like the people who posed as her parents. She inherited nothing from them even when they had no other heirs. They didn't treat her as a daughter; they treated her like a boarder. Someone to house and feed. And then there's that picture of her. It is Katherine, I know it."

"Well, what about her letters?"

Rebecca's eyes dropped. "I haven't found any papers."

"How can you write your thesis without papers? One picture isn't enough. There has to be something —"

"Do you think I'm not aware of that?" she snapped, pushing past him to the garage door. She opened it, stepped through, and slammed it behind her before he could even move.

He waited for a few moments, scripting an apology for kicking his wife when she was down. She'd expected the letters to be in plain view, and they weren't. She needed to find them, not be lectured by him about what a poor choice she'd made. He moved to the garage door, pulled it open, and took the two steps to the concrete floor. Looking up, he thought he recognized the place.

"I've been here before," he said, turning about to stare.

"What? When?" asked Rebecca, off to his left. "When have you been here?"

"This is her work area, isn't it?"

"The belt sander tip you off?"

Ian ignored her for a moment and moved to the middle of the room. It was exactly like being in Howard Kepler's darkroom in Utah. There was an orderliness to the place, a sense that everything had been arranged specifically for a purpose. Film stock, calipers, and chemical baths had been replaced by varnish, T-squares, and table vises, but the feeling was the same. It was the third time Ian remembered feeling this way: first Kepler's darkroom, then a limestone Presbyterian church he had attended after Howard's funeral, and now here.

He looked to Rebecca and shook his head, amazed.

She walked to his side and asked what it was he saw.

"Can't you imagine her *being* here?" he asked.

Rebecca nodded, but Ian could tell she didn't understand. It was more than just a place to work or a place to go. It was being able to enter into something bigger than that. It was a secure spot to find communion, to reach toward something and not be aware of children crying around you or a sudden draft or a ringing telephone. It was a place of work and creation and more than either of those, worship.

Ian slipped an arm around his wife and assured her that they would find Katherine Jacoby's letters.

"But how can you be sure?" Rebecca asked, just the slightest catch in her voice, the worry making itself more evident now.

"I just think that someone who creates and builds and sees life so clearly that she mimics it in her art wouldn't go around throwing out letters."

Rebecca nodded and said, "But there's only four weeks until my thesis is due."

Ian laughed, "And I've got a novel expected in less than seven. Aren't we the pretty pair?" He squeezed her once more and repeated that they would find the notes.

Allowing herself a smile, Rebecca pulled Ian toward the far wall, saying she had a few more items to catalog before they were done. As Ian followed, he was aware for the first time of strange shapes covered in white sheets that lined the wall. Rebecca walked to the first and when she pulled back the linen Ian saw an enormous vase, grand and nearly four feet tall. On the sides, as on Grecian urns of old, were carved images. These, however, weren't of lovers frozen in eternal embrace or Olympian moments of sport. There was neither love nor joy on this vase.

On one panel were twisted bodies, corrupted and melting into what looked like flames. A second relief showed men brandishing sabers. The final image was a single crying face. Ian walked around the great container three times before he saw the dates carved in a ring around the bottom: 1933–1945. Ian asked Rebecca what it was called.

She looked at her list, tried to pronounce the word twice, and then just handed it to Ian.

Gleichschaltung.

Ian shuddered and looked to the next entry, which was called *Many Mansions.* Rebecca lifted the sheet, and there was a great shallow bowl carved from pine with a rounded beam sticking from the middle to a height of about five feet. At the top, pegs of varying lengths each held a birdhouse by a precious few links of chain. Ian had no idea what it meant.

Next to the bowl, Rebecca unveiled an enormous book.

Ian couldn't believe it, but the thing was the exact duplicate of the smaller version they'd found in the library. Same title, same portrait, same raised letters. Staring at the picture, Ian was even more certain that he remembered the woman. He pictured himself at the Labor Day party, asking her if she'd like ice for her soda.

Rebecca moved on, unwrapping an elegant swoop of curved metal that hinted at the shape of wings. Ian asked what that one was called, and Rebecca replied that it was *Angel.* Ian nodded. Next to the wings was a brutal and simple cross fashioned of sea-tossed logs with railroad spikes driven deep at the foot and on the crossbar.

Rebecca, standing in front of the cross, stretched both arms out to see if she could touch the spikes, and for an instant Ian felt a deep sickness touch him. He winced and then Rebecca brought down her arms and moved to the final sculpture, sweeping the sheet from it as though she were displaying a new car.

She turned and blanched, her reaction instantaneous.

Ian stared, mouth open. This, too, he had seen before.

It was a ravaged and open rib cage, pieced together with fishing line dangling off a smooth, arched stand. Each piece hung from its own strand to form the outline of a skeletal chest cavity like some demented mobile. Rebecca walked away from it quickly, not hiding her displeasure, and as she did the air she stirred swept the carved bones together and the pieces clacked dryly against one another.

"That's sick," Rebecca said. "The museum's not taking that one."

"It's a wind chime, I think," Ian replied, not really hearing his wife. "What's it called?"

Rebecca looked down. *"Ezekiel."*

Ian walked over and stirred the mobile, thinking of Howard's image of the rib cage half buried in the desert sand. He stared into the open space where the lungs would have inflated, then shriveled with each breath, and where a glistening heart would have pulsed. He even brought his own fingers to his chest and dug through muscle for a trace of his bones. After a few seconds he turned away and walked back to Rebecca, wondering how many times he would come across the empty skeleton of a human body before finally understanding what it was trying to say.

EARLY MORNING. TUESDAY, JULY 23

A lick of black parted the rushes, then disappeared. Ian pulled Cain to a stop, knelt behind a blind of reeds, and stared across the pond. Bullfrogs called to one another from across the banks, and water bugs skated on the surface of the water. A family of mallards — five ducklings trailing in the wake of their emerald-crowned father and tawny mother — circled in the shallows at the far end, and Ian flicked his eyes from them to a high batch of scrub where he'd seen, or imagined he'd seen, the local fox.

The ducks changed course a bit and swam directly in front of where Ian swore the fox had disappeared, but nothing happened. The father quacked, but it seemed not to mean anything. Cain whined as Ian held her to the ground, and after three minutes Ian felt the soggy earth about his knees for the first time. He rocked into a squat, his eyes fixed on the paddling line of ducks. Again they crossed by the tuft of reeds, but once more nothing happened.

Cain pulled tight at her leash, and Ian turned to try to make her still.

Behind him there was a single squawk and a tiny splash of water.

Ian looked back. Nothing much seemed to have changed, but again he saw that flick of black and red tail and the quick parting of tall grass as something slipped away from the pond. The ducks were now gliding out to the center of the pond, and he counted — one, two, three, four — ducklings in tow. Three times he counted just to make sure his eyes weren't again slipping focus, but the fifth yellow puff had disappeared. Ian and Cain stood and walked to the far side of the water. There wasn't so much as a tuft of down or a bit of yellow to be found.

Ian showered the moment he got home from the walk, and Rebecca was still there when he came downstairs, reading through her report on the Jacoby estate. She'd been working on it the past two days and was supposed to turn in her recommendation to the museum today. Ian asked if he could see her summary and she handed it over.

Furniture, housewares, tools, appliances, clothing, and the majority of the books would be sold at an estate sale, the proceeds of which would go to the museum. Two sculptures — the angelic curve of wings and the Star of David — would be donated, under the auspices of a foundation, to the permanent state collection. Twenty sculptures, including the odd birdhouse artwork, the toothbrush, the sewing cabinet, and the large book, would become part of the museum's permanent collection. The remaining sculptures — anything from the urn to the bread to the rose — would be added to the catalog for the auction being held in a couple of weeks.

The last five pages of the proposal contained a more detailed plan for the creation of a Katherine Jacoby room within the museum. The display, centered around the spectacular faux fireplace, would be permanent and could be used to display a rotating number of the smaller pieces. A limited number of potentially saleable items, such as the mantel clock and an armchair, would be held simply to complete the room. Or so were the suggestions of Rebecca Merchant. Her signature underscored the final sentence, and when Ian looked up she was watching him.

"I present it to the director today. If he approves, it'll go before the board tomorrow."

She said this with little enthusiasm, but Ian knew she was proud of the proposal and thought it would go through. The missing papers weighed on her in a way Ian hadn't seen since they'd visited doctor after doctor, specialist after specialist, eight years ago. All this grand anticipation followed by the agonizing understanding that things wouldn't be working out as planned. In fact, they wouldn't be working out at all. He wished he could do something. He wished he could go into Katherine's home, turn over a dresser drawer, and uncover the vanished writings. Instead he stroked his wife's arm and told her that the board would accept her plans without a change.

She murmured something Ian couldn't understand under her breath, stood, and moved across the room to her bag. When she passed by the table once more on her way to the garage, Ian leaned over for a kiss. Her lips grazed his, but there was no thought in the action. Just a dry brush of skin and haunted eyes searching for answers Ian couldn't provide.

The police had no answers, either, when Ian called after lunch. They'd hoped to find some fibers, a fingerprint, anything that would give them a lead, but both the Cherokee and the note looked clean. Detective Oakley asked if Ian had contacted a home security company, and Ian said he'd scheduled an appointment for the upcoming week. Oakley was about to hang up when Ian mentioned dinner. The men decided to meet next Tuesday, and Ian said he hoped not to see Oakley before then.

For a few moments after he returned to his den, he read the concluding paragraphs in his newest chapter. One sentence needed a small adjustment in rhythm, but for the most part they seemed to work. Ian took a deep breath, spaced down the page a few lines, and typed: *Chapter 4.* Events had been set in motion, and now Ian needed to introduce his hero, the man who would save Joshua Yardley from the crimes of his daily life.

His fingers hovered above the keyboard but would not move.

He watched the cursor blink, its steady pulse keeping rhythm as though it was his heart laid out on the screen. The cursor never wavered.

His heart began to race, and a sharp aftertaste of coffee came to his mouth. Though the screen had only been blank for a few moments, it felt as though he'd hit not only a block but some impenetrable wall, miles wide and high.

Ian pushed himself away from the computer, moved into the kitchen, and called for Cain. He needed the whip of a fresh breeze and the inescapable brightness of the sun to scour the dark corners of his mind and allow him to face this thing full on. Cain shook off a yawn as she wandered in from the hall, and her eyes brightened when Ian produced her leash. They headed out into the high afternoon, Cain in bliss at being on her second walk of the day.

Ian let his dog lead and faced the emptiness of his situation. He'd been looking for a hero, some squared-jaw amalgam of uncommon resourcefulness and grit, but no such creation existed in his mind. There was no good guy anymore. It would be so easy to simply create a Dirk or Jake to sweep in and save the day, but the words sounded hollow and he didn't want that.

From the depths of the woods to the north, Ian was distracted by the sound of a woodpecker drilling a dead tree for insects. The tommy-gun precision of its search was the only sound besides the early drone of cicadas and crickets. Neither duck nor frog nor fox stirred at the pond when they reached it. Occasionally a breeze tripped the surface into ripples, but that was the extent of the motion. Ian found a shady patch of ground on the high bank that bordered a grove of trees and sat, unhooking the leash from Cain's neck so she could roam a little.

Ian leaned against the closest tree and closed his eyes. He heard Cain pace through the high grass in front of him; he heard gnats buzz about his face; he heard the stirring of a sweet breeze and felt it lick at the sweat beading on his neck and cheeks. Cain's shuffling pursuit ended for a moment, and Ian imagined that she was tasting the air, sniffing about with her eager nose.

His thoughts returned finally to the meltdown he'd experienced just moments ago, and he was surprised that the panic and worry had dissolved into a pale kind of relief. Howard's death and the other explanations about his writer's block had just been excuses. This was real; he no longer believed in heroes. He wasn't sure why yet, but Ian knew that his days of writing fiction were over. The thought went through his mind again, but instead of dread and nausea, Ian felt freed. He knew what would happen next.

Opening his eyes, he stood, blinked a bit in the afternoon sun, and whistled for Cain. She bounded back to him, her paws wet from straying too close to the pond, and he clipped her back onto her leash. Together they traced the outline of the pond, again passing the thicket where the fox had disappeared that morning with the duckling. As they did, Ian thought about tomorrow's meeting with Louis. He knew his latest ghost story would never be completed, but he didn't want to make any rash choices. Bringing the finished chapters along seemed to be the best option for this week. Louis wouldn't be thrilled with them, and perhaps he might even bring up the stalking memoir again. Ian would show him the notes and agree that this was the book on which to focus.

Cain and Ian passed the baseball fields. A mean, hot breeze was snapping the loose dirt of the base paths into clouds. Crossing into the cover of an inviting shade tree, they rounded a corner into the entrance of Ian's small development. Empty trash cans lay at the entrance to each driveway, and red plastic flags stood waiting for the postman to make his daily rounds. As Ian and Cain made their way up the hill toward home, Ian glanced down the winding drives. He caught only glimpses of doors, windows, and eaves. The rest of the exteriors sat hidden behind sculpted shrubbery and evergreens.

Near the top of the hill, Ian looked toward his own house and saw first the chimney, then the sloped roof, and finally the wide face of the house. It looked smaller under such a high sun, the loss of shadows somehow stealing depth at the same time. They crested the hill, and an unexpected glare caught Ian's eye. He caught the full reflection of the sun against a car's rear window. His eyes teared and shut. Behind his lids he saw two green squares that looked like the fierce glowing eyes of some predator. He opened his eyes into a squint and gasped.

Forty yards ahead sat a brown sedan. It

was hidden behind a shrub so it couldn't be seen from the house, but Ian had a perfect view of its taillights.

Jerking Cain's leash, he fled behind a small stand of thin dogwoods. Hidden from sight, he began shivering. Small beads of sweat that had emerged during the walk now felt like icicles, and he had to kneel to get out of the breeze. He took three great swallows of air to calm down and forced himself to slow his thoughts.

He had spotted the stalker. The person in the car was surely watching the house and may or may not have seen him. He could see the entire lower half of the car, and it hadn't moved. The driver either didn't know he had been spotted or didn't care. Ian saw two choices — stay put or flee down the hill to a house.

Ahead there was a small rustle, like a shuffling of feet, and Ian's head snapped up. He expected to see a pair of brown work boots, but it was just the scraping of two branches stirred by the light afternoon wind. Cain strained hard at her leash and nearly toppled Ian from his crouch. His knees and thighs burned. He had to leave, had to slip down the hill and have a neighbor phone the police before his legs cramped up and he couldn't stand.

With a small groan he rose and began backing out of the trees, his eyes fixed on the sedan's bumper. Step by step he made his way down the hill, each second taking him farther away from the car. When it was finally out of sight, Ian pulled at Cain's leash and broke into a jog toward one of the homes. He rang the bell, waited for a few seconds, heard nothing.

He thought for a second, then made his way through the landscaping to the house next door. That home was quiet as well. Ian skulked his way through the yards of all six homes at the bottom of his community, but no one answered at any of them. As the echo of the final doorbell faded he realized he was alone. The neighborhood was empty.

Turning to face the road, Ian saw raspberry bushes and remembered seeing deer hidden in their depths last fall. Hesitating for just a second, he decided it would be best to hide away. Crossing the road, he pushed at the bushes, finding a broad opening through which he and Cain could squeeze. After forcing the dog inside, he held off as many thorns as he could and shoved his way next to her. Cain had long ago stopped whimpering and among the dead leaves she merely panted, worn from the exertion of the day. Ian rubbed her muzzle and kept watch on the road.

Two minutes became five, and five minutes became fifteen before finally he heard the sound of an engine approaching. Cocking his head as he listened, Ian could tell it wasn't coming from up the hill.

A square little Jeep wheeled around the corner and pulled up to the first house across from Ian's hiding place. Idling for only a moment, gears soon caught again and it rolled to the next house. Ian blinked.

It was the mailman. And he was driving away.

Letting go of the leash and wrapping his arms over his head and eyes, he bulled his way from the bush, thorns snatching at his shirt and face. Ian felt one tear at his cheek. Still, he shook himself loose and ran shouting after the Jeep. Behind him he could hear Cain yelping as she tried to wriggle herself free from the bush, but Ian kept running. He caught the Jeep halfway up the hill. The mail carrier jumped out from his driver's seat to see what was the problem.

"You're bleeding," the man said, pointing to Ian's face.

"I'm being followed, Chet," Ian replied. Without hesitation, the postman pointed to the Jeep and they climbed in, Ian pushing empty mail crates out of the way to sit.

Chet turned the vehicle around to head back down the hill. At the bend, Ian asked him to stop, freed himself from the passenger seat, and went to disentangle Cain, who lay wailing within the thorny grip of the bush. Ian undid the leash, which was as knotted as a noose, and unstuck her as best he could. The worst thorn had been buried in one of the dog's floppy ears, and she whimpered as Ian released her and then carried her back into the postal Jeep as well. Without asking, Chet pointed the vehicle toward the police station and took off.

On the short ride Ian only once caught a glimpse of himself in the mirror. Chet was right — he was bleeding. The bush had traced a single thick scratch from his left temple back toward his earlobe and a single line of blood had worked toward his jaw during the action. Staring at himself, Ian realized this was first blood. From here it seemed it could only escalate.

After Ian hung up from his conversation with the desk sergeant that night, Rebecca insisted he repeat every word exchanged. He said he'd tell her as they got ready for bed and headed out of the kitchen to the stairs. His legs and knees ached from the effort of the day, and he relied on the banister on the way up. He felt old and tired as he climbed toward his bedroom, and it saddened him because he didn't even have enough energy to feel angry at what he'd learned.

"So?" Rebecca asked as she passed him on her way to the closet.

"The car was abandoned," Ian sighed. "There was an expired registration that they traced back to a vacant apartment in Brooklyn. No fingerprints, no clues of any sort. They think the guy drove it here, left it to scare us, and walked away."

"Oh," she said, returning from the closet in her sweat shorts and T-shirt. Her eyes were soft with pity and that, more than anything else, brought the heat to Ian's face. He turned his back on his wife, stripped off his shirt too quickly, and gasped as it brushed the cut on his face. Rebecca rushed to him and wrapped her arms around him as he collapsed onto the bed.

"Stupidstupidstupidstupid," he muttered into the bedsheet.

Rebecca tightened her hold and whispered for him to be still.

"You did the only thing you could."

"I did nothing," he answered.

She sat up and when she spoke, her voice was firm.

"That's what you're going to keep doing, Ian," she began. "This isn't one of your books; I don't want you risking yourself just to be a man."

Ian moaned as Rebecca rubbed his shoulders. He felt the whole ridiculous weight of the day ease away under the movement of her strong fingers. The fear went first, followed by this newfound anger. After another moment all that was left was the dull throbbing of an aching body.

He knew Rebecca was right; he couldn't go out of his way to confront the stalker. At the same time, so many things suddenly rested on this whole situation continuing. He'd given up fiction and was left only with this unfinished story and a thousand small scratches from a raspberry bush. He hoped it was the last of his injuries, but he had the smallest suspicion it wouldn't be. There was to be more pain ahead, more moments of paralyzed fright, and with it would come his book. While before the presence of fear had provided energy for his novels, now it meant another chapter was playing itself out before his eyes. And all he needed to do was write it down. There'd be no story without it.

WEEK 3

MID-AFTERNOON. WEDNESDAY, JULY 24

Ian accessed his answering machine messages from his cell phone as his train rumbled out of Penn Station and away from the streets of New York. Over the clack of rails he heard Rebecca reminding him about her class at the university that evening, Michael Oakley notifying him that he'd gotten some interesting information on Norman Gruitt, a clerk from the frame shop promising that his picture would be ready tomorrow, and a lawyer named Bud Siegel calling in regard to Howard Kepler. Ian replayed the message twice to note the number, slipped the phone into his briefcase, and leaned into the side of the car, taking just enough pressure off his right haunch to stem the ache of yesterday's exertions. Outside, the world glowed in a golden light.

A few more minutes down the line, a

knock sounded and Trout slid back the curtain to offer beverages. Ian requested an iced tea, and Trout took only a few seconds to pour the drink and return.

He raised an eyebrow as he set the drink down and said, "Get into a fight with a cat?"

"Raspberry bush," Ian sighed.

"Should I ask?"

"You'd be the first," said Ian. "Everybody else just stares at me and then pretends I don't have a big scratch on my face." Trout laughed and left, saying he'd be back in a while.

Ian sipped his tea and glanced outside. He could see a very dim reflection of his face in the window. He wondered if the scratch would scar, if journalists would add it to their list of macabre details.

Louis had been the only one at the office to demand the story, and he'd seen it as simply a great chapter to Ian's book. There had been no fuss at all about switching topics, not that Ian expected any. He wasn't a writer anymore, he was a hack having his story written for him. He'd stepped from the realm of fantasy into the real world, and from now on his imagination meant nothing. In the stores, this book would go in the True Crime section along with the sordid tales of mayhem and slaughter.

Ian turned away from the window and concentrated on his tea. Stray thoughts like that and like those that kept his eyes open wide last night kept sneaking up on him. As if the stalker wasn't enough, his own mind now lay in wait for him, lingering until the perfect moment to provoke some dark idea into consciousness. It reminded him of the small voices of doubt that plagued him throughout his early months of writer's block last year. They'd gotten so insistent that he ended up on a plane and entered the life of Howard Kepler in the hope that this complete stranger could help him. And the man did by giving him an answer larger than his problems. Now he needed Howard's guidance once again, and all he had was the phone number of some lawyer.

Ian finished his iced tea and was surprised to hear the beverage cart rattle down the aisle. Looking at his watch, he realized he'd been lost in thought for over an hour. Trout slipped Ian's glass into a bin before returning to the compartment, where he now stood staring at Ian.

Ian examined the man's face and wondered how he would describe him in a novel. Would he have to say he was looking at an elderly black man or could he paint a picture with words — the full, freckled nose, heavy-lidded eyes, tight salt-and-pepper hair — to get the image across.

After a few moments of staring at each other, Trout spoke. "You remind me of a story I haven't thought on since I was a kid working construction," he began. "A friend of mine got caught swimming in a lake when a storm blew in. He saw it coming, but it arrived quicker than he expected.

"Anyhow, my friend got out, headed for home, but the weather really laid in and so the only place to hide was in this mess of saplings. He squeezed himself in, put his head down, and waited.

"Well, the thunder came as it does, and so did the lightning, but what really let loose was the wind. Every time a big gust came through, a branch would snap down across his back. He showed up at work the next day, and in three minutes I saw tears running down his face and blood soaking through his shirt. Couldn't barely even lift a hammer.

"Boss comes up to see what the problem was and makes my friend take his shirt off. I tell you I ain't never seen anything like it outside pictures. I mean, we all seen pictures, a black man tied to a pole, that sort of thing. Well, this — it looked the same.

174

No meanness behind it maybe, but pain is pain."

Ian grimaced. "I remind you of that?"

Trout shrugged. "No. But it's the only other time I remember seeing someone get beat up by a plant, other than falling out of trees. But mainly that's just stupidity and gravity."

Ian smiled just a little.

Trout nodded to himself and said, "Poor fella. We called him Switch after that." He laughed at the memory and said, "Funny how it is about nicknames."

Ian asked what he meant.

"Just that a nickname is supposed to help you remember something you would never forget anyway. I'm sure Switch'll never forget that storm. His back sure don't forget, I know that."

"How about you?" asked Ian. "Why do they call you Trout?"

The porter shook his head and slipped the velvet back so he could exit. "Can't tell all my stories in one day now, can I?" he said, stepping through. "Nobody ever goin' to buy a drink if I don't have something to tell them."

He let the curtain fall into place, and Ian heard the cart squeak as Trout rolled it up the aisle.

After departing the train, Ian spent his few minutes at home treating his cut, changing clothes, and gathering his chapters for the writers group. He knew he'd be early for the meeting, but he wanted to take advantage of the fine evening — a sky filled with clouds colored cherry, plum, and peach sagging low on the horizon. Sailors and fishermen were no doubt making plans for tomorrow based on the palette of dusk, but to Ian it only meant that the days were beginning to shorten. Even at this hour — a week still left in July — the street lamps would soon snap on, adding their glow to the lowering sun.

After parking, Ian made his way down the street, passing an antiques store and a book shop. He found himself outside A Doll's House, Anne Oakley's shop. An orange square in the window said the store was closed, but Ian stopped anyway to look at the dolls staring out into the street with ever-vigilant marble eyes. He was about to walk away when a cat roused itself from a basket in the window and yawned.

Ian tapped at the window twice to get its attention, but it just glanced at him and began grooming its slender forelegs with its tongue. A light snapped on in the back and Ian saw a shadowy figure moving. Not wanting to be caught leering into the window, Ian stepped behind an elm planted at the edge of the sidewalk.

Oakley's wife stood visible in the window, rubbing the cat and staring blankly through the window, her mouth moving up and down as she talked to the tabby. Her high forehead and slender nose mirrored her mother's, and Ian remembered how the old woman had stood the same way, eyes unfocused and cloudy. It could be a glimpse of the future, what lay in store for Oakley's wife, or perhaps an image of the past, the mother as a young woman with memory. Ian watched a little longer until Anne stepped out of view. He checked his watch: still fifteen minutes to kill.

Crossing the street and taking one of the side alleys, Ian reached the store he had intended to visit and was pleased that it was still open. He stepped inside, the jingle of a bell announcing his arrival, and looked around. Just like Katherine Jacoby's library, the room was heavy and dark with books.

A bespectacled man looked around his computer screen, gave a slight wave, and then stopped, squinted, and stood up. Grabbing his cane, the clerk stepped out from behind the counter and walked to Ian with a full smile.

"I owe you some thanks, Mr. Merchant. Some thanks."

Ian took the man's offered hand, wondering if they'd met before, and asked why.

"Your books, of course. You keep me in business. People have always been fans of your novels, and the horror fans especially. I've had folks fly in just to buy a first edition in the town where Ian Merchant lives."

Ian thanked him and explained to the dealer that he had stopped in for a particular reason. When the clerk asked what, Ian explained how his wife was looking for anything on Katherine Jacoby.

"Ah, the sculptor. Well, no, there's never been a book on her. I think I may have some old town records, though, that might be of service. Probably just copies of what they have in the Historical Society, but I can check." He shuffled back to a shelf marked Local Interest and insisted that Ian look around to see if there was anything else interesting.

Ian passed up and down the crowded aisles, staring up at the cracked leather spines and frayed stitching. The store smelled of what Ian assumed was tired ink and mildewed vellum. Many titles were so worn as to be illegible, but every once in a while there was a book he recognized — Hemingway, an early Fitzgerald, Harper Lee.

Passing through another row and to the front of the store, Ian found his own works. More recent first editions sold for just dollars more than retail; however, there were six first editions of *Monster* that could be had for $175 and a Portuguese translation that was three times higher. Next to the bookshelf was a glass-covered table. Ian walked to it and shook his head. An assortment of memorabilia, often signed by his own hand, lay arranged beneath glass and plastic, but he recognized none of it. There was a Boston Red Sox cap he'd autographed at some point, the typical glamour shot of him straddling a chair, and even an old *Esquire* in which he was interviewed. He wondered who would ever buy the stuff, and the only answer that came to mind made him shudder — the same person who'd steal a brown sedan just to park it outside his house.

From the counter the clerk called to Ian and showed him two thick books, both with green leather covers with a dated registry stenciled in gold on the spine. Ian decided to pass for the moment but promised he would tell Rebecca about them. When he turned to leave, the clerk stopped him.

"Since you're here," the man began, "I was wondering perhaps if you could do me a favor."

Ian paused at the door, his hand on the glass, and looked back over his shoulder. The man was holding a marker. It did no good to snub people who depended on his books, so he crossed back to the counter, and the man bent down to get something. When he came back up, Ian nearly gasped.

MERCHANT

The man set a small stack of note cards on the oak countertop. Ian picked them up and flipped through each one. Each had the same thing chiseled on it in black letters. Ian closed his eyes and shook his head.

"You don't need to sign them all," said the man, worried. "One or two would do."

From a pay phone outside DeCafé, Ian called the police, and Oakley confirmed what he'd just seen.

"That was the interesting news I wanted to tell you about," the officer said. "Norman Gruitt did draw those cards, but it was for a bookstore promotion."

Oakley continued, his story matching

exactly with what the bookstore owner had told Ian. As a promotion for the release of *Mason's Road,* Horror-able Books in New Haven and the used bookstore here in town paid the artist to draw 150 MERCHANT notes and one MONSTER note. Attendees of the party drew a card from a basket in hopes of getting the single MONSTER note and winning a first edition of Ian's debut novel.

Here Ian interrupted. "Since the MONSTER note showed up on my doorstep, all we have to do is find the winner of that contest, right?"

Oakley said it was not quite so simple. They'd already tracked down the winner — a video store clerk from Rye, New York — and the fellow had no recollection of what happened to his winning ticket. Said he probably handed it over to claim his book.

"He didn't even have his prize anymore," Oakley added. "Sold it on eBay a few months ago. We saw the completed auction notification."

The detective had nothing else of importance to pass along but promised to keep Ian updated. As Ian hung up, a nearby clock chimed the half hour. He was now very late.

Passing through the door of DeCafé, he

paused a moment to let his eyes adjust to the harsh light and saw the others seated in the far corner of the room. He threaded his way through the maze of tables and apologized for being tardy. The three men turned to him, and in unison Kevin and Jaret pointed to his cheek.

"It's nothing," Ian said. He'd already found a better story.

Kevin nodded at what Ian and the police had discovered about Norman Gruitt and seemed relieved that the painter's involvement was peripheral. For a moment there was silence.

"Get a chance to read the chapters amid all the hubbub?" Pete asked finally.

Ian nodded and brought out his portion of *Quinlin's Estate.* Though he'd made comments throughout, the group was focusing on the fifth chapter this evening and began their discussion by talking about setting. This chapter strayed away from the central Pennsylvania factory town for the distant shores of New Zealand where Gabriel Quinlin would meet his untimely demise in a horrible train accident through the Tongariro Crossing. Each man had the same comment about the scene: good sense of place, poor sense of time. It seemed like a far-off land but not a past decade. Pete took notes as the discussion continued.

They talked about changes in point of view, about unique character traits, and about the subtle use of sensory description that deepened the pages with unexpected sights, sounds, and smells. For ten minutes Kevin and Jaret argued whether a character's actions should be portrayed as truly altruistic and whether altruism existed at all, anywhere. The discussion rolled on in waves, and it was only as they were nearing the end of the chapter that Ian realized how fulfilling the entire meeting had been. He wanted to say it was because there'd been no talk of money or market saturation or publicity campaigns, but that wasn't quite true. Instead, the past two hours had been gratifying because, for the first time in a long while, he'd returned to writing without it being the source of his problems or concerns. There were no deadlines, no writer's block or self-doubt, no stabs at his nascent conscience. He hoped sometime in the future even his own writing would treat him so kindly.

The evening ended with a debate on a repeating scene: the notion of having something looking down on you. The estate towered over the town, there was a plastic Santa Claus keeping watch over a trailer park, and a snow-capped trinity of volcanoes guarded over the final resting place of Gabriel Quinlin. The men agreed that they liked the repetition and encouraged Pete to keep an eye out for further opportunities. He nodded, and something in his eyes convinced Ian that the man never had a problem understanding that very fact. There is something very grand that looms large over all of us.

EARLY MORNING. THURSDAY, JULY 25

After Ian and Cain limped through a short walk, he returned to find Rebecca gone and a note propped against the centerpiece. His wife said it was a great interview and the first one in memory where he hadn't told the stupid disappearing child story. Ian grabbed the paper and found Cheryl Rose's story as he poured his juice. A grainy black-and-white portrait grinned from the front page, and in bold type above his picture a headline read: *SHOPTALK WITH IAN MERCHANT.* Could have used a better title but at least it didn't say *bizarre* or *macabre* or any of the other twenty-five-cent Halloween words that normally turned up in articles about him.

Returning to the table, he scanned the feature quickly and then settled in to read. Seven minutes later he'd finished and was impressed. Cheryl had received valuable column inches, and Ian was glad to see she knew how to use them. The article was well-composed, intelligent, and, for once, accurate. As promised, mention of the stalking was buried in a section on all the odd knickknacks he'd received and mentioned little more than the fact that two notes had mysteriously appeared at his door.

Two more paragraphs about critical and social commentary — including a quote, Ian was surprised to see, from anti-Merchant psychiatrist Noel Buford — ended with Cheryl summarizing her thesis. *Ian Merchant is neither ghoul nor hobgoblin, warlock nor spook. He is a man borne of imagination who has released his skeletons from their closets and pegged them to the wall, who has swept the monsters out from under the beds and set them upon his filing cabinets. He is one who calls darkness by its true name.*

Ian nodded to himself and folded the newspaper up. Cheryl had done a fine job with the article, and Ian realized if he could create a hero half as credible as the character she had imagined, he would be able to work again on his stalled novel. But he knew her hero all too well, and though he might give names to horror, it was only while running away, eyes white with fear, pulse jamming blood through his veins.

Ian spent half of his afternoon reading through his notes and trying to think up a unique lead into his story. Most of the ideas he'd concocted, however, relied on knowing the end of the story. Though Ian hoped he could predict a quick trial and jail time for the stalker, there was no way to be sure. In the end, he put the notes aside and returned to Titansburg to retrieve his framed photo of the Great White Throne.

By the time he returned, Rebecca was home, and he asked for her help in hanging the image. She agreed, but in a murmur that told Ian her heart was still heavy over not finding Katherine's letters. She'd been given one more week by her thesis advisor, but it seemed just to be delaying the inevitable.

"How about the library?" Rebecca suggested after the photo failed to look good anywhere downstairs.

With its odd mishmash of colors and shapes, the library seemed as likely as any room in the house, and it turned out that the frame fit neatly just above two small bookcases Rebecca purchased last summer. With his wife's help, Ian checked off a target for his hammer and pounded a hook into place. The photo slid into place, and suddenly the Great White Throne towered over the room from the wall. Ian couldn't help but think of Pete's story and wondered if Howard had been going for the same effect.

Rebecca slipped her arm through his as she stared and leaned against him. When she spoke, her voice was a sigh.

"I wish I had been with you."

"We can go sometime," Ian replied and saw his wife lower her eyes.

"It's not that," she said. "I just wish I had been with you."

Ian nodded but didn't say anything, trying to imagine what it would have been like. The long talks with Howard. The retreat to the park and the night under the stars, watching the moon finally hide itself beneath the shelf of the great monuments. The early-morning baptism where he'd been taken by the current. What if she had been there? Would she have come running after him, fear draining the blood from her face, or would she have stood there laughing as Howard had?

Rebecca shifted a bit more of her weight against him, and Ian knew she was waiting for a reply. He wanted to give her the answer she needed, but the words failed. No matter how hard he tried, he couldn't imagine her as part of that weekend. She just wouldn't have understood.

Ian said none of these things. Instead, he pulled his wife close and she tucked her head under his collarbone. They stood that way for just a few seconds until the silence lasted too long. Rebecca moved first, slipping out of his arms.

"Shut off the light when you come," she said softly.

Ian followed quickly, but the last thing he saw as he shut the door was the ghostly image of that enormous rock. It seemed strange that so small a room could contain it.

Ian read for the remainder of the evening, while Rebecca furthered the Labor Day party plans and made some phone calls to family. They spoke little, and when Ian finally looked up from his novel, he realized the day had slipped by without police interference or the threat of violence. He wondered if the rest of the summer would be like this: sporadic bursts of terror surrounded by a vain attempt to pretend everything was normal. It was just another thing for which he had no answer, and when Rebecca headed upstairs to bed, Ian soon followed.

By the time he made his way upstairs, Rebecca had already covered the bed with an assortment of papers. He recognized her notebook from class, the list she had compiled of Katherine Jacoby's estate, and what looked to be blueprints. As he stepped into the room, she was flipping back and forth from the house plans to the list.

"You really think the letters are still there?" he asked.

Without looking up she replied that they had to be there or her thesis and possibly her degree were shot.

Ian walked to the foot of the bed and stared as Rebecca traced the navy outline of the building with her steady finger. He didn't know what she was looking for — a hidden crevice, a sunken hold, a secret room — so he simply watched. After a few seconds he realized she wasn't sleeping anytime soon and decided a glass of milk might be nice. Leaving the room, he asked if she'd like anything, and she said that water would be great.

Ian made his way through the dark down

the spiral staircase and into the kitchen, where he could he see that the answering machine light was blinking. Five minutes ago he'd gone upstairs. Five minutes ago he'd silenced the phone for the evening, and yet somebody had managed to call. Ian pressed *Play* and grabbed glasses.

The voice on the message cleared its throat loudly and spoke in a vague southern accent that Ian couldn't place.

"Mr. Merchant, this is Bud Quincy in Springdale. I promised to call you regarding the Kepler estate but lost track completely of what time it was. I'll leave my number and if you get a chance and could call me, that would be fantastic."

Ian jotted the number with ease as the lawyer spoke with the speed of a Utah tortoise. Next, he erased the message from the machine and turned the volume to mute so he wouldn't be disturbed. Grabbing the drinks and heading back to the bedroom, Ian couldn't help but wonder what Howard Kepler had left as an estate. The man rented a trailer home, pawned kitchen appliances for money to invest in photography equipment, and passed any profit from his art on to a local youth center that reached out to at-risk reservation children. If anything, Ian realized, the lawyer might need money to settle leftover expenses. Caskets and the rest never came for free.

As Ian reached the top of the stairs, he noticed an odd whirring sound that broke his concentration. The mantel clock in the kitchen chimed eleven times before he could identify the noise, but when the final gong faded to silence Ian heard a click, and then a labored buzzing. The answering machine. It was probably the lawyer again, but Ian refused to look downstairs, crossing the final few feet of dark hallway to the bedroom.

"Howard Kepler's lawyer called again," he said, pushing the door open, but Rebecca didn't respond. Her head hung to her chest and despite the lights, her body rose and fell with the pace of sleep.

Ian watched her for a bit, papers spread out over the bed like an enormous jigsaw, her finger still marking a particular spot on the blueprint. Then, setting the glasses down, he shuffled the loose papers into a pile and slowly pulled the house plans from under her palm. Freed, they would not fold neatly back into one square, and he ended up having to go into the bathroom so that he wouldn't wake Rebecca with his rustling. When they were folded, he set them on top of the other papers, shut off the lights, and climbed into bed. Rebecca still leaned against the backboard, so Ian grabbed his glass and sat up next to her, sipping his milk and watching as Rebecca's head lulled to some unseen rhythm of dreaming. It was only after he'd swallowed the last gulp of milk and lowered himself under the covers that she startled, her body tense, her eyes open to the dark.

She reached for his hand under the covers and slid down next to her husband.

"Did you bring me water?" she asked.

Ian reached out to the nightstand for her glass and lifted it to the shadow of her outstretched hand. She tilted it to her mouth and Ian could hear her swallow — two, three times until she drained the glass.

She set the glass on her bed stand and said, "Did you say something when you walked in, something about Howard Kepler?"

"His lawyer called," Ian said, rolling to face her. "I thought you were asleep."

"I was," she answered, "but somehow I heard that and started dreaming about us in Utah. The three of us, or at least us and a little bearded man. It had to be Howard."

"What were we doing?" Ian asked.

"Walking through the desert toward that stone tower in the photo."

"What for?"

"I don't know," she said. "I woke up before we got very far."

Ian apologized for rousing her.

"Wasn't that," she said and then turned on her side, her face only inches from his. "It was the heat. My lips were cracking from the sun." She whispered this.

Ian reached out and patted her hand.

"But you brought me water," she said and leaned forward to kiss him on the cheek, her lips still hot as coals.

Early morning. Friday, July 26

Ian turned to face the nozzle and was pleased that the water didn't sting. A scab had toughened over the cut and it appeared that it wouldn't scar after all. Only the memory.

He'd just finished scrubbing his chest when he heard the creak of the bathroom door and saw a blurry image of Rebecca through the frosted glass. Her head was lowered and her shoulders quivered, and Ian had barely a chance to turn around before she pulled the door open, stepped inside, and wrapped her arms about him in a tight embrace.

He said her name twice and tried to loosen her grip, but she just tightened her grasp and refused to budge. He couldn't see her face, but from the way she trembled and gasped in his arms, he knew she was sobbing. Her flow of tears simply pooled with the rest of the water flowing down his chest.

For a minute or two they stood like that: Rebecca fully dressed, her denim skirt now navy and sopping, and Ian naked and wet, his back beginning to ache from the heat of the water. Finally he managed to pry her away, shut the water off, and face his wife. Tiny beaded strands of sopping hair clung to her face. As he smoothed them away she managed her first words.

"Oh, Ian," she said, voice nearly breaking. "The message. The horrible message."

After heading to the police station with the answering machine tape, Ian listened to the message three times in hopes of recognizing the voice. With its slight, birdlike quality he knew it was the stalker but could say nothing more. Oakley suggested one more listen, but Ian shook his head.

"I've memorized the thing, Mike," he grumbled. "Another listen won't do any good. What I want to do is call Rebecca, make sure she's okay, and then get out of here."

It had come out angrier than he'd intended, but Oakley didn't seem offended. He just pointed into the hallway and told Ian to use the phone in his office. He'd be right behind. Ian headed the way the officer had motioned and as he left the electronics room he heard that pale, fragile voice begin to chirp again.

A drink before bed, Ian? I hope you're not having trouble falling asleep. . . .

He found the office and was soon connected to his wife's line at the Historical Society. She claimed to be fine but sounded on the verge of tears, her voice flat and pinched. They talked for just a moment, Ian telling her what the police would be looking for in the message, before she was paged for another call. Ian pledged his love and hung up with the dull shimmer of her voice still in his ears. He had to take his mind off the hurt he felt he'd caused and began looking at assorted wall hangings that decorated the room. He wondered what the reporter Cheryl Rose would make of Detective Oakley's belongings.

On the far wall was a black-and-white photo of three dirty-faced boys glaring at the camera as though it had just stolen their ice cream. To its side was an image of a younger Oakley in a Redbirds warm-up suit, dressed for the ballpark, a wooden bat cocked at his shoulder. There were a number of family portraits, Mike and Anne first without, then with, their son, and a wedding photo of the grinning couple looking over their shoulders from the front seat of a gleaming Mustang convertible. Finally, there was a picture of Anne hugging her mother in front of a spurting Poseidon fountain. The older woman's eyes were bright and surprised, and Ian guessed this had been taken before the Alzheimer's. He was staring at the picture when Oakley entered.

"Isn't that great?" the officer asked, handing Ian a Styrofoam cup of gray coffee. "Anne's mother was a terrific lady when . . . well, when she was with us. It's just killed Anne and me to see her this way."

Ian nodded.

"Your parents still around?" Oakley asked.

"Mother is; she lives outside Ithaca. My father died when I was four."

Oakley frowned. "I lost mine when I was three. Killed in Korea. Got a stepfather a decade later, but I never had much use for him. Did you reach your wife?"

Ian said he had and that she sounded frightened. He attempted a sip of coffee and waited for Oakley to respond. The officer said nothing, however, and seemed to be waiting for something. When the phone rang, Ian realized the man had been expecting the call.

"The boys in tech want us down there," he explained and waved for Ian to follow. Together they headed back down the hall to a glass door marked *Electronics.* Two officers stood holding headphones to their ears, staring with blank expressions as they listened.

"Got it." One of them grinned and handed Ian the pair of headphones.

He slipped them on, and there was silence. None of the cops talked, and Ian stared at his shoes waiting for something to happen.

Then, without warning: *A drink before bed, Ian?*

The tape started over, and though Ian strained, he could hear no difference for the first few lines. The voice continued on and soon there was the faintest ringing noise that had been isolated. Ian looked up at the officers and motioned for them to rewind.

He closed his eyes.

— have such — DONG *— worries though —* DONG *— Ian. Some of —* DONG *— us sleep soundly —* DONG *— at night —* DONG

Ian put his hand to his mouth and tried

to slow his breathing. It was the clock, his own mantel clock, tolling eleven. The caller had been right outside.

It surprised Ian to find Rebecca's coupe parked neatly at the bottom of the driveway as he pulled up to the house with police vehicles trailing him. She hadn't mentioned needing to return home early, and he hoped that the officers soon to be scouring the yard for clues to the caller's identity wouldn't interrupt any work she'd planned to complete in the silence of an empty house. As he made his way up the walk, the two younger officers under Oakley's command began listening to orders.

Inside, Ian found Rebecca watching the activity from the comfort of her favorite chair. The museum had been filled with five busloads of seventh graders on summer school trips, and the ruckus proved too much. She had an assignment that didn't require any of the resources in the office and had decided that a half day at home might not be a bad idea.

"Why are you back here?" she asked.

Ian told her, and she pulled her legs up under her and shut her eyes. She sat that way for only a moment before a shudder arched her spine. Ian moved to comfort her, but she stood before he reached her, the green of her hazel eyes scorching.

"This is going to stop."

Ian saw the tight line of her jaw and the white of her knuckles. There was often exhaustion in fear, but Ian knew he wasn't seeing that. He was seeing anger: a rage born of the futility in fighting a nameless enemy. He had no energy to match it and could only stand beside Rebecca, stroke her shoulder, and say he hoped she was right. He hoped it all stopped.

Oakley knocked on the glass of the French doors soon after, and Rebecca motioned for him to enter. As they headed to the kitchen to meet the officer, Ian caught a glimpse through the window of the two officers pacing to their assigned portions of the backyard. Ian could only hope that they found nothing gruesome, nothing to add to this already painful day.

When the Merchants and Oakley had taken seats at the kitchen table, the detective updated them on the little progress that had been made and asked if they had any questions. Rebecca didn't hesitate.

"How dangerous do you think this situation is?"

Oakley nodded in approval. "As hard as this may be to believe," he began, "we've got no proof that this will escalate any further than harassment. A violent, confrontational personality would have exhibited different behaviors, different approaches than we've seen so far. That said, we can't rule it out. I don't want to be caught making light of a dangerous situation, so we'll continue to approach this from a worst-case-scenario standpoint."

"What is the worst-case scenario?" Rebecca followed.

"Someone who wants to do your husband harm rather than simply scare him."

A brittle quiet fell over the table, and Ian wondered if he'd ever written as frightening a sentence as the one he'd just heard. It was the kind of thing with which to end a chapter, sitting at the bottom of one of his own neatly typed pages. Leaning back in his chair, he waited for someone to break the silence.

"Why is this happening?" Rebecca asked finally. Ian first thought the question might be rhetorical, but she was looking right at Oakley. She wanted an answer. What was going on? Why was their life suddenly the stuff of dime-store novels and slickly filmed Hollywood thrillers?

Oakley answered that it looked like a case of hero worship, what with all the references to Ian's books and the use of the notes given away at the book release party.

"Your husband is a popular guy," he continued. "Most everyone I've talked to at the station has read one of his books. With so many copies out there it's inevitable that one would fall into the wrong hands." He paused, then added, "It's not like he's writing fuzzy bunny nursery rhymes either, if you know what I mean."

Before either Rebecca or Ian could respond, one of the officers knocked on the kitchen window and motioned for Oakley to come outside.

The Merchants sat in silence. Rebecca worried a fingernail down to the skin, and Ian stared at his hands. Soon they'd be putting to paper everything that was happening, but for the moment they simply sat still, and Ian was glad he didn't have to hide a tremble.

Oakley returned a short time later and suggested he follow them. When they made their way outside, he began pointing out little things to the couple. The shallow impression of a work boot. The broken stem of a dahlia. The greasy smudge of a fingerprint on the window. He held up a plastic bag with a cigarette butt and said that it had been found on a narrow pathway cutting through some shrubs and out toward the stone wall. He also pointed to a small patch of matted grass near one of the arborvitae and said that the guy had relieved himself there at some point.

Ian couldn't help but laugh. All this and the guy urinated on the lawn. Gall was the only word for it.

Rebecca asked what it all proved.

"We can guess that you've got a short, slim, right-handed fellow on your hands. We know he smokes. We'll find out from ground over there whether he uses drugs or drinks. Alcohol explains the boldness; drugs confuse everything. If there are traces of anything, that becomes a wild card."

Ian and Rebecca both stood quiet with surprise.

"How in the world . . . ?"

"It's actually pretty simple," said Oakley with a laugh. "I just like playing Sherlock Holmes every once in a while." He went on to describe how a heavier man would have left a far deeper footprint and how only a short man would be able to see in through the kitchen window without stooping down too low and how the fingerprint was of the right finger and it was likely that whoever touched the glass used his stronger hand.

Ian nodded, a little amazed at the deductions, and said that was terrific. But what did it mean? "There are a lot of short, slim, right-handed men in the world."

"It's a start," said Oakley and they began to walk back around the house to his cruiser. He talked about further precautions that should be made, including a separate, unlisted phone line to give to family and friends so that only the stalker would use the other line.

"And courtesy calls, of course," Oakley added and seemed content to leave on that light note. He walked to the other side of his car and opened the door. He was about to step in when he stopped, appearing to have remembered something.

"Tuesday," he said. "Anne's free on Tuesday. Would that be all right for dinner?"

Rebecca and Ian looked at each other, and he knew she was thinking about the little joke she'd made at Patrick Henry's. An eyebrow twitched and her lips flickered with a grin, but she didn't say anything, so Ian turned back to Oakley and said that would be fine. Seven on Tuesday at, say, Marzipan.

Oakley nodded, said he didn't know where it was but would find out. Then he gave a little wave, got into his car, and pulled from the driveway.

They didn't talk about the incident for

the rest of the day. Ian worked at his desk, trying to find the best description for the stalker's odd, almost womanlike voice. Rebecca labored over a project for the museum for a few hours before turning her attention once more to her blueprints. In the silence between them, though, Ian felt a great weight. It wasn't the casual quiet between a long-married couple. This was a forced silence brought on by circumstances beyond their control. He'd felt it before, most strongly after the crushing report from the obstetrician a few years back, and knew it would pass in a couple of days.

Day passed to night, and as the cold shard of moon crept above the tree line, Rebecca announced she'd finished working for the evening. Ian followed her lead and they were soon ready for sleep. For a few minutes they lay apart, but Rebecca soon reached over to him, her fingers light against the inside of his arm.

He pulled her close and she ended up falling asleep with her arm draped over his chest. Ian felt content for the first time since his morning shower; it was always a terrific privilege when Rebecca curled up next to him in sleep. Something, though, wouldn't let him find rest of his own. Something kept his eyes from shutting, kept the blood alive and wild in his veins. Fear and silence were one thing when the sun shone and everyone walked about, but here in the dark they were another story, amplifying the sounds of the house and tightening his neck at his shoulders. He didn't want to scream or run — he simply wanted the bright light of day or the voice of his wife. It was all he could do to keep from stirring her awake.

MORNING. SATURDAY, JULY 27

Saturday morning the crew from Home-Safe arrived and began installing the security system. Ian tried to keep Cain away from the men while calling around for other changes to the house. Sears could install security lighting next Thursday, and he received a pleasant surprise when Bell Atlantic reminded him that the house was already wired for a second telephone line. All they had to do was assign a number and open the switch: it could be completed by noon. Ian immediately began calling friends and family to let them know of their new number.

That afternoon they received their first call on the new phone line. It was from Rebecca's sister, and she thought that they had moved without sending notice. Rebecca assured her they were still in Connecticut and glossed over the reasons for the change in number, saying they were sick of getting calls from every long-distance carrier in the country. Unlisted was better.

A few hours later, the crew from Home-Safe finished and went over the operating procedures with Ian and Rebecca. There were keypads to access and pass codes to remember and motion sensors that would alert the command center if anyone tripped them. As a bonus, Cain had been fitted with a special collar so that she could roam throughout the house without setting off the alarm. All the doors and windows of the home had been secured, and starting immediately, their house was now under the protective umbrella of the Home-Safe company. Ian thanked the men, sent them on their way, and then spent ten minutes with Rebecca practicing how to enter and exit the house. When they finally returned to the living room and took up their reading again, Rebecca seemed changed.

"Just that one thing is so reassuring," she said, and for the first time in a day Ian didn't see the scrim of worry clouding her face. Even talking about her final plans for finding Katherine Jacoby's papers, Rebecca appeared more relaxed. This moment of fear had passed. Ian hoped there would be no more.

As if in reply, the phone rang. The old line. Ian looked to Rebecca, but this didn't faze her either. She shrugged, said lots of people still had their old number, and suggested that he wait for the machine to pick up. He nodded in agreement but walked to the kitchen anyway, feeling it was better for some reason to be near the phone.

The tape clicked on, Rebecca's voice telling the caller to leave a message, and a slow, heavy voice started explaining that he was calling from Utah. Ian jumped at the receiver, fumbling to shut off the machine at the same time.

"Hello?" he said, hoping he hadn't disconnected Howard's lawyer.

"Mr. Merchant," the man said, Ian's name coming out as *marchent,* "glad to reach you. I figured my best shot might be a Saturday."

They talked for a while, the lawyer explaining how Howard had signed over a good deal of his personal belongings to Ian in case of his death. Ian asked what kind of belongings but the lawyer couldn't answer in specifics, saying that one package would be arriving next week sometime and that a second and final shipment would be made in about two weeks, assuming there were no unexpected problems.

"And you can't tell me anything?"

"I do know there were an awful lot of photographs. That's part of the reason everything is so late. We've got two clerks cataloging everything, and we're still digging out. Legally, Mr. Kepler was ready to die, everything in good order, but materially, he wasn't as prepared. It's like sorting for needles in a haystack when you want to feed the horses and do some sewing."

"Come again?" asked Ian.

"Just that you need the hay as much as the needles, that's all."

Ian asked a few quick questions about any estate taxes he might have to pay and legal fees for representation, but Bud Siegel explained that nothing Ian was going to receive added up to any substantial value. "A whole lotta junk" was the phrase he used.

Ian smiled to himself as he walked back to the living room and Rebecca asked what he was grinning over. He repeated the conversation for her and laughed again when he finished. He didn't know what was going to arrive, but he could almost guarantee that it would be interesting. The most boring thing about Howard Kepler was his name, and that was only if you didn't include the middle one: Ezekiel.

Rebecca went back to her book — borrowed, she admitted, from Katherine Jacoby's grand library — while Ian said he was going to head to his office. On his way he looked over at the title and saw that it was the collected letters of a man named Dietrich Bonhoeffer. He recognized the name but couldn't remember in what context. A cross and a swastika on the cover placed the book in World War II, and Ian guessed that it had something to do with the dead sculptor having been the daughter of a Nazi officer.

In the den he settled into the leather chair, pulled out his portfolio, and removed the most recent chapter of Jaret's manuscript so he could get a jump on his critique before Wednesday. This chapter, Ian guessed, having now read the first six, would explain how the father of that kneeling child became a believer. Like the others it was titled only with a single name. This one was called *Ted*.

Ian read for a while, turning through page after page of Ted's early life — loss of an early love followed by an imploding marriage of convenience, a long time of wandering after divorce, a chance encounter with a Christian folksinger who had written music for all of the psalms — until, all in a hurry, he wasn't reading about Ted anymore, he was reading about himself.

The folksinger's thoughtful explanations of each of the poems and the way they seemed to open doors in the character's mind, that was Howard talking over a campfire and Ian understanding for the first time. Understanding the movement of his own life and the loneliness of his heart. Understanding the length of time one could wander in a desert, full of desperation and longing. Understanding love and acceptance.

Ian paged through the manuscript faster and faster. Words blurred together, but Ian barely even needed to read them; they were as recognizable as a memory, as real as the images he saw when he closed his eyes and thought about Utah. Somehow the kid had gotten his story and put it down on paper. Even Ted's baptism, a sloppy affair in a shallow ditch on the side of the road, echoed his own submersion in the stream the night after the northern rains washed down in a tumbling froth of murky water.

Had he told Jaret his story?

He hadn't mentioned anything, he was sure of that. Perhaps he'd been wrong about Pete being the prophet of the group, those searching eyes looking through you as though he were seeing something you'd never see — something light and easy and good for the soul. Perhaps the real prophet was the kid, looking for all the world as though he still had a heap of growing to do, yet still a seer.

What was it Howard had said? *Being a prophet has less to do with the ability of man than with the foolishness of those around him. Jeremiah, Ezekiel, Isaiah: They were surrounded by some wrongheaded folk.*

The thought struck Ian, and he rolled his chair over to a large filing cabinet. There he pulled out a drawer tumbled full of papers, manuscript pages, fan mail, a cassette tape or two, and finally a framed photo with the words *Self-Portrait.*

As he rolled back to the desk, Ian looked at the picture, the featureless silhouette of his own face carved into the dimming gray of a Utah evening. Howard had caught him off guard and snapped the photo as Ian stood staring at some great, floating bird circling on the high drafts of air above the canyons. He held the photo up now and tried to match the angle of his head, tilting his head back so that he looked at the corner where the ceiling and wall joined, and then tilting back in the chair so he gazed crookedly into the upper corner of the room. A cobweb danced in the breath of the air conditioning, and Ian watched it for a few seconds until a voice surprised him.

"What are you doing?"

He whirled in his chair, banging his knee on the desk, and placed the photo face-up on the blotter. Rebecca stood in the doorway, leaning, her hands folded. He didn't know how long she had been there.

"Found this picture of me," he said, pointing to the photo. "I'm not sure I ever showed it to you." He stood to hand her the framed image, sat back down, and watched her expression.

She read the words on the photo and looked at Ian. "It's a wonderful picture, but the quote isn't very flattering." She looked down again and read it once more. "He sure picks out odd portions of the Bible. 'Here is a trustworthy saying that deserves full acceptance. Christ Jesus came into the world to save all sinners — of whom I am the worst.' "

"Howard said that all the time."

"That you're the worst of sinners?" she asked.

"No. *'Trustworthy.'* Instead of 'great' or 'wonderful.' Everything was 'trustworthy.' He said it when I was baptized."

"It's from Paul," said Rebecca. "I remember the nuns reading it in school."

Ian nodded, and they stared at each other for some seconds. Sitting there looking at his wife as she remembered her days dressed in wool and he remembered his firelight conversion, it seemed to him that they weren't just husband and wife. So often that was all he thought about when he saw her, but now he saw a woman, one he knew to be sure, but a distinct person, her heart beating and her lungs filling with air. Their eyes met and Ian couldn't help but remember the first time he'd seen her, sitting with a crowd at a diner across the street from his college's student union. She wore green ribbons woven through her hair and they didn't manage to say more than "Hello," or "Pass the salt," but when their eyes met over a basket of fries, neither looked away too quickly.

In the doorway Rebecca shifted her weight to her other leg and stood upright, the picture held flat in front of her with both hands. With that shift in posture, Ian's memory of her changed. She looked now, for all the world, like the woman who had waited in the doorway of their first bedroom, holding his manuscript out after she had read through *Monster.* Ian remembered waiting for her to laugh or sigh, but instead she nodded, placed the pages down, and crawled into bed next to him, shivering a bit in his arms.

"What are you thinking about?" she asked now, and he focused his eyes on her once more. It was difficult to see her face because of the bright light behind her.

"Old times," he said. "You?"

"Something a nun once told me."

Ian waited.

"She said, 'A man can't change himself. Only God can change a man.' "

Ian looked to the photo and then back to her.

"You've changed, Ian," she said quietly, and shrugged, eyes moist at the corners.

He wanted to tell her that he was still the same guy, still the same Ian, but the words caught in his throat. He could only stand, walk to her, pull her close, and whisper both her name and that he loved her.

It was the thought he'd never finished that afternoon that kept Ian up when he should have fallen asleep. The same notion that had made him look for that Howard Kepler portrait now stirred his restless mind. He went over it again, trying and trying to simplify his thoughts, and when he finished he was left with three words.

I believe it.

He believed in prophets pointing out the way toward God. He believed in the stupidity of man. He believed, most of all, in his own ignorant ways and his own disbelief. For the first time he realized why Howard had given him the picture — the man had known Ian would end up believing it at some point.

He stared at the ceiling for a second and found himself thinking of all the other things he needed to be believing. For the second time in three weeks he made a list of things in which he believed, only this time it was in his head and most of the things were what he'd call pleasant. He started with the important things — God, Jesus, Spirit, resurrection, Bible — moved through sin and mercy and some concepts that he couldn't quite explain, and then ended with a list of people who had helped him on his way. He believed them and believed in them.

Rebecca.

Howard.

His mom.

Louis.

Pete.

Oakley.

Each name brought a face to his mind, and for some reason he started smiling as he thought about the assortment of friends and family. He smiled in the dark for a long time before finally closing his eyes. He expected his happiness would bring sleep, but there was still something keeping him awake, so he started the only prayers he knew.

Now I lay me down to sleep . . .

Our Father, who art in heaven . . .

He got four lines into the Lord's Prayer and couldn't remember any more. It had been a weekly ritual growing up, but now he wasn't able to find the words. In his mind he heard the drone of a bored congregation — that rumbling half-chanted sound that went hand in hand with the prayer — but he couldn't pin down the words themselves. Whatever smile he'd had before was now gone and he flipped over onto his stomach, hoping the right position might lure him into sleep. Instead, his mind continued to search almost feverishly for that elusive next line, and when it still wouldn't come he was left with a feeling not of guilt, but of loss. He had forgotten something that should have been extremely important. And the only thing to do was to get it back.

Ian turned over twice more, played with

his pillow, and finally, when he had just gotten comfortable, Rebecca stroked his shoulder and asked, her voice a murmur, why he was wrestling sleep.

Whispering, he said, "Maybe we can go to church tomorrow. Or I might, at least."

Rebecca didn't respond, just stroked his shoulder a few times before her hand fell still against his back. He felt it there, warm and solid, and without even turning he knew she had fallen asleep again. He knew her mouth was parted just a bit and her left eyelid wasn't quite closed, as though she wanted to be ready to see or talk if the need arose. Still though, she was asleep and whether it was the music of her breathing, the warmth of her against him, or the night far gone, he soon faded into rest as well.

MORNING. SUNDAY, JULY 28

Ian woke, looked at the clock, and groaned. It was half-past ten, far too late to get ready and head out to a church service. Rubbing his eyes, he propped himself up in bed and looked about his empty room. Heavy sun broke through the curtains, and Ian knew that his alarm clock wasn't lying; it was late.

He finally made it downstairs and found a note from Rebecca saying that she had left

217

for the Jacoby house to do some poking around and would be back for lunch. He crumpled the note and tossed it in the direction of the trash basket, but it missed, skittered across the floor, and ended in Cain's nook, stopping a few inches from the sleeping dog's nose. She opened one drowsy eye, snorted twice, decided the paper was neither edible nor threatening, and grumbled herself back to sleep.

Ian fixed himself breakfast — grapefruit, coffee, a few leftover strawberries — unbundled the Sunday paper, and began reading the events of the week. Two stories in, the phone began ringing.

"Saw the article," his sister-in-law said. "Is everything all right?"

Ian asked what article and she said the one about the stalker. It was in the celebrity watch column. He assured her things were fine and promised to pass her concern on to Rebecca. He hung up and began searching through the paper for the *Entertainment* section. Before he had found it, the phone rang again — the old line, but he picked it up anyway. It was one of his fraternity brothers calling from Columbus, Ohio. He too was just checking up.

"I'm fine," Ian said. "I haven't even seen

the article yet."

After a quick chat, Ian hung up and began paging through the movie ads, the CD reviews, and a long article on a blues singer who had just passed away. He found the celebrity blurbs, searched for his name, and found it three paragraphs down, bold and eerily reminiscent of the notes left about the house.

He read through the inch-long statement and sighed in relief; it was nothing more than a gloss of the mysterious notes. It even got it wrong, mentioning that two notes had appeared rather than three. Nothing had been leaked; this was all old news.

Old news to him, at least. To friends and extended family who hadn't been notified, it seemed like good gossip, and the phone continued to ring throughout the morning. The questions were always the same — "Who? Why? Are you okay?" — so Ian constructed a few simple answers and tried to get off the line as soon as possible. He didn't need people finding out the situation had deteriorated from notes to phone calls and lurking.

Rebecca arrived home a little after noon while Ian was on the phone with one of her aunts from somewhere in Michigan. The woman refused to believe that either Ian or

Rebecca was safe, and the only way Ian could get off the phone was by passing the receiver over to his wife. For ten minutes she handled the questions, assuring her nervous aunt that the devil hadn't sent a minion to punish Ian for writing tales of horror and madness.

She hung up and twirled her finger near her ear. Aunt Nell was still seeking guidance from visions of her dead husband, Stan, apparently.

"At least that one was interesting," said Ian. "All the rest have been the same boring conversation."

"All the rest?" Rebecca asked, and Ian pointed out the AP wire story to his wife. She read it and shook her head, asking how many of her relatives had called.

Ian counted them out on his hands and remembered at least fourteen.

"They all seem sort of pleased, as if they expected this to happen sooner or later."

Rebecca laughed a little, and as if in response, the phone rang. They looked at each other and neither moved. They let the machine pick up and listened to one of Rebecca's friends from high school. Same story: three questions and then a request that Rebecca give a call if she needed to talk.

"Do you need to talk?" asked Ian.

Rebecca shrugged, stood, and walked to get some water. Her back was to him but she spoke, talking about how frustrating it was to be in Katherine's house, to know the papers were there and not be able to find them. She finished one glass, then a second, turned, and came to sit with him. Her cheeks were flushed and there was a thin strand of cobweb spiraled about her neck. Ian picked it off and took Rebecca's hands. She squeezed his in return, said she'd had one more day left to look because she couldn't go at all tomorrow. Everything was moving quickly: The curators would begin installation of the permanent room at the museum and she needed to be there to guarantee they followed her instructions. She shrugged as if there were nothing more to add, took her hands from his, and grabbed the paper again to read through the tiny news story.

"Any idea who sent it in?" she asked finally.

"Louis," Ian said without hesitation. "Or someone in publicity. Had to be." He looked at Rebecca, but she didn't look so certain. "Why, who do you think sent it in?"

She said she wasn't sure. It didn't seem like Louis's style, though, something so small and so wrong. If someone at the publisher had been in on it, there'd be more than just a little paragraph.

Ian passed the afternoon on the patio, hunched over a caterer's menu, discussing the best theme for this year's Labor Day party with Rebecca. At first it seemed that they might go with a nautical theme, but Rebecca remembered the town lobster bake was late this year and said people might be sick of seafood. Ian decided then to go to the other extreme and suggested Mexican food. Rebecca wavered, thought a second, and proposed Southwestern.

Ian looked at her and blinked. "South. West. Sounds like Mexico to me."

Southwestern would combine Mexican and Native American flavors, she explained, and flipped through a couple pages to show an entire menu covering the theme. Ian looked it over, noticed the word *chipotle* more times than he'd ever seen before and started getting hungry.

"You can hang some of Howard's pictures out if there are any landscapes in the package you get from the lawyer."

Ian agreed. He was liking this idea more and more.

Instantly, three more folders came out.

One was filled with pamphlets on where to rent cacti the size of trees, a second with brochures on mariachi bands that sang authentic Mestizo folk songs, and a third from a company that would display desert fauna to the delight and wonderment of your guests. Taking the brochure on the animals, Ian just shook his head.

"Tarantulas?"

She nodded, excited.

Paging through, Ian realized they were all there: scorpions, kangaroo rats, sidewinders, diamondback rattlers, gila monsters, even coyotes. Rebecca took out price lists, suggested layouts, and environmental requirements. As she began putting the party together Ian realized this must be an escape for her — planning and researching something and having it work out. He hoped that she could find Katherine's papers in that stupid house, but he knew time was running short. Just one more looming deadline.

Crawling into bed that night, Rebecca voiced the thought that Ian had been saying to himself ever since they had come upstairs:

"This has been a great day."

Maybe it was just that for two days they hadn't seen Oakley, hadn't heard from the stalker. Perhaps it was finalizing the plans for the Labor Day picnic, though Ian didn't think so. Most likely, it was just a good day, plain as that. There could be good days once in a while, despite not finding Katherine Jacoby's papers. Despite news of the stalking being printed like a coupon for everyone in the country to read. It could still be a good day.

Of course, something still could happen. The doorbell could ring. A car could pull up and idle outside the house. A window downstairs could shatter. He could wake up and glimpse the cold shadow of a man slipping into the room. There'd be a flash of steel and then the sound of screaming.

Ian turned on his side; this was ridiculous. His mind catapulted back and forth from simple pleasure at a day well spent to sudden terror at what might be creeping through the shrubbery out back. He couldn't just enjoy the one without some internal alarm warning him of the lingering threat.

After ten minutes, Ian fetched a glass of water. On his way back to the bed, he remembered other times he'd had trouble sleeping. Almost without fail, each occurred when he was about to start a novel. Ideas or character traits or opening lines would push any other thought out and quiet only when

Ian gave them voice. He realized he would have to do that now as well. He'd finished looking through his notes and was ready to start his memoir about this stalking. Perhaps in writing, the persistent worries would vanish and the deepest hours of his night would be left in peace.

LATE AFTERNOON. TUESDAY, JULY 30

Rebecca arrived home early, her hair dusty and tangled from a day's exploration of Katherine Jacoby's attic and basement. The moment she pushed open the door — eyes red from dust and dirt, shoulders rounded and heavy — Ian knew she had not found the papers. They had escaped her final search, and she would have to speak with her advisor and change back to her original thesis topic. She would have to secure a cubicle at the library and hit the books for the next three weeks straight.

Rebecca smiled at him as she trudged past and said that she needed to get cleaned up before they met the Oakleys for dinner. Normally Ian would have made a joke, but this time he stayed silent and simply touched her shoulder as she walked by. A few minutes later he heard the shuffle of Rebecca at her mirror, so he returned to the tablet of notes he had made about the stalking, skimming through it to find phrases he'd marked that afternoon.

One idea, one expression stood out, over and over, in what he'd written.

I was wrong.

He looked at the sentence and realized he had his opening line. He'd written something true, something that impacted every part of these maddening weeks, something on which he could expand. He'd been wrong about many things and now had a chance to get things right.

As he closed the notebook, Rebecca called for his help in zipping her dress. Ian pushed the pad and pen to the middle of the table, crossed the kitchen to the stairs, and took them two at a time. As he reached the hall, Rebecca stepped through the doorway, holding her hand behind her neck to keep her open dress from slipping off her shoulders. Ian stepped behind her, zipped the back of her dress to her neck, and kissed her there. She turned in his grasp, slipped her arms around him, and gave his waist a squeeze. Her eyes were still bleary and red, and for the first time Ian wondered if it was more than simply the dust and her allergies.

She said nothing about it, though, and walked into the next room. Ian passed into their bedroom, grabbed a clean Oxford from the closet, and began searching through his ties. It felt good to be dressing up for something other than an uncomfortable meeting downtown. Dinner would be a chance to unwind, and lately they needed every chance they could find.

Ian and Rebecca arrived two minutes early for their reservation at Marzipan and found the Oakleys waiting just inside the door. Ian introduced Rebecca to Anne, and the two couples were seated immediately at a table in the middle of the restaurant's single sprawling dining room. They shared small talk for a few moments while looking through the menus, stopping only to give their orders when the waiter appeared. Conversation moved simply and easily from the day's weather, to favorite local beaches, and even to hometowns.

When Rebecca asked what had brought them to Titansburg, Anne told the story of the doll shop, and as she mentioned her mother's illness Oakley slipped an arm around her shoulder. Anne didn't let the subject remain open very long and admitted to Ian how much she enjoyed his writing. He thanked her and answered a few questions about writing. By the time he'd finished, their meals had arrived.

When conversation resumed, Anne asked, "Are you working on anything new?"

Ian thought of the single sentence scrawled in his crooked lettering at the top of the note pad that sat on the kitchen table. It wasn't much — three simple words — but it meant he wasn't lying when he nodded in the affirmative. Anne asked what, but, as always, Ian had to decline answering. Until the first draft landed on his editor's desk, he had to keep all information under lock and key.

Anne finished her meal first, looked at her watch, and stood, saying that she needed to visit the ladies room. Rebecca finished and said she'd join her. As the two women walked off, Ian heard his wife ask about Anne's barely showing pregnancy and hoped the sight didn't sting as greatly as it used to.

Alone with Ian, Mike Oakley said, "I saw that blurb in the paper. Your publisher put that in?"

Ian shook his head, said that though Louis was thrilled with the publicity, someone else had leaked it. Oakley grunted and finished off the remaining chunk of his wife's swordfish.

After another minute, Rebecca returned and said Anne was giving the sitter a call.

Oakley nodded and explained that she was a little nervous about leaving Jay with the neighbor girl since he'd just gotten over chicken pox.

"Still hot under the collar that he got sick during summer vacation." He said this with a smile, but when Anne returned to the table — her serious eyes worried — Oakley stood and asked what had happened.

She waved him down and then lowered herself into her chair. "Jay is fine," she said. "The sitter said he fell asleep in the middle of one of his videos and has been snoring for a half hour." She tried to smile at this, but her lips were tight and unconvincing. "She also said that my father called. Mom slipped out of the apartment again. They found her at the old jetty, sitting on the rocks watching the tide come in."

Oakley asked if anything had happened, but Anne just shook her head. "It's just the idea of her wandering around like that," she said, staring across the table at her husband. He nodded and reached to take his wife's hand. Ian saw Rebecca look away, so he did too, and for a moment the group sat in silence.

Anne broke the quiet by apologizing and, to change the subject, asked Rebecca what new things would be appearing at the museum. Perhaps during lunch, she could slip on over and get a tour.

Ian saw his wife's face light at the question, and as she began explaining the new Katherine Jacoby display being constructed, Rebecca sounded as though she were talking about a close friend.

"Installation began yesterday," she said, "but the opening won't be until a week from Saturday, the same day we're having a big fundraising auction. Hopefully a lot of the collectors will fall in love with her art."

Oakley asked who Katherine Jacoby was and Rebecca told as much as she knew, asking him finally if he remembered seeing the big driftwood sculpture in the town hall. The officer nodded and Rebecca said that was one of Katherine's works.

"You know a lot about her," said Anne.

Rebecca nodded, a little embarrassed, and admitted that the woman fascinated her. She loved Katherine's sculptures, the unique vision the woman had of the world.

"I was going to use her for my thesis, but a master's degree in archiving without letters isn't worth all that much."

"What happened to the papers?" asked Anne.

Rebecca shrugged. "I searched that entire house and I couldn't find a thing. Just the one picture of her as a child. That's it."

At this Oakley leaned forward and asked if there were any places to hide papers.

"Michael," said Anne, "the woman searched the house. If she said the letters weren't there, they weren't there."

"People are good at hiding things, that's all," said Oakley.

"You're a detective," Rebecca said, almost to herself, and Ian realized what she meant. She turned to look at the officer, and he nodded. Without a word being spoken Ian realized dinner would not be followed by dessert, but by a visit to Katherine Jacoby's house so they could give it one more search — this time, a professional search.

After Oakley dropped Anne off at home to relieve the babysitter, he followed Ian and Rebecca to Katherine Jacoby's house. Rebecca didn't speak much on the ride over, and Ian guessed she was trying to keep any flicker of hope in check. The day's earlier disappointment would have certainly been enough.

They arrived at the small Cape Cod a little after ten, and Rebecca let them in with the key she would surrender tomorrow when the final belongings were removed from the house. As they entered, their footsteps echoed through the vacant rooms, and Ian smelled the sharp, pungent odor of bleach and what might have been a rug shampoo. As Rebecca led Oakley on the tour, Ian found himself surprised at how much the house had changed.

Before, color and pattern swarmed through each room, and with Rebecca playing her game of hide-and-seek with the sculptures it had seemed as though the house were more than just the earthly remains of this dead woman. Now, though — its walls scrubbed and gleaming, its carpets crisscrossed with the tracks of industrial steamers — the home felt tiny to Ian, as if removing those elusive sculptures and their strange dimensions caused the entire house to shrink.

"Ready?" Oakley asked, startling Ian from his thoughts. The man pulled a small penlight from his pocket and moved to the living room to begin his search. Ian and Rebecca followed to observe.

Oakley first checked the fireplace. Movers had dismantled the elaborate fake piece she'd created, so now it was only a small, dark hole with two bricks' worth of facing around it and a slight marble hearth that stretched out level with the carpet. He fiddled with the flue for a second, rapped his knuckles on the facing, and motioned for them to follow. Room by room they searched, neither speaking nor even looking at one another. Oakley tapped on walls, pulled at the carpet, ran his fingers over the length of vents. He shone his light into the ducts, opened every closet, rustled the light fixtures, and explored all the corners of the rooms. He found nothing.

Oakley asked if there were anyplace else to search.

"The only thing that's left is her workroom," Rebecca said. Her words were slow and heavy with the weight of sighs. She pushed open the door and walked through, switching on the light as she did. Oakley and Ian followed, closing the door behind them.

The garage, unlike the house, had been virtually untouched during the cleaning. Ian saw that the same row of sculptures stood covered against the right wall, and though the sawdust and wood chips had been picked up, the tools and equipment still hung on nimble hooks. Ian heard Oakley whistle as the officer walked a grid through the room, staring at the cluttered workbench and the host of carving tools.

Rebecca asked if he had a plan for searching and if there was any way she could help.

Oakley didn't say anything at first, just stared at the belt sander, the high-bore router, the assortment of reciprocating saws that were mounted like stuffed marlin on the pegboard. Finally he turned to her and asked what kind of sculptor this woman had been.

"All sorts," said Rebecca, but she motioned to the tools and said that Katherine had worked mostly with wood in the last years.

Oakley nodded. He said it looked like his father's woodshop, the one the old man had left in the basement when he went off to Korea. For years afterward nobody bothered to touch it, and he would sometimes steal downstairs and sit in the dark.

"It smelled like this," he said, waving a hand. "That burnt smell of cut lumber and machine grease. I'd close my eyes and make up stories about him." Oakley shook his head then, as if to clear his thoughts, and looked around him.

He tackled the workbench first, picking up a rag to open each drawer. Rebecca asked why he covered his hand and Oakley looked down, as though surprised. He grinned then and said it was habit. He'd almost forgotten that this wasn't a crime scene. He needn't worry about leaving fingerprints. Ian and Rebecca laughed at that, and then they began to search the room as well.

Ian walked to the back of the garage where a tall brace of metal shelving stood wedged beneath the ceiling. Each row had a small model on it, and after a while Ian recognized that they were miniatures of her larger sculptures. These had been put together with plaster or clay, however, and Ian assumed they were studies, rough miniatures that Katherine used before starting her originals.

He saw the angel wings, the odd bowl sculpture, and even a delicate version of the rib cage. There was a rough cross fashioned from pieces of what looked to be firewood and then a number of models of originals he had never seen. Two rows of skulls lining what looked to be either a sleeping figure or a corpse. A tree with strings of barbed wire passing through its trunk. A rough nude of a woman sculpting. An apple with bite marks in it that formed the silhouettes of two faces: man and woman.

Finally on the bottom shelf nearest to him was a model of the book. This study was smaller than even the replica that Rebecca and he had found in the library, and the portrait was indistinct and unrecognizable.

Something in the model seemed different, though, than either of the sculptures he had seen before. Ian picked it up to get a better look. Immediately, the portrait, which had only been resting on the front, slipped from the book and clattered off the shelves and to the floor.

As Ian bent to pick it up, Rebecca shouted for him to be careful. She walked over from the boxes she had been searching through fruitlessly and asked if he had broken anything. Ian said no, the top had just slid off. He held the pieces to her and explained that the portrait had been like a lid. The center of the book was hollow.

Rebecca stared at it for a second, turned, and walked over to the enormous original, pulling off the sheet with a snap of her wrist. Oakley crossed the garage to her side and asked what she had found. She said she wasn't sure, but perhaps the sculpture was hollow.

Oakley shrugged, lowered himself so his ear was near what would be the front cover of the book, and began tapping. He worked slowly, stopping every few inches to knock twice on the book's smooth wood. The officer's arm slid along the grain of the sculpture and his ear remained pressed to its side. Rebecca and Ian barely breathed.

Suddenly Oakley's eyes widened and he worked around a small area for about twenty seconds.

He rapped one more time with his knuckles and stood. His eyes were electric.

"It's hollow, or part of it is, at least."

Ian thought Rebecca might break into laughter, but she had simply put her hand over her mouth and stared. It was Ian who asked how they could open it.

Oakley shook his head, said he didn't know. Perhaps there was a secret lever.

For minutes all three scoured the surface of the book looking for anything that might let them in. Ian tugged at the portrait, since that had acted as a lid on the model, but it wouldn't budge. When he moved around back, he thought he had found a button but it turned out to be a dead fly wrapped snug and tight in a spider's web.

Rebecca was on the side of the book when Ian saw her finger slip into a crease of some sort. She got a strange look on her face, part pleasure, part disbelief, and told the men that they'd been thinking too hard.

"It's a book," she said, standing. "It opens like a book." She grabbed the corners of the massive sculpture and pulled up. Oakley helped and soon the front cover swung open. Katherine wasn't hiding her papers;

she'd put them in the most obvious spot.

Ian moved to the open sculpture and looked in. Ring binders lay stacked within the hollowed cavity, and Rebecca withdrew one and opened the cover, paging through the contents. Letters stuffed into plastic sleeves filled the notebooks along with postcards, drawings, photos, and even ticket stubs and brochures.

Ian and Oakley looked at each other, reached into the book, and began unloading the binders, one after the other. When they had finished Ian counted thirty-six notebooks: three across, four down, and three deep. The book had been constructed to hold all of Katherine Jacoby's letters and memories.

The title was dead on; it truly was an autobiography.

Ian, with Oakley's help, swung the front cover closed once more, and they both took some time to look at the portrait on the cover. The face, smiling and warm, stared out at them as though pleased they had found her secrets.

Ian turned to Rebecca, expecting to see his wife glowing with delight, but instead her chin was lowered to her chest and her shoulders trembled. Ian slipped his arms around her. He wanted to whisper something into her ear but couldn't think of anything to say. He had no idea why she wept, so he simply held her to his chest and rubbed the small of her back with his palm.

Oakley walked quietly away from the couple, and Ian saw him give a flat, sympathetic smile before turning to fiddle with some of the tools.

For a minute more Rebecca cried into Ian's shirt, and then the heavy sobs became something different, higher and closer together. He loosened his arms around his wife and stared at her flushed, puffy face. Her eyes had begun to swell and she still sniffled, but tugging at the corner of her mouth was the beginnings of a smile. The tears turned toward laughter, though it still surprised Ian how similar the two sounded. He saw Oakley look over his shoulder at the sound, and then the officer made his way back to the sculpture.

They stood that way for a while — Ian holding his teary, laughing wife, Oakley a few feet away, arms crossed behind him — until Rebecca unfolded herself from Ian's arms, bent down, and let one hand stroke the covers of the binders. Then she let out one long, deep sigh, her face and eyes smiling with a glow that nearly outshone the

single, naked bulb dangling from a high
socket and bathing the room in light.

Week 4

For the first time since he'd started these weekly trips into the city, Ian was finally able to enjoy the opulence of the train. He'd glanced at the velvet curtain before but hadn't taken the time to feel its easy weight. He'd looked past the chiseled scrollwork on his bench every other trip and had never bothered to notice that the molding throughout the first-class car was inlaid with filigree gold. Today he'd had a productive session working with Louis outlining the early chapters of the memoir, and though a deadline still loomed, the nervous worry of the past months seemed to have vanished. Ian rested, and once the train rumbled from its last tunnel into the long shadows of the late Connecticut afternoon, he pulled Jaret's story from his case and read while waiting for Trout to appear.

The closing pages of the chapter still

241

mimicked Ian's life with an eerie accuracy, and he had just read the kid's introduction to the talented folksinger again when he heard the clank of the beverage cart rolling down the aisle.

"Get you a drink?" Trout asked, pulling back the curtain.

Ian asked for ice water, and as it was being poured, he studied the face of the old man. Trout was an impressively large man, and his eyes looked as though they might have stared another man down from opposite corners of a ring. The porter's hands, though, were the most impressive part. Wide and thick, they were like two baseball mitts, leathered and tough, but while the ground underneath him moved, he could pour out drinks without spilling a drop. He could have been a fine shortstop with the combination of size and fluid dexterity.

"You ever play ball?" asked Ian.

The man shook his head in a way Ian couldn't read and said he'd been too busy working to bother with a thing like sports. His carefree days ended with the Crash. He was one of eight kids, and only the last two got to play sports of any kind. His youngest brother even went to the University of Hartford on scholarship as a defensive back, but that was a long time ago.

"You need anything more at the moment?"

Ian shook his head. He still wanted to hear the story of how Trout got his nickname, but that could wait.

"I'll be back around a little later then," the old man said, "to collect that." Then he stepped from the room and headed back down the aisle.

Ian paged through a bit more of Jaret's chapter and skimmed a stack of four memoirs Louis had given him before giving up the pretense of wanting to stay awake. He slumped into his bench and let the haze of sleep fall over him. The last thing he remembered hearing were the clanging bells of a railroad crossing as the train passed through a clogged intersection.

Padded footsteps and the clink of glasses awakened him, and when he roused, Trout was creeping softly from the room, glass and napkin in hand. Ian cleared his throat and stretched a bit, and when Trout heard him rustling he turned and apologized for making too much noise.

Through a yawn, Ian said, "No problem. I needed to get up and make myself pretty anyway."

Trout smiled at that, slipped the glass into his cart, and returned to see if Ian needed anything else. When Ian asked for the story of Trout's name, the old man just grinned a little and shook his head. It wasn't anything much of a story, the man protested, but when Ian insisted, the porter smiled and steadied himself in the doorframe.

"My grandmother started using it when I was a baby, and everybody in the house picked up on it eventually. She said it was because my skin is speckled." He held out a spotted hand to show Ian. "Like the brook trout we used to catch from a stream near our house. And because I didn't crawl like a normal baby — just wriggled around like I was swimming on dry land."

Ian's mouth must have been open and his eyes perplexed, because the next thing Trout said was, "Weren't expecting that, were you?"

Ian shook his head. He'd anticipated a boyhood tale of catching some mythically large fish. "What's your real name?"

"Jedidiah," Trout answered, and then added with a proud smile, "It's biblical."

"Sounds it," answered Ian, understanding a tad more why folks called him Trout.

"Old Testament," Trout continued. "It's a nickname too; it's what God called Solomon to let the people know he was blessed. Means 'loved by the Lord.' "

Ian looked at Trout's smiling face and guessed that the name was appropriate.

A whistle blew from the locomotive, and Trout's smile vanished. He chastised himself for spending so much time yapping away like a woman and told Ian that it had been good chatting but he needed to finish up his rounds. He gathered his cart and pushed it down the aisle toward the caboose.

Ian leaned back, and his first thought was how much comfort it must give a person to have God reach down and give you a name that said He would always love you. But then something Trout said last week passed through his mind: *A nickname reminds you of something you were never going to forget anyway.*

Ian was sitting in the back room of DeCafé looking up at the words brushed in ink by Norman Gruitt when Kevin walked in. They nodded to each other but said nothing. Kevin stood in front of one of the words before taking an armchair opposite Ian with a low groan that Ian barely caught over the air conditioning. Ian looked up to see if he was all right, but Kevin had already removed Jaret's story from his book bag and was reading it. Ian did the same and the only noise in the sitting room, besides the hum of the vents, was the rustle of turning pages.

Ian had just reread the first conversation between the folksinger and Ted the wanderer when Kevin mumbled something that made Ian look up. The teacher wasn't looking at him, just at the wall, so Ian guessed that the mumble hadn't been meant as conversation after all and looked back down.

Kevin's voice, louder this time, said, "I never did introduce you to Norman Gruitt, did I?"

Ian looked up. This time the teacher was staring his direction. Ian shook his head.

"You want to meet him?"

Ian was about to say no, it didn't really matter, when he realized that this would be perfect for his book about the stalking. An interview, a meeting with the man whose art became the notes that started the whole affair. He thought one more second and nodded, said he'd love to meet him.

"Friday all right?"

Ian held up a finger, asking for a second, and checked his day planner. Friday afternoon was free and clear, so Ian penciled the meeting in and asked where they should meet.

"Do you know where Cold Cuts is?" asked Kevin. When Ian nodded, the teacher explained that the deli wasn't too far from Norman's studio. They could meet for lunch.

"Remind me how you know him?" asked Ian, but Kevin only laughed. Said all things would be explained in time and then laughed some more.

Ian wanted to talk about the ending of Jaret's story — how the wonderful connection that the wandering man made with the psalms that had been put to music was truer and more real than any other conversion story he'd read in the genealogy. He had written his notes, had even scripted a bit of what he wanted to say, but hadn't been able to put a word in yet. Kevin kept talking about the first portion of the chapter and the devastating effects of unrequited love while Pete kept chiming in about the middle section and how the man's wandering, random path had actually been a search, an unconscious hunt to find meaning and fulfillment. Nothing was being debated fully, and Jaret was getting frustrated.

"Can we do this in an organized fashion?" he asked after Pete and Kevin had traded non-sequiturs three comments in a row.

Kevin said sure, and Ian nodded.

Pete apologized for being out of hand.

"It's just that this chapter really hit home for me," he added.

Ian and Kevin both looked at Pete at the same time.

"You?" asked Kevin. "It practically mirrored my life."

Ian said he saw a lot of similarities to his own life as well, and then all three men looked at Jaret. Ian wondered if the others felt as jealous as he did. He thought the story was special and personal; instead, everyone at the table seemed to have a connection to it. All except Jaret, that is, who shrugged and said, "Well, none of this stuff happened to me. I just made it up," and proposed that the group spend five minutes on each portion before calling it an evening.

Ian spoke last, as he had connected with the concluding portion of the chapter. Like the men before him, he tried his best to talk only about the text without bringing too much of his own life into it, and for the most part he managed. At one point, however, when questioned by Kevin about the possibility of forming a lasting friendship with a stranger, Ian could only think about Howard and say, "It's possible."

As the group closed, Kevin handed copies of his newest chapter, one week late, to Jaret and Pete. He looked at Ian, apologized, and said he had photocopied his whole manuscript but had left it on his computer chair at home. Could he bring it on Friday?

Ian nodded, a bit curious as to what a man like Kevin would write — probably something political or militant. He tried to peek at Jaret's copy as it lay across the table but couldn't read the printing upside down.

The others straightened their bags as well, rearranging books and notebooks, but when all that was done nobody moved from his seat.

Pete finally spoke up and said that Ian was looking a sight better than last week. The cut certainly had healed fast. Ian said thanks and noted that plants don't exactly leave deep wounds.

"I saw the blurb in the paper on Sunday," Pete added. "Everything going all right?"

Before Ian could answer, Kevin jumped up as though he'd been bitten.

"That's right!" he shouted. "The story! I forgot to tell you."

The others waited.

"Our girl got in," he said. "Cheryl made it onto the Associated Press wire!"

Ian groaned, and Pete asked who Cheryl was. Kevin explained how one of his students had interviewed Ian, and that when the story went to print, the editor suggested she summarize it for the celebrity wire. Three days later the Associated Press picked it up.

"Good for her," said Jaret, then almost apologized when he saw Ian's face.

"Good?" said Kevin. "It's great. She broke a story and it ended up going national. That's the sort of thing that gets you into the bigger newsrooms right out of college. She's going places, that Cheryl."

He smiled then and turned to Ian, who stifled a groan.

"And she owes it all to you," said Kevin, and Ian could keep it in no longer.

Outside Ian caught Pete before he got into his car and asked the question he'd been thinking about since getting up late last Sunday: *Where did he go to church?* Pete looked surprised, then smiled and said at the Titansburg Church of God at the middle school on Faulty and Wayne. Ian raised an eyebrow, surprised the service was in a school, but asked if that's where Jaret attended. Pete nodded but said the kid often used the weekends to visit his fiancée.

"Didn't know you were looking for a church," Pete said after they had stood quiet for a moment.

"I haven't gone in a long time," Ian replied. "Nor my wife."

"Not much has changed," Pete replied. "Hymns, prayers, sermons, and offering plates. You won't feel too lost."

"And you'll be there on Sunday?"

"Eight-fifteen sharp, surrounded by blondes." He paused. "Wife and daughter."

Ian said he'd be on the lookout, waved a quick good-bye, and turned to walk to his car. After a few steps he turned back to Pete, who stood watching with a look of amazement on his face, and asked if there was anything else he should know. Anything for which he should be ready.

Pete thought a minute and said, "We've got basketball rims rather than stained-glass saints. Just wanted to warn you." Ian nodded and watched Pete stuff himself into his hatchback. As he pulled past Ian into the night, he beeped, and all Ian could do in return was wave before heading to his Cherokee.

The weather was fair and breezy, so Ian lingered in the evening air, thinking about the men in the group and how four weeks ago the people he knew, really knew, in the town wouldn't form a basketball team, let alone a group of friends. Folks from Titansburg were always invited to the Labor Day parties but, like Katherine Jacoby, Ian had shaken their hands, forgotten their names, and moved on to a colleague from the city or a relative who'd made the trip from Buffalo. Now, though, names and faces and occupations and family and cares and worries and all the rest were sticking, and he was getting to know people. Ian realized he'd been wrong in the past for not branching out — add it to the list of things he'd been mistaken about — and had managed to hurt himself more than he thought possible. And maybe Rebecca as well. Wrongs were being righted these days and errors corrected. Ian drove home happy, singing along as the Beatles explained the one thing money couldn't buy, and found his wife asleep on the bed, lights blazing, surrounded by a wall of Katherine Jacoby's binders. Her capacity for slumber amidst clutter impressed him once more.

Somehow she stayed asleep as he cleared off the bed. The moment he crawled in next to her, she moved to him, gave him a sleepy hug, and mumbled that she loved him. She would never remember saying it, Ian knew, but he also knew that he would never forget. It was just one of those moments.

Cain had the energy of a puppy this morning, and whether digging after moles or chasing leaves floating before her on the summer wind, she did everything with a spirit Ian hadn't seen since their tangle with the raspberry bush. She pulled him through their walk in what had to be record time, and when Ian stepped inside he noticed that Rebecca hadn't even made it downstairs for her breakfast yet. Taking advantage of the chance, Ian started a pot of coffee, poured juice, and set out two bowls of cereal. As he turned to retrieve spoons, he heard Rebecca's footsteps rounding the corner. He turned and smiled, and she gave what was almost a shy wave in return before taking a seat. A few bites into breakfast, Ian asked how her advisory meeting went. Had she beaten the deadline?

"I dropped two of Katherine's binders on her desk, said there were thirty-four more like them, and asked if that was enough."

"What'd she say?"

"She said thirty-six *letters* were enough. Thirty-six binders was a doctorate in waiting."

Ian waited for her to comment on that but she continued, saying how they decided she should concentrate on the letters detailing Jacoby's past and the question of her parents' identity.

"Whether she was really the daughter of a storm trooper."

Ian stood to pour the coffee and asked what Rebecca guessed she'd find.

His wife sat thinking over the question for a bit, her eyes focused straight ahead. But Ian knew she wasn't looking at the centerpiece or the clock on the far wall or even imagining the inside of the garage. She was somewhere else, imagining the doors that would open until she had her answer. Ian repeated the question.

"Oh," she said, rousing herself, "I know she was that man's daughter. And I'm almost positive she knew about it. I'm just not sure when she found out or how it changed her life."

Ian said, "Can you imagine something like that coming up from your past to bite you?"

Rebecca shook her head, said it must have shaken the very foundation of Katherine's life. She paused, as though to say more, then looked down to her cereal and finished what remained. When the bowl was empty, she stood, kissed Ian on the top of his head, and wished him a good day of writing. Ian didn't even have a chance to respond before she was out the door and into the garage. The house was empty and quiet once more, but for the moment that was okay. He had writing to do. He had to explain all the things about which he'd been so wrong.

I was wrong. I forgot there were monsters, and they have thrived.

The first sentence came out in a burst of typing, and others soon followed. For an hour Ian wrote furiously, as though it were his one chance to get the words out. He didn't look at his notes on the stalking, didn't even take a break to check his thesaurus. Pages filled with his dawning recognition that somebody was watching him, waiting for him, and before Ian knew it, the installation team from Sears had arrived with his lights.

He returned to his computer after showing the men where he wanted the lights and moved on just as briskly as before. The three eerie scratches on his garage door, the mysterious car, and the first note all made their appearances, as did his writer's block, Rebecca, and Cain. He'd never had it so easy before — a full cast of characters had been laid out before him without a second of thought. For another thirty minutes he filled in some back story about his own novels before a dry throat and eager stomach led him to lunch.

After checking the progress of the security lights, he headed to the kitchen and had barely gotten his sandwich put together when the doorbell rang. Ian and Cain jogged to the door together.

Chet the mailman stood holding a package. "Didn't want to leave it on your front stoop, what with people around," he said, hinting with a nod to the workers gathered around their van for a noontime break.

"Good idea, Chet," said Ian, taking the box. It was heavier than he expected and felt as though it'd been packed tight. Ian smiled when he noticed the postmark: Springdale, Utah. It was the first shipment Howard's lawyer had promised.

Ian thanked the mailman and was going to shut the door but Chet spoke up, said that Ian looked like he'd healed pretty well and wasn't that just a crazy afternoon. Ian nodded and agreed that it certainly had been.

Chet leaned forward. "They ever catch him?" he whispered.

"No, Chet, not yet."

The mailman looked disappointed, as though somehow he might've missed out on a reward, and so he just shook his head and turned to go.

"Well, good luck with that," he called, walking back to his van. "And let me know if you need more help."

"Will do," said Ian and shut the door. God help him if he ever needed Chet the mailman's help again.

Ian settled himself outside on the patio with his sandwich, a sweating glass of water, and Howard Kepler's box. He took a bite of roast beef, a sip from his water, and hoisted the package onto his knees. Looking at it, bouncing it a little to feel the weight, he guessed that it had to be close to twenty-five pounds. He pulled out a penknife to slit open the taped flaps.

A note rested on top of packing peanuts, and Ian glanced over it briefly, noting that the lawyer used the word *client* in referring to Howard. It was as absurd a description as he could imagine of the old photographer. Clients spoke in complete sentences, asked well-phrased questions, and signed their signature with metal pens that matched the varied shades of charcoal and gray worn to the office. They did not make a meal of fried corn bread, wouldn't consider a sleeping bag the bedroom, and owned more than the three pairs of wool socks Howard kept.

Ian shook his head, folded the letter, and began scooping handfuls of packing peanuts to the ground. Cain, who'd been content to turn an occasional eye to Ian's sandwich, rose to sniff the Styrofoam in case it might be edible. Finding nothing to her taste, she sighed and slumped onto Ian's feet with a grumble.

Three inches under the packing Ian uncovered two photograph albums lying side by side. He took them out and set them next to his chair. Under each lay another pair, and these he removed as well. Twice more he emptied albums from the box until all eight stood in two towers next to his chair. He couldn't even touch them, only stare. This had to have been what Rebecca felt when the sculpture had been opened and the binders of letters were set before her — happiness, for sure, but a quick realization, too, that this was all that remained. Neither eight albums nor thirty-six binders would ever equal the person who had once taken the time to fill them.

Ian took a sip of his water and opened the first book.

He was not surprised.

Photographs filled each book, pages upon pages of pictures developed over Howard's lifetime. At first glance it appeared that they were simply black-and-white images, but looking closer Ian noticed that each had writing across it. They were the same as all of Howard Kepler's art that he'd seen — monochrome pictures with Bible verses inscribed over top. Turning back to the first page, though, Ian realized that Howard had a much bigger plan than just taking photos.

In the beginning God created the heaven and the earth . . . read the writing on the first image. The next was also a verse from Genesis. The third was as well. Ian glanced through the rest of the albums and saw the same pattern.

Howard Kepler had been photographing the Bible.

Or at least, that was what Ian could make of the book.

Each page of the album was crowded with eight 3 × 5 black-and-white prints. On every one was written a passage of scripture — some of which were so long that Ian could barely make out the original image beneath. It appeared as though the entire Bible might be transcribed over Howard's images, and Ian was stunned at the project's immensity.

The man had copied the Bible. Not only that, but he'd taken a corresponding picture for each passage.

Here in a verse about tax collectors from one of the last books, Ian could see a telephoto shot of a burnished penny half covered in dirt. In Jesus' prayer in the Garden, there was a photo of three men in tank tops sleeping on lawn chairs, mouths open in exhaustion. A second copy of the image he knew as *Cage* with its barren horror — empty rib cage, piling sand — graced the pages with other psalms, and Ian wondered how someone else had managed a reproduction of the work or if Howard had purposely copied some photos to be sold. Remembering the other photo given to him — the silhouetted profile of his face — he searched through the albums until he found the words in Paul's letter to Timothy. It was not his image, however, that filled the space.

Instead, under the same exact verse, a subtle and beautiful picture of Howard himself graced the page. The face was younger than Ian remembered and the hair was cropped close to the skull, but in the eyes and those grand ears, Ian recognized his friend. No other landscape or reference point was available in the picture, just Howard's face cropped right below the chin. Ian removed it from the page and turned it over. From a line of cramped writing, Ian could read the photo was taken in Springdale, 1943. Next to that was the title, *Self-Portrait.* He'd called the image the same thing and Ian realized that the title didn't refer to the photo itself but to the verse. Before God, everyone would declare themselves the worst of sinners. Ian sat back a moment, hoping to think this over, but the doorbell rang. He figured it was the men from Sears, finished with their installation. He didn't want to leave the albums, not when he had just started paging through them, but he knew he would have all the time he'd need to look through the photos later. They were his gift, and he could linger over them as long as he liked.

Sitting in bed that evening, Ian and Rebecca traded albums and binders back and forth, pointing out interesting facts, unusual photos, and other things that caught their eyes as they worked their way through their respective collections. Rebecca said she was finding more than enough letters that talked about Katherine's history, but only a handful dealing with her father and his connections to the Nazi party. Ian discovered that Howard had not managed to complete the entire Bible after all; in fact, he was far from it. Entire books, many from the Old Testament, were missing, and as Ian compared the albums to his Bible he wasn't surprised. He wouldn't have known how to photograph the genealogies or the technical requirements of the law either.

About eleven, Rebecca said her eyes had suffered enough for one night and that she was going to get some rest. Ian agreed and they both set their binders aside and switched off the lamps. Under the sheets, Rebecca's hand sought Ian's and gave it a squeeze. He moved toward his wife, and she met his touch with a smile that disappeared only when Ian stopped her mouth with a kiss. The darkness of the room meant nothing, and they found each other with a simple ease that made it difficult to remember what it was like to be awkward newlyweds discovering each other with tentative hands and fumbling caresses.

Afterward he held onto her hand for a while, saying nothing, just content to feel her settling pulse as it slowly unwound toward sleep. Ian lay in silence, trying to remember the last time their love had poured forth from such happiness and joy, and almost missed Rebecca's voice when she spoke, her words barely comprehensible through the pillow.

"I'd like to buy some of Katherine's sculptures at the auction next Saturday."

Ian tightened his hold on her hand, and she murmured something else that Ian couldn't hear. A moment later, she turned on her side and slipped her hand from his. A slight breeze rustled the curtains and Ian felt the chill of the room. August had come — not with the heaviness of summer but with a yearning for autumn. He pulled the sheet up about his cheek to fight the cold, but the thin fabric did little. He edged himself over to where Rebecca lay asleep and folded himself against her body. Together they were warm, and Ian no longer felt the night.

Early morning. Friday, August 2

After Cain's morning walk, Ian joined Rebecca for muffins. They discussed the museum auction and which sculptures might fit best in their home. Rebecca wrote a few quick notes to herself, stood, and reminded Ian to mail the Labor Day party invitations that afternoon. He nodded and was rewarded with a quick kiss before she left him to silence and work. Ian moved to his den and reminded himself of today's goal — he hoped to make it at least as far as the discovery of the third note before his lunch meeting with Kevin.

Shutting his eyes, he let his thoughts drift. Quick glimpses of his wife's pale, drawn face stained by the whirling strobes of police cars flashed through his mind but didn't stay. Instead, each was replaced by some more recent vision of his wife. The dazed enrapturing look that took her when Katherine's book was opened. Her sincere exhilaration at knowing she'd have papers around which to base her thesis. The smile in her eyes last evening.

The fear of recent weeks had been overrun these past days, and it now seemed clear to Ian the ugliness of his current task. He had to put aside the joy and pleasure he felt and center his thoughts to everything horrid that had come before. He had to ignore the blessing of Howard's gift and Katherine's letters to bring attention to what was probably some half-baked thug who meant not a lick of good.

The scary thing was that he knew how to do it.

Every novel he'd written had followed the same pattern. He'd set aside months of happiness with his wife to conjure up some evil the color of nightshade. Book after book he'd done that until he realized that to do it once more would send him down a path he did not want to see. And now it was happening again.

Ian stopped, scrolled up to the first page of his memoir, and gave himself three lines to write. He was not going to do it again. He wasn't going to sacrifice joy on the altar of sales and money. If he was going to write this memoir, it would be the way *he* wanted it — stalker or no stalker.

Cold Cuts sat four blocks west of the ocean on a rarely visited side street between a camera store and an insurance agency. The place tried to pull off New York deli but the floor was polished to a spit-shine, the signed photos of celebrities were forgeries, and the whole place was silent despite a scattered number of customers. Ian didn't see Kevin right away, so he took a seat in a booth. The teacher soon appeared from the men's room, waved, and slowly made his way across the floor, his limp more noticeable than ever. As the man sat, Ian asked if he was okay.

"Shin splints," he answered. "Bought a new pair of running shoes, and my legs have been killing me."

That was all he said on the subject, just leaned back and began his gentle rocking, while a waitress arrived to take their order. After she hurried toward the kitchen, Kevin reached into his book bag, pulled out a thick stack of paper, and slid it to Ian. On the cover page were written two words: *Evangeline Strong.*

"Your novel?"

Kevin nodded almost shyly and didn't seem to be ready to offer anything further, so Ian set the pages aside and asked what he should expect from Norman Gruitt during their interview.

As the waitress returned with their lunches, Kevin repeated a little of what he'd already told Ian about the artist and then suggested that Ian should read the manuscript, since the whole story was in there.

"Your novel is about Norman Gruitt?"

Kevin shrugged and said, "Years back, when he could see, Norman painted a portrait of a woman that was just amazing. Then I met the model and she was just as incredible." His voice faded into longing, and it took a second for him to catch himself. He waved his hand as though to make the memory disappear and concluded, "But that was a long time ago."

Ian nodded as if he knew what Kevin meant, but sat stunned. Peter Ray, the world traveler, he knew, had a depth of stories to

him, and Jaret, though young, had the ability to get into other's people lives, but Kevin
he'd never gotten a handle on. So driven
and focused that he wouldn't even stop running despite shin splints, it just seemed he
wasn't cut from the same cloth as most writers. Now Ian realized why — Kevin was a
"storyteller." He had one tale to chronicle
and that was it. The others might write for
ages, volume upon volume, but Kevin
would stop and the ink would dry and his
story would be told.

Ian tilted his water glass at Kevin finally
and said, "Here's to stories from long ago."
Kevin snorted a bit but grabbed his glass
just the same and said, "And here's to
stories from right here in the present. May
they all end happily."

After lunch, Kevin and Ian headed to Norman's studio three blocks east. A narrow
staircase led up from Holton Street to a pair
of second-story apartments, and Kevin
knocked on the second door. A voice called
for them to come in, and as Ian entered the
apartment he was staggered by an unexpected burst of light, as though someone
had just taken his picture. It wasn't that —
it was just the room. He squinted and
looked around. Where he had expected a

dark, cluttered hovel crammed with crooked easels and rolls of canvas waiting to be stretched, Ian had found a profoundly bright and open space covered by thin gray carpet. There was a tiny kitchen, a door that must have led to a single bedroom, and a large living area, half of which was sectioned off by two sofas. The rest remained vacant except for a single easel, its empty canvas waiting to be filled.

A man decked in a white smock, hair silver and wild, emerged from the kitchen and approached with his hand raised. Kevin made a quick introduction. In a voice as brittle and thin as gathering ice, Norman Gruitt said it was a pleasure to host Titansburg's most famous resident. Ian took the man's hand and thanked him for agreeing to an interview, all the time trying hard not to stare at the man's lifeless eyes, unhidden by dark glasses. Ian and the artist sat diagonally from each other on separate couches, and after a moment of silence Ian realized there were to be no pleasantries. He ignored his first question for the moment and instead asked one that had come to him the moment he'd walked in: "Why is the room so bright?"

"I can still see shadows," the artist answered. "If the room is bright enough, I can get around." Norman went on to explain how the retinal nerve degeneration that had started in his thirties had taken most of his sight by 1980, but never quite finished the job.

Ian nodded, brought out a pen and his note pad. One by one, he asked his questions and received his answers.

Norman was hired by the proprietor of Horror-able Books for a publication party. He never did find out how this bookseller had heard of him.

He'd written MERCHANT on one hundred seventy-five cards. MONSTER on two. The owner came in and selected one hundred fifty of MERCHANT and the best MONSTER. The rest ended in one of his storage boxes and might be found if needed.

Ian jotted quick notes until he had just one question left, the one thing that had been on his mind since he'd heard about all the notes: Had Norman grown bored writing the same thing over and over again, the name of a stranger nearly two hundred times?

The old artist grinned at this, and with his dim, lifeless eyes staring vacantly across the apartment he looked like the dolls Ian had seen gazing from the store window.

"Do you want to see?" Norman asked,

and without waiting for an answer, stood up and crossed the room to his easel. "Choose a word," he croaked after taking a bottle of ink from a cabinet.

Neither Kevin nor Ian responded.

"C'mon, just say a word. This isn't brain surgery."

Ian was about to say his wife's name when Kevin spoke.

"Memory."

Norman nodded, then approached the canvas by inching forward until he could feel the fabric.

Ian watched as the man scoured the cloth with his fingers, deft and quick. It was the way Ian had always imagined Braille must be read. Norman stood completely still as he caressed the canvas, and it was only as he altered his motion and began sweeping his hand across the page in a wave — up and down and up and down, from edge to edge — that Ian realized the man was measuring for the word. Space enough for six letters opened every pass. Soon the word and the movement became one and it was as if Norman need not even paint the letters.

Still, the artist grabbed the brush, dipped it, and held it before him, bristles smothered in a shimmering ink. After bringing the brush centimeters from the canvas, Norman began sweeping the brush in that same wave motion until he stopped suddenly in the middle of the movement, circled from right to left with a furious stab of the brush, and then pulled away. So abrupt and unexpected was the motion that it took Ian a second to realize that the perfect black circle now on the canvas was the word's second vowel.

Norman, feet and shoulders perfectly still, sank his brush once more into the ink and, after three passes, plunged and carved an *E* onto the canvas. And carving was not a bad description, Ian thought, for it seemed as though Norman, with his violent, rhythmic motion, was uncovering letters hidden deep in some hard stone, trapped like *David* in Michelangelo's marble, waiting for the master to carve him free. Four more dips into the inkwell, four more passes across the canvas, four more incisions into the staid fabric, and the word appeared.

MEMORY

Ian could barely believe the word hadn't been there all along and could say nothing when Norman asked how it came out. Kevin pointed out that the *R* had blended into the *Y* a fraction but otherwise looked good and asked if Norman was going to hawk it at DeCafé — another word for the elliptical little sentence running through the back room.

"No," Norman said, "I think this one I'll give to your friend here." He turned his face toward where he thought Ian stood and said, "If he'll have it." He then stepped out of the way to give Ian a clear look at the canvas and waited, eyes directed over Ian's shoulder into the empty studio.

"As a sign of good faith," Norman said after Ian failed to respond, "because I know some of my work was used against him. This would be his." He spoke as if Ian weren't standing next to him, but Ian didn't mind. He stepped toward Norman, grabbed the old painter's hand, flecked as it was with ink, and shook.

"Sure, I'll take it," he said. "Of course." Reaching out, he caressed a little of the untouched fabric near the corner and could almost swear that it felt hot.

Time had passed in a very different way in the studio, falling not in quick ticks of a second hand but in chunks, minutes lost mesmerized by Norman's darting hand, and when Ian looked out the window he was startled to see how low the sun had fallen. Evening was still hours off, but the high heat of day had fled. Before the men left, though, Ian thought of a question.

"Why words, Norman?" he asked, turning back to the artist. "Kevin said you'd been quite a portraitist and landscape artist in your day."

"Well," sighed the artist, pulling a bit at his hair with his fingers, leaving it in stiff greasy wisps like a fine meringue. "Do you know what happens to people who go deaf slowly, how they end up talking louder and louder until all you get are sounds? Well, the same thing happened to me." He paused and thought awhile.

"I used to see sentences and paragraphs and the rest, but after a time things just kept falling apart. Lines became a sentence or two, which became a phrase. Soon I concentrated just to see one single word. They just became bigger and louder than ever before. Real painting was impossible so I just started writing them down. People still don't know if what I do is painting or writing." He stopped as if thinking and then concluded, "I say it's seeing."

Ian watched the old man's vacant eyes wander from the doorway to the floor and back and tried to imagine what he was seeing now, in the silence, in the blackness. He didn't ask, just said his thanks, shook the old man's hand again, and stepped to the stairwell.

Kevin stood waiting with the same flat smile he'd had all afternoon. "Quite a guy, isn't he?"

Though Ian nodded in agreement, it didn't sound as if Kevin quite believed it. The two men made it back down the flight of stairs to the street and stepped outside. "I was wondering how he was going to treat you."

"It was great . . ." Ian began, but seeing Kevin shake his head, stopped.

"He lied to you, Ian," the teacher said. "That whole story at the end about seeing words — it's a lie."

Ian started to open his mouth to reply, but Kevin interrupted. "It's not right for me to bring up something that far back. I wanted to give him the chance to tell you."

"Tell me what?" Ian asked.

Kevin looked to his feet, then lifted his eyes and met Ian's gaze. "Beginning in 1962," he started, "Norman Gruitt was a sign painter in Millville State Prison. I met him there in 1977 as a volunteer through a prison literacy program. He was an amazing artist at that time — they let him do some landscapes and portraits in his cell — but even then his eyes were going. Seven years later when he got paroled, he came to me for help, and I got him set up where he is now. Can't paint a lick anymore, but those twenty-two years of writing signs, they sure taught him to write a word black and neat." He scoffed, a mean laugh. "And those idiots at DeCafé, they think it's art."

Ian blinked a few times and tried to take the information in. His whole perspective on the man had been turned upside down, and he didn't know what to think. Kevin stood waiting. Finally Ian asked if Norman had a part in the stalking after all.

"No," Kevin answered. "What he told you about the notes was true. And I was there when the police spoke with him — he told them everything. Even showed them the extra notes."

"But why would he lie?"

"Don't know," Kevin said. "Sometimes he tells people, sometimes he doesn't. For some little reason he just doesn't seem to trust you."

Ian shook his head slowly. "I know how he feels."

MORNING. SATURDAY, AUGUST 3

Ian swung the front door open to take

Cain for her walk and found a bearded man with black eyes glaring at him. Waiting for him. Ian screamed out in surprise and took an involuntary step back, but the man didn't lunge. Rebecca called down asking what was the matter, her voice thick with worry.

"It's me," Ian shouted back. "I'm outside."

Rebecca didn't stay around too long once the police arrived, and Ian noticed that she refused to even look at the life-size cardboard cutout left standing on the front porch. It was her husband, but from a time long ago, and she ignored it entirely as she made her way to her car, out the driveway, and down the road to the local mall.

Alone in the house, Ian waited. He collapsed into his armchair and couldn't even manufacture enough energy to turn on the radio. The screaming — that awful release — had left him void and paralyzed with exhaustion. He'd emptied his body, and so far nothing had filled it again. He sat worn and wasted until Oakley entered, dragging the marketing promotion behind him. He left it standing in the hall and came into the living room.

Taking a seat opposite Ian, he said, "The boys found nothing."

Ian nodded; he'd expected nothing else.

Oakley took out his notebook and pointed over his shoulder at the two-dimensional Ian Merchant propped in the hallway. "What's that thing's story?" he asked.

"Promotional piece for *Semi*," Ian answered. "They went to stores that preordered a certain number of books."

Looking down and writing, Oakley asked, "How many of them were made?"

Ian thought. 1989 was a different world of publishing. Lots more independent stores. He shrugged. "A couple hundred, maybe more. Marketing would know."

Oakley penciled that in his notebook and asked if anything had been changed with the cutout.

"Wish there had been," Ian replied. "I hate that thing."

Oakley looked up and asked why.

"Reminds me of a bad time," he began. As he moved to the image of himself, he said, "For a few years in the mid-eighties they really tried to market me as a nut-job. Horror novelists were coming out of the woodwork, so they tried to sell me as the real thing."

Ian stopped in front of himself. It was like staring into some ghastly looking glass — the leer, the curled lip, one blackened fingernail hooked around a mock-up of

Semi. He remembered how he had thought it was fun, but now it just seemed pathetic. For the first time since screaming he felt something surge. Deep in his stomach a wild heat was building. He could feel the anger rising like a fever.

Oakley rose from his seat, took a few steps, and leaned against the doorframe. "Did it work?"

Ian barely heard the man. Staring at this absurd doppelganger, he was forced to listen once more to the litany of stupid things that had come from his mouth — the mean jokes and cheap threats. He saw the trip-wire temper that flashed like thunder over the stupidest things. He felt the molten rage that seemed to live in his blood and suddenly realized he wasn't just remembering anymore. That furious, scorching heat knotted his fingers into fists, and he felt one small bead of sweat on his brow. A steady pulsing of his heartbeat pounded in his head.

He took one deep breath, and for a moment his thoughts were clear. Then, for the second time that day, his wires crossed. His fist flew, slamming into his own leering face. There was no crash, though, no crunch of bone on bone, just a small slap before the cutout tilted back and slid to the floor.

Ian's hands remained as fists. Where was the release, the sign that he'd hit something? That . . . that had been like punching the air. Frustration piled onto his anger, and Ian drove his hand hard into his own thigh. That was better. That was pain.

Something moved at his shoulder, and Ian noticed Oakley standing beside him. He expected the man might try to speak words of comfort or even touch his arm, but there was only the sound of their breathing until the cop nodded at the flattened image. With a thin smile he said, "Knock yourself out," and all Ian's rage vanished into a laughter he wasn't able to keep back.

"This is the climax of it all," said Ian, loading a tape into the VCR. "This was from a segment taped in 1995. After this, I stopped using the weird persona."

He pressed Play and after a few seconds of static, theme music began. Ian hadn't watched this for nearly four years. He wondered if his stomach would still twist in knots.

A blonde was talking on the screen. "Up next on 'Out and About Hartford,' special reporter Kyle Turner takes us one on one with master of the macabre, Ian Merchant, in a rare interview you won't want to miss."

Ian fast-forwarded through commercials until he found the blonde again. She reintroduced the story and there was a cut to a strapping fellow in a polo shirt, his jaw as chiseled as a comic-book gumshoe. Ian winced as the man's deep timbre explained how a meeting with Ian Merchant was, indeed, a descent into the company of madness.

"Man," Oakley muttered. Ian didn't turn, the worst was yet to come.

Onscreen, Ian sat in a chair across from the interviewer. His beard wasn't trimmed and his shirt was loose and greasy. Ian shut his eyes; he couldn't watch. Embarrassment and guilt swept through him in equal parts, and he felt his face chill. The heat of anger was gone. He heard the questioning on the video — normal questions about writing and the newest novel — and then came the first unexpected one.

"Critics have said that you've created an idealized killer in your new book. What was it that drew you so closely to this character?"

He heard himself flounder on the reply. He could mouth the words right along with it. In his mind he saw himself sitting across from Kyle Turner. He was sweating. Ian opened his eyes. A close-up of him filled the screen. Beads of sweat glistened on his image's brow.

More questions. Once a subtle jab by Kyle that intimated that Ian might profit from the rising homicide rate in Hartford by finding an idea for a new story.

Onscreen, Ian spluttered. The act of madness was gone. Ian looked at himself and saw a face of rising confusion.

Then Kyle again, this time quoting a psychiatrist whose studies on the creative mind and the culture of horror showed that there was a greater incidence of affective response to violence and a disassociative reaction to acts of violence perpetrated on others around them, even loved ones. The nature of the creative act, then, seemed not so much cathartic as latently sociopathic. Kyle asked if Ian had a response.

Only now did Ian understand it. Onscreen, he said, "Repeat the question."

"Violence breeds violence," Kyle began, and then Ian heard his wife's name being spoken. He shut his eyes once more. He knew what came next: the insinuation, his own look into the studio wings where his wife stood with tearing eyes, and then his own body hurtling across the screen toward the man, fists flying, chairs tumbling until the tape snapped to an end. Electronic snow filled the screen.

Ian shuddered, opened his eyes, and stabbed at the remote so the tape would stop. He looked down at the carpet for a while and then at Oakley. The officer seemed stunned.

"That didn't seem like you on the screen," he said finally.

Ian shrugged.

"How did it end? He sue you?"

"And I sued him. Assault vs. defamation. We both won and our settlements canceled each other out. He's got a restraining order against me, though. I can't come within two hundred yards of him."

Oakley shook his head. He looked into his notebook and then at Ian. He asked why he'd shown him the video.

"I feel," Ian began, then stopped. He glanced at the cardboard cutout lying on the hallway tile and tried to pin down the feeling. It had started when he'd received the second note, but today simply confirmed it. Oakley waited without saying a word, and Ian finally captured his thought. "I feel like I'm being punished for what I was. Like somebody's trying to remind me so I never forget."

Oakley nodded slowly. He made no reaction for or against the idea. Just thought for a few seconds before moving to the hall to leave. When the door opened, Ian felt the sticky heat of a humid day. He was about to offer his hand when Oakley spoke.

"He deserved it, you know, saying those things about you hitting your wife."

Ian froze, couldn't say anything, and the officer said his good-bye. When the door shut, Ian got a sick black feeling in his stomach, as if everything he'd tried had gone wrong. He'd wanted Oakley to see one thing, and the man had seen something else. The officer had patted him on the back and shaken his hand for something that Ian wanted only to forget. He wanted to be a *different* person, not a changed person, but more and more it seemed as though he was neither.

Ian spent the rest of his Saturday alternating between a book, napping, and the first game of a Sox doubleheader on television. Occasionally his mind would pull back to that morning — the surge of fear and dread — but for the most part the distractions he'd chosen worked. The book was interesting and Pedro was pitching a gem at Fenway, so the only time he found himself really having to think about what had happened was when Rebecca walked in a little before dinner. Seeing her tired eyes brought it all back, and he related as much as he could about what had happened after she left.

She listened without comment and asked no questions when he'd finished. When he asked how her day had been, she opened the bag she'd brought home and removed a long, willowy dress the color of a Douglas fir.

"For church tomorrow," she said.

"You'll go with me?" Ian asked. He just needed her to say it one more time.

"Yes," she answered. "You left me here when you went to Utah. I'm not letting you do it again."

Ian hugged her tight for a few seconds before she squeezed from his arms to head upstairs and hang up her dress. When she returned downstairs, Rebecca fixed a quick sandwich and told Ian she would be spending the evening working on her thesis. Ian wished her luck, then sequestered himself in his den to work on his own writing. Three times he read through what he'd written so far, and all three times he was reminded of the feeling he'd had yesterday that something was missing. Yesterday he thought it was joy. Today, however, he noticed how little his remorse over who he'd been came through. For an hour he tried to add a sentence here or there, but the whole thing failed to come together. He was about to shut down and log out when a quick glimpse of Howard Kepler's photo albums made Ian realize that it was Kepler who best personified both Ian's joy and remorse. In Howard, he'd found —

He stopped.

It wasn't in Howard that he'd found those things. Howard had led him to them, but he wasn't the source. Howard was just a man.

Ian tapped a finger on his keyboard a few times and realized he was going to have to rewrite this chapter yet again. He paused for just a moment and then started anew.

Morning. Sunday, August 4

Ian awoke to find Rebecca stepping into her new dress. Her hair was already styled and there was no steam on the mirror when Ian stumbled into the bathroom, so he guessed his wife had been awake for a while. After showering and donning a shirt and tie, he joined her for breakfast and found himself watching her every move. None of her typical mannerisms of concern or anxiety — clenching her jaw, worrying her fingernails — drew attention to themselves, but Ian wasn't convinced. He knew she hadn't been to church in years and had only set foot inside a Protestant sanctuary three or four times in her life. He wished he could comfort her, tell her what to expect, but he was just as in the dark. They ventured forth with only a minimum of conversation.

The church itself, as Pete had promised, was a middle school gymnasium. Nobody had tried to make it look like anything else. Only a sincere-looking greeter and a trio of microphones seemed the least bit out of place, and without really trying Ian found himself remembering seventh-grade phys ed and the torturous things stubble-faced hoods could do to you with a playground ball. The sound of his own name being spoken finally lured him from his reverie. Pete and his young wife were crossing the foul line with smiles on their faces. Peeking from behind her mother's legs was Greta, and Ian surprised himself by remembering her name.

Introductions were made quickly because a guitarist had just taken his place behind a microphone. As the group settled into their seats, he began to play. Ian had never heard the song before, but a PowerPoint slide with lyrics soon appeared high on the white cinder-block wall facing the audience. Voices joined the guitar, and church had begun.

Throughout the service, Ian's thoughts flickered between two topics: concern about whether Rebecca was enjoying the service and his own realization that this was what he'd been missing for so long. To hear, just for a moment, a man, a stranger, call on the name of the Lord quenched some longing Ian didn't even know he'd been having. The music, the prayers, the Scripture reading — even the sermon, though Ian didn't understand everything — all seemed fraught with meaning, as though he was supposed to have heard each and every word. When the service came to a close, he looked at Rebecca one last time. She turned to him and her eyes were comfortable, her smile easy. They stood together for the benediction and, for the first time since their marriage vows, Ian realized, received a blessing as a couple.

Outside, it appeared that the men and women split into groups to mingle, and so Ian followed Pete and was introduced to the pastor and a second fellow with the alliterative name of Bob Bringle. Ian learned that the church was awaiting a new sanctuary that was supposed to be completed mid-September, heard about some plans for a picnic, and received a hearty invitation to come back anytime. He and Pete split off, found their wives, and said they'd meet up again on Wednesday.

As Rebecca turned, Ian thought she looked worried, but she just slipped her arm though his and said not a word. They edged around the corner of the school, Rebecca finding Ian's hand with hers, and strolled in the fine morning air until they found the car.

Ian unlocked the Cherokee, climbed in, and started it up. He was just about to make a comment about how he'd had a very nice time indeed when he noticed Rebecca was crying. Soundlessly crying. No sobs, no sniffles, just red eyes and tears. He asked what was wrong but she just shook her head and asked him to drive.

Two more times he asked what was bothering her but she said nothing, so he grabbed her hand. She took it and Ian realized, almost thankfully, that it was nothing he had done. He drove that way, right hand in hers, left hand steering through the light morning traffic until they reached the driveway and he needed both hands to make the turn. Parked and idling outside the garage, Ian turned once more and asked what was the matter.

Rebecca stared at him hard, her eyes narrowed and her mouth opened as if she thought he were joking. Finally she said, "You have no idea, do you?"

Ian answered, voice raised just slightly, that if he had an idea he wouldn't keep asking.

She shuddered and tears spilled from her eyes.

"Sometimes you're in your own little world."

He tried to slip his arm around her back, rub a shoulder, let her know that he was here, now, but she leaned away from him and glared. Ian threw his hands up, and his lips tightened. He killed the engine, opened his door, and stepped out. He wanted lunch; he wanted inside.

Rebecca whispered something as he walked by her door, and he whirled to face her.

Her face was still and serious. The tears had stopped, yet her face seemed the sadder for it. She looked at him with searching eyes and said, "A woman said terrible things, Ian. I can't believe you didn't hear them."

Her words weren't what he was expecting, and he could only stare. After a moment he realized he still didn't know what had been said. He touched Rebecca's shoulder through the open window of the Cherokee and asked what she'd heard.

"That it was a disgrace." She didn't look at him now. "It was a disgrace that you would even dare show your face at a church."

Ian didn't move, but his grip tightened and Rebecca had to let him know that he was squeezing too hard. He apologized and patted her shoulder, stroked it over and over, while he stared across his Cherokee and into the garden. Butterflies swarmed on a damp patch of dirt, and for one second there seemed to be no ugliness there, only the fluttering wings of a thousand insects. That lasted no more than a moment, and when the next breeze licked across the grass, a swarm of insects took to wing and the mud was visible once more. Ian watched for another moment before opening Rebecca's door and letting her out. They embraced and she rested her head under his chin. Ian said nothing; it was only her letting go that led him into the house at all.

Sunday, sinking like a ship taking on water,

never righted itself, and as the hours passed Ian felt more and more like a captain going down with the boat. Two reporters called, leaving impolite messages on the Merchants' machine, demanding interviews and feature articles about the stalking. Cain chewed up Rebecca's favorite pair of moccasins, leaving slimy, chewed-up bits of tan leather about the upstairs hallway. A bird smashed into the bay window, dying in the shrubs below as Ian and Rebecca tried to pass a quiet hour simply reading. Worse, every quiet moment simply opened up an opportunity for Ian to think about the words Rebecca had overheard outside the church. *"Disgrace,"* the woman had said, and Ian didn't know if he'd ever been called something so ugly. Critics had their own names for him, but this faceless woman had branded him an affront to God. He turned these thoughts over and over in his mind until they were all he could hear. He needed an escape, any escape. The *Entertainment* section of the Sunday paper lay near, and Ian opened it to the movies.

Ten minutes later he and Rebecca were out the door, escaping the impossibility that Cain had become that afternoon and pulling from the driveway to catch the last matinee of something called *Rainbow's End* at the local art house.

"I heard this was good," Rebecca said, and Ian said he didn't care so long as there were no moping dogs, angry church members, or looming manuscripts in it.

Rebecca said it should be right up his alley.

"Good," he replied, "What is it about?"

Rebecca smiled. "The end of the world."

"Fitting" was the only thing Ian could think to say.

The film was a miasma of science-versus-faith themes that made for good conversation over hoagies afterward. Content to stay away from Cain and the rest of their worries as long as possible, Ian and Rebecca sat across from each other and talked as they hadn't in weeks. Even the morning's service came up, and Rebecca surprised Ian by balancing the anger she felt at this unknown woman with the thanks she felt for Pete's wife and the others who had welcomed her so warmly. She still wasn't sure if she wanted to return, but they could always try someplace else, someplace away from the idiotic words of mean-spirited people.

Ian agreed, and they both decided to let the topic drop, moving on to Rebecca's surprise at how quickly her thesis was coming together, her pleasure at the tremendous progression of Katherine's exhibit installation, and even her thoughts on what she might wear at the auction on Saturday. Ian talked about possibly changing the focus of his book, how they hadn't visited Louis and his wife, Elaine, for a while, and his hope that Oakley's mother-in-law was doing better. They ate and talked and laughed until they'd finished their subs, got back into the car, and finally headed for home. Darkness had dipped low over the land, and as Ian flipped on his headlights he switched the radio on as well.

A Beatles song came on as they turned out of Titansburg and Ian turned the volume up, opening the windows to let in the fresh night air. As husband and wife they sang the words to the vanishing light of day, and Rebecca let the wind whip her hair into knots. Buddy Holly crooned his devotion to Peggy Sue, and Richie Valens finished singing about a girl named Donna as Ian turned up their hill and headed for home. He crested the rise and immediately slammed on the brakes.

Neither of the two cruisers had their lights on, but in the dimming night Ian could make out the shadows of a few men — one crossing the yard, some leaning in a group against the car, a couple talking into radios. Ian edged his way into the driveway, and the Cherokee's headlights shone first on words painted in streaks of red across the bay window of their house and then the head and shoulders of a man stuffed into the back of one of the police cars. Ian looked back to the window.

YOU CAN NEVER ESCAPE THE PAST!

Shutting off the engine, he read the words, then glanced at the squad car again. Rebecca turned to him and when he faced her, Ian could see deep lines carving worry into her face. This is what they'd been talking about — how each fine moment shattered into something mean and painful. Ian had just one hope this time and he made sure Rebecca saw it too — a person sitting in the back of the squad car.

As Ian stepped from his car, a cop, nobody Ian recognized, lifted the beam of a flashlight to Ian's face and asked for identification. Ian closed his eyes and turned his face away from the glare, yelling that he owned this house and where was Detective Oakley. The officer apologized, switched off the lamp, and said he would go find someone who could help. Ian thanked him and opened his eyes, seeing white spots. Slowly his eyes came into focus and he wasn't seeing spots anymore, but a face staring at him from behind the window of the squad car.

Ian blinked. It was the man, the stalker — eyes spooked and a thin stubble across his jaw. The skin of the man's cheeks and forehead was pale and bloodless. One cruiser's spotlights flashed on, and the face seemed to glow. Ian wanted to look away but he couldn't. He stared, noticing a dark smudge or cut at his cheek, dirt perhaps or maybe blood. The man stared back, and Ian noticed that his eyes never blinked. White and round as a full platinum moon, they gazed through the window as if blind. Then the man licked his lips into a vicious grin, and Ian stepped back in reflex.

Two people called his name, and he saw Rebecca approaching from the car and one of the officers beckoning from the squad car closest to the garage. Ian grabbed Rebecca's hand, moved his body between her eyes and the ghost in the backseat, and escorted her to the waiting officer. To their right, close enough to see the red drips, Ian looked at the words again.

YOU CAN NEVER ESCAPE THE PAST!

He wondered if it was blood — oh, how he hoped it wasn't — and moved the final few feet to the car. The detective, on the radio now, motioned for them to take a seat. They collapsed to the bumper and leaned into each other. Ian looked up: All his security lights were on. The glare, the sound of anxious voices and commands, the cool breeze, it all brought back a quick memory.

The concert. His second date with Rebecca.

It had been a music festival where you stayed all day for five bucks, got a sunburn, and heard band after band. He remembered kissing Rebecca after she made a good joke and holding her hand, thinking that the world could just stop. Twenty minutes later, though, the rains came, wind and thunder following soon after. Lightning arrived last, but swiftest, and the fairgrounds had no time to empty. They ran for his car, but the downpour was too heavy and the ground slick. Vans and cars honked and spun their tires. Just when Ian was on the verge of true panic — his car nowhere in sight, bolts of lightning pounding the earth — the rear door of a Crown Victoria swung open, and a couple they didn't know yelled for them to jump inside.

They waited out the storm in silence,

didn't even introduce themselves.

When it had blown over, Ian and Rebecca made their way to a black police van where volunteers were serving coffee to the stranded. Clutching their Styrofoam cups and taking eager little sips, they slumped against each other and then to the cold bumper where they sat. *"That was frightening,"* Rebecca said finally and wrapped her arms around his chest, burying her face in his soggy T-shirt. Ian said it certainly was and held on to her tight, thinking he might just marry this girl.

Now, feeling the cool plastic bumper against his legs and hearing the sound of so many men running about, he could do little but hold her hand. She looked at him and asked what he was thinking.

"Just about the fairgrounds," he said with a sigh.

"All those poor people," she said, voice barely heard over the crackling radio static. Ian sighed; he had overlooked that part once again. Six dead, struck by lightning. They didn't know about it at the time, but the papers did a full write-up the next day. College freshman. Ticket taker. Gray-haired professor. Stationery store owner. Mother and daughter; they'd been the saddest. Six dead. Ian always forgot them. He thought about what he might be forgetting now and the answer came to him, slow and sickening.

Cain.

He looked to the house, the front door ajar, and remembered the stain slashed across the man's cheek. Ian jumped from the bumper, racing to find anyone who could help.

MORNING. MONDAY, AUGUST 5

Ian roused a little after nine and couldn't believe he'd slept so long. Perhaps it was knowing the stalker was in jail or having the vet's assurance last night that Cain would recover from her stabbing. Most likely, though, it was just the exhaustion of dealing with this whole terrible mess. Either way, all signs pointed to this impending week being a washout, and only the sound of his wife pacing around downstairs drove him from bed.

The phone rang as he dressed and Rebecca, who'd taken the day off, yelled up that Oakley was on the line. Ian picked up and said hello as best he could.

"Sorry about your dog, Ian," Oakley said as an introduction.

Ian assured him that things were fine. He

was just glad she made it to the vet so quick. "Without you," Ian said with thanks, "she might've lost too much blood."

Oakley said nothing and Ian asked what they had found out from the stalker.

The officer sighed and grumbled to himself. Ian heard papers being shuffled and then Oakley finally spoke.

"He's asleep, Ian," he began. "We threw him in the pen last night and this morning he was fast asleep. Still hasn't come to. He's got tracks up and down his arms and we found a vial of meth on him. Looks like he's sleeping off a bender. Unfortunately, he's got no ID on him and fingerprints didn't get us anywhere. Sorry."

Ian nodded into the phone as if Oakley could see him, and the officer continued. Reporters were calling this morning asking for details. Someone had leaked the story, and he just wanted to warn Ian that there might be some on their way.

Ian said thanks for the warning, hung up, and grimaced at the phone. As if in reply, it rang. Ian picked it up with a sigh — a voice on the other line said he was from the *New York Times*. Ian said he had three minutes to answer questions. He looked at the clock. The second hand circled three times and

Ian hung up in the middle of a question. More calls came in. Ian said "no comment" more than he ever had in his life. Finally a call from a voice he recognized: Louis. He sounded scared — genuinely concerned.

"Are you all right?"

"He got my dog," Ian answered. "Broke in, busted up a few things, and slashed Cain across her left haunch."

"Who was it?"

"The stalker," Ian answered. "Who else?"

Louis said of course, and then asked if there was anything he could do to help out. Anything at all.

Ian thought for a second and then asked the old man to issue a formal statement on behalf of Ian that could be sent to the press. "I'm sick of answering the phone."

"I'll page Mark in publicity and tell him to get right on it."

Ian said thanks.

Louis coughed and, after talking around in circles for a bit, came out and suggested that perhaps one in-depth interview might not be such a bad idea. Let the public get the full story. It'd be good pre-press for the book.

"Just one?" Ian asked.

Louis assured him one would be enough.

Ian thought for a second and consented. He could handle one interview, so long as it could be taped at his place. He didn't want to leave Rebecca or Cain when they picked her up. Louis agreed, said something would be set up soon, and said good-bye.

Ian replaced the receiver and turned to walk away. The phone rang again and he whirled back, slid his hand up the cord until he had a firm grasp, and yanked. It felt like snapping a snagged fishing line. The cord popped from the phone jack and fell to the floor in a neat pile. There was silence in the house: no ringing phone, no buzz of policemen, nothing.

Ian stared at the knot of phone cord on the floor and remembered the last time he'd done something so rash, after he'd heard that Howard Kepler had died in that lonely Utah hospital. Always the same reactions. Over and over, he always did the same things. The same anger, the same feeling of wanting to hide, break communication. History repeated itself, and Ian realized that the words he'd seen written on his house in paint might be true. Perhaps he never could escape the past.

MORNING. TUESDAY, AUGUST 6

To make up for yesterday's absence,

Rebecca left early this morning and Ian passed a quiet breakfast reading the paper before leaving for the veterinarian. Twenty minutes later, with the help of a thick-armed assistant, Ian loaded Cain into the back of the Cherokee. Tape and bandage swaddled her left haunch, and though her eyes opened occasionally as she worked through a recent shot of pain-killer, they seemed not to register anything. Ian rubbed her snout for a minute, but she did not bother, or could not manage, to lick his hand. He hoped the car ride home wouldn't prove too difficult and kept his speed to a minimum, checking in the rearview mirror for any signs of distress. Luckily she slept the entire way, and only as Ian turned into the driveway did he wonder how he was going to get her into the house without jarring the wound.

A poor excuse for an answer was uprooting the pachysandra about his house: a video news crew from "Out and About Hartford," complete with ace reporter Kyle Turner, who stood knocking at Ian's front door, microphone cocked at his hip like a pistol. The entire team turned in unison when his Cherokee appeared, and Ian saw two cameras pointed his direction. He punched the seat beside him, swallowed twice, and got out. Recording lights on both cameras switched on.

The first words from Kyle's mouth when Ian had made it close enough to hear were "Louis Kael said it was all right," the second were "so don't punch me." Then he turned, suggested to one of the photographers that a shot of Ian bringing the wounded dog into the house would be "Emmy."

He turned to Ian and smiled, teeth bared. "Emmy means great television."

Behind him two cameramen fought for angles on the driveway, tearing leaves and slicing branches of shrubbery off with their tangle of electric cords. Ian said there would be no shot of the dog unless someone helped him, and Kyle yelled for a skinny, embarrassed-looking kid to get off his duff. The boy introduced himself as Steve the intern, and as they moved to the Jeep he said, "I'm sorry, sir. I know this must be difficult."

It was a bad start, but cameras were rolling so they heaved Cain from the Cherokee and, stepping gingerly over wire after wire and cord upon cord, reached the open garage. Kyle had shadowed their every step, firing questions as they walked. Now Ian interrupted him and told the reporter to shut up until they were inside the house.

"Answer a question first."

Ian said nothing.

"A source from the Titansburg Police Department said the man arrested on Sunday appears to be a copycat rather than the original stalker. Do you have any comment to that?"

Ian's pulse buckled. Copycat? He stared at Kyle and couldn't say a thing. Cameras recorded him from almost every possible angle.

"Any comment?" Kyle asked.

"I was not aware of that," he said, the words almost choking him. Ian punched in the security code. The door swung open, and Steve the intern and Ian made their way to Cain's bed. It was folded in two, and with Cain in his arms he could do nothing. He looked at Kyle.

"Another question first?" asked Kyle.

Ian nodded.

"Is it true that you are working on a memoir about the recent events?"

Ian recognized it as a Louis question. Had to be.

Ian crooked his head and found a camera.

"That is correct," he said, addressing the lens directly.

Kyle asked if he'd like to elaborate, and

Ian said not until the man straightened his dog's bed. The reporter sighed, as though bored, and straightened out the corduroy mattress. Steven and Ian lowered the dog. Cain opened her eyes, blinked, and fell to slumbering again. Ian thanked the intern, who could barely lift his eyes, and both made their way into the kitchen. Two cameras glared at him when he turned. Ian gathered a breath and said, "I don't recall inviting you inside."

"We're not vampires, Ian. We can come in without invitation. Besides, we'll just be a minute," said Kyle with a flash of teeth.

"Sixty seconds," Ian answered and looked at the clock. "Go."

"Do you know why anyone would stalk you?"

Ian shook his head.

"Do you feel that you've brought this upon yourself since many of your readers might get the ideas from your books?"

"I am not responsible for their behavior."

"But you are responsible for the words which may have incited them to come after you. Is that correct?"

"My novels have nothing to do with this."

Ian looked at the second hand: twenty ticks left.

"What about the quotes taken from your

works? We have it on record that each of the appearances of the stalker has been linked with something that you have written."

"I wasn't aware of that," Ian replied and then looked at Kyle. "Last question."

Kyle cocked his head, as though searching through a memorized list, and then smiled. "I just want to make this clear. You refuse to take responsibility for the danger that you have put not only yourself into but your wife and even your poor dog as well. Is that correct?"

Ian felt the warmth gathering deep inside again. He smelled Kyle's expensive skin lotion, and it seized at his stomach. The cameras waited.

"From the beginning," he started, jaw set, "I have made every effort to afford myself and my household security and protection. Every precaution has been taken."

"And yet that wasn't enough," said Kyle, but Ian had already walked away and was trying to shoo the crew from his home. One of the cameramen had almost made it to the garage when Ian heard Cain yelp.

Ian rushed around the corner and pushed his way into Cain's nook.

A second cameraman was bent over Cain's rump trying to turn her around.

"What are you doing to my dog!" Ian

shouted, the heat high in his throat and eyes now, and grabbed the man by his shoulders. The fellow's weight shifted back and he toppled onto his back.

"Easy, dude, hands off," said the man, but Ian kept pushing and finally the man scrambled to his feet, bolting out of the kitchen and into the garage.

Ian stormed after him. "Get off my property," he shouted at the crew, but his voice died among the garage's high ceiling and it sounded empty and small.

"I was just getting a shot of the bandage," the fellow mumbled, walking away.

Kyle squeezed past Ian and gave a little laugh.

"Glad to see you haven't changed, Merchant."

Ian said nothing — everything was red and burning.

"Hey, Jack," said the reporter to the last cameraman coming from the kitchen, "I thought people were supposed to mellow in their old age."

The video man laughed but didn't answer, just looked back at Ian as he passed him and shook his head. Kyle fell in next to Jack, turned and saluted Ian, then spun once more and passed through the open garage door. Before they got too far away, Ian heard him ask: "Did you get that footage? Did you get him going nuts?"

The man said nothing, only patted his camera, assuring everyone he'd caught each second. Ian watched them pile into their vans, and as they drove off he let loose a scream of rage that seemed without end. No words, just sound and violence and blazing heat.

Ian's phone call to Louis soothed him not at all, and hearing the editor explain how Kyle Turner had gotten the nod hurt in a new and deeper way than anything yet that day. It was all about exposure, and not even friendship could stand in the way of that. Only in dialing up Michael Oakley for his explanation did Ian get the slightest reprieve from his fury.

"Blast, blast, blast" were the detective's first words, followed by an apology. "Ian, I promise, we just finished interviewing the guy early this morning. I haven't been home yet."

A quick image of Anne, staring out a window like her lost mother, flashed through Ian's mind, and the heat retreated. As always, weariness followed, and he had to sit down for the rest of the call.

"How'd they find out?" he asked.

"A leak here," Oakley answered. "All good reporters have their point men."

Ian didn't want to hear Kyle Turner called good, so he asked about the stalker.

"Copycat," answered Oakley. "No doubt. He had no idea what was in the first notes, didn't know there even was a third note. What he knew, he got from the paper."

"But why'd he show at all?"

Ian heard Oakley sigh; the man hadn't been home yet.

"He talked for hours," the officer began. "Once he woke up and we put him into an interview room, he just started talking. He had some priors on his record and spent some time under psychiatric care. Most likely, he'll be going back."

"So . . . what now?"

"Same old, same old, Ian. Sorry, but the stalker — the real one — is still out there."

Ian nodded into the phone, told Oakley to visit a bed, and hung up. The shivers set in not two seconds afterward.

Rebecca took the news better than he had. Never having gained any sense of relief from the man's arrest, her fear was not renewed by the understanding that the stalker had never disappeared. She was, however, far more distressed about Cain's condition than he'd expected of her, and every half hour or so that evening she stopped working on her thesis to check on the dog.

The mood was heavy and grim that night, and Ian spent most of his time preparing for tomorrow's meeting with Louis. He thought about taking the man to task for helping bring Kyle Turner down on his back, but Rebecca warned him off that idea, and so he passed his hours by reading the chapters he'd written and thinking over how he would write his latest chapter.

The room was quiet and with nothing to distract him, his mind whirled. Rather than play things as they'd happened, he found himself lingering over portions of the day. Color rose to his face as he saw all the places he had acted poorly. How he could have answered the questions differently. How he shouldn't have pushed the cameraman. How he'd felt like punching out every capped tooth in that Cheshire smile of Kyle Turner.

Ian shook his head. He needed a distraction and began searching through drawers. Nothing interested him until he remembered Howard's photo albums. Ian picked one off the pile stacked on the bookshelf, opened it, and began reading randomly. Finally, after five verses, his eye caught an image he didn't remember seeing before, a photo of a cracked pocket watch. He read the verse. The relevance of the watch meant nothing to him, but the words stopped his breath.

You were taught, with regard to your former way of life, to put off your old self, which is being corrupted by its deceitful desires; to be made new in the attitude of your minds; and to put on the new self, created to be like God in true righteousness and holiness.

Ian saw himself swearing at the cameraman, tumbling over chairs in the studio, pulling phone cords from the wall, crying into the dark night at the loss of a friend. He saw himself doing the same things now and in the past, saw himself glaring from the same leering eyes. He recognized himself in the cardboard cutout and in the words of each note. He heard again the words of the woman at church accusing him of being a disgrace, and it all began to make sense. Whatever had happened in Utah wasn't real. He'd slipped under the water and come up again, but the old Ian remained. The new one was nowhere to be found. He was the same old person. Ian read the verse one more time, shut the album, and went to bed. Rebecca called after him to see if he was all right, and he responded with a wave over his shoulder.

Even now, he thought, trudging up the stairs, *even now I'm the same person. Afraid and lonely. Running away and hiding in sleep.* The thoughts barely slowed his feet and soon he was in bed, in the dark, shutting his eyes tight against anything else that might happen that day. He fell asleep quickly, face buried in his pillow and one hand clenched in a tight fist.

WEEK 5

Louis remained uncharacteristically quiet during their meeting; his offer to accompany Ian to the train station could only mean the editor had saved his comments for private conversation. During the taxi ride he said little, just chewed his nicotine-laced gum and stared out the window. Only in the dim recesses of Penn Station, after Ian had exchanged his reserved seat for a spot on the local express leaving in fifteen minutes, did it seem that Louis was going to speak.

Even then he didn't. Instead he just stood next to Ian and looked into the swarm of people, his eyes flicking from face to face as though searching for something.

"What do you see, old man?"

Louis looked over, smiled. "You never call me that anymore."

Ian sighed. "That's because I'm an old man too now."

Louis tilted his head a little at the comment, thinking for a moment. "You put a lot of pressure on yourself, my boy," he said. Then after a moment added, "It worries me sometimes."

Ian didn't know what to say. He hadn't heard that sort of thing from Louis in seven years, since he and Rebecca stopped meeting with the Kaels for occasional dinners. He looked at his watch and then at Louis again.

"I'm the same guy I always was, Lou."

The editor shook his head, "No, no, no, no, no, no. You're not the same guy at all." He sat down, looked in his briefcase, and pulled out the manuscript they had gone over. "I've never seen this Ian before," he said, waving the paper. "Since when were you ever wrong before?"

Ian felt his blood chill — he was finally going to hear the editor's opinion.

"It's what I'm feeling," he answered, sitting down next to Louis.

"Wrong?" his editor asked. "You're feeling wrong? What kind of way is that to live?"

The public address system crackled to life, announcing a train bound for Philadelphia. Ian hoped it might mention the arrival of his train as well, but the system fell silent, and Ian was left sitting without an answer.

He squeezed a knee with his hand and scratched an itch near his jaw.

"Guilt isn't attractive," Louis said finally and stood. Ian knew the man had a meeting to attend. "I don't want this project to turn into a big confessional. There are enough of those stupid things published as it is."

Ian looked up at Louis and asked what it was the man wanted.

Louis sighed and closed his eyes; he looked tired.

"Ian," he said, "you're the best horror writer I've seen, ever. You scare the pants off people. That's what I want to see."

"I don't know if I can do it anymore."

"Why?"

"That's what I'm writing about, Lou. Haven't you read it?"

Louis nodded, and his face was serious.

"I have read it," he said. "And I'm speaking as an editor now when I say that you don't explain anything. I haven't the slightest idea what's happened to you."

Ian shut his eyes. The chill returned, but he knew it was the truth.

"It'll all work out," he said, almost in a whisper. "Everything will clear up in the end."

Louis nodded. "I hope it does." He took a few steps toward the stairs and then turned again. "In the end, all I'm looking for is a heck of a story, Ian. That's it."

"You'll get one," Ian shouted, but Louis had already disappeared into the crowd, and his words were swallowed by the shrill announcement that Ian's train had just arrived at Track B2. Ian stood, slipped his portfolio strap over his shoulder, and pushed his way into the crowd. One last battle with the people of the city before he could go home.

The train ride home proved to Ian just how spoiled he'd become in recent weeks. The express was faster, but he missed the solitude, the service, and even the stories he'd received on the luxury line. Stuffed into a row with two other businessmen, he tried to think over what Louis had just said, but the constant shifting of the passenger next to him distracted his thoughts. Finally he was left only to stare down the aisle and wait for the whine of the train coming to a halt in Titansburg.

Thirty-two minutes later it did, and Ian faced his first free Wednesday afternoon in weeks. Unsure quite what to do, he returned home to check on his recuperating dog and was happy to see her both awake and alert. Cain still had no real desire to stand, but at least the pain seemed less today. She even licked his hand a few times as he stroked her muzzle. Assured that she was doing better, he made plans for the rest of the afternoon.

The day went quickly.

After listening to messages from Oakley, the Utah lawyer, and Cheryl Rose, he spent a moment setting up a follow-up interview with the cub reporter before heading down to the police station per the detective's request. There, pen in hand, he signed off a number of pages formally pressing charges against Marcus Graves and read through the ninety-page deposition Oakley had taken during the offender's five-hour-long rambling interview. Little of it made sense, and both men agreed the man needed to be under psychiatric care.

"He was there a few months ago," said Oakley.

"Put him back," Ian answered. He stretched his hand once more and continued signing his name in all the appropriate boxes. When he finished he shook Oakley's hand, walked from the man's office, and headed outside into the brightest of days. He wrenched the Cherokee to life and pointed it to the nearest burger joint for a very late lunch.

■ ■ ■ ■

While finishing the last of his fries and quarter-pounder, Ian read through Kevin's story for writers group that evening. Despite knowing what the tale was about, despite having read it a few days ago, Ian found himself surprised once more as he paged through the five chapters Contrade had provided. The writing was fluid and tender, so unlike the man who had written it that Ian could barely link the two together. Kevin Contrade, off kilter and edgy, was writing a thoughtful, meditative piece on both the discovery and loss of love. It stunned Ian, and he found himself running out of new ways to word his praise in the margins.

Wonderful control.

Perfect description.

Terrific rhythm in this paragraph. This is elegantly written.

He finished his remarks, checked his watch, decided to drive to town a little early, and headed out of the restaurant to his car. Five minutes later he found himself in the crush of downtown and was sorry he'd come in early. Parking was clogged, and he drove around until he finally found a spot when a Taurus pulled away from the curb at the north end of Titansburg.

Ian made his way down the sidewalk past a small ice cream parlor, a pet supply store, the frame shop working on Norman Gruitt's word, and finally A Doll's House. Though it was still early, a *Closed* sign rested in the door, and Ian couldn't go in and say hello. In the display window, porcelain faces stared out as always, but this time most of their eyes were shut. He looked again just to make sure he was seeing things right, but it was true. Someone had taken the time to close all the hinged eyes, plastic lashes tight so the flecked marbles inside were hidden. It was strange to see them that way in the dark, as if they might all be sleeping, and Ian wondered who had taken the time to put them all to bed. A small girl perhaps, playing in the window? Anne? Her mother? He turned his back on the store and walked away briskly. It was the kind of thing that might have sparked a story a few years ago. Dolls who closed their eyes, who needed sleep. Now the thought simply made him shudder, and he picked up his pace until he reached the bookstore. Here the display window wasn't so much eerie as it was depressing. More books written by people other than him.

Bestsellers lined the display, and Ian was surprised to see the number of non-fiction titles. It used to be that the latest espionage tale or ghost story would crush anything real-to-life, but these days that didn't hold. Two more memoirs — one from an Israeli Jew and the other from a country music star — filled the shelves along with a new diet fad based on your birthday, an instruction manual for beating Wall Street, and one title that was a dialogue between an Episcopalian priest and God. This was a tiny, robin's-egg blue book and was by far the thinnest in the window. Apparently talking directly with the Creator was worth only a hundred and fifty pages or so. Ian shook his head and walked away. If only it were so easy.

A few people turned to give him looks as he continued his walk toward DeCafé, but most ignored or didn't seem to recognize him. Ian was glad. He entered the coffee shop without saying a word to anyone and was happy to see the place mostly empty. How they stayed in business, he didn't know, but the solitude was fine as long as it lasted.

He ordered coffee, sat at a table in the back of the café, and used the solitude to think over what Louis had said to him before he boarded the train. The editor hadn't enjoyed the chapters he'd received, had barely even understood the direction Ian had taken. Using the stalking to point out all the ways in which he'd been wrong had seemed like an interesting twist, but it lacked overall cohesiveness. One does not, after all, simply wake up one day realizing he was wrong about his life unless there's a compelling reason. Ian had that reason, and yet it hadn't made it into the narrative. He needed the months of worry that followed the holidays last year, the odd discovery of Howard Kepler's image of bones in sand, and Ian's eventual meeting with the elfin photographer. More than that, the story needed a glimpse of that final spark that lowered Ian's eyes, bowed his head, and called him by his true name. He needed to explain the calling of his faith to step into water and let it wash him clean. In the same way that Ian had needed a new beginning, his story did. Louis would probably like it even less than the rest that Ian had turned in, but it had to be done.

Just then Pete stepped through the door, and Ian noticed his hands were empty. No backpack, no manuscript, not even a pencil and scrap of paper.

"Glad I came," he said, approaching and taking a seat. "Kevin left a message backing out for tonight. No explanation, just said he couldn't make it. I let Jaret know, but didn't reach you and thought you might come here right off the train."

"Took an early train today, but I still wasn't at home."

"Glad I came," Pete said again, then looked as though he'd remembered something. "How'd you and Rebecca like church on Sunday? Didn't get to talk to you too long afterward."

"Well," said Ian, but that was all he could manage. He didn't want to offend Pete but he couldn't lie either, and he could still see his wife in tears. He felt color come to his cheeks when he thought of the way she cried.

"You can tell me," Pete prompted. "I won't get upset."

"I'll just say that it was not a pleasant experience."

Pete leaned in now, his arms nearly halfway across the small table, and stared for a moment as if trying to read the answer in Ian's face. After a second more he sat back and took his arms off the table. "How so?"

Ian's stomach began to tighten, and a low heat began to creep through him. His wife had been brought to tears because of his name. He'd dragged her to church and she'd come home weeping. He tried to think of some way to say it without anger, but nothing would come. *How so? How so?* He took one deep breath and then the words came.

"My wife heard some women talking."

Ian heard himself say it and was relieved. The words were not angry, but sad. And that's what he felt now, the warmth of anger subdued by a glum fear that the first time had ruined it for Rebecca, ruined it for him. Pete had told him not to expect miracles from the church, but he hadn't expected antagonism either.

Pete cocked an eyebrow and asked Ian to continue.

Ian shrugged. He didn't want to sound like a complainer, as if he was put upon.

"My wife overheard someone make a comment about me. . . . That's it."

"A comment?" asked Pete. "A bad comment?"

"You really want to know?"

Pete nodded.

"A woman said it was a disgrace that I would come to church only after the stalking began and how my being there . . . how just my being there mocked the whole thing."

At this Pete's jaw snapped shut. A wide angry vein bulged in his neck, his knuckles went white, and there was a tremor at his lips as though trying to keep words from flying out. And the eyes . . . those gray eyes now looked hard as steel. The transformation was swift and staggering, and for a few seconds Pete could say nothing. Finally, he looked at Ian and said very softly, "You're not coming back, are you?"

"I don't know."

Pete nodded and rubbed his jaw with a hand. "We make it hard sometimes, don't we?"

Ian wasn't sure what the man meant.

"We're always talking about reaching our neighbors and friends," Pete started. "Then someone who's really searching shows up, and suddenly he's not the right kind of neighbor or friend. Burns me."

"It's Rebecca I worry about most," Ian said when Pete had finished. "I've dealt with critics my whole career; it's almost my job not to be liked. But she takes things very personally, even things that happen to me."

"Well," began Pete, who didn't seem to know what to say, "just don't give up searching."

Ian promised he wouldn't and changed the topic to Kevin Contrade, telling Pete the story about meeting Norman Gruitt and how Kevin seemed devoted to the man though he didn't seem to even like him. Pete nodded and said that was Kevin to a T.

"Stubborn, devoted, and a perfectionist."

Ian nodded, but added he didn't know the man that well yet.

"Well, here's a fact for you," said Pete, leaning in once more. "This," he said, pointing to the chapters, "is the third time Kevin's written the same story. He's finished the thing twice and burned all the pages."

"The same story?"

Pete nodded.

"Have you ever read the whole thing?"

Pete shook his head.

"Do you think we ever will?"

Pete thought a second and said, "Doubt it very much."

Ian arrived home an hour early but was pleasantly surprised to find Rebecca waiting for him. Her class ended early and she had just walked in moments before. She kissed Ian with parted lips, then smiled at the impulse. Coaxing him into a chair, they caught up on the hours spent apart, and as usual Ian did most of the talking. She took

Louis's comments with a nod, as well as Oakley's description of the copycat stalker. Pete's kind words and concern for her brought an appreciative smile, but Ian still saw her eyes flash when the church visit was mentioned. Finally, he talked about his own wearying thoughts and the possibility that he'd been leaving something out of his book that might tie it all together — his desert conversion in the rain-swollen Utah stream.

As usual when Ian mentioned his writing, Rebecca said nothing in response to his plans. He saw her eyes narrow in the slightest when he told her and her lips purse, but couldn't be sure what these things meant. Finally he just asked what she thought of the idea.

After thinking, she said, "It will certainly make it a different book."

"Is that okay?"

Rebecca nodded. "Unless this is just a phase — some Bob Dylan conversion — it has to affect who you are. I'd be more concerned if you *didn't* include it."

Ian thanked her and finally they got to her day. The smile that had greeted him returned, and she said that things were going so well with her thesis that she was able to spend some time preparing for the upcoming auction.

"They asked me to give a five-minute talk this Saturday about Katherine and her work. Before her stuff goes up for sale."

Ian smiled and squeezed her shoulder.

"Plus, I've copied some of her letters where she talks about her sculptures. They're going to use them as descriptions in the auction catalog."

Ian asked if she had picked out the pieces she wanted to buy yet, and she nodded, said she had some ideas.

"It's going to be a fun day. Anne Oakley stopped by the museum today during her lunch break. She and Mike are definitely going to be there on Saturday."

Ian gave his wife a quick hug before standing to finally put his portfolio away. Another day was gone — some hours lost, some given to conversation and reflection. Tonight he wanted nothing but some quiet moments with his wife. Setting everything aside for the evening, he joined her in the library, sat next to her, and let the rhythm of her typing calm him. Tomorrow would bring its own set of worries, but tonight he would find solace in his wife's faith in him and God's willingness to provide instruction through the lives of men like Peter Ray, despite Ian's own doubts. For the moment, it seemed tolerable to have more questions than answers. God was responding in the same ways He had before, and Ian realized he was starting to recognize His handiwork.

EARLY MORNING. THURSDAY, AUGUST 8

Cain wobbled a bit upon getting up but seemed strong enough to take a short walk for the first time since the stabbing. Ian was more than happy to accompany her outside. The stroll lasted only a few minutes, and once back inside Cain collapsed into her bed. At least she was recovering. Ian then kissed Rebecca good-bye as she readied for work and headed to his den for an hour or two of writing. His intentions, however, did not lead so easily to results, and the time was spent trying to figure out the best way to enter the story of his conversion. He tried beginning with his shallow baptism but that seemed too abrupt. Introducing Howard Kepler only confused the issue and led him back to receiving the photograph of the rib cage as a Christmas present. Pushing further and further back, he had just come across the first time writing horror had seemed like a bad idea when the doorbell rang.

In the hall, Cain stood at attention, eyes focused on the doorknob. Ian decided not to take chances and checked the peephole. It was Cheryl Rose, right on time.

"How come you agreed to this second interview?" she asked, even before they were inside.

Ian smiled, said it was because he was such a nice guy. She laughed with him but didn't buy it, and he waved her into the living room. There he told her about Kyle Turner and the ugly incident. He said he knew that crew was going to do a hatchet job on him, so he wanted at least to get his side of the story out there.

"Besides," he added, "you did a fine job with the other interview. First time I didn't come off looking like a psycho."

The reporter lowered her eyes at the praise and couldn't help but smile. She recovered quickly and asked if Ian thought Kyle had a personal vendetta against him.

Ian shrugged. "Off the record, I don't think Kyle cares enough about anything to carry a grudge. It's all about ratings for him, and my name resurfaced."

"Anything on the record?"

Ian sighed and said, "I can only hope Mr. Turner has the ability to forgive. I hope this isn't part of some deep-seated resentment."

Cheryl moved then from the television reporter to the newest information on the stalking. She made sure it was kosher to write the whole story this time, and Ian said it was fine. She asked whether reports that there were now two stalkers were true, she asked what steps Ian was taking to ensure his safety, and she asked how the stress was affecting his professional and personal life.

"Has it given you any ideas for new books?"

Ian nodded. Louis had okayed his talking about the work in progress to drum up some early publicity, so Ian told Cheryl about the memoir.

"You're writing about the stalking?" she asked, scribbling furiously to capture all his words.

"About the stalking, yes, but more about things that I've learned recently."

Cheryl looked up and Ian waited. He didn't know if she was going to ask what he had learned, and he didn't know if he was going to answer. This was something he talked about with Rebecca and with Louis, but to start blabbing about it to the world seemed desperate. They stared at each other for a few seconds, and then she asked: "What things have you been learning?"

Ian decided to give the easy answer. He talked about how the stalking had taught him things about the nature of fear and terror. He'd written books about them before, but much of those books had been wrong.

He shrugged and said that he'd been wrong about a lot of things and that this newest book was going to address those areas.

Cheryl was about to ask a follow-up question when the front door opened and Rebecca entered. Ian stood immediately and asked if everything was okay, but his wife shook him off, saying that the office was simply too crazy and she needed a quiet place to work for the day. Relieved, Ian motioned to Cheryl and introduced her as the woman who was going to save his reputation.

"As if there's anything left to save," said Rebecca, stepping past Ian to shake the reporter's hand. "Nice to meet you, Cheryl. I don't want to intrude any longer, but make sure to talk to me before you leave. I'll let you know what your next feature article could be."

Cheryl thanked her, and as Rebecca left for Ian's den, he asked the reporter to repeat the last question. She looked in her notebook, asked why the stalker was quoting from Ian's old stories, and readied her pen.

"I don't have an answer for that," Ian said. "It's the same reason, I'm sure, that he's stalking me in the first place. I don't know if we'll ever know the answer."

■ ■ ■ ■

Two more pages of questions were asked, and Ian didn't know how many pages his answers filled. Cheryl turned to a fresh page and asked Ian if he had any closing thoughts. Something she hadn't asked about. Ian thought for a moment, came close to addressing the stalker directly, but gave it up.

"No," he replied, "I've said my piece."

Cheryl stood, preparing to leave, and suddenly said, "I know something I forgot. I saw Mr. Contrade last evening. He wanted me to say hello to you."

"You saw him last night?" Ian asked. "Where? He skipped out on our writers group."

Cheryl looked nervous, as though she might have just told a secret. She slipped the shoulder strap of her bag over her neck and said that she'd seen him at the county library.

"The bum," said Ian.

"Did I get him in trouble?"

"No, I just thought he would make a little more effort to make it to the group. That's it."

"Well, I'll yell at him the next time I see

him," she said and double-checked to make sure she had everything. Before she made it two steps to the door, however, Rebecca emerged from the den carrying her laptop, a legal pad, and one of Katherine Jacoby's binders.

"Do you have time for an early lunch?" she asked Cheryl.

Cheryl said she did, and Ian knew that he was now old news. He wished them a good meal, entered his den, and started up his computer. Waiting for the PC to boot, he looked around.

Things were different.

Rebecca hadn't been in here writing, she'd been rearranging. A box of fan mail that he'd been using as a footstool was now pushed way under the desk. One of the reading lamps he'd surrounded with old manuscripts was now completely accessible, the stacks of paper nowhere to be seen. The tower of Howard Kepler's photo albums on the floor had been turned into a single neat row on one of the bookshelves, and Ian couldn't even remember what had occupied that space originally. Most likely just a dozen or so paperbacks. Maybe a hardcover first printing of one of his newer novels.

Ian gave up trying to figure out all the things she'd switched around in her hour alone and turned back to his monitor. Once again he opened an empty document, set the margins, and tried to capture the thought Cheryl's arrival had interrupted. The colored map hanging on his wall helped provoke the memory.

Each country in which he'd sold a book carried a small monogram. He spanned the globe from Canada to New Zealand to South Africa. Foreign translations had been released in over twenty-five languages, and those countries received their own coloring. Finally, red ink covered a small band of countries in the Middle East and Southeast Asia. These were the countries that had banned his books. Louis had singled them out as a joke, but now, looking at the massed conglomeration of them from the United Arab Emirates to Iran to Burma, Ian felt sickened. Millions of people across the planet would know him only as the man who penned words too violent to read. *Hunter* was no exception, but unlike the rest of his books, *Hunter* had no happy ending. The killer got away — there was no hero strong enough to stop him. In the only interview he gave about the book, the reporter kept asking whether this vicious nihilism was a new phase that would mark the rest of his books. Ian couldn't answer, but he told himself he hoped not.

For a week after that interview, Ian did nothing but reread *Hunter.* He remembered Rebecca's anxious looks as she returned home night after night from work and found him laboring over pages he'd seen just yesterday. After the week was finished, he had sat down with his wife and they talked about what he'd found.

"It's dead," he'd told her. *"This book has no soul. It's cold and brutal and mean."*

Rebecca nodded; she said she'd thought so all along.

"I can't keep going in this direction. There's got to be something more."

Rebecca had pulled him close to herself and told him that made her happier than anything she'd ever heard him say.

"What now?" Ian then asked, but for this his wife had had no response.

The memory ended, and Ian realized that during it his fingers had managed to type out at least one phrase he'd been thinking through. On the screen, in the thin black lettering he'd seen for more days that he'd like to remember, waited the words: *There's got to be something more.* Ian nodded. This was his entrance.

"She agreed to write it," said Rebecca, bursting into the den.

Ian finished his sentence, shook his head to clear the cobwebs, and looked at the clock. He'd been writing for five hours. He looked to Rebecca and she was beaming, her face bright and excited. She stood in the doorway waiting for Ian to reply, but all he could do was look at her: hands on her hips, hair falling into her eyes.

"She's going to do the story," Rebecca repeated. Cheryl was a big art lover and would start her research by coming to the auction on Saturday to see some of the sculptures. After that she'd spend some time with the letters and interviewing folks who knew Katherine and see what she could create.

Ian looked at his wife. "Isn't that what you're doing for your thesis?"

She shook her head. "Cheryl is going to focus on Titansburg and Katherine Jacoby as an artist, rather than her history. I think it will be fun."

Ian said if she was happy then he was happy and turned back to the computer. Rebecca came and stood behind him, asked what he was working on.

"I found my way into the new entrance for the book," he explained. "It's going to begin with that terrible week when all I did was read *Hunter*."

"I remember that week," Rebecca replied, voice grave. "You were almost someone else."

Ian saw himself, unshaven and dressed only in boxers, flipping wildly through pages of a disintegrating hardcover. In a way she was right, it hardly seemed like him at all. On the other hand, he'd never felt like he had such a pure glimpse at himself. "That was the breaking point," he answered finally.

She murmured her agreement, wrapped her arms around his shoulders, and crushed him with a hug. Her face was warm against his neck, and he could feel the whisper of her eyelashes glancing softly against his skin as though she might be blinking back tears. When she pulled back, though, her eyes were clear and light. He knew she wasn't thinking about where they'd been, but where they were now, and he had to agree with her. Every answer he'd looked for hadn't appeared, but, if only for having met Howard Kepler, his life was improved. And it amazed him that he could forget this so easily.

After meeting Rebecca for a quick lunch downtown, Ian passed by A Doll's House and decided to finally stop in. No chime greeted him as he entered, and the store was silent. All around were quiet faces staring back at him. There were infant dolls in bibs and dressing gowns, toddler dolls with rubber sneakers and coveralls, and children outfitted for some activity — horseback riding, swimming, even sledding. A good percentage were historical — decked in little gingham dresses, satin frocks, or gowns ready for a waltz. One doll, Ian swore, was fashioned after Scarlet O'Hara. He would have asked, but no one had yet come out from the back room, and the store was still silent. He looked at his watch, but before he could leave, a voice apologized and asked if she could be of service.

Ian looked up. It was neither Anne nor her mother, but an eager-looking woman of about thirty-five. She asked again if she could help.

"No," said Ian, "I'd never been in before and just wanted to stop by." He realized how ridiculous that might sound, a man his age, so he added, "I'm friends with the owners."

"Oh," the woman said, putting a hand to

338

her mouth. "I'm covering for Anne today. Her mother went into the hospital this morning."

Ian's stomach clenched, and he asked the woman if she knew what had happened.

"I think she hit her head. Took a fall when she was out walking. She's not supposed to be on her own, you know."

Ian said he did. He rocked on his heels for a moment, thanked the woman, and said he wouldn't take up any more of her time.

"Not a problem . . ." the woman replied, her voice trailing off. She looked hard at Ian, and then her eyes brightened. "Hey, I know you. You're the horror writer. There was an article about you in the paper recently, right?"

Ian nodded.

"Hold on a second," the woman said and came around the counter. "There's something you should see. Anne just got it in last week."

She searched first on a lower shelf and then, not finding what she was looking for, moved across to one of the crowded higher shelves. Before she could point it out, Ian saw what she had been searching for — a Katherine Shade doll based on a character from one of his novels. The woman saw it too, brought it down with the box, and handed it to Ian.

The doll was redheaded, just like the girl in the book, and wore a denim jacket with a sun patch on one sleeve and a moon patch on the other. It was her favorite piece of clothing in the world, and Ian was glad to see the toy maker had gotten it right. He'd heard the dolls had been made, remembered signing his name years back to authorize it, but had never seen one. Now a molded plastic face and synthetic eyes stared back at him. It was the closest he'd ever get to meeting one of his characters.

The woman pointed to something on the doll's back, and Ian turned it over. A pull string; he'd forgotten that. This doll, like many others, talked. Only — because Katherine Shade was blessed with a form of ESP — what she said was a prediction of some sort. Ask the doll a question, pull the string, and she'd tell you the future.

"Will I be rich?" the woman asked and pulled the string.

"Not a chance," squeaked the doll in a voice that sounded light with helium.

"How much is it?" Ian asked, and the woman checked the box.

"Eighty-five dollars."

Ian whistled, handed the doll back with a small smile, and walked to the door. Behind him, the woman asked the doll a question that he couldn't hear, but as he pushed the door open and walked out he caught the sound of the shrill voice box: "I'd be careful if I were you, I'd be careful if I were you, I'd be careful if I were you."

It was the mantra, the warning that Ian's telepathic little girl repeated right before some horrendous prophecy rained down in violence upon the person to whom she was speaking. He tried not to shudder as he walked down the street, but a quick breath of wind blew through his light cotton shirt, and he shook despite himself.

Back in his den, Ian found it difficult to return to work. Partly it was an uneasiness at hearing his own dire words coming back to haunt him, and part of it was for the sake of Oakley's mother-in-law. Mike and Anne seemed so hamstrung in their ability to care for the woman — like him, they were going through an unbearable period of waiting for the worst. Minutes passed, yet he couldn't shake the image of that confused woman toppling to the ground, her eyes blurry and not even aware of the trauma about to occur. He wished he could reach out to her, catch her some way, but she kept on falling nonetheless. Finally, powerless to do anything else, Ian spoke the name of God and asked for the old woman to be saved. He said little else if anything, but when he finished, his troubling visions disappeared and he found his quiet. Work seemed possible after all, but before he could begin the doorbell chimed.

Ian walked to the door, checked the peephole, and saw a uniformed courier waiting with a package. After checking the Utah return address and signing for it, Ian carried the package, which was smaller than the first, to the kitchen and slit it open. Again the box was neat and orderly, and like the other, there was a note on top. Ian didn't even bother with the letter, just reached inside and dug out three things: a thin black book, a jeweler's box, and an old portrait of a group of men dressed in coattails and ties. Ian tried to recognize Howard in what looked like a wedding party, but all the men appeared too similar.

He assumed the book to be Howard's Bible. Upon opening to the first page, however, he found that it was a kind of journal, page after page filled with inscrutable handwriting in an ink so dark it seemed to cut holes into the page. Ian leafed through some of the pages, trying his best to read the words, but it was too much of a struggle deciphering the nearly hieroglyphic writing. Even with the book inches from his eyes he could only make out some dates for the entries. It started in Baltimore of March 1943 and finished in August of that same year in Springdale, Utah. Working for two minutes, Ian deciphered the first words of the first page — *"I left this morning and nobody saw me go."* He realized this thin leather volume in his hand was Howard's notes as the man crossed the country forty-odd years ago. Unfortunately it would take hours of translation to read, so he set the journal aside and opened the jeweler's box. Inside lay a tangle of silver chain and beneath, a pocket watch with a cracked face. Ian took it from the velvet box and let the watch dangle from its length of chain, holding it until it spun to a stop.

It made no sense. An old journal was something you kept, likewise a family portrait, but a watch with a smashed crystal seemed like junk. Or at least something that you got fixed rather than left damaged. Howard's life was so spartan and uncluttered that the watch confounded the whole thing. Ian ran his fingers over the spider web of cracks on its face and shut the velvet lid. Once before he'd made the mistake of thinking Howard was a simple man. Perhaps, he realized, he was doing it again.

Ian was still leaning over Howard's journal when his wife returned home a little after six-thirty that evening. Daylight was failing now, and Rebecca chided him for attempting to ruin his eyes. It was said, though, with a small grin, and Ian assumed that plans for the auction had come together well today.

Handing the journal to his wife, he told her about the box. Then, as she looked at the watch and photo, he mentioned the news about Anne's mother.

She wasn't surprised. "Anne called me. Just to mention that they might not make it to the auction after all."

They were silent for a moment, and Ian then had an absurd desire to tell his wife he'd prayed for the woman. Instead he said nothing until Rebecca began gathering food for dinner. Insisting that she'd worked enough for the day, he pushed her from the kitchen and said he'd fix the meal. Without protest, she disappeared into the living room, and soon Ian could hear the low murmur of the television.

Dinner, a light salad with grilled chicken, came together quickly, and by a quarter to eight Rebecca was back in the living room as Ian loaded the dishwasher. They chatted across the rooms about buying a card for the Oakleys and where Ian should sit during the auction and on which sculptures he should bid. As he finished cleaning up, Rebecca returned with an odd look on her face and her hand behind her back.

"What's up?" he asked. "What are you hiding?"

She hesitated for just a second before showing him what she held. It was an unmarked video with a small portion of tape played out. Ian didn't understand what she was showing him.

"Want your good mood ruined?" she asked. " 'Out and About Hartford' just ended."

"Nuts," Ian said, hands dropping to his side. He couldn't decide what else to say or do. Finally he just reached for the video. It was still warm from being inside the VCR.

Nothing good could come of this. The last time a story aired about him, Rebecca ended up in tears and he ended up with a lawsuit and assault charges. This last taping had passed without anything quite that dramatic, but Ian felt that whatever Kyle Turner pieced together came with an agenda. He shook his head a few times and sat down, looking up at Rebecca's face.

"Did you watch it?"

She shook her head, said she had wanted to wait for him.

"Isn't there a bad TV movie or a wrestling match we could watch instead?"

Tugging at his arm, Rebecca promised it'd be okay. "Besides," she said, "who needs wrestling when I'm sure there's a shot of you tackling Turner in here somewhere?"

And there was — but except for his responses to questions about the stalker and his tussle with the cameraman, most of the segment came from old footage.

Ian pressed Stop on the remote and looked at his wife, who sat beside him, a throw pillow clutched to her chest. When he asked what she thought, Rebecca studied his face for a moment to make sure she wouldn't say the wrong thing. "It wasn't as bad it might've been," she said. "Most of that stuff is water under the bridge." Ian nodded and she added, "Though the shot of you swearing at the video man was new."

"He was hurting Cain," Ian answered, and immediately Rebecca grabbed his hand, said she knew, said she was on his side. She rubbed his fingers for a moment and looked at her watch. She said she had spent enough time with Kyle Turner for one day and needed to practice her speech.

"You going to watch it again?"

Ian nodded.

Rebecca kissed him on the forehead, stood, and headed upstairs. When the sound of her footsteps disappeared into the bedroom, Ian took two deep breaths and started the rewound cassette. Immediately, the jarring theme song came on and he fast-forwarded, stopping only when Kyle's square jaw appeared onscreen. He caught the man in mid-sentence.

"— *past has come back to haunt him. Tonight we bring you a closer look at Connecticut's most horrifying writer, Ian Merchant.*"

Then the clips started.

A home video of Ian yelling at some tourists to get off his lawn.

An introduction he'd done for one of the miniseries based on his books showing him rising from a tomb dressed like a zombie.

More of the home video: Ian, wearing only running shorts, chasing the tourists with a rake.

Answering questions about the stalker as he tried to get his dog into the kitchen.

Rolling his eyes back into his head so only the whites appeared.

A talk show panel on which he admitted to sacrificing chickens in college.

Saying he was writing a book about his experiences.

Cackling like a madman at a mid-'80s book signing.

Swearing and shoving the cameraman.

Tumbling over chairs to take a swing at Kyle Turner.

The montage ended, followed by a short interview between Turner and psychiatrist Noel Buford. The shrink said that horror writers brought themselves into proximity with a very unstable portion of the population and that it was only a matter of time before something terrible happened. The doctor kept getting interrupted by the hospital intercom. Still he persisted and made a final comment.

"The past is something that you just can't get away from."

The interview ended and the video returned to Kyle Turner sitting at the studio anchor desk. He promised viewers that "Out and About" would continue to follow the Merchant case and report on any new developments. When a blonde with high cheekbones thanked Kyle and began introducing the evening's next story, Ian shut off the VCR. It was now nearly half past eight, and dusk claimed the Connecticut night.

Ian sat alone in the dark wondering what

to do next. If anything, watching the video had the opposite effect from what he'd expected. Seeing all those old images of himself — he knew he wasn't that person anymore. He did yell at the cameraman, but in the context of protecting Cain, that was almost justifiable. Maybe he'd changed after all. Maybe the thoughts he was typing about his search for an answer to his longings and the solution he'd found in the desert were more than just another gathering of words.

For another few minutes Ian sat in the dim light of his living room before locking up the house for the night. Sleep was still hours away, but right now he just wanted to be with Rebecca, listening to her practice her speech. Together they would face this night together, celebrating their little victories.

EARLY AFTERNOON. SATURDAY, AUGUST 10

Katherine Jacoby's living room now filled a corner of the Titansburg Historical Society. There was the fake fireplace, the single carved rose, and the sewing cabinet, along with a real rocking chair, real lamp, and a few obvious sculptures — the cat blending into a dog, two arms twisting into each other, the odd birdhouse configuration. Rebecca was working, so Ian visited the display alone, enjoying the conversations of other patrons as they passed. Some took time to read the descriptions, but most just glanced at the obvious pieces and then walked away, oblivious to the subtleties they had missed. Younger people seemed to pass more quickly than the elderly, who took their time and often exclaimed in disbelieving voices that the sewing table or fireplace had been formed from wood.

"Do you believe it?" a white-haired gentleman asked Ian.

"I've touched them," he replied, and the old man smiled, seemingly pleased that the sculptures were as amazing as they seemed.

"Are you guarding the exhibit?" asked another voice, and Ian turned to find Anne and Mike Oakley. They were holding hands as if each needed the other's strength just to stand.

"How's your mother?" Ian asked. "Is everything okay?"

"She took a fall during one of her escapes. Banged her head a little but didn't hurt herself too badly. They kept her in the hospital just to make sure."

"Where did they find her?"

Anne sighed, said the old woman wandered through the grounds of the retirement community and was found leaning against a fence. There was a house nearby with a swimming pool, and she was just watching the family splash about.

Ian had nothing he could say to that, and neither Anne nor Mike looked like they wanted to talk about it any further, so Ian directed their attention to the exhibit. Each was impressed by the woman's skill and artistry and spent time reading the placard descriptions about Katherine Jacoby's life and work. By the time they finished, only ten minutes remained before the auction. Ian led them through the museum to a large auditorium.

Onstage, near the podium, Rebecca stood chatting with another woman. Ian wanted to wave, catch her attention, but she didn't look over, so he and the Oakleys made their way to a row of open chairs near the front. About them some patrons mingled near the stage, scouting the offerings, but most merely looked through the afternoon's program. Ian double-checked the list of three sculptures on which he was to bid and showed them to the Oakleys. Soon the lights dimmed for a split second to warn that the afternoon's presentation was about to begin.

The director of the Historical Society, a thin, neat man who didn't look his fifty years, gave the opening address, and then the stage was turned over to the curator, who talked about the exquisite reproductions of antiques from their collection that would be auctioned off first. Ian was only bidding on the sculptures later in the program, so he didn't pay much attention to what was being said and looked around the crowd instead. One face caught his attention, and he realized Cheryl Rose was standing along the far wall, notebook in one hand, program in the other. She met his gaze and waved. Ian nodded, and there was the banging of a gavel. The auctioneer approached the podium, introduced the first item — a reproduction tall-clock based on a 1734 Louis Heinz model — named the starting price, and waited for the first bid.

The first lot consisted of twenty items, and bidding for them lasted nearly an hour. Finally, after the last one sold — a tri-corner hatbox starting at a ridiculous seven hundred dollars — the auctioneer took his seat. Ian saw Rebecca begin to fidget in her chair and checked the program — she was next. The director introduced the second lot as a holding from the estate of Katherine Jacoby and said that Mrs. Rebecca Merchant, archivist with the Historical Society, would introduce the woman, her art, and her world.

Ian watched his wife stand and realized everyone else was looking at her as well. It felt different, odd in a way, to be only one pair of a hundred focused eyes. He wondered if this was how she felt when his picture made it into a newspaper or onto television. One in a crowd.

She smoothed her skirt and crossed the stage to the microphone. His eyes were on hers, and suddenly she was looking at him. The briefest smile crossed her face and then she looked at her notes, cleared her throat once, and nodded to the back of the room. A slide appeared on the screen behind her. It was the picture of Katherine as a baby in her father's arms. Ian heard murmuring as the audience realized what they were seeing.

"Katherine Jacoby was born to William and Greta Schmidt. Her father served as a captain in Hitler's SA. He sent his only daughter out of the country at the age of two to live with a Jewish aunt and uncle. This one decision can be seen as the fulcrum on which Katherine's development as an artist and person rests. At first it caused her to hide her past. Raised by her aunt and uncle as a devout and practicing Jew, she ignored and ran from her true identity. It is only later, as a young woman, that she

353

became reconciled to her past."

A second slide appeared, this one of Katherine, her eyes crossed at the camera.

"At the age of thirty-six she began to read more about World War II and the Nazi movement, coming across the writings and letters of Christian theologian and martyr Dietrich Bonhoeffer. For a year she struggled with reconciling her Jewish faith to the understanding she was gaining through Bonhoeffer. In the fall of 1967, she began her life as a Messianic Jew."

Around Ian there were more murmurs. Rebecca stood tall, her head held high and her voice rising clear and strong. Her eyes were electric.

"At this point her art and life took a dramatic turn. Instead of focusing on the fragile notion of image and surface prevalent in her early *trompe l'oeil* pieces, she began to explore her own history and the life of her father. Again and again in letters, she describes how she was unable to solve his enigmatic place in her life. She could never defend the choices he made in devoting his life to Hitler's cause. However, it was his choice to send her away that ultimately cost him his life. Assassinated as part of a brutal purge on what is known as the Night of

Long Knives, her father, Katherine came to believe, was killed for not remaining true to the Nazi cause, to the pride of Germany, by sending his daughter to live with a Jewish relative. He sacrificed his life for her freedom and safety, and Katherine's struggle came to a climax in a powerful piece called *Gleichshaltung.*"

An image of the urn with its frantic, fearful carvings filled the screen.

"This marked the beginning of a new period in her art that explored, sometimes with painful honesty, the notions of her faith and truth about her life."

Rebecca nodded once more, and a final slide appeared — a portrait of the artist as an elderly woman. Sawdust and wood chips powdered her hair, and her face held a contented smile. Ian imagined the woman planing a board or chiseling her own pleasant face into the grain of a wooden book.

"Katherine Jacoby's legacy is one of willful perseverance and hearty faith. Her sculptures are monuments not only to her skill and artistry but to her devotion and industry. She gave all she had to her art and her beliefs, and often the two intertwined so tightly that even she didn't know where one ended and the other began. I'll close with a passage from her journal.

" 'I finished the cross this morning and fell into tears. The thing was so terrible and lovely, so heavy and wonderful. I think I finally know what it means to be forgiven.' "

The carved urn *Gleichshaltung* as well as the Star of David were bought by a doctor from New York City whose eyes were blood-shot with tears as the sculptures were handed over to him. The small book came next, and Ian bought it for $800. He took a break while the wooden loaf of bread was being auctioned and then joined again in the bidding for the cross. Three others bid against him, and Ian could hear the crowd buzz with excitement as the price climbed.

This was the one sculpture Ian and Rebecca wanted most, though, and he would go as high as necessary. One fellow dropped out at $7,500, but the other traded bids back and forth with Ian until $11,150. The auctioneer repeated the price three times and then banged his gavel. It was sold to the Merchants. When the audience burst into a congratulatory applause, Ian could see his wife allow herself a brief smile. He watched her for a few moments, ignoring the sale of a few smaller pieces. Again and again the prices rose, and each time the gavel crashed down applause filled the auditorium.

Finally the sculpture Ian wanted was wheeled on stage. Bones swayed and clacked together with a hollow scraping that sounded like branches clattering through a storm. All around people whispered about how odd and grotesque this one was, not at all like the other pieces. Even Anne winced at the sight of the hollow chest.

Rebecca caught Ian's eye and stared. He winked at her and she shrugged, knowing what was about to happen. The auctioneer shouted a starting price of two thousand dollars and the room fell silent and still, the only motion that of the swaying bones up front. Ian lifted his number and looked around.

"Going once . . . twice . . . sold," yelled the caller and the hammer crashed down. This time there was no applause, only an uncomfortable silence from the audience. The only thing Ian heard came from about two rows back. It was a man speaking, and it was just one word.

"Figures."

After the auction, Rebecca met Ian and the Oakleys on the patio outside for wine and cheese. They complimented her on the talk, and Ian found he couldn't keep his eyes off his wife. Her speech, her research, her poise, her passion — it all had stunned him, and he felt like he might say something incredibly stupid and gushing. Thankfully, Anne spoke first.

"We were just talking about where you guys were going to keep the sculptures."

"Probably in the basement for now," Rebecca answered. "Especially the wind chime that my husband here felt compelled to buy." She squeezed his arm, and Ian knew she was pleased.

A few strangers interrupted to add their congratulations, and when they disappeared Mike leaned in and said, "So what's *Gleichshaltung* mean?"

"Consolidation, basically." Rebecca answered, then popped some more cheese into her mouth. Ian waited for her to continue. He realized in his worries about his book and the stalking and Kyle Turner that he'd simply neglected asking his wife any questions about her research. He was almost ashamed that he was hearing all this for the first time.

"It was one of Hitler's ideas," Rebecca began again. "It gave him the freedom to get rid of anyone he wanted — Communists, Jews, anyone — in the name of unifying the country. He ordered hundreds of men killed so that his own private army and the national army could be combined."

Ian and the Oakleys stared a moment at Rebecca.

"So Katherine's father was one of them just because he sent his daughter to safety?" Anne asked.

Rebecca shrugged. "That's what Katherine believed. There's probably more — secret alliances in the SA with the wrong people — but we'll never know. The only evidence is one final letter that her father had mailed to his sister, which hinted that he knew what was coming. It said something about someone finding out about Katherine. Even if they needed a reason, which they didn't, that would have been enough."

"Man," said Oakley, and nobody else added anything more. Conversation paused for a moment, then swung to other more pleasant topics. At five-thirty, Anne decided they needed to go rescue friends from their son, so she and Mike said good-bye and strolled hand-in-hand from the museum. Ian watched them leave and thought they looked livelier than when they'd arrived. He wondered if the day had diverted their fears for the moment.

Rebecca said she was ready to go also, and once they arranged for delivery of the sculptures, they left for home with only the small carved book in hand. It sat between them on the seat as they drove, and all Ian could do was tell his wife how wonderfully the whole day had gone.

Ian awoke to the sound of bells, and it took a few seconds before he realized he wasn't dreaming. Soft, sweet chimes drifted through an open window along with the breeze; it was a sound Ian had never heard this far from town before and he could only assume some change in weather carried the tune in his window. Whatever the cause, it appeared that ringing bells meant a mild, pleasant day, and Ian climbed from bed without waking Rebecca. He looked at the clock, then the closet. Something about the bells seemed to beckon him to church, so he slipped into slacks, buttoned up a solid Oxford, and went downstairs. After leaving a quick note for Rebecca, he got in his car and began to drive. He would find a service that was about to start and go to it.

Problems began at the Baptist church two miles away. Their service had started already, and Ian didn't want to walk in twenty minutes late. A nearby Presbyterian church had only one service during the summer and it wasn't for forty minutes. Ian passed by a Congregational church and two Methodist sanctuaries, but all of those had already started as well. Ian checked the dashboard clock and took a hard right. It was the last place he wanted to be going, but then again it was the only option remaining. The Church of God was beginning in ten minutes. He could slip in, sit in the back, and not cause a scene. The woman who had made his wife cry wouldn't even notice.

Ian parked, entered the gym through a side door, and slid into the most remote row of chairs. An older man fiddling with the stem of a pocket watch was the only person who looked up at all. The man said nothing, just nodded at him seriously the way farmers might before a storm and went back to his timepiece before Ian could even nod back. As he read his bulletin, Ian tried to place an odd scent that floated through the room and seemed quite familiar. Scanning the list of prayer requests and ministry announcements, his mind kept tugging back to a memory of the bathroom ceiling in his childhood home. He flipped one more page and read the order of service.

It wasn't a regular Sunday service but something called an "All Baptism Sunday." Music started, and Ian looked up. There was no choir, no worship leaders, just the pastor singing his way through a hymn from start to finish. When it ended, there was a brief welcome. Then the pastor requested that everyone follow him to the pool. The congregation stood and began filing through the rows of chairs and across the three-point arc to a narrow doorway. As Ian shuffled his way into line he felt the first wave of humid warmth and pinpointed the elusive odor — chlorine. The scent never reminded him of other pools or summers spent swimming with his cousins but of the time he passed out in the bathroom after washing the tub with bleach and ammonia. His mother rescued him that day, but the high ceiling mottled with unreachable mildew stains was forever tattooed in his memory.

After settling in at the end of the highest row of swim-meet bleachers, Ian scanned the crowd, wondering if anyone else thought this the least bit odd. A few men in linen suits tugged at silk ties in the heavy, wet air. Everyone else seemed unaffected until the first person was called forward to be baptized. As the woman tiptoed up to the microphone, the group leaned forward almost imperceptibly, waiting. The woman — a frail lady named Lois dressed in Bermuda shorts and a black T-shirt — spoke, turned, climbed down the ladder into the shallow end of the pool, and moved to the pastor's waiting arms. He said a blessing, lowered her into the water, and brought her up once more, dripping and smiling.

Over and over, people — some just children, some older than Ian — gave their story. One fellow talked about time he'd spent in prison. A girl cried as she explained how God rescued her from an eating disorder. Some spoke with excitement and joy while others were intense and grateful. Ian watched as twenty people slipped under the water, were held a moment, and then pulled back up. Twice he heard others around him sniffling, and once, when a seventy-two-year-old man named Charlie called to Jesus for forgiveness for the first time, he thought he might break down himself.

Ian listened to the men and women and children tell their stories and watched their faces, and he knew that's how he had been those few months ago in the desert. He saw himself struggling to find purchase on the slippery bottom of that flooded stream bed, and he heard Howard Kepler roaring with laughter all the way upstream. Others talked about the forgiveness and absolution granted by God, and Ian felt the words in a deep place he'd forgotten since his trip to Utah. One final man stood dripping, arms raised in triumph, and Ian crept from his seat, out a rear door open to the cool air, and into his car.

Something electric filled his mind, and he

found himself smiling at what he'd just seen. It was like Jaret's book coming to life — a great gathering of believers telling their stories to others for no other reason than to publicly thank God for the changes wrought in their lives. The most important thing was in the speaking, and Ian knew his restarted chapter was the way to go. He needed to tell his story as well. The time for wishing others had been alongside Howard in the desert was over. It was now time to write the tale, to evoke visions of sand and heat and tell others what they would have seen: a man, brought to his knees, calling on God.

Rebecca seemed surprised to hear that Ian had gone back to Titansburg Church of God after their experience the week before, but showed genuine interest when Ian described the service to her and tried to explain how it made him feel. Most of her questions were directed at what it would mean for his book.

"Are you going to stop writing about the stalking?"

Ian shook his head. "The stalking is still there, but it's tied too closely to other things — my problems writing, my visit with Howard — to focus on it alone. It's all the same story. And for the first time I feel like

I'm approaching it from the right direction."

"Do you think Louis will want it?"

Ian paused, but just for a second. He knew the answer.

"No. I don't think Louis will want this at all."

"But you're still going to write it?"

Ian nodded. His choice was to write these words or silence.

"Go to it, then," Rebecca answered and reached out to touch his hand. He took it and for just a few seconds they sat together in silence. His wife was standing by him the only way she knew how, and Ian couldn't think of anything more important at the moment. So many other things would fade away and disappear, but this was something important. Five seconds more he held on to her, then squeezed her hand and headed into his office. He had a story to tell.

Ian spent two hours finishing his introductory chapter and saved it. Tomorrow he would come back for an edit, but for now he wanted to think about anything else. His escape came in the inked clottings of scratches that masqueraded as Howard Kepler's penmanship. Five pages took him half an hour to decipher, but finally a pattern was coming clear in the writing and a story was emerging from the pages.

At the age of sixteen, Howard runs away from his home in Baltimore. The year is 1943 and something the boy has done makes him too ashamed to ever show his face at home again. He has a duffel bag with clothes and a little money that he uses to buy food when necessary, but for the most part he bums rides, works for meals, and makes his way across the country. After two weeks, the journal entries start reading the same: place, date, a short worry about where he'd find food, and a general lament that he was so alone. A second entry would tell of the people he'd met who had been kind enough to feed him or give him a lift. Twice in the early portions he talks about dodging the police, but for the most part his disappearance goes untraced, and he wanders alone.

A month after sneaking away, Howard enters St. Louis. The land has begun to open up, and he decides to spend a little time in the city, perhaps even make enough money to board a train. The first night he sleeps under a tree in the park. The next day, hungry and chilled, he wanders around town stopping at shops to inquire about work. A baker, a grocer, an undertaker, and a dime store owner all turn him down before he stumbles across a photographer. The man offers a cot to sleep on, a couple of dimes as salary, and some food for helping lug equipment around. Howard agrees and works there for three months. The journal entries are less frequent now that he has daily bread and acquaintances. He mentions learning how to take portraits, and soon he buys a used camera from the photographer, taking images of the city and landscapes to sell at the gallery. June ends with Howard purchasing a rail ticket to Denver, Colorado. He now has two suitcases and a camera bag. He doesn't mention missing anybody or his family or even what he had run away from. He is focused on moving West.

Ian slipped a bookmark into the journal and closed it a fourth of the way through. Setting the book aside, he turned to Rebecca, who sat reading in the armchair across the room. She kept reading for a few moments before the weight of his stare must have distracted her, and she looked up. He had no real reason for staring, so he just winked and she shook her head a bit, then buried her nose once more in her reading.

Ian didn't look away, though. He watched

Rebecca read — watched her pull her legs up under her, watched her furrow her brow when a sentence made no sense, watched her absently stroke her chin — and thought there was nothing else he'd rather be doing. Since the middle of last week his world had gained a certain normalcy that was welcome after the terrible things that had come before. Things as simple as the success of the auction and the wonderful baptismal service and time spent with Howard Kepler's diary seemed all the richer simply because moments like them had been few and far between recently. On top of it all, Ian had finished a chapter of which he was proud — the first thing he'd written in nearly a year that felt good appearing on screen. Picking up the journal once more, Ian felt that things could stay this way for a good long time.

After he arrives in Colorado, Howard contacts a friend of a friend to get himself settled in Denver. He gains employment as a photographer's assistant and works for a few weeks with barely an entry in his journal. That all changes on July 23.

The day starts out typically with Howard helping develop photos and running errands when necessary. Then late in the day he is handed an assignment to shoot a family portrait for a reverend on the other side of the city. Howard makes it to the place just as dinner is being served, and the family asks him to join them. He does and ends up being put on the spot by the pastor's wife, who grills him about his family.

I tried to lie at first, but my answers came too slowly. I couldn't think fast enough, and that woman just kept staring at me like she knew I was telling stories. Just like Momma used to do. Finally I just blurted out the truth that I'd left home a few months ago and was making my way in the world just fine.

She asked about my family some, and what I told her was mostly the truth. She wondered if I went to church back home, and I said that we were part of a Brethren church but that I didn't put too much stock in that sort of thing. She smiled some and then left the room. Soon she came back with a Bible and asked me if I had one. I said no, so she set it in front of me and told me to keep it. The world could be a lonely place sometimes, and this would mean I'd always have somewhere to turn. She also said it gave lots of answers to any questions or worries I might have.

Then she served up dessert and I got the portrait taken.

Howard returns to his room that night and pages through his new Bible. He reads through Genesis and starts to cry when it says that a man would leave his family to be united with a woman. He admits for the first time that he misses his home.

Entries now deal mostly with what he finds in his Bible, which he is reading, as he would any other book, from start to finish. Many are questions without answers and most are short and incomplete. Howard doesn't understand Isaac's surrender to his father's knife or Joseph's brutal brothers. He gets tangled in the laws and bored by the genealogies. The psalms interest him, but it is the prophets who catch his attention.

How is it possible they are talking to me? How do they know me so well?

Howard finishes reading through Isaiah in August, and by the time he receives a week-long vacation for Labor Day he's nearly finished Jeremiah. It is evident that he's planned a trip to see the Grand Canyon with his free week, and for a few days all his writings are about the blasted landscape and the arid weather. From the Grand Canyon he makes his way north into Utah and decides to spend one week fasting and wandering in the desert. He brings only his journal, a canteen, and his camera along. Writing little but of his hunger, he picks his way through southern Utah and on the fifth day finds Zion National Park, the Court of the Patriarchs, Angel's Landing, and the Great White Throne. That same night he reads the conclusion of Jeremiah and writes a fragment of Scripture.

> " 'In those days, and in that time,'
> saith the Lord, 'the children of
> Israel shall come, they and the
> children of Judah together, going
> and weeping; they shall go,
> and seek the Lord, their God.
> They shall ask the way to Zion
> with their faces toward it, saying
> come, and let us join ourselves to
> the Lord in a perpetual covenant
> that shall not be forgotten.' " (50:4–5)

At the Throne, Howard looks for a way to commemorate the occasion. Something beyond merely writing it with words. He thinks of building a tower of stone as the Israelites did after crossing the Jordan but decides on something else.

I smashed my watch. That time is over, something new has begun.

Howard spends two more days in the desert, but the complaining is over. Now he writes only about how many changes are going to be made in his life. He sees the future in front of him and confesses over and over the wrongs that have come before. On day seven, at an entrance road to the park outside Springdale, Utah, he mentions taking his self-portrait and then heading off to do whatever God may will. The journal ends with three verses from Psalm 73.

Ian stood, stretched, and walked to his den where he retrieved the pocket watch and one of Howard's scrapbooks. The stopped hands read 9:12 and suddenly it seemed very odd to Ian to see, to hold, the precise moment of his friend's conversion. He set the watch aside and opened the album to the self-portrait of the skinny kid with the big ears, checking the date on the back. Ian realized that this was the photo. This was Howard Kepler as a new believer, his cheeks ruddy and burnt, his hair shaved to a crew cut. The smile was dazed and loopy and his eyes, his eyes stared out as if they were focused on something very far away. Something you didn't want to take your eyes off. Ever.

EARLY MORNING. TUESDAY, AUGUST 13

When he found Cain waiting for him at the bottom of the stairs, eyes bright and tail wagging, Ian realized this was just one more sign of life regaining equilibrium. He rubbed her ears twice before turning into the kitchen to grab a quick glass of juice. His first notion that something was wrong came when Cain barked. She'd been trained — hours of obedience school — to remain quiet inside the house, and Ian was so surprised by the noise that he nearly spilled his drink. He made to turn for her, but as he did a small motion outside the kitchen door caught his eye. There, approaching the house, walked a man carrying something in front of him. A man with a loose, uneven smile, slick black hair, and a brown pair of work boots. Ian's breath escaped in a wheeze and he remembered those scuffed boots, remembered them approaching him once before in the garage.

He took two steps back and still the man came. Time seemed to slow. Ian could see the fellow's hollow cheeks now, his liquid eyes and the slender fingers curled under the corners of the box he carried. The box.

The man carried a white cardboard box. It read *Walker's Point Auto Repair* and one corner was frayed. The fingernail of the man's left thumb was black. That same twisted smile tangled the man's lips like a wolf snarling.

Ian took another step back. He heard the slap of boot on the first step of the porch. That sound, heel against wood plank, shattered Ian's paralysis and he turned, grabbing for the phone, and fleeing from the kitchen, the hollow thump of the man striding across the porch following him.

Cain barked and Ian raced upstairs, dialing 9-1-1 as he ran. Breathless by the top, he gave the operator his information in a wheeze, slipped into the bedroom, and locked the door, holding one ear to its wood. He waited for the sound of shattering glass, waited for the muffled kick of a revolver. He heard only Cain bark and, behind him, the splash and patter of Rebecca's shower. Then, sirens — a cruiser must have been close.

Warmth flooded his body in a rush and Ian collapsed to the rug, aware for the first time that his arm was wet. Dazed, he looked down and realized he was half soaked in orange juice. At some point, his morning drink must have tumbled all over him. He knew the interview was coming next and he knew he had to remember as much as he could. Ignoring his wet arm, he closed his eyes and pictured the face of the man who walked toward him. The arching cheekbones. The sloped chin. The wide and urgent eyes staring at Ian.

Then, the kicker.

The man had no eyebrows. Somehow, in the hurried moments before, it had failed to register. But now, picturing the stalker's face in his mind, Ian realized the man had no eyebrows at all, not even a penciled line drawn where they should have been. And somehow that made everything so much worse.

Sirens blared to a stop outside the house, and, for the first time, Rebecca spoke.

"Ian!" she yelled, worried.

"I'm here," he called back. "I'm okay."

"No eyebrows?" Oakley asked, entering his office and holding up a computerized rendering of the stalker for Ian to see. Ian could barely lift his eyes; he would see the man's face in his dreams. "Wonder why no eyebrows?"

"What about the box?" asked Rebecca. She'd called off work.

"Clean," the detective replied. "No prints. Some trace elements, but I doubt they'll help."

"But I saw his hands holding it," Ian said, his voice almost a squeak. "His thumbnail was black."

"Must have wiped it when you turned your back."

Ian groaned. "Well, what was inside?"

Oakley motioned for Ian and Rebecca to stand, waved them to the hallway, and said they needed to be at their house for the answer to that. They moved down the hall to the front entrance. Ian and Rebecca had ridden in a squad car to the station, so they climbed into Oakley's cruiser and in a few minutes were pulling toward their house. The ride was silent. Ian kept imagining horrible things peeking out from under the box lid. Rebecca was looking out the back window. More sad thoughts, he imagined. They'd returned so quickly.

When they arrived, all three entered, and Oakley moved straight to the kitchen table. Another cardboard box — different from the one Ian had seen the stalker carrying — was in his arms. He put it down and removed a sheaf of papers from inside.

"Do you keep copies of interviews and such?"

377

Ian nodded.

"Get your books, too." He pointed to the packet of papers. "Fifty-six articles," he said. "Each has a quote written on it. We want to identify each article and the quote. It's a long shot, but at this point we're looking for anything."

Ian looked at the first article, recognized it as a profile written for *People* magazine, and read the quote scrawled with a messy hand at the bottom of the page.

Believe me, I will make sure you never forget that such a thing happened.

It was from *Monster.* He left for a moment to gather up paperbacks and when he returned, found the quote and showed Oakley. The cop nodded, said that he thought it would go easier with two experts on the case.

Rebecca and Ian split the photocopies between them and began to identify both the interview and the quote placed with it. Most took about a minute, and it was strange to Ian to see how easily he remembered portions of his own writing. He knew not only where a quote would be in the context of the book, but usually where it would be printed physically on the page. He and Rebecca both flipped through the first ten without problems while Oakley took notes. Once the officer turned a copy of *Semi* over to read the back copy. Ian watched him and, from the expression on his face, knew better than to ask for an opinion.

Rebecca asked for assistance.

"Things have a way of sneaking up on you," she read aloud, and Ian paused. It was too short. It could have come from any of his novels. He gave her suggestions and she checked each one. Was it from Katherine Shade's dad's death? Or possibly the time the truck ran over the motorcycle cop parked behind the billboard? Or when the hand reached out from the lake and nearly grabbed the grandmother in *Mason's Road*?

Paging through the final book, she gave a shout. It was there. Ian turned back to his articles. Each time, he gave Oakley the name of the publication, the approximate date, and the page number for the quote. Most of the quotes were from *Monster* or from the early novels, and most of the interviews were torn from major magazines. Rebecca found one that had come from a small Connecticut paper, but that was as close to a lead as they could get. On and on they worked until fifty-five articles had been finished. The last gave Ian problems, and after ten minutes he had to take a break. After a quick walk to the sink to get a glass of water, he returned to find Oakley and Rebecca looking at the quote.

The more you change, the more likely you are to lose yourself.

"Think that's true?" the officer asked.

Ian shook his head. Right now he didn't even remember writing it. He stared across the kitchen table at nothing, trying to remember writing those words.

"Our guy seems pretty intent on reminding you about what happens when people try to change."

Ian nodded.

"Are you trying to change, Ian?"

Ian looked up. Oakley and Rebecca both stared at him, each as intent as the other. Some small part of him wanted to laugh at the resemblance, but he didn't. Since that face shocked the morning, he'd been unable to raise even the most slender of chuckles.

"I am. I don't want this anymore." He waved at the pile of quotes and notes before him.

"Why?"

"Because . . ." Ian began, then stopped. A

notion struck him. "Do you remember Rebecca's talk about Katherine Jacoby, how at one point she stopped painting *trompe l'oeil* sculptures completely? I understand that. For so long she saw the world as this illusion, this dream-of-a-giant kind of thing. Then she became a Christian, and her perspective changed. Suddenly, illusion didn't matter anymore. She fought through that and ended up having to dedicate her life to something new." It had come out in a stream, but he realized that he believed every word. It was part of what he'd felt in her workroom that first day. Part of why he bought the sculpture.

"For a long time," he continued before Rebecca or Oakley said anything, "I saw the world in terms of horror and grief. It sounds bad, and I guess it was, but it's the truth. I followed it to the very end — *Hunter* took my vision as far as I could take it. And when I got there I found out I was very wrong. My answer, my vision, had been wrong. For Katherine there was something more than illusion. For me there was something more than horror. I now know that I can't return."

He looked at the quote again. *The more you change, the more likely you are to lose yourself.* A bell rang for him, and he grabbed a copy of *Hunter.* He saw the words, as he had with the other quotes in a general position in the book. He remembered the chapter and paged through, searching until he came to where he expected them to be.

Only they weren't there.

He flipped a few pages forward and began scanning the text. Nothing.

"Can't find this one," he said.

Oakley waved him off. "We've spent enough time on it today."

Ian shut the novel and leaned back. Rebecca and the officer were still looking at him. It was Oakley who spoke first.

"Well, I need to be going. We're going to have an officer stationed here tonight so you folks don't need to worry. I'll touch base with you tomorrow to discuss some longer-term precautions, but right now I should be getting home."

"Everything okay there, Mike?" Rebecca asked.

"Not really," answered Oakley. "But what are you going to do? Anne and her father argue a lot about caring for Anne's mother. He swears he can take care of her, but she keeps getting out." He sighed, weary. "No winning this battle."

He stood and Ian stood with him. Rebecca told the officer she'd stop by the store if she could, say hello to Anne. Oakley thanked her and moved down the hall. He said nothing more, just shook Ian's hand and went out the door to his car, looking little like a man armed with badge and gun. Ian wished him well, got a wave in return, and then shut the door. When he returned to the kitchen, Rebecca still sat at the table.

"You really identify with Katherine Jacoby?"

The question didn't surprise Ian. She'd been looking at him oddly ever since he'd mentioned the woman.

"Sort of," he answered. "Really, she reminds me of Howard, and I've always identified with him. But Oakley wouldn't have known him."

Rebecca looked as though she understood. She asked nothing more, just stood and wrapped her arms around Ian. In a very bad way it seemed as though things were all starting over again.

The notion did not dim through the night. As the dark cloak of evening fell, Ian could not turn his mind from the terrible face he'd seen that morning. Every movement outside a window seized at his throat, and the knowledge that a pair of officers sat directly outside his home meant nothing.

Rebecca sat with him and tried to keep him occupied, but he kept becoming distracted and couldn't even follow the simplest of conversations.

"I'm glad I didn't see him," his wife said after he failed to respond to a simple question. There was a frightened relief to her voice, that of somebody who's just avoided an accident.

Ian, meanwhile, felt as though he'd barely crawled alive from the wreck. Ten o'clock came without even a hint of sleep, and when Rebecca went upstairs twenty minutes later, Ian was alone downstairs for the first time since that morning. Immediately he went to his windowless den. Books they'd used hours ago cluttered his desk, and straightening up was the only thing he found to keep himself busy.

Out of habit he walked to the bookshelf but found Howard's albums clogging the shelf. Rebecca had put them there the other morning, and so he walked to the storage closet and pulled out the box in which he'd found the paperbacks. A stack of paper lay inside, and when he looked closer he saw it was a late draft of *Hunter*. The pages curled, and he almost dumped them into the trash when a thought crossed his mind. Somehow the pages were familiar.

Ian pulled the draft out and skimmed through it. Fragments and sentences flashed up at him, but only one thing stood out in his mind: the sentence he couldn't find earlier that day.

The more you change, the more likely you are to lose yourself.

Pages riffled by, and just like earlier in the evening, Ian thought he could see the words on the page. They were near the top, perhaps the second line. He turned four more pages and stopped.

The more you change, the more likely you are to lose yourself.

The words were crossed out in red ink.

Ian blinked and grabbed the paperback copy of the novel, turning to the corresponding page. The words weren't there. They had been there in the final draft, but Louis had cut them at the last moment. Too mumbo-jumbo, he'd said.

Ian stared at the words. He had no idea how they'd made it into that malicious box of notes and letters. Did the stalker somehow own a draft of Ian's work? Was he that obsessed? Or could it be somebody from the publisher? A janitor who'd stolen the pages from Louis's desk while vacuuming?

The gaunt, bald face glowered at him from his imagination, and Ian's jaw clenched tight. He'd never seen that face before. A person remembered a face like that, remembered the vicious eyes of depravity staring at him, sizing up his soul. Ian promised himself that he'd ask around tomorrow, but he expected no answers. He'd never come across this person in his life. Such things change you. Change your days, and change especially your nights.

WEEK 6

Ian woke late after a night interrupted by cold visions of the bald-faced man and rushed to make his train. No new box awaited him on the porch, and when he glanced out the bay window, he saw the police cruiser still waiting in silence. Gulping some juice and calling that breakfast, Ian grabbed his portfolio, headed to his Cherokee, and, once the police officers pulled out with a wave, sped toward the depot, making it with just moments to spare.

Climbing aboard, Ian saw a surprising face. Trout, whom he'd never seen on his ride into the city, stood preparing the luxury car beverage cart. Ian greeted him as he squeezed down the aisle, and the porter's eyes lit with recognition. When Ian asked what he was doing on this train into the city, the man explained that he was just doing a favor for a co-worker. Switching routes just for the day. He assured Ian he'd be by soon with drinks, but Ian said not to bother.

"Gotta sleep," he explained. "Just make sure to wake me up."

Trout promised and Ian slipped into his compartment, letting down the velvet curtains and lowering the window shades. Even before the train began to move, he settled himself across the seat and tried his best to relax from the rushed morning. Soon a whistle sounded and the train eased forward. Ian thought once about the fellow who'd risen from the morning mist with his slick hair and sullen mouth, but that thought soon dissolved in his need for sleep, and he found the comfort of rest.

The wheezing shriek of the train whistle that alerted its arrival into the city woke Ian. He tried opening his eyes, but there was a tremendous blinding light shining in and he thought the shade on his window might have been raised, the morning sun pouring through. Squinting did nothing so he squeezed his eyes shut, a blurred and greenish afterimage filling his mind. Dark and indistinct at first, it took only an instant to sharpen.

It was the outline of a person.

He opened his eyes to slits. At once it all

made a kind of sickening sense. They were under the city, about to arrive at Penn Station. The light wasn't from the sun, it was from the seeking beam of a flashlight.

"Ian," the figure holding the light said in a terrible, birdlike flutter of a voice, and then there was an unyielding scream.

Only as he jumped up did Ian realize that he was screaming, that it was his own terror unleashing itself with unspeakable volume. For just a second he stood face-to-face with the stalker, but the man ducked low and the light disappeared. Ian couldn't move. He felt the brush of velvet and heard footsteps down the aisle.

There was another whistle, the shudder of the train braking, and then light flooded the space, a jaundiced glow from the lamps illuminating Penn Station. Ian collapsed onto the seat, unable to gather enough breath. The train rolled to a halt, and Ian could see expressionless crowds milling about outside, waiting to board. He couldn't gulp enough air, and just when he thought he had, there was more shouting from down the car. Crowds outside pulled back, expressions of shock on their faces. Ian knew something had happened, and he guessed he was part of it.

He stood, pushed out into the hall, down

the aisle, and out of the car. A group of people stood huddled on the platform. One man knelt. Sprawled in the midst of them, Ian realized, was a body. He saw a leg, twisted and still. Ian jumped off the train to the tile and took two steps. He saw maroon cuffs around the leg and the person's thick black ankle. Without taking another step, he knew it was Trout.

A policeman appeared almost instantaneously, and a strong-looking fellow carrying a toolbox that said *NYCTA Paramedics*. The group backed off a little, and Ian could see Trout's blank face, the pool of blood spreading across the tiles from his head.

"I saw what happened," a man in a Yankees cap shouted to the police. "Some guy pushed his way to the exit, and the old guy went to stop him. Got shoved right off and cracked his head."

"The fellow was wearing jeans and a white T-shirt. Black hair," called another.

"Yeah, the guy jumped from the train and took off across the platform before anyone stopped him."

More officers arrived and began taking statements. Ian stood waiting, tucking his chin into his collar so he wouldn't be recognized, until a policeman approached him.

"I think I know who it was who did this," he told the cop. The officer pulled out a pad, but before Ian started talking, he pulled out his phone, made a quick call, and told Louis's secretary he was going to be late.

When Ian finished twenty minutes later, two officers discussed whether to bring him to a precinct station for more detailed questioning, but finally decided he could head on to his meetings at the publisher. Before leaving, Ian asked one of them if he knew the status of the porter. The cop shook his head.

"Do you know where they might take him?"

"Probably Roosevelt or St. Clair," said one of the officers and walked off.

Ian shouldered his portfolio strap and passed through a small flock of people still waiting to be interviewed. One or two turned to watch as he passed, but most just talked among themselves.

Ian walked across the tiled room, up the stairs, through the main entrance to Madison Square Garden and out onto West 33rd. People and taxis swarmed together in the street, and all around horns sounded. Clouds filtered what little light made it past the skyscrapers, and though it was still morning it was as dark outside as it had been in the train station. Ian elbowed his way through the jam of tourists and New Yorkers and beckoned a taxi. All he could think about was that slow, thick blood creeping across the floor from the head of an innocent man.

Inside the publishing house, Ian wondered if word had already spread about the accident. Nobody greeted him with smiles or friendly waves. They just stared as though he'd been recently raised from the dead. The receptionist even shuddered a little when he approached and said that Louis was waiting for him in the office. He couldn't believe news traveled so quickly, but guessed a staffer had seen it and come running all the way just to be the first one to tell the story.

Editors, copywriters, and administrative assistants stared as he walked to Louis's office. Only his editor's secretary was able to give him any sort of smile at all as she buzzed to let Louis know he'd arrived. She pointed to the door, saying that they were waiting inside.

"They?" Ian asked, but the door was open, and the woman pretended she didn't hear. He passed her desk and entered the room.

Louis sat behind his desk as usual, only today he wasn't wearing a suit, but a cream cardigan over a maroon Oxford. Two thick-necked men rested in chairs in front of the desk, and in the middle sat an empty seat Ian assumed was his own.

"What's going on, Louis?" he said while sitting, leaning the portfolio against the chair. The two men turned to the editor as if waiting for his answer. When he didn't respond, the fellow on Ian's right offered his hand and introduced himself.

"I'm Lieutenant Phil Brown," he said as Ian shook the officer's meaty palm. "And that's Detective Ed Chambers."

Ian turned, but Chambers only lowered his chin as a greeting. Ian nodded in return and then looked at Louis. His editor, his friend, wouldn't meet his eyes. He stared at a piece of paper in front of him and then at a corner of the desk.

"We're from the police department, if you haven't guessed. Mr. Kael summoned us this morning. He wanted —"

"No," Louis said, interrupting, "I'll tell him."

The editor took a deep breath, and Ian noticed that a day's worth of stubble flecked the old man's wrinkled chin.

"It was me," he said finally, his voice

catching. "I planned the whole thing."

The full confession took less than three minutes.

Faced with sagging sales and a delinquent book, Louis hired someone to stalk Ian in hope that the resulting press and possible story might inject some life into the horrible quarter. There was never supposed to be the actual threat of harm; it was all supposed to be controlled and managed. Except . . .

"Except what?" Ian asked.

"Except yesterday the man I hired decided he didn't want to work for me anymore. He said you deserved something worse than just phone calls and threatening notes."

Ian gagged. The tie around his neck felt as if it had shrunk three sizes. An elegant noose choking the air from his lungs. He coughed to clear his throat, and his voice was ragged when he spoke.

"What are you saying?"

"I'm saying," said Louis, wincing, "that it's real now. It wasn't before, but now it is." He leaned across the desk and whispered in a frightened voice: "He's after you, Ian. I'm so, so sorry, but he's after you."

The police began asking questions and the

editor answered.

Louis said the man's name was Martin Hanover. He described the man in detail, gave the address and phone number where'd he been contacting him, and even said that he had a high, almost feminine voice. Like a child in a way. Throughout, Ian had tried not to shudder, but this last fact chilled like a sliver of ice slipped down his shirt. Both the officers and Louis asked if Ian was feeling well. He looked at his shoes, thought a second, and then told the morning's story. How Hanover had appeared in the doorway of his railway compartment and then bolted down the hall. How Ian had tried to follow but was too late. How Trout had taken the worst of it and Ian didn't even know how the old fellow was doing.

Detective Chambers left the room to make a call while Lieutenant Brown continued to make hurried notes. Louis had put his head in his hands, and Ian thought he might be crying. The lieutenant stood and walked from the room. When the door slammed behind him, something shattered inside Ian. He felt the pieces cut like glass, and he knew it was the disintegration of a lifelong friendship. He couldn't sit still.

"Are you kidding me!" he shouted, jumping to his feet. Louis startled and looked up. Ian could see that he hadn't been crying at all, just hiding, and that made him even angrier. "Are you kidding me?" he shouted again, and when Louis didn't answer he yelled it a third time, louder.

"I never thought —"

"You certainly didn't think," Ian shot back. He started to pace the room. Curses and anger surged through his mind, but he just walked. Back and forth, back and forth, trying to find the right thing to say.

"Ian —" said Louis, but stopped silent when Ian held up his hand.

Finally Ian stopped, walked to the desk, and grabbed it with both hands. He was close enough that he could keep his voice low.

"Do you know how many times in the past week Rebecca has cried because of how scared she was?"

Louis lifted his eyes, shook his head.

"That's right, you don't! Because you didn't consider that kind of thing, just organized your little game."

"I know," the editor whispered, chin dropping to his chest.

"What?"

Louis looked up. Tears now filled both eyes, and the editor didn't even wipe them away. They pooled heavily and coursed down his cheeks.

"I never thought it would hurt you. Or Rebecca. But then that copycat came, and I thought about calling it off."

"But you didn't."

"I tried, but even then I started losing control. Martin kept making wilder and wilder suggestions. He was the one who wanted you to see him deliver the box. I didn't know what to do." He sniffled before finally wiping the tears off his face with trembling hands.

Ian turned from the desk and took once more to pacing.

"Ian," said Louis, but Ian didn't turn. "Ian, I didn't do this only for myself. I did it for you as well."

A harsh laugh escaped Ian's lips. Here came the excuses.

"It's true," the editor insisted. "Think about it. The sales. Your problem with finishing the book. We're both in a rough spot. I figured this would be a way we could both benefit. I did it for you."

"You're repeating yourself."

"Ian," said Louis, coming out from behind the desk for the first time. He was wearing wrinkled slacks that looked as though they'd been slept in and socks that didn't match. The last evening must have been rough for the old man. "Have I ever done one thing to deliberately hurt you? Haven't I always treated you like a son, my own son?"

Ian said nothing, just stared.

"I did the wrong thing. I thought it was an answer but it turned out so, so wrong. Ian, I apologize. I'm sorry for scaring Rebecca, and I'm sorry for frightening you. I'm most sorry for sacrificing our relationship. I need you to understand that I never thought it would turn out this way. Tell me you believe that."

Detective Chambers walked back and looked at Louis and Ian. Finally he asked if everything was all right. Ian nodded and asked if he and Louis could have just a minute or two more of privacy.

The detective nodded, backing from the room. Before he shut the door he said, "By the way, I asked our sergeant. Nobody knows where the EMT brought that porter. They were going to interview him, but it's like he disappeared." He shut the door, and Ian shut his eyes.

After a brief silence Louis asked if Ian was all right.

"I knew that porter. He was a friendly guy."

"I'm sorry," Louis whispered.

"Yeah, well," Ian said, "you should be."

Nobody knew what to do next. The police continued to make phone calls to the precinct in order to formulate some plan of action, and they assured Ian that finding Martin Hanover was the top priority. He requested they contact Mike Oakley with the Titansburg Police Department and share all the information they had. Detective Chambers said he'd get right on it and bolted from the room.

Lieutenant Brown sat down on one of the chairs opposite Louis. The editor glanced up at him from writing on a note pad and then returned to his thoughts. The officer swiveled in the chair to face Ian.

"So what are we going to do with Kael?" he asked, jerking his thumb toward Louis. The editor looked up at the mention of his name and stared at Ian.

"What do you mean?" Ian asked.

"Do we arrest him?"

Louis gasped a little at the notion and his eyes widened. Ian stopped pacing and looked to his feet. He hadn't even considered that Louis might be arrested. He stared at the editor and tried to imagine putting him behind bars. The thought saddened him.

"Let me put it this way," said the captain. "Are you going to press charges? If not, there's no point in taking him in. He's been cooperative so far."

Louis remained silent, didn't even nod at the policeman's endorsement. Ian thought he looked frightened.

"There has to be some punishment. . . ." Ian said finally, but the words sounded flat. "I mean, things can't just resume as if nothing happened."

"Things won't be the same," said Louis.

His voice irritated Ian. He had no right to speak at this moment, even to say something in his own defense. Ian glared and asked the editor how he could be so sure.

Louis held up the piece of paper he'd been writing on and handed it to Ian, who read through it once and then again to make sure he understood what it said. He looked at Louis, and the old man stared at his desk. Dark rings had deepened around his eyes, and he looked battered and worn. Ian saw the scuffed wedding ring on the man's finger and the photo of his wife perched on the file cabinet in the corner of the room. His anger started to ebb, and he began to recognize how there had been other things shattered today. The man's wife must be nursing her own wounds. Too much had been lost already, and Ian didn't want to surrender anything else. He stared at Louis until the old man looked up.

"Will you do this?"

Louis nodded, twice.

Ian handed the paper back and told him to type it up. He looked at the cop then and said he wouldn't be pressing charges. Louis's resignation would be punishment enough.

On the local express back to Titansburg, Ian could only remember Louis's trembling hand as he signed a battery of police forms and finally put his pen to his withdrawal from the publishing house. Idle chatter from two porters interrupted his thoughts, and he heard them mention the old fellow who got pushed off the train this morning. Ian waved one over and asked if they'd heard anything specific. They looked at him funny and he had to explain that he'd been on that train and, as a regular passenger, knew the porter. Neither could give him an answer, and the worry added to the weight of his problems. Only when they arrived in Titansburg and Ian remembered that he was supposed to attend the writers group tonight did his mind wander off his worries about Trout and his anger over Louis. He took a few minutes to drive to DeCafé and drop off copies of his chapter at the coffee bar. The barista knew whom to give them to. Ian had no energy to visit with the men tonight.

Arriving home, Ian found three messages on the answering machine: two from the publishing house vice president and one from the company attorney. Ian took a few notes, unplugged the phone, and walked to the couch. Alone in the quiet, the worst thought of the evening dawned on him — Rebecca wouldn't be home until after her class tonight. He had nothing but empty hours before him.

He knew the silence would drive him mad, so he moved back into the kitchen, plugged the phone back in, and made his call to the publisher. Soon they'd arranged a conference call with two attorneys, the vice president of editorial, the company CFO, and the publisher himself. Ian couldn't believe he had these two women and three men groveling before him. It was so sad.

For forty-five minutes they discussed his future with the company, and when he hung up, most of the important decisions had been agreed to. His relationship with the publisher was finished, and it looked like there would be no lawsuits. He'd keep the advance for the final unpublished book of his contract and be free from any further obligations to the house. A clean break, it was decided, was best for all.

Headlights appeared at the top of the hill as Ian walked back into the living room, and he hoped that it might be Rebecca, home early from her last class at the university. Instead the car pulled into a neighbor's driveway at the last moment, and Ian realized exactly how much he wanted his wife to be with him right now. To stroke his head or merely look his way and nod while he plugged holes in the sinking boat that was his life. That would be everything. Ian closed his eyes and thanked God for Rebecca as he'd never done before. She was the greatest portion of his happiness and the one part of his life that made sense anymore.

MORNING. THURSDAY, AUGUST 15

Rebecca called Louis every name she could think of and then made up a few more on the spot. She rattled dishes in the sink, slammed a few doors, and even yelled at the dog for getting in her way. Cain slunk outside when Ian offered her the choice and watched from the safety of the porch as Rebecca continued her rant.

"The worst part of it," she said, her voice lowering into a quiet tremble, "is that it isn't over. It's not over, can't you see that? He's still out there."

Ian tried to wrap his arms around her shoulders, but Rebecca refused any easy comfort and slipped from his grasp, ducking to the other side of the kitchen table. Ian could see she was fighting back tears, and his own anger at Louis began to rise again. Perhaps the man had gotten off too easily, perhaps he deserved a greater punishment. Before he could second-guess himself anymore, he tried to explain it to her.

"I did what I thought was best."

She snorted.

"Bec, listen. I've severed my relationship with the house. They wanted me to stay, but things have been so rough these past months that a clean break seemed easiest. They're going to give me the advance on the final book as a settlement. Louis resigned and apologized. What more could I ask?"

Rebecca's lips tightened and Ian knew she was thinking hard, trying to come up with something more that could have been done.

"It was a terrible day, but I couldn't send Louis to jail. Think of Elaine. What would it do to her? Is that what you would want?"

"I want him to feel sorry for what he did," she said and slipped into a chair. Ian took the seat across from her and reached out his hand. She paused a second and then took it. Ian could feel the heat of her anger in the damp warmth of her palm. He stroked her fingers for a few seconds, and as they sat he could feel his wife's pulse softening. The flush lifted from her cheeks and she sighed.

"I need to go to work."

Ian squeezed her hand and then let go. They stood and Ian walked over to the garage door to give her a hug. He told her to give him a call if she got upset again. She nodded and moved to her car. Ian watched as she pulled out and shut the door. He sat at the kitchen table for a moment trying to collect his thoughts when he heard a bark at the door. Cain woofed again and then wagged her tail when she saw Ian moving to let her in.

Ian pulled open the French doors and Cain bounded inside. Walking outside onto the porch, Ian took in the day. Darkening clouds filled part of the sky, while other patches were blue and high. The weather could go either way, but as he stepped back inside and swung the doors closed again he said, "Ah, let it rain."

Out of habit Ian went to his den after breakfast, but when he sat at the computer he realized he no longer had anything to write. He could still work on his tale about the stalking, but he was now without contract or deadline. He spun around in the chair a few times, stood, and walked out of the office again without even turning on the computer. He was unemployed, and for a day or so he was going to act the part.

Stopping at a bookshelf, Ian pulled down the book of letters by the German pastor, which Rebecca had been reading. It intrigued him that Katherine Jacoby could understand the love of God and the sacrifice of His son through a journal written by a prisoner. Three letters in, he felt weary and saddened once more. There was so much hope in the early letters the man had written from prison, yet he knew the horrible ending. He knew the Nazis would kill Bonhoeffer. Ian closed the book and stood wondering if a similar fate was playing out in his own story. Was there some inevitable ending toward which he and this stalker were straining?

Before he could help it, yesterday's encounter played through his mind — the first it had since finding out about Louis's betrayal. He remembered the dawning realization that somebody was hovering over him in the dark. The voice speaking his name sounded like the whisper of death, and in his mind, Ian could see himself rising from the bench, a scream bursting from his chest.

He had to stop. Lingering over it only made it worse. Ian stood and looked around his house, jittery. It was like being uncomfortable in his own skin. Finally he thought of something he could do. Moving to the kitchen, he grabbed the phone and the New York City white pages and looked up both hospitals where the cop suggested Trout may have been taken. He scribbled down their numbers, sat at the table, and dialed St. Clair. When the receptionist answered, he asked to speak with the emergency department.

When the line clicked through, Ian introduced himself and said he was trying to locate a man who might have been brought in yesterday morning for head trauma under the name Trout.

"Trout?" a woman asked. Her voice sounded as though she'd gotten crank calls before and knew how to deal with them.

Ian said that it was a nickname and he

couldn't remember the porter's real name. He knew the fellow had told him, but the name wouldn't come. He tried giving a description to the nurse, but she just laughed.

"An older, black gentleman with a cut on his head? Sir, do you know how many people we treat every day here? I can't find anyone just by a description."

Ian said the fellow was a porter on the *Coastal Express,* but the nurse still couldn't find anything. Finally she recommended that Ian get the man's name and call back later. She had more important things to do than play hide-and-seek with a missing patient.

Ian hung up and tried Roosevelt. This nurse didn't even let him give a description — no name, no chance. Ian dropped the phone on the table and swore at himself for forgetting Trout's name. How could he know something like that was going to be important? He tried the railroad's human resources department but got an overly suspicious manager on the phone, who insisted that personnel information remain strictly confidential. After pleading for a minute, Ian hung up.

He tried once more to remember but

could recall only that it was in the Bible and it was a nickname God had given to someone else. Which meant there was one place he should look. Moving back to the bookshelf, he pulled down his Bible. Before even opening it, it seemed appropriate that he might ask for help, so he said a quick prayer for guidance, cracked the spine, and started to search — *In the beginning. . . .*

Ian had scanned fifteen chapters of Genesis when the phone rang. He thought it might be Rebecca or a lawyer and was surprised to hear Pete Ray asking how everything was going. Ian said fine, just fine, at once realizing how huge a lie that was. He was sitting here searching through the Bible for the name of man whose head was cracked open.

"Actually, not so good," he admitted but said it was a long story.

"Well," Pete said, "I called to check in, since you didn't make it to group last night. I was wondering if you could make lunch. Could you tell your story there?"

Ian made a move for his calendar and realized he had absolutely no plans. Getting away from the house might be the best thing for him. He said he'd be there, hung up, and returned to his search.

Page after page passed beneath his eye, but no name rang a bell. In fact, after a few minutes all the names began sounding alike, and as lunch approached Ian decided to give up the chase until he could get some assistance. Pete knew his Bible and might be of help. The kid, Jaret, certainly could give him suggestions. Before leaving, Ian called his wife to let her know where he'd be, then headed out the door to the Szechuan Tiger.

Pete arrived a minute after Ian, and as they waited for their order Ian asked how the store was doing. Pete said it was fine, just fine. It was the line Ian had used on the phone earlier, and he wondered if it meant for Pete what it had for him.

After the waiter reappeared with the appetizers, Pete cleared his throat and said that he had seen Ian at the pool service on Sunday but didn't get a chance to speak with him.

"I took off right as the service ended."

Pete nodded and asked if Ian had liked it.

"Yeah!" said Ian, surprised at his own enthusiasm. "I'd never seen anything like it. You know, it reminded me of Jaret's story. All those people talking about becoming Christians, telling about who guided them. It was like his story come to life."

Pete smiled, said he hadn't thought about it that way but agreed. Then he said he had read Ian's chapter when he'd gotten home from the coffee shop last night.

Ian stopped chewing and realized he felt unaccountably nervous. He searched Pete's face for a reaction, but the man was expressionless. Ian wondered if he'd said anything wrong in the pages. Or maybe the chapter made no sense. He tried to sound casual when he asked what Pete thought about it, but his right knee took to pumping like a piston.

"Was it what you expected?" he inquired.

Pete burst with laughter. "Not at all," he said. "I was expecting more of the transparent man story. Or a chapter from the memoirs you mentioned starting. Anything but your testimony."

The food arrived before Ian could respond, and after Pete blessed the meal he started in with a few questions he had about Howard Kepler and the timing of certain events that came across a touch unclear in the chapter. Ian, nerves restored, cleared up things as much as he could and asked how the writers group had gone.

Pete said the group had gone fine, though Kevin was pretty rattled.

"He really wanted to talk to you about

something, but he wouldn't say what."

Ian tried to think of anything the teacher might have to discuss with him, but the only things they had in common were Norman Gruitt and Cheryl Rose. He wondered if it had to do with one of them. Another request for an interview perhaps. He stabbed at a water chestnut with his fork and watched as Pete plucked a tiny cashew from his plate with chopsticks. He asked where Pete had learned that.

"China," said Pete.

"Good place to learn."

"Spent some time there in the early eighties," the man answered but didn't explain.

They ate for some time in silence before Pete finally asked Ian to tell the long story that had kept him away last evening. Ian closed his eyes and stopped eating. He placed his utensils on his plate as he thought, and Pete said not to worry about it if it was too stressful. Ian lifted his head, said it was fine, and began recounting his day, ending with watching his editor — his friend — sign an apology and resignation. Pete remained silent and just shook his head when Ian finished. He started to say something about the pain of being betrayed, stopped, and asked how long Ian had known Louis.

"Over twelve years."

"I'm very sorry," Pete said finally, and it sounded to Ian like he was. What more could the man have said? The check came and Ian grabbed it first, so the two men made their way to the register.

"Glad I called," Pete said after the bill had been paid. He reached for two fortune cookies from a basket and handed one to Ian. "I wanted to get together and say how great it was to read your story. A couple weeks ago you said you weren't sure, but I can tell you that I'm convinced."

As Ian opened his cookie he said, "It was one of the hardest things I've ever done. I just feel like I understand so little." Pinching out the slip of paper, he glanced at his fortune — *Take time in your day to smile* — and ate the cookie.

"Just concentrate on the basics as Howard explained and you'll be all right," Pete said. He paused a second and added, "If you ever have any other questions on the Bible or the church, you can always come to me or Jaret. He'd be thrilled to answer."

Ian smiled, said he had one right off the bat. Pete waited.

"Do you know any nicknames given by God to people in the Bible?"

At home Ian continued his search. Pete's suggestions had intrigued him, but he knew they weren't what he was looking for. Jesus had given the names Peter and Paul to those two apostles, but Ian knew Trout's nickname was something long and out of the ordinary. Something from the Old Testament. Skimming now, Ian paged his way through Exodus and then Leviticus before coming to Numbers and the census. He made it through one chapter before he began laughing: The whole book was nothing but names.

After dinner that night Rebecca started to do the dishes, but Ian waved her off. She was the breadwinner in the family now, so he would take care of cooking and cleaning and soap opera watching. Rebecca laughed and put in no argument, just sat at the kitchen table and sipped her iced tea. She said she'd had a good day at work, but Ian could tell something was bothering her. Her laughter sounded light, but it dissolved too quickly, and her smiles lasted but a moment this evening. He tried to ask her about it as he filled the dishwasher, but she didn't offer any concrete answer, just stared through the kitchen door into the yard.

Ian closed the dishwasher and sat down next to her. Her expression was serious, and Ian couldn't tell if it was edging toward fear or sadness or simple contentment. Twice she sighed heavily.

Ian asked what she was thinking about.

"Louis," she replied. "What might have made him do such a thing?"

Ian didn't reply. She knew he didn't have an answer.

"We stopped seeing him," she continued. "Except for the Labor Day party and the Christmas bash." She sighed again. "Remember when we'd go over to their old brownstone, and when they were both in the kitchen we'd pretend that we were the owners of the place?"

"Yeah," Ian answered, "and how we always hated driving back to our little apartment."

Rebecca turned to him and reached out her hand. He thought she was going to remark on how long past those days seemed now, but she remained quiet so he said it instead.

"But we're happy now," she said. "Things are better. Most things at least."

She didn't have to explain. Ian knew she meant the stalker. He also realized that things were better between them. The fights and arguments still came but without the ferocity of old. And he felt like he'd learned so much more about his wife in recent years. She wasn't just Mrs. Ian Merchant. At the same time he wondered why the same hadn't held true for Louis. The same number of years had ticked by, yet he had fallen further and further from their lives. And now he was gone.

The impending storm hadn't yet come, so fireflies continued to gather in the lawn outside. Rebecca switched off the kitchen light and lit a vanilla votive candle resting on the table. When she sat, she took Ian's hand, and together they stared out into the darkened yard at the flickering lights of a thousand lightning bugs. Occasionally one would pass right by the French doors, and Ian wondered if it had become confused by the candle's flame burning there on the table. He knew that feeling, chasing something that just wasn't right, but sitting there, holding his wife's hand in the still of evening, Ian felt that he was right where he should be. He had the love of his wife and the love of his God. Concentrating on the warmth of Rebecca's hand and the strong outline of her face as it glowed in the light of the dancing flame, he felt he'd been led right to this very moment.

The morning brought no such peace. For the second night in a row sleep had been wracked by terrifying visions, and this time Ian remembered, if not each one, a good portion of them. Scenes of his books had played through his dreams all night, and each time the villain would step out from the shadows it would be Martin Hanover. Eyebrowless, gaunt, and sneering that the old black man had just been the start. Twice Ian had awakened clutching the bedsheet tight up to his chin, and once nearly cried out when something fluttered by the corner of his eye. It turned out to be just the curtain billowing with the breath of a steady night breeze.

The blustery night blew away any lingering threat of storm, and the morning outside looked crystalline, but Ian couldn't rouse himself enough to appreciate it. He lingered over breakfast, saying little to Rebecca, and made slow work of the morning paper, reading stories he'd normally skip by without a glance. In the middle of an article about the United States Post Office's pressing decision about whom to include in their newest set of commemorative stamps, Rebecca kissed him good-bye and suggested a nap. Ian nodded, wished her a great day, and wondered if going back to bed at eight in the morning could be considered a nap.

Before she made it to the garage, Rebecca turned and reminded Ian that Ed would be accompanying her home from work with the sculptures today.

With that, she left and Ian turned briefly back to the paper. The *Hartford News* had nothing about Louis's resignation, but he bet the *New York Times* might. The thought, though, of driving to the tobacco store in town just to pick up a newspaper and read a third-person account of his own crumbling life seemed like too much to bear, so Ian closed the paper and decided to count this day as a wash. Trudging upstairs with heavy shoulders, he hoped only for an uninterrupted passing of hours in bed. Like some horrible equation, fear without consequence had left him exhausted, but he didn't know if the weariness was great enough yet. Or would he have to wait even longer? Climbing into bed, Ian closed his eyes and hoped the answer didn't tarry.

Voices drifting up from the lawn roused Ian from the deepest sleep he'd gotten in two days. From his bed it sounded as though two men were conversing right on his front

418

stoop, but he couldn't discern either of the speakers. Rolling from the covers, he shuffled to the window and peeked out from behind the curtain. He could see nothing from this angle and was about to walk away when someone stepped back from his front porch.

The man looked all around as though searching for something, and it seemed to Ian that he'd seen the face before. Those slack eyes and the odd way the fellow moved his tongue about in his mouth even when just standing still. Suddenly the fellow looked up, caught Ian's eye, and started pointing. A second man, this one much taller and better groomed, appeared and Ian had his answer.

"Good morning, Ian," called Kyle Turner. "Sorry to wake you, but I was wondering if we could have a few words?"

"No comment," Ian shouted.

Kyle whispered something to fellow next to him, who disappeared for a second, then reappeared with a video camera.

"Three questions," shouted Kyle. "None of those sucker punches, either. Turns out you were the victim after all."

Looking down at himself, Ian grumbled. He couldn't go on television in tatty bed shorts and an old T-shirt. Still, the idea of being justified on Kyle's own television show appealed to him.

"Gimme ten minutes," Ian shouted. "For once I'd like to not look like a wacko on your program."

Kyle grinned at that, and Ian raced to the bathroom to shower and shave.

Fifteen minutes later he opened his front door.

The videographer jumped into position and gave Kyle the thumbs-up.

Turner assumed a grave expression and asked Ian three scripted questions about the confession and resignation of Louis Kael. Ian gave the shortest honest answers he could, and Kyle motioned for the camera to cut.

"That was painless, wasn't it?" he asked.

Ian said it was.

"I was talking to Dave," Kyle sneered, and the video man, the one Ian had shoved, guffawed. Both men walked by Ian to the van. Before he jumped in, Kyle turned back.

"My sympathies, Merchant. I was screwed once by someone close to me too. You just never see it coming." He climbed in the van, backed from the driveway, and headed down the road. Ian looked at his watch and saw that only fifteen minutes had passed.

He felt spared. It had been painless.

Ian spent the afternoon reading: first Bonhoeffer's letters and then his Bible. He hadn't given up hope that he might find Trout's real name. More and more he found himself reading rather than skimming, even though he realized the significance of most of the stories went flying over his head. He just enjoyed immersing himself in the bizarre tales of the early books.

Closing the Bible after reading in the Book of Joshua about the crossing of the Jordan, Ian understood what Howard was trying to express with his broken watch. He pulled the journal off the table and looked up the entry. It matched perfectly. Howard had seen God's intervention in his own life as clearly as the men of Israel had seen the waters of the Jordan River ebb so the ark could be carried into the Promised Land. Ian liked the idea of creating a memorial so that the works of God would never be forgotten, and he couldn't help but think of his own book. Who said a monument had to be of rock and clay?

It was the first thought he'd given to writing today, and it was a comfort to him that it felt so appealing. He might not start writing this very moment, but he would soon. It was a constant in his life, and with the direction his memoir was taking, it was also providing him with a unique opportunity to explore a faith he didn't always understand.

Sunlight reflecting off a car caught his attention, and he saw Rebecca's coupe pull into the driveway, followed by a large white conversion van. The sculptures had arrived, and he knew his help would be needed, so he met his wife outside. She introduced Ed, the driver, who swung open the back doors on the van. Ian saw the enormous cross and a small bundle of towels he assumed was protecting the bone sculpture, *Ezekiel.*

"I'll need a hand with the cross," Ed said over his shoulder as he got into the van.

Ian nodded, stepped up to the bumper, and gave a tug on the sculpture. It didn't move a bit.

"It was a little heavier than we realized," Rebecca whispered, slipping by to grab the towel bundle. "I'll take this since it's so light."

For the next few minutes, all Ian knew was heaviness. Lurching through the garage, his hands straining desperately to keep hold of the sculpture, he wondered if Katherine had melted down railroad spikes and added them to the piece. It must have weighed two hundred pounds.

Fingers searing from the cutting edge of the cross digging in, Ian maneuvered around the corner of the kitchen toward the basement door Rebecca held open.

"Down here for now," she said.

Taking his first step, Ian realized his arms and fingers wouldn't make it. The strain on his arms was too much. Bending as low as possible, he slipped his shoulder into the angle of the arm and then tried to stand. He couldn't make it all the way upright, but his knees and back now carried most of the weight that his arms had once held. He took another step, then a third, and Ed followed. Slowly, slowly they descended the stairs until even Ian's back began to burn and ache. He took two more steps and then felt the smooth, cool cement of the basement under his feet. Laboring for the nearest corner, Ian shouted for Ed to drop his end first and then Ian powered the cross upright by heaving himself toward the wall. Both men gasped for air, but the cross had made it. Ian tried his best not to think about having to carry the thing up a hill by himself.

When they returned upstairs, Rebecca had unwrapped the pile of bones and was untangling the knot of fishing line that held the pieces together. She offered Ed a glass of lemonade for his assistance, but the man declined, saying he'd better be getting home.

When Ed had left, Ian bent down and began helping Rebecca sort through the web of crossed lines and the maze of snarled connections. Each bone seemed connected to three others, and it took them twenty minutes working together to sort the whole thing out. Rebecca stood then and held the sculpture at arm's length so that the pieces would fall into place. Each bone swayed and swung and clacked against another. And though she tried her best to hold it still, the thing rattled like a dry cough.

Afternoon. Saturday, August 17

The caterer arrived to finalize the Labor Day menu carrying a full-color album with photographs of all the foods Ian and Rebecca could order. She'd just gotten past the entrees — hickory grilled chicken breasts, tortilla-crusted pheasant, glazed pork loin with rhubarb chutney — when the phone rang. Ian excused himself, reaching the receiver on the third ring. It was Oakley.

"I've been on the phone all morning with the city police," he said. "They wanted me to give you an update."

Ian said he was ready.

"Martin Hanover has disappeared. They

checked the apartment he'd been renting, they even found his car, but he hasn't shown his face at all. Seems he caught wind of Louis's confession and got out of there."

"Are people searching for him?"

"Absolutely. We had a thorough background check done and a number of jurisdictions are working together on this one. If he goes to any of his associates, we'll grab him."

"What if he comes here?"

Oakley said that they'd maintain surveillance around the house during the night hours and increase daytime drive-bys. It wouldn't be twenty-four-hour, but most of the time someone would be ready and watching.

"The thing is . . ." said Oakley, his voice trailing off as though he wasn't sure he should say more.

Ian asked what the cop was thinking.

"It's Hanover. I've read his arrest report, and it wasn't what I expected. He's been put up a few times, but they've been things like breaking and entering and larceny, not assault or anything violent."

"But Louis said he'd hired the man thinking he'd be easy to control, and Hanover turned on him."

Oakley agreed. Plus, Hanover's record did

show a slow progression and amplification in the seriousness of his crimes. They would be prepared for anything.

Ian thanked the officer for all his help and realized it'd been a few days since he had talked with the man. He asked if any decision had been reached with Anne's mother. Oakley grumbled and said that Anne's father had gotten stubborn and made the decision to keep his wife in the apartment with him even when it was clear he couldn't take care of her anymore. Anne had been so upset by the whole mess she closed the shop for a few days.

"And this is prime buying time, what with people ending their vacations," Oakley said. "We'll need a few more sales this summer to break even for the year and keep the shop running."

Ian tried to give him some words of encouragement, but Oakley assured him things would be fine. He closed by returning Ian's encouragement, insisting that Ian and Rebecca not worry. He would be in touch if any news came through.

Ian hung up and made it back to the meeting with the caterer just in time to sign a check. The appetite he'd been building earlier had vanished, replaced by that constant dull worry which had been a part of his life for nearly six weeks now. He wondered if he'd even get to enjoy his own party come Labor Day.

An hour later Ian felt even worse. He'd spent the sixty minutes searching for Trout's name through the book of Joshua and the first two chapters of Judges without even a hint of coming close. Perhaps it was the bad news of Hanover's disappearance, or perhaps it was Oakley's own obvious worry about his mother-in-law, but Ian's hunt through the Bible now seemed hopeless. A man probably was lying shattered in a New York hospital, and Ian was left thumbing through a book he should have been reading all along. A day that had started with such gorgeous descriptions of food now seemed ruined. It didn't help at all when the doorbell rang.

"That's the event coordinator," Rebecca said, hurrying in from the kitchen to open the door. Ian stood, and peering in from the living room he could see a Panama hat and a tiny man beneath it pale as the stem of a mushroom.

"Ty Caller," the man said, shaking Rebecca's hand. "You have wonderful grounds. We'll work magic here."

Entering, Ian received the same introduction and praise, and without another word the diminutive fellow whisked Ian and Rebecca outside to begin sharing his vision for the party. With the right assortment of decorations, he and his crew could turn their yard into a "festive desert mesa."

Over the next thirty minutes, and with the help of a photo album so beautiful it could have doubled as a coffee table book, Ty Caller wove a vision of what was to come.

"Cholla, yuccas, some barrel cacti, and possibly a saguaro or two," he said, pointing at pictures of the plants. "Sagebrush, some Mormon tea, maybe a creosote bush or two, and some well-placed tumbleweeds. Voila!" He snapped his fingers like a magician about to make the illusion appear before their eyes. Before Ian or Rebecca could respond, he moved on to geology.

"We can do some fake buttes, maybe an arch or two. Like in the national parks out there. That wouldn't be a problem at all." Jotting notes to himself, Ty finally allowed an instant for interruption. Rebecca asked about fauna.

"Ah," Caller said, putting the pen to his lips. "Animals." He thought for a second, and soon Rebecca had signed on for a birds of prey exhibit — falcons, an owl or two — handlers walking around with armadillos, jackrabbits, and a tame coyote, and terrariums filled with an assortment of reptiles including some rattlers, a gorgeous Mesa Verde night snake, something called a chuckwalla, and a gila monster. Ian tried not to think of how many might be poisonous.

A few papers were signed, a check written, and after Ty slipped the money into his briefcase, he gathered his things and said how great it was to be working with them. Rebecca agreed and offered her hand. Ty took it and then shook Ian's as well and said that he and his men would begin setting up on Sunday, September 1. If there were no problems they would be back then. Ian and Rebecca nodded and accompanied Ty to his car.

When he had left, Rebecca turned to Ian and smiled. "You know why I'm doing this, right?"

"So I take you with me the next time I go to Utah?"

"Absolutely," she replied.

Evening swept in a few hours after Ty Caller left, followed with the swift curtain of night. The days were getting shorter; it was noticeable now. It wasn't a change Ian felt good about. More chances for Martin Hanover to hide out. More black corners in which to lurk. If a month passed without his capture, Ian decided that he and Rebecca would spend their winter somewhere else. Perhaps some small western college would accept him as writer-in-residence for a semester or two.

Thinking his lonely thoughts about the possibility of fleeing, Ian hadn't even noticed that Rebecca had finally finished reading Bonhoeffer's letters. Only when her shadow fell thick across his open Bible, across the story of Gideon, did he look up.

"You find your man?" she asked.

He didn't respond and let that be answer enough. She didn't seem to mind. His wife's eyes looked as though they were focused miles away. "You okay?" he asked.

"It's just those letters," she said, pointing back to the book she'd left on her chair.

Ian couldn't tell what she meant, so he just agreed that they were pretty horrible and tragic.

Rebecca's expression turned odd, as though he'd said something impossibly silly.

"It's really a triumphant story, Ian," she said, and when he asked her to explain she tried. Too quickly, though, she got flustered. Hope and joy and redemption all got tangled for her, and she finally just said he should read the book. He'd understand then.

"Can you see why it hit Katherine so hard?" he asked.

She nodded, and he realized the question he should be asking was could she understand why it was striking home in her own life so much. He didn't want to frustrate her further, though. She'd already struggled through one conversation. Before she went upstairs, however, she said one simple thing that made Ian know that she was thinking about the book and her own life quite a lot.

"Wake me if you get up for church tomorrow," she said, ready to climb the steps. "I think I'll join you."

In seconds she was out of view. Still her words lifted Ian out of the funk he'd slipped into with Oakley's phone call that morning. Such advances and retreats. Such small victories and defeats. Sitting alone in his living room, the glint of the garage lamps reflecting off a police car parked for his safety, Ian realized yet again how quickly he forgot the important things. He wondered if his entire life would come down to this: forgetting and remembrance, neglecting and recollection.

"Forgiven and forgiving," the pastor proclaimed in a stentorian voice bold enough to fill even the high ceilings of the middle school gym. He continued, telling the congregation to look at the name of the person they had chosen and spend the next few moments of silence in prayer — "for that person and for yourself."

Ian looked down at his bulletin and the name he'd written in the space provided — the person he needed to forgive. It was the obvious choice and the only name he could think of.

"Allow the promise of God's forgiveness to you through Jesus lead you into a ministry of reconciliation with the people around you."

Ian tried to pray, tried to think how he could even approach Louis, but neither inspiration nor words came, only the fierce grip and heat of resentment. He felt his stomach begin to clench and his color rise, and he knew this was not the path to being able to forgive. His thoughts drifted elsewhere — to the nylon nets and glowing orange rims, to Pete's bowed head one row in front, to the pressure of Rebecca's thigh against his own. Soon Ian felt his pulse fall smooth and level, and he stood to receive the benediction.

Immediately after the pastor said "Amen," the guitarists commenced with an intricate postlude duet and the congregation began to disperse. Pete and Christine turned to face Ian and Rebecca. Pete asked if any more news had come down from the investigation, and Ian shook his head. Things were pretty quiet for the moment.

"Not sure if it's good or bad," Ian added.

Two couples approached to say good morning to the Rays, and so Ian and Rebecca turned to each other. She asked Ian if he wrote the same person on his piece of paper that she did on hers, and Ian said probably. Rebecca then stared over Ian's shoulder and said she hadn't seen the woman that had said those things a few weeks ago.

"You would recognize her?" Ian asked.

Rebecca snapped her fingers. "Like that," she said.

Pete interrupted then and introduced Ian to a bearded fellow who worked for an advertising firm in the city, not far from the publisher. The men, joined by a fourth who introduced himself as Paul, talked about the hassle of commuting into the city and some favorite lunch spots. Behind them, Ian could hear Rebecca in animated conversation about the auction and guessed that she met somebody who had attended it.

Ian and the men chatted for another ten minutes before a few noticed the time and said they had to be getting to their Sunday school classes. Women joined their husbands once more, and the couples began splitting for the various homes and restaurants where groups were meeting during the church construction. Paul and his wife — the woman with whom Rebecca had been speaking — invited them to a study on Ecclesiastes, but the Merchants begged off and said perhaps next time. Ian gave Pete one last wave as he crossed the gym floor to the rear entrance. Rebecca pushed open the door and they were outside.

Bells chimed, like the ones that had roused Ian last week, and he noticed they were coming from down the block. He couldn't place the church that had set them ringing and told Rebecca he wanted to drive by on their way home. She agreed and grabbed his hand. As they walked toward the car, Rebecca saw one of her co-workers. They stopped to chat and the woman, Cathy, said that she and her husband had just started looking for churches as well, and wasn't this a coincidence. After another minute or so, Rebecca said good-bye, and she and Ian strolled to their car, got in, and pulled from the parking lot.

"I think that's what church is supposed to be," Ian said, making a right into traffic so he could track down the bells. Rebecca agreed, and as they pulled up the block she pointed to a squat, stone building tucked amongst a thick grove of trees. Ian slowed the Cherokee as much as he could, but traffic was heavy and he didn't get a good look.

"Did you see what the sign said?" he asked his wife.

"Church of the Savior. Ever hear of it?"

Ian said no and Rebecca said she hadn't either but it looked like a place they should visit some Sunday. After agreeing, Ian took a hard left and swung the Cherokee back toward home on a narrow lane that emptied a half mile from their street. Shadows danced across the road as the light and breeze played with the branches, and in an open field a family was taking advantage of the gusty day to teach their young boy to fly a kite. Ian wasn't sure what his own day would hold but made plans to get outside for at least a portion of it. He'd been too much indoors lately, and the house was beginning to feel like a prison.

Ian's opportunity to enjoy the fresh sum-

mer day came in the worst possible way —
Oakley called and said they'd found something in the woods beyond Ian's property.
He'd be right over and together they'd go
take a look.

Hanging up, Ian stood by the French
doors leading to the deck. Sunlight, which
had seemed as warm and bronzed as honey
tea, now looked harsh and mean as it
poured through the backyard and into the
kitchen. He stood staring out into the yard
without seeing a thing for ten minutes until
Oakley and another officer arrived.

Rebecca, already in boots and a fleece
vest, greeted the men at the door and called
for Ian. He joined them, and soon the four
were walking around the back of the house
and cutting a diagonal across the lawn to a
far patch of woods. Every so often Ian
would turn around to glance back at the
house, where he could see Cain sitting at
the porch doors watching them, a mournful
expression on her face at being left behind.
There was nothing pleasant about this walk,
though, and an energetic dog would have
gotten in the way.

Reaching the border between Ian's yard
and the first stand of trees, Oakley pushed
some brush out of the way and found an
opening through the old wall that traced

the back of the property. Ian had walked this area countless times, but always from the other side. All four slipped through the crumbling brick and angled their way back along the wall for twenty feet or so before stopping.

Everybody was looking down except Ian. He stood staring through a cleft in branches and leaves that allowed for a perfect view of his house while still remaining mostly hidden. Even without binoculars he could see the outline of his dog still waiting at the glass door. This would be the ideal place for surveillance.

"Recognize anything?" Oakley said, and finally Ian's attention was drawn to a small pile of rubbish near the base of the wall. He bent for a closer look. A convenience store bag and two plastic soda bottles littered the ground, along with empty corn chips bags and two tins of tuna. He was about to stand up when a small piece of paper caught his eye. It was a train ticket.

Leaning closer, Ian checked the date — August 14. He shuddered and got up quickly. It was from the day Martin Hanover appeared to him on the train. This was the ticket. The man had been here. He'd camped here and watched.

Ian suddenly felt nauseous and cold.

"Hanover was here," he said to Oakley.

The officer nodded. "That's the bad news. The good news is that he hasn't approached you. Our surveillance is working. He's been afraid, and now that he made this mess it's just one more place we can watch."

"I'd like to go," Ian said. He was finding small comfort in Oakley's reassurance.

Rebecca grabbed Ian's hand, and together they took a few steps back toward the opening in the wall when they heard a sound. From deeper in the woods. It was the crack of a branch. Both turned, but the officers' responses were even quicker.

Oakley moved to Ian while the other cop was already moving off into the woods, hand at his holster, feet barely stirring the leaves.

"Get back to the house, Ian," Oakley said, a ferocious look in his eyes. He turned to follow the other officer.

Ian didn't think twice. With Rebecca at his side, they made it to the hole in the wall, back out of the woods, and were across the lawn when they heard some muffled shouts and a flurry of twigs snapping. Somebody was running.

Ian and Rebecca stopped to listen.

The next sound defied comprehension. It was a car. The distant sound of a car engine growling to life from the deepest part of the woods.

Waiting not a second longer, Ian and Rebecca finished their walk across the yard and let themselves in through the French doors. Cain stood staring at them, a hurt look on her face as though still saddened at being left, but Ian didn't pay attention. He just stood staring at his wife and tried not to think about what would have happened had they taken a walk by themselves that afternoon as he'd planned.

Twenty minutes later, Oakley and the other officer returned to the house. Both were tired, with leaves and twigs stuck to their clothes. Their shoes were black with mud, and they left them on the deck to dry while Rebecca offered some lemonade.

"There's a bog back there," Oakley said, motioning to the woods. "Took too long to get around. Once we did, the guy was gone. He probably knows a quicker path that we missed. We found where the car was parked, though. There's a service road back through there with a small turnoff. From the looks of it, the place is known by a bunch of teens. There were beer cans, a few vials, some empty condom packages lying about. Found some fresh tire tracks, though, so we'll get them run, bag up the evidence outside that wall, and see if we can't find Hanover's fingerprints."

"Do you think you've scared him away?" Rebecca asked.

Oakley turned serious. There was nothing in his face that reminded Ian of the man he was beginning to call his friend. This was Oakley the officer, sworn to protect and serve.

"Rebecca, I wish I could say yes. But after all this time I don't think anything's going to scare that man away. He just needs to be caught."

Morning. Monday, August 19

After Rebecca left for work, a crew from Home-Safe arrived to ensure that every point of entry in the home was wired for security. Serious and intent as ants, the men, led by Don the supervisor, scoured the house, rechecking the first installation. When the inspection was finished, Don made his recommendation.

"The two big areas that aren't secure right now are the attic and the basement. The question is, how safe do you want your home?"

"Impenetrable," Ian said.

Don nodded. "Do you use either area much?"

440

Ian shook his head, said mainly for storage.

"What we can do is treat the primary doors, then, as entry points to the house. That means the basement door and the pull-down ladder in your attic will be wired. They'll lock so that you'll only be able to get out by knowing your pass code."

Ian said punching a few numbers would be worth the added assurance and sent the men to work. When they disappeared, he headed to his den. It was a small act of habit, and when he'd shut his door, he realized he had no reason to be there. Nothing needed editing. No chapter required a polish. He didn't even need to read through typeset proofs back from his publisher. Last week it had all seemed a dream. Today, sitting alone on a quiet Monday, it seemed much more real.

To pass the time, Ian picked up the closest thing on his desk and began reading his chapter that would be discussed on Wednesday evening. In the aftermath of everything that'd happened last week he hadn't given much thought to the piece, except for that one short conversation with Pete over lunch. Sitting back in his chair, Ian began to read. Even though he'd written the words a week ago, they seemed new to him. They spoke of Howard and Utah and of the confusion that had led Ian to the desert in the first place. Reading, Ian could almost hear the echo of his old friend's voice as they talked through faith and art and what it means to see past the horror of this selfish world. Ian tried to reconcile what he'd learned from Howard with the new revelations discovered in the man's own journal. Why had his running away from Baltimore never come up? Nor the circumstances surrounding the family wedding photo? An answer came suddenly to him, and he was surprised by its inherent sense. If they'd wasted talk on other things, or strayed too deeply into the complexities and struggles of Howard's own faith, Ian might never have bowed beneath the pain and longing. It was a matter of time and the right words needing to be said. After all, Howard would fall just a few weeks later.

The whole thing left Ian with an odd feeling. Here he'd written his first piece of nonfiction, a work in which he'd done no plotting of his own, and yet he couldn't help but feel that, in some way, the piece *had* been designed. There seemed to be purpose behind every moment in the story. The clearest example was a portion that left Ian holding his breath.

Howard watched me read. He'd suggested I look through John's description of Christ's death, and as I did he watched, sitting cross-legged on the floor. My first response was from the gut — "It's a pretty grim and terrible story."

"Yeah," he replied. "But get past that and it's the triumphant part that matters."

It was the conversation, almost to a word, that Rebecca and Ian had had last evening. He was still pointing out the obvious and being reminded that just below the surface rested a measure of impossible victory that could be nothing less than sacred. Letting his breath out, he realized how wonderful it was to have his own wife sharing in that mystery.

Perhaps his writing was not quite through. Perhaps the tangle of events complicating his life right now were integral to some story line even he didn't understand at the moment. All he knew was that he wanted to write, to add on with another few chapters to the story he'd already started.

That night, after the final alarm installations were complete, after Rebecca had come home from work, after dinner was eaten and they'd retreated to the living room, Ian found himself watching his wife almost constantly. After a few minutes she caught him and asked why he was staring at her. Not wanting to admit that he was waiting for another opportunity like the one he'd missed last night to talk to her about tragedy and triumph, he just said that after a lonely day with only Cain at his side, it was nice to see her.

"You didn't do anything today?" she asked.

"I wrote a little. Polished up a few lines for the chapter the writers group is discussing on Wednesday."

Rebecca set down her book. "You're still planning on going? Even with the deadline over?"

Ian paused. He'd forgotten that the deadline was one of the reasons he'd joined in the first place. It had turned out to be a good group of guys, and he enjoyed their discussions. It never occurred to him to quit.

"It's fine, Ian," Rebecca said. "I just didn't want you to feel guilted into it."

"I think I'll stay for a while," he said. Then, with a smile, he added, "Maybe they'll have something good to say about my chapter."

"Wouldn't know," Rebecca said and picked up her book. The effect was immediate and unmistakable.

"Are you bothered?" Ian asked, though he knew the answer. He was hoping she might explain why.

Turning to him, she took in a great breath and let it out slowly. "Ian, when was the last time you gave me anything to read? I used to be your first opinion, and now I rate below a bunch of townies you meet for lattes." She was half kidding, but Ian realized it had been a while since he'd slipped a chapter or two her way.

"Your class . . ." he started, but gave it up before finishing. Standing, he walked immediately to his den and picked up a copy of his chapter off the desk. In the living room, Rebecca was already closing her book and readying herself for the pages.

"What's it about?" she asked when he returned. "Is this about the stalking?"

He handed over the pages and told her no hints. Tucking her feet beneath her on the couch, she began the first page, and Ian slipped back into his chair across from her. He had been giving an occasional glance to the Bible this evening, but that didn't even come into play now. He just watched as his wife's eyes moved across the words he'd written and she turned to the second page.

Another two minutes passed and another

page as well. Her expression betrayed nothing.

Ian couldn't bear it anymore, so he stepped out of the living room to fill his water glass. Cain met him at the refrigerator, and he figured a dog eager for love beat the slow torture of watching his wife read. He scratched Cain's ears and muzzle and chest and rubbed each leg until her tongue lolled out of her mouth, pink and moist. Ten minutes had passed. Given that the chapter was fifteen pages, Rebecca would be just another minute or two.

He was surprised when he heard her clear her throat and stand.

She walked to the kitchen and stood watching him. She was a master at controlling her expression, and Ian hadn't even a guess.

"I'm proud of you, Ian," she said finally. "It couldn't have been easy to write that."

"Easier than you'd think," he said. "Starting it was the tricky part."

"Are you going to continue with it?"

Ian nodded. He'd decided that very thing while sitting in his den alone this afternoon. He didn't know if more than four people would ever read the story he had to tell, but for the first time ever it was something that he felt *he* needed to write.

"For as long as it goes," he said.

Evening. Tuesday, August 20

"Ian, this is Mike Oakley," voiced the answering machine message. *"Anne wanted me to call. Or we both did. We know you're a religious guy — we wondered if you could pray for us. It's Anne's mother. She's disappeared."*

There was a pause, followed by a sigh. *"Thanks."*

Week 7

Morning. Wednesday, August 21

Five minutes after waking up, Ian remembered yesterday's awful news. Lois Gavell, Mike Oakley's mother-in-law, had vanished from the retirement community apartment where she and her husband lived. John had taken a nap shortly after dinner and roused only when a neighbor poked her head in to find out why his front door was open. By then, Lois wasn't to be found and the subsequent search turned up nothing.

Ian remembered Rebecca's immediate tears and the way she'd turned to him after hearing the message from Oakley. He remembered their quick phone call to Anne and the panic in the woman's voice as she whispered how very scared she was for her mother. He remembered her request before hanging up that Ian and Rebecca pray, please, please pray. And he remembered praying. Sitting side by side with his wife on

448

the living room couch, he'd just started talking. For ten or fifteen minutes he talked, and not just about Lois Gavell. He prayed about Louis and about Trout and about the search for Martin Hanover. He remembered all of it and one more thing. He remembered feeling, in the midst of his prayer, not that something good was going to happen but that this simply *was* good.

He tried to turn his thoughts to the morning ahead but couldn't. Each time they'd flit to some small detail of yesterday — the mascara smudge across Rebecca's cheek after she wiped a teary eye, the red thumbprint she'd left on his palm after holding hands for so long, the simple quiet way they'd come together in the dark of night as though being as close as possible might cure the sadness even for an instant. She'd cried after that as well.

Mostly, Ian came back to Anne Oakley's request for him to pray and the way he'd taken Rebecca's hand after hanging up and led her to the couch. Thinking on it, picturing it in his mind, was like staring into someone else's memories. He barely recognized himself — but what he did identify, he liked very much. The decision had been instantaneous and right. For this one moment he didn't need the consultations of

Howard or Pete. He didn't need, even, the constant reassurance of being slipped beneath water. He'd acted because he'd known it was right, and that, more than anything else, gave him the trust that his faith in something greater than himself truly was bigger than the exertions of just one man. More and more he was beginning to feel as though he'd gotten it right after all.

Rebecca called in the afternoon, and Ian was glad that she had news of her own to share rather than asking him what he'd been doing. It would have been hard to explain that for a few hours he'd just been sitting around reflecting, praying some more for Lois Gavell, and scouring the Bible for more hints to Trout's name. Especially after he'd talked about getting back to writing.

Rebecca never asked, though. Instead she repeated the conversation she'd had with Anne, who'd called just an hour before. No hint of the woman had been found, and police were now beginning to broaden the scope of their search. Rebecca said Anne sounded weary rather than frightened and figured a sleepless night would do that to you.

"They go hand in hand," Ian said, thinking of his own restless nights torn open by dreams of a man without eyebrows. It was the first notion of Martin Hanover he'd had today, and he wanted it gone. "And how has your day been?" he asked Rebecca.

"Okay," she said. "Katherine's exhibit is getting a lot of attention and lots of favorable comments, so that's nice. The library was awful, though, this morning. I had two old men doing historical research on ancestors who'd fought in the Civil War. Connecticut men only fought in a few regiments, so they went after the battalion registers at the same time. You wouldn't believe the grousing that these two guys went into. I swear you'd have thought it was a couple of two-year-olds fighting for a lollipop."

"Finders keepers?" Ian asked.

"Not quite, but one of them did say, 'I was here first.' Then they started pulling on the book. A hundred-and-thirty-year-old journal, and they were having a tug-of-war. I felt like Solomon with the two mothers."

Ian's breath caught. He knew the reference, but there was something else in the phrase that rang for him. He repeated it to himself a few times while Rebecca told how she had to set thirty-minute blocks of time for each man to use the book.

"Solomon," Ian said aloud.

"What about him?"

"Did he," Ian asked, thinking aloud, "have a nickname?"

After hanging up, it took Ian five minutes to track down Solomon's birth in 2 Samuel, and he realized it would have taken another week or so of hit-or-miss searching for him to have gotten this far had his memory not been jogged. Moving to the kitchen, he found the telephone numbers of the hospitals and added a new word below them — Jedidiah.

The name was unusual enough that they should be able to track a patient down, but after a minute of searching, the receptionist at Roosevelt was unable to find anyone checked into the hospital by that name. So Ian tried St. Clair.

"Who?" the receptionist asked when Ian said the name. "How do you spell that?"

Ian made sure he read the name exactly as he'd written it. He heard typing and then silence. More typing came over the line and then the woman's voice.

"Room 257-C, Jedidiah Respert," she said. "He was admitted last Wednesday."

"That's him!" Ian knew his voice was too loud, but he couldn't help it.

"Would you like me to transfer you?"

Without thinking, he said yes, thanked the woman one more time, and found himself on the end of a ringing phone. Why was he calling? Would the man even know who he was? What if something had gone wrong? Before another question could spring through his mind, the phone was answered.

"Hello?" It was a young woman's voice.

Ian was too surprised to speak.

"Hello?" she asked again and he knew she was about to hang up.

"Excuse me," he said and then introduced himself as briefly as possible. He said he knew Jedidiah from taking the train into the city and he wanted to check on the man's condition.

"Are you a lawyer?" she asked. "Because we're not bothering with that sort of thing."

"No," said Ian and then tried once more to explain why he was calling.

"Hold on," the voice said, and then after a few seconds a new voice answered. Another woman, older this time.

"This is Mrs. Respert. To whom am I speaking?"

"My name is Ian Merchant," he began. "I rode the train with Trout — I mean Jedidiah."

"Yes?"

"I wanted to know how he was doing."

There was a pause. Ian waited while voices murmured on the other line.

"Mr. Merchant . . ." the woman began, and Ian knew she didn't trust him.

"I took the Wednesday-afternoon train from Penn Station to Titansburg every week," he said. "I was almost always the only passenger, so your husband and I spoke quite often."

"Are you the fellow who got torn up by the bush?"

"Exactly!" Ian shouted. "That was me."

"Oh," Mrs. Respert replied, and Ian didn't like the sound of her voice. "Mr. Merchant, I'm sorry but my husband isn't doing so well. There's been some swelling around the brain. He roused for a day or two last week but has been unconscious since Sunday."

Ian sucked in his breath and held it. Having seen the blood, the sprawl of the man's body, he should have been expecting it, but faced with the news, he found himself without an answer. "I'm sorry" was all he could manage, and then a weak, "Can I help in any way?"

"We'd appreciate any prayers," the woman answered. "Nothing else to do but wait."

Ian said he would pray and wished his best to the family before hanging up. When he replaced the receiver, he wasn't filled with that same urge to pray as he had been last night. Instead he stood leaning on the counter, filled with a deepening dread. He had caused Trout's injury. Hanover had pushed Trout, but Hanover had only been there because he knew Ian would be on the train. Without Ian, Trout would still be serving riders and telling stories of long ago.

Ian finally sat down, but when he closed his eyes he wasn't sure whether to pray for Trout or pray for his own forgiveness. He tried both but the words sounded pale and pallid compared to last night. Maybe he wasn't quite as fit and ready as he thought.

Over the next few hours Ian calmed himself and thought through the events of the past day or two a little more fully. For a time he seesawed between which moment represented the true Ian Merchant — his time of prayer or his moment of self-pity. Finally he realized that with such extremes, the truth most likely lay somewhere in the middle. The one thing that cheered him was that, while he'd often fallen into pits of self-obsession before, he'd never spontaneously prayed. And if that was the direction in which he was moving — in which he was being taken — so much the better.

The chapter waiting for him in his den

confirmed, better than any thought he'd had that evening, his realization. This wasn't a matter of on and off, it was a process — one that began in the waning daylight of a Utah desert, or perhaps earlier, and would continue tonight in a small coffee shop. Checking the clock, Ian realized it wouldn't continue without him being there, so he grabbed his keys and headed to his Cherokee.

The roads into Titansburg were crowded that evening, offering Ian the first escape from his thoughts. Blinking yellow lights and crowded intersections meant he could forget about Trout and Anne's mother and simply focus on dotted yellow lines and sharp curves and braking at crosswalks.

After parking and crossing the street, he looked up the block and saw that light spilled from the doorway of the Oakleys' store, though most other smaller shops had closed against the coming night. Ian thought about checking in, making sure everything was all right, but knew the place was open just in case the old woman wandered back to her store. The lights wouldn't dim at A Doll's House that night.

Entering DeCafé, he noticed that new lamps had been added at each corner of the restaurant, and the room seemed to glow in a warm golden light. Cello music, round and full of sorrow, added to the room's burnished warmth, and Ian felt as though he'd been away more than a week.

Kevin entered a few seconds after the music skipped into a livelier piece and joined Ian at the table without bothering to stop for a drink. He shrugged off his backpack and sat, all the while glaring at Ian.

"Hi, Kevin," Ian said finally, since it was clear that the man wasn't going to offer any easy explanation.

"You didn't get in touch with me," the teacher said, his knee bobbing up and down with each word. "Didn't Pete tell you I wanted to talk to you?"

"This has been a bad week, Kevin," said Ian. Kevin's face immediately softened. He apologized but didn't ask any questions, just leaned forward and lowered his voice.

"I helped Norman Gruitt clean two Saturdays ago, clear out the clutter. Guess what I found in one of his boxes?"

Ian said he had no idea.

Kevin pulled a slip of paper out of his pocket and passed it across to Ian. It was a copy of an invoice with Norman's name at the top. Payment was due for two items — 150 Merchant notes and one Monster note.

"So?" As far as Ian could tell it just

confirmed what they'd known all along.

"Look at the bottom," Kevin said, reaching across to point.

Ian looked down. There, in neat script, it read: *Thank Louis K. for me. It was good of him to recommend me.* He glanced up. Kevin sat waiting, expectant.

"He confessed, Kevin," Ian said, folding the letter and slipping it across the table. Hard evidence seemed too tough to hold right now.

Kevin's mouth dropped open. When he finally tried to speak, a jumble of words fell out at once and it took him a moment to sort his thoughts. After a few seconds he asked Ian to repeat himself.

"Louis Kael turned himself in. He didn't mention this, but he admitted to setting up the stalking."

Kevin slumped back in his chair, more than a little disappointment evident on his face. "I thought I'd found a clue," he said. "And here the case is over."

Ian nodded but knew it wasn't over by a long shot.

After Pete and Jaret arrived, they launched right in to Ian's chapter but soon found themselves stalled because nobody could decide what to talk about. Jaret wanted to talk about Ian's description of baptism and conversion, while Peter wanted to concentrate on the winding tale that led Ian to meet Howard Kepler in the first place. Kevin, loudest of all, demanded to know when he'd agreed to become part of a Bible study and what had happened to Ian's novel.

"Why all of a sudden am I reading about some desert photographer who thinks he's John the Baptist?"

Jaret said that the prophet Jeremiah or Elijah was actually a closer fit, and Kevin rolled his eyes and asked why he was reading about *any* kind of long-dead prophet. Jaret tried to explain that Elijah never actually died, but stopped when Kevin's eyes flashed bright as coals. Pete joined the conversation and said anyone who led another person to Christ was, in the most basic sense, a prophet since he was taking the time to explain God's words.

"But —" Kevin tried again when Pete interrupted.

"The problem," said Pete, "is that we're trying to critique something that can't be changed. This happened. We can comment on whether the writing is efficient and powerful or whether there are digressions in the story, but we can't make Ian change his tale."

Jaret nodded for Pete to continue, and Kevin leaned back in his chair, frustration forcing him to tug at his beard. Pete seemed not to notice.

"This is a testimony. The written word is okay for this sort of thing but, really, you've got to hear somebody tell his story out loud. At least that's what I always feel. Anybody can make words on a page sound pretty, but it's a whole different matter talking from your heart." He was looking at Ian now, expectantly.

"You want me to tell my story?" Ian asked.

"That's the way we see if you put the right stuff into it."

Ian looked at Kevin and Jaret to see if they had any opinions, but both of them simply stared, waiting. Ian asked if this was all right, and when Jaret nodded, he turned and looked at Kevin.

The teacher shrugged, said he would listen if Ian wanted to talk, but that he wanted to get a coffee first. Pete agreed that was a good idea and suggested a drink and bathroom break before hearing Ian tell his story.

"Need anything?" asked Pete as he headed toward the counter. When Ian shook his head he said, "Well, then, take some time and think over what you want to say. I know one person at this table who could really use a story about God changing lives."

It took Ian a few seconds to realize the man was talking about Kevin and not about Ian himself.

"I'm going to borrow from the chapter I wrote to tell this story," Ian began, "but I hope it won't be too boring for you."

The others nodded, said they didn't mind, and leaned back in their chairs to listen.

"This all started around Christmas last year. I was supposed to be working on a new novel and found that I just couldn't write anymore. Nothing. I had just finished *Hunter,* and the book wiped me out. I was dreaming about it — nightmares, actually. I realized that the book had taken some feelings I'd been having about evil and punishment to their logical conclusion, and what was there scared me. Scared me and also made me realize that, at my heart, I didn't believe in it. I didn't believe in a world without meaning. The whole thing unnerved me, and I decided to take a four-month hiatus to get my marbles back in the bag. The publishing house wasn't crazy about the idea, but they wished me the best.

"Every Christmas Eve Rebecca and I go to a 'white elephant' party thrown by an old friend of mine up in Boston. Do you know what they are?"

Pete nodded, but Jaret and Kevin shook their heads.

"Basically," Ian explained, "the idea is to give the most hideous gift you can find. It's all for fun, see who can find the most bizarre thing. Three years back I got a full-size inflatable rhinoceros, and last year" — Ian thought a second — "two years ago was a bug collection that was supposed to have belonged to Buddy Holly. It's all gag stuff.

"This past year I got a picture. It's the one I mention in the chapter, an empty rib cage half buried in a sand dune. On it was written what I thought were lines from a poem or something. Usually everybody laughs at the gifts, but nobody even chuckled when I opened this one. It was too morbid."

Ian paused to sip from his water and sort through the tumble of images in his mind. He saw the barren image of *Cage* and wondered if he should say more about it. Or he could talk about the blank screen of his computer that had stared back at him for so long and even Howard Kepler's face, though he hadn't even reached the photographer yet. None of the others said anything, so Ian took one more drink and then jumped back into his story.

"Fast forward three months. My sabbatical was almost over but I still felt groundless, as if I had no idea what the next word was going to be. Rebecca suggested therapy, and I tried that for a couple of weeks, but I still couldn't type more than a few sentences without becoming totally frustrated. Publishing colleagues tried to help — one even volunteered to write a book for me — but I knew I had to do it on my own.

"So I started rereading my books. One after another, trying to figure out the secret of how I'd written them before. When I had finished — late March maybe — I was at probably my lowest point. Not only could I not write, but I was just saddened by everything that had come before. It all seemed so wrong, like everything I'd done was worthless.

"On April Fool's Day I walked into Louis Kael's office and asked for a three-month extension. He laughed for two seconds and then realized I wasn't kidding. We talked for three hours that day, and he tried everything he could to help me get my confidence back. We ended up getting into a bit of an argument, and things went downhill from there with him . . . but I guess that's another story, isn't it."

Ian paused for a sip of water. His mouth was starting to dry up from talking so much, and words seemed to stick on his tongue.

"One day I was searching through my storage closet looking for some old books when I found this framed photo of the rib cage. I'd thrown it there after the party because it was just too disturbing to have on display, but what amazed me when I found it the second time was how it still spooked me. The thing just gave me chills. I must have stared at that picture for half an hour thinking, 'What is it that makes this thing so effective? Why does it have such an impact?'

"I didn't get an answer that night, but I did hang the frame on the wall. Four days later someone visits, sees the picture, reads the words, and says, 'That's from the Bible.' We did some searching and found out that the passage was from a psalm. I read the words and was just blown away. Here I was having problems writing horror, and before my eyes, in supposedly the holiest book on earth, there were these horrendous descriptions. I knew right then that I had to meet the photographer. I had talked with all these other people, but now I had to talk to the person who took this picture. I thought anyone brave enough to interpret the Bible this way would have some answers.

"I knew the picture was taken in Utah by a man with the last name of Kepler, because it was written on the back of the photo. I used the Internet and e-mail to make some contacts and eventually came up with Howard Kepler. I was able to arrange a visit to meet Howard as part of my attendance at a writers conference. My time with him changed my life forever."

"How?" asked Pete. It was a set-up question, and Ian almost smiled at the man.

"My first question to Howard was about the rib cage," he said. "I wanted to know what his vision was behind this horrific image. He looked at me like I'd called the earth flat.

" 'Horrific?' he asked. 'It's the most beautiful thing in the world.' "

"Why would he say that?"

Kevin asked the question, and all three men looked at him at the same time. He ignored their stares and focused on Ian.

"That was my question, Kev: 'What in the world are you talking about? How can the image of a man dying and suffering be beautiful?' "

Kevin looked at Ian and waited.

"Do you know what he said?"

Kevin shook his head.

"He said, 'This image is beautiful because it means the end of horror.' "

"I don't understand."

"Neither did I at the time. Basically, though, through that weekend, Howard talked to me about Jesus' death on the cross and how it was predicted in this psalm. We talked all about crucifixion and read the verses. It's an exact description. But then he went on about the resurrection and how because Jesus overcame the suffering, we have the promise of eternally overcoming ours. 'Horror isn't anything but the fear of death, the fear of the unknown. Jesus' death buries both of those. Death is overcome and everything is made known.' I still remember all those words he said to me."

Kevin protested. "There's still horror in the world, Ian."

"Not quite. There's still pain. There's still suffering. There's even still death. But through Jesus there doesn't need to be any more terror. I believed that way back in December, believed that there was something stronger and bigger than the tales I could write. Now I simply knew what to call it: God's mercy and Jesus' death."

Nobody moved. Jaret and Pete both looked at Kevin, but the teacher didn't change expression. Ian watched the three men, wondering if he'd said the right things, wondering if he'd made any mistakes. Part of him wanted to go back and add more to the story: all the conversations Howard had led out in the desert, his own tumbling baptism, the struggles he'd had with what he believed since he returned.

Jaret finally broke the silence. "Howard's dead now?"

Ian nodded once. "He took a fall in the desert," he explained, "and wasn't found in time."

Pete sighed. Then the room was quiet. Even the music had been shut down for the evening.

Then Kevin spoke. "You don't call that horrible?" he asked, looking at all three men. "This man's life is spent in honor to God and then he's left to die in the desert like some animal, and you don't call that horrible?"

Jaret and Pete didn't move.

Kevin looked at Ian, who said, "I don't know. I can't."

"Yeah, well, I can. And I do."

At that he stood, gathered his things, and

said good-night. He left before the others could even turn in stunned wonder. The door swung shut in his wake, and with it blew a chill draft that swept the ground around Ian's ankles.

AFTERNOON. THURSDAY, AUGUST 22

As Ian searched Titansburg for a small present Rebecca might like for her graduation, a third face was added to his thoughts of Martin Hanover and Jedidiah Respert — Kevin's. The man's abrupt exit last evening had left Ian, Pete, and Jaret speechless, and today Ian felt a growing sense that he'd said the wrong thing. Or not said enough. Or hadn't had the proper answer for Kevin's question. Clearly the man on some level was right. Horror and terror meted out vicious judgment every day in the world. Trout and Hanover, the two faces haunting him day and night, were shining examples of that. Still Ian couldn't shake the vague sense that Howard's teaching had been right. The end of horror had come. He couldn't explain it for himself yet, and certainly couldn't explain it to others, so he just hoped the understanding would come soon.

At the end of Chestnut Street, Ian turned and walked toward a curio shop. As he did, he remembered the china hutch he'd bought here years ago that matched a piece in Rebecca's grandmother's dining room. It was perhaps the best gift he'd ever given, and the memory of his wife's face brimming with joy made him all the more eager to find something wonderful. Not just an expensive memento, but something that would speak to his pride in her. It needed to voice how impressed he was with her as an intelligent and capable woman. It needed to capture the wonder he'd felt when he'd watched her present the life of Katherine Jacoby at the auction.

Pushing in through the stubborn door, Ian found himself engulfed in bric-a-brac. This and that cluttered dark aisles. Strange tin cans with men in blackface filled a shelf. Trunks covered in travel stickers blocked a row. The place was a mess, utterly without organization, and he was about to turn around and walk out when a wall of clocks caught his eye. Ringed in aluminum and brass, they looked like something that might have hung in a mechanic's shop during the fifties. Stepping over a Radio Flyer filled with glass Christmas ornaments to take a closer look, Ian found Rebecca's gift, but it wasn't a clock.

Hanging on the wall to the side was a portfolio bag crafted from weathered leather the color of a bombardier's jacket. Its shoulder strap wrapped around a hook, and Ian slipped it off and held the bag to his nose. The skin smelled warmly of oil and travel and was soft as the belly of the cow who'd died for it. He knew it was similar to his own briefcase, but this one was a veteran, of a vintage his could only hope to achieve. Brass zippers shone as though they'd been recently polished, but the strap and handles were rubbed smooth and golden. It had character and a story behind it. Rebecca would love just wondering whose letters the bag once held.

A young man at the counter shook his head in disappointment when Ian approached and said he was hoping that the bag might have remained a few more weeks. He'd been thinking about buying it for school.

"For my wife," Ian answered as if in apology, and the fellow at the register seemed to accept that.

While the charge was processing, the clerk asked Ian if he wanted to know the story behind the portfolio. Ian nodded.

"Well," said the young man, "there were two owners. The first was an organist who lived in New Hampshire. He used to walk from his house to the church every day with this portfolio carrying the music he had to learn, a newspaper from Boston, and a flask of whiskey. Eventually his drinking and some hard times caught up with the guy, and he ended up killing himself."

Ian must have blanched, because the clerk waved his hands and said that the bag had nothing to do with his suicide.

"The last thing anything heard about the fellow was on his gravestone. Just a string of musical notes carved across the face."

"Bizarre," Ian said, signing the receipt. "Who was the second owner?"

"Oh, his name was Mitchell Standing. He was a journalist for the *Globe.* Toted the bag across most of the continents and all of the States. He started out writing blurbs for the police log and ended up covering the Treaty of Versailles. I think he retired sometime around the Korean War."

This was what Ian had been hoping for, and he shook his head, amazed. The bag had seen more people, more history, than he ever would. He slipped a finger across its mellow grain and then asked for it to be boxed up. Years of wear had worn the leather smooth and light, and it seemed to Ian as he walked down the street that the box he was holding was weightless, a few

471

ounces of story and stitching, a vapor of history held together by worn seams that had seen it all.

As Ian approached A Doll's House he could see Anne Oakley through the open door. She was assisting two small girls and their mother, but the stoop to her shoulders gave him the answer he might have been coming to get. Still he entered and waited until the customers had finished their purchase to approach the counter. Anne gave a small, tired wave.

Ian placed his box on the counter and asked if there was any news about her mother.

Anne's face tightened, and Ian could see the muscles in her neck begin to work. She nodded eventually, and it was a strained motion. A hospital twenty miles away took her mother in on Tuesday evening, she said. Because the woman had been carrying no identification, it took a while to make the link to the missing person's report Mike had released on Monday. They'd gotten the call yesterday and had her moved back to the nursing unit in her retirement community. Anne said she'd been at her mother's bed-side for almost the entire time and had just escaped to the store for a reprieve.

"She's in pretty bad shape."

Ian murmured how sorry he was to hear that and asked, "Do you know where she went?"

Anne didn't move. Finally she said, "She's bruised pretty badly and has the beginnings of pneumonia. The doctors think she might've stayed the night outside on Monday." She shook her head as if trying to shake the image of her frail mother shivering through the cold Connecticut morning, then thanked Ian for all his prayers and support.

"It would have been even worse if we hadn't been able to go to some people. You and Rebecca were a real comfort."

They were quiet for a moment before Anne asked what was in the box. Ian explained how Rebecca was graduating on Saturday. Opening the lid, he asked if Anne thought it was a good gift.

"It's a beautiful bag," she said, "You got it at Merchantile Curio?"

"Just a few minutes ago."

Anne laughed, an honest and light burst of pleasure, and asked if Ian met Jack. Ian said he wasn't sure.

"Oh, you'd remember Jack. He's one of the shopkeepers."

"Young guy?"

Anne grinned. "He looks young, but he's really thirty. He's a wonderful guy, sweet as can be, but he has some psychiatric problems. He's a raving liar, tells stories like you wouldn't believe."

Ian could feel the warmth of embarrassment begin to color his cheeks. "He makes up stories?"

Anne nodded. "About all the antiques, about the history of the town, about the history of the state. Weird stuff that you wouldn't ever guess was false. I've heard tourists come in repeating stories he told, and I just let them be. I guess if he convinces enough people maybe the history books will have to change."

Ian nodded but didn't say anything.

Anne looked a little more relaxed now, and when a new customer entered the store, Ian began replacing the portfolio in the box and said he needed to get going. Anne thanked him once again and told him to give Rebecca congratulations on graduation. He said he would pray for a quick recovery for her mother. She didn't respond as if it was likely, so Ian left and let Anne get to her customer.

EARLY MORNING. FRIDAY, AUGUST 23
With a police escort shadowing their every

move, Ian took Cain for her morning walk. It used to be such a commonplace thing, but now he found his thoughts scattered, torn between keeping an eye on his protection and examining the land for signs of autumn's approach. Acorns littered the ground, and everywhere spent pods and burst sacs lay scattered among the carpet of helicopters and chestnuts. Squirrels skittered through the woods in a nervous fever gathering stores for the hard months ahead. Ian wondered when his hard months would end.

They threaded their way over the ragged, exposed roots of trees and back along a thin dirt path that would emerge opposite their house. Twenty or so yards from the road Ian heard the squeal of tires, a small thud, and the idling of a car. The officer who'd been shadowing him jogged up from behind, slipped past, and headed to the road. There was the sound of the car coming to life and pulling away. Ian watched.

For a few seconds the officer stood looking left and right. Finally he waved Ian along.

"What happened?" Ian asked as they made it to the curb. Cain was tugging at the leash, straining to go down the road.

"Guy must've hit the brakes," he said and

pointed to the crest of the hill.

For a second, Ian could see or hear nothing. Then he heard a yelp. His eyes turned toward the sound, and he saw the same lick of black that had caught his eye weeks ago. Cain, sensing what Ian guessed, gave up her effort and relaxed at Ian's side. The two men and dog stood staring for another few seconds and then walked across the road to the house. Ian realized that, often, the hard times came without any warning at all.

After showering, Ian poured a cup of juice and headed to his office. He worked for an hour or two revising his story, but he still couldn't get Kevin's last statement out of his mind. As well, continuing worries about Anne's mother and Trout kept him from fully focusing. Using any excuse to stand up and walk around, he made several trips upstairs. From the bedroom, he heard the two-doorbell signal that the police had set up to let him know they were at the door. He ran downstairs and opened the door. A large officer named Quentin stood tapping one finger on his thigh.

"He says he knows you," Quentin said and stepped aside. Louis Kael stood, arms in front of him, on the front stoop. Ian felt the breath go out of him, and the officer must have thought that a bad sign because he reached one large arm toward the editor. Ian saw it and waved him down.

"Yeah, I know him. Come on in, Louis."

The editor sidestepped past the officer and into the house. Ian thanked Quentin and, as he closed the door, heard the man exclaim that it had started to rain.

Ian turned and pointed Louis to the living room. After they both took seats they sat in silence. Ian determined not to say the first word, determined to make Louis speak, so he just stared at his former friend, former colleague, and wondered if the man had aged as much in the past week as it looked. Perhaps it was just the hair, which Louis seemed not to have run a comb through that morning.

"I have to get something on the table," the editor said suddenly, startling Ian. "I am here for a reason. A couple of reasons, really, but one that I want you to know up front." He sat with rigid posture, his back barely even touching the cushions of the couch. He crossed his legs at the knee and Ian was surprised that the man hadn't bothered to put on socks. He tried to push the thought out of his mind and trained his eyes on Louis once more, nodding for the man to continue.

"I'm here partly for selfish reasons. More than anything in the world I want to apologize and try to set things straight, but the purpose for my being here *now* is that there's been more talk of bringing charges against me."

Ian narrowed his eyes and watched his editor. He wasn't sure if the man was accusing him or asking for help.

"The publisher — a few of the executives — talked over initiating some sort of prosecution against me. They blame me for losing you."

"They're right."

Louis swallowed. "I know they're right, but I'm scared to death about what might happen." He stopped, waited for Ian to look at him, and said, "Ian, I can't go to jail."

Without even thinking, Ian sighed. This was proceeding all wrong, and it was going to be tougher than he imagined. He lifted his feet onto the plush ottoman at the base of his chair and tried to think.

"Ian —" Louis started, but Ian waved him off. After a few seconds he started as slowly as he could.

"Louis, I've already said I don't want you in jail. That does nobody any good. But my ties with the house are through. If they pursue something against you, which I think they have every right to do, I don't know what I can do."

"Forgive me," whispered Louis, and for a moment Ian thought it was an apology. When the editor repeated it, he realized it was something totally different. Not an apology at all, but a request.

Ian wasn't sure, but the silence might have lasted five minutes.

Louis's head was bowed the entire time, his eyes on the ground, and Ian's own eyes were focused above the man's head out the window. The rain had arrived now, tumbling lines of it that swept across his lawn, twisting and turning in the swirling winds. He stared out the glass without any answers, without even a notion of what to say. Then he looked at the man, ragged and worn on his couch, and the words came.

"I will forgive you, Louis. I do forgive you."

Louis raised his head like someone expecting the worst and mouthed a thank-you.

"Do you know why?"

Louis shook his head very quickly and watched Ian with a wary eye.

"Do you remember those chapters about my life I'd been bringing you, and how you said that they weren't part of a good story?"

Louis didn't respond.

"Well, you may or may not be right about how intriguing they are, but the one thing you have to realize is that it's *true.* I couldn't change it to make something up."

The editor raised an eyebrow. Ian knew he was confused. The man had come here asking for forgiveness, and Ian wanted to talk about writing.

"What chapters are we talking about?"

"The ones about my life. About Howard Kepler and the baptism in Utah."

"Ah yes."

Louis regained a little bit of his energy, and he straightened himself up once more. For a moment Ian thought the man was going to lecture him about meeting the market needs and not throwing a curve ball at them with these spiritual ramblings, but Louis kept still and waited for Ian to continue.

"I'm a Christian —" Ian began.

"So am I," Louis interrupted, and Ian had no idea what to say. He stared at the man sitting across from him and didn't know whether to argue the point or ignore it. He knew the man went to church on holidays, but that seemed like a scant reason to consider oneself a Christian. Immediately another thought reminded him that faith wasn't about *doing* at all, but about believing in Jesus' death and rebirth.

Finally, Ian just started talking.

"I need to forgive you because of God," he said. "This all has to go back to that. If it were up to me I probably wouldn't do it, but I realize how my life was so messed up and I remember how good it felt to be forgiven. I know I need to give that to you. I need to be reconciled to you." He took a deep breath as though he might say some more and then realized there was nothing left to say.

"So you'll talk to the executives at the house?" Louis ventured.

"I'll say I forgive you. I don't know how much weight that'll hold."

"Just tell them I don't deserve to be punished." It was almost an order.

Ian bristled: "You do, though, Louis."

The man's mouth dropped open.

"That's what I've been trying to tell you. You deserve to be punished. I'm forgiving you anyway. That's the whole point. God did it for me, and I'm doing it for you." He wanted the man to see — to see how being forgiven when you don't deserve it is the best gift of all. How it could change your life. How it could change everything.

"But that doesn't help me out at all," the man whined.

Ian only sighed and said he was sorry Louis felt that way.

Thunder and lightning greeted Louis on his way out and Rebecca's return home forty minutes later. Ian promised it would blow over for graduation tomorrow, but when the lights went out a little after eight o'clock he wasn't as sure. The night was spent talking by candlelight, and the darkness occasioned an early bedtime.

Sleep didn't last, though. At 11:58 p.m., every light they'd forgotten to turn off came on with the renewed electricity, and the security alarms sounded their screaming wail. Something about the loss of electricity must have confounded the system, and now a racket that sounded like the end of the world had broken out.

It took Ian five minutes to phone the security switchboard, assure an operator that things were fine, and convince her to shut the alarms off. She apologized for the foul-up and scheduled a maintenance crew for Monday to check the wiring. Seconds after he hung up there was a silence so sudden that it took a moment for Ian to realize the ringing echoes in his ears were all he was hearing. Stumbling upstairs, dazed and angry, Ian tried to quiet his thoughts so that sleep would come soon. After all, tomorrow was a big day.

LATE AFTERNOON. SATURDAY, AUGUST 24

Rebecca graduated. The weather had cleared as promised, and for perhaps the first time in the history of commencement ceremonies the officials kept a steady, quick pace. Fifty-two master's degrees were handed out in less than an hour, giving Ian and Rebecca more than enough time to make their dinner reservations back in Titansburg.

During the drive Rebecca fussed with her hair which, she claimed, still looked flat from wearing the mortarboard, and Ian watched her out of the corner of his eye. All morning she'd been quiet and was just beginning to come to life. Perhaps she'd been remembering the years' worth of work; the long hours in the library poring over indecipherable letters trying to pin down an author; the commute once a week to class and back no matter the weather, no matter how difficult a day she'd had at work. He'd often feel exhausted and quiet at the completion of a book and guessed she was feeling a similar weariness. Her words as she folded the mirror into the sun visor surprised him utterly.

"What would you think if I went back to school next semester?"

She wasn't looking at him, just staring out the windshield at the passing road.

"Wow," Ian said because it was the only thought he had.

"My thesis advisor brought it up to me again when she saw me this afternoon. She said that my thesis was excellent but that Katherine's letters and life have a lot more hidden in them and that she'd sponsor me for a doctorate if I wanted to pursue it."

"Do you?" Ian asked.

Rebecca laughed. "No. Not in the least."

Her response caught Ian off guard, and he was about to ask why she'd brought it up in the first place when she continued.

"I don't want to pursue the degree — I couldn't care less about it — but I feel like I should keep going through Katherine's life. I probably would anyway — she was a great woman — and at least in this case I'd have some academic authority behind me."

Ian nodded. Her choice made all the sense in the world to him. After all, he was the one with a dead man's photo albums taking up one whole shelf at home. Katherine was to Rebecca what Howard had been to Ian.

"So you're okay with it?"

Ian took his right hand off the steering

wheel and reached to his wife. She took it between both hers and held it. They said nothing more as the Cherokee slipped past the sign for the Titansburg town limits and made its way through a quick snarl of turns to their waiting dinner. Silence with his wife had become a joy to Ian recently, a new-found blessing so very different from his earlier life of words, words, and more words.

Dinner passed in quiet elegance and ended with Ian presenting Rebecca with her gift. She loved the portfolio and, just as he guessed, asked immediately about its history. Ian tried as best he could to remember the lies he'd heard at the store, figuring they were better than nothing, and knowing that any story would be fine with his wife.

Outside they began walking through town on the way to the parking lot where they'd left the Cherokee. Tourists were gone for the evening, and the sidewalks were filled only with couples walking hand in hand to the beach or small enclaves of teens who obviously had nothing better to do than hang out against the brick face of a building.

As they strolled Ian listened to Rebecca talk about how excited she was now for the Labor Day party. Before she'd had too much on her mind, but in just the past few days she'd been thinking about it and couldn't wait to see Ty Caller transform their yard into a desert.

Ian was about to reply that Ty Caller had more of a chance of turning Cain into a guard dog than he did their lush yard into a barren wasteland when a face leering from a drugstore window caught his attention.

He stopped.

The man had the same brow, the same penetrating eyes, and the same barren forehead. He stepped closer, and Rebecca turned as well. It was a drawing of Martin Hanover, just a crude pencil sketch with the words *Have you seen this man?* above the portrait. The shop was still open so he stepped inside, got a cashier's attention, and asked why the picture was in the window. The cashier had no answer but used the intercom to request a manager, and soon Ian was speaking with Randy Klimmer.

"Oh, the picture. Yeah, I had one of the kids here draw it up for me. The guy just walked in two nights ago right before closing, grabbed a couple of things, and bolted before we could even move. It was strange."

"What'd he take?"

"That's the odd part," Randy said. "He

got some razors, a toothbrush, some batteries, and we think a box of hair dye. But because he didn't even get twenty dollars' worth of stuff I didn't bother to call the police. I put the sign up mostly for the other shop owners. A guy like that will hit more than one place if he sticks around. Hopefully seeing his picture around will scare him away."

Ian thanked Randy for the information, wished him good-night, and headed for the door with Rebecca. The manager called out a question, but it was too late and the door shut without Ian having to turn around. With Rebecca at his side, they made quick work of the final block and found safety in their Cherokee. The good day, the fine feelings, were over. Ian started the car and headed for home mindful, for the second time in two days, that the bad times could come without any warning at all.

MORNING. SUNDAY, AUGUST 25

Church of the Savior, the tiny chapel sitting hidden behind the trees that they'd passed just a week ago, seemed nice enough, but Ian couldn't concentrate on the sermon, the service, or much of anything. He was too busy thinking about what Martin Hanover could do with razors, hair dye, and batteries.

Maybe the next time Hanover approached it'd be as a blond man with a goatee and penciled-in eyebrows. Or as a redhead with a trim mustache. He could be sitting in this very service watching from the back pew, waiting for his chance to strike.

Ian's thoughts plagued him even to the benediction, and he had little to say to Rebecca on the way home when she asked what he thought. He mumbled a few words about feeling welcome, deflected the question back to her, and was surprised when she answered so quickly.

"I liked the Church of God better," she said as they made their way east out of the parking lot. "Maybe it was as simple as knowing Cathy from work and recognizing Pete and his wife, but last week I felt more comfortable there. That's one thing I missed growing up. The diocese we were assigned to was a different one from most of the families and kids I knew. Going to mass was just week after week of strange faces. I like feeling a part of something."

Ian pulled hard on the wheel to round a sharp turn and flipped down the visor against the morning sun. It amazed him how two people could be living so closely and have such wildly varying thoughts. For months he'd been consumed with God and faith, and Rebecca hadn't had the slightest inclination toward it. Now he was haunted by a man without eyebrows, and she was feeling the same spirit he'd felt earlier this year. He turned and said, "I'd love to go back sometime if it's the place you feel comfortable."

They smiled at each other for a second before Ian turned his focus back to the road and made the slight left into the back entrance of their road. A slim pillow of mist still buffered the shallows at the bottom of their hill, and the Cherokee pulled through it, up the incline and to their house. Inside Rebecca jogged straight upstairs to change, and Ian moved directly to the phone. His first call was to the Titansburg Police Department. Church or no church, fine feelings or none, it was still true that Martin Hanover was in town. Not even the great joy of listening to his wife's interest in faith could keep Ian from forgetting that the man might be making himself unrecognizable at this very moment.

The phone call from Oakley came as a surprise, because the officer who'd taken Ian's message assured him that the detective was off duty all day. Ian had taken that to mean that he was with his family and, most likely, with his family at the sickbed of his mother-in-law. He'd been right about that as Oakley was calling from Bethesda Fount, the nursing facility where his mother-in-law was recuperating.

"Got your message, Ian. Thanks for calling. We'll talk to the druggist and get the word out." His voice could barely be heard through the crackle of the line. Bethesda must have old pay phones.

"How's Anne's mother doing?"

"Not so good," Oakley said, sighing. "She seemed to be recovering yesterday, but it's gone downhill since then. Who knows, at this point."

"We'll keep praying," Ian assured the officer.

"For Anne," Mike replied. "Pray for Anne." Then he hung up.

Rebecca had come downstairs during the conversation, and Ian just gave a small frown and shrug when she looked at him, waiting. She was dressed for lunch with Cheryl Rose and had more of Katherine's notebooks along with photos of the woman's sculptures under her arm. The reporter needed more information for her feature on Katherine Jacoby, and Rebecca looked thrilled to help.

"Nothing new?" she asked, moving to the door.

Ian shook his head.

"I'll be back for dinner, then. You be good." She slipped out the door, and Ian was left in silence with an order he had no problem at all obeying. He could be good in his sleep — but could he be good and find something interesting to do all at the same time?

The search ended before it got started. He realized, after not being able to get Oakley's voice out of his head, that he should head down to the nursing home and pay the family a visit. That's what caring people do. That's what friends do. Without another thought, he was out the door and on his way.

Bethesda Fount was the sort of place where Ian didn't want to die but knew he probably would. Prim and pristine, the neat bungalows and tidy apartment blocks looked like the plastic dollhouses lining the shelves of the Oakleys' store.

Inside, the distracted on-duty nurse pointed a finger in the general direction of Lois Gavell's room. As he walked down the hall he heard a woman begin to shriek from

491

somewhere along the back of the wing, but with the click of a closing door the cries fell silent. Ian threaded his way between two heavy canvas carts and found the doorway to Mrs. Gavell's room.

He knocked on the frame and leaned in. A tiny woman with yellow skin and darkened eyes looked up from the pillow but didn't speak. There was nobody else in the room. He retreated to the nurses' station and asked if the Oakleys were nearby. The woman said he'd just missed them. The whole group had left to find lunch.

Ian paused, not knowing what to do. The nurse waited for a second and, when it was clear he had no questions, went back to entering something into the computer. Ian took a few steps toward the exit and realized that was silly. He could visit the woman, what harm would it be? Turning, he headed back to the room. She was still staring at the doorway when he entered.

"Are you here to see me?"

Ian couldn't believe that the wasted figure on the bed could even draw enough breath to speak, but he nodded and took a few steps into the room. A bright bouquet of daisies and fragile wild flowers guarded the windowsill, and there was a guest book next to it. The woman raised a finger and pointed for Ian to sign in.

After he scribbled small hopes for a return of health, Ian took a seat and introduced himself and explained that he knew her daughter and son-in-law. The woman made no reply to his name nor to Anne's and Mike's names. She simply closed her eyes and focused her attention on inhaling. Ian could hear each bitter, ragged breath.

Ian watched the trembling covers as the woman fought for each gasp and wondered what the chances of her dying right here and now were. His legs twitched, but he didn't move. He wanted to say at least one thing to this woman, something more than his name.

"I heard you weren't feeling so well," he tried, but his words echoed in the empty room, and the woman didn't even open her eyes at the sound of his voice.

"Perhaps . . . perhaps there's something that I might be able to pray about with you?" It was what he'd promised Oakley.

Mrs. Gavell stirred at this, and it seemed to Ian that she was trying to turn over. He stood, anxious and ready if anything might happen, but the woman just blinked slowly.

"Are you here to see me?" she asked.

Ian swallowed twice and left the room without a single prayer. She wouldn't remember he'd been there and he had no idea what good he would have done. Mike had been right — Anne needed the prayers most of all.

At home Rebecca still hadn't returned, and Ian began to feel guilt over abandoning Lois Gavell's room so quickly. He tried to occupy his mind but reading failed because he couldn't get comfortable, and writing failed because he kept accusing himself of weaseling out of a difficult situation without doing the one thing he'd promised. And so, before he tried anything else, Ian prayed. It was halting and simple, but he prayed. For Anne and Mike and Anne's father. For the caretakers at Bethesda and for Mrs. Gavell herself. He prayed that somehow, through all this, she might not be quite so lost to the family who loved her.

When he opened his eyes Cain stood staring up at him, a puzzled expression in her eyes. Words uttered to an invisible God, no matter how omnipresent, would likely strike a dog as strange. Ian smiled as he called her to him and rubbed her muzzle. She snuffled his hand and gave a big sigh before flopping in pleasure at his feet. Left with the quiet, Ian turned to the only things handy, Howard's photo albums.

For the most part the photographs had to be symbolic of something, though many times Ian could barely even make a guess. A picture of a raven straddling the center line of a New Mexico highway coupled with a portion of Levitical law must have made some sense to Howard Kepler, but Ian preferred the images he could reason out. The fork of lightning accompanying a verse about God's promised deluge. An ugly, stained shirt covered by a scripture about new and old wineskins. A broken porcelain doll as an image of martyrs for God being stoned.

The images Ian liked best — the ones his eyes lingered over — were the self-portraits of Howard Kepler. Flat-topped, fresh-scrubbed whippersnapper. Serene middle-aged photographer with a lens held to his eye. Gnarled old goat with wiry hair. The verses Howard chose to illustrate with pictures of himself seemed mostly to be random. In all there couldn't have been more than fifty of them throughout the binders, but there always seemed to be a brutal honesty lingering in each gaze. Worst of sinners. Child of God. The dichotomy came through in the deep liquid eyes of the man, regardless of age, and the photographs of him as an older man seemed to reveal it even more. Howard had the far-off gaze of one comprehending something even angels would yearn to know.

Toward the end of the last album, in the photos covering the epistles of Peter and John, Ian discovered the one image that truly puzzled him. It didn't seem to be symbolic — a close-up of a rusted seat belt from a scrap-iron junker — yet Ian couldn't understand why Howard had chosen it.

The passage, a section from 1 John, read, "I write to you, fathers, because you have known him who is from the beginning. I write to you, young men, because you are strong, and the word of God lives in you, and you have overcome the evil one."

It made no sense. Like Lois Gavell's fractured mind, it held a story never to be told. Ian stared at it for a few moments and shut the book, surprised by the fierce grief he felt thickening his throat and singeing his heart. There was something in the longing that spoke of family and loss and sorrow, and he realized that perhaps he too needed a prayer of understanding and sympathy.

A little after five o'clock, Ian began to wonder what was keeping Rebecca. He couldn't imagine her discussing Katherine

Jacoby for more than four hours on a follow-up interview and began to worry. The first ugly thought was a simple vision of a man stepping from an alley and reaching for her slender wrist. The second was more involved and included a tense car chase over the hills of Connecticut. Before the third could arrive he saw her coupe pull into the driveway. As quickly as they'd come, the dark visions were gone and he waited for his wife to enter the house.

Only she didn't come in.

For minutes Ian waited and just as he was about to check again, she entered. She smiled at him, but Ian knew something was amiss. After years of marriage, they'd developed a sense of rhythm and timing. He knew the syncopation of her walk and the short time she'd hold her breath before the punch line of a joke. Tonight, in just the slightest of things — her coming home late, the way she didn't enter the house right away — something felt different. Even the set of her jaw. It looked as though she was thinking about something quite complicated.

"Ian," she said, moving to him and wrapping her arms around him. This also he hadn't expected.

"Everything okay, Bec?"

She lowered her head for just a slight second, raised it, and held out her hand to him. In it sat something smooth, round, and dark. Like the whorl of a snail's shell.

He stared at the object she held, not recognizing even an angle or curve until in a blink the image shifted. Like one of those poster illusions the item suddenly gained depth and relief. He swallowed once and looked back to his wife.

"She made it" was all Rebecca said.

Ian looked back down to the carved figure in her hand. Ian traced his finger over the curve of the back and touched the tiny bent head of the figure. Hands were clasped together at the forehead, and Ian thought he'd never seen a more beautiful image of a person crouched, bowed and genuflecting, in his life. He lifted it from Rebecca's hand and the sculpture felt as though it weighed nothing. It was an apparition — airy as shadows, slight as a memory.

"It was the book," she said.

Ian looked up.

"I was telling Cheryl about finding Katherine's letters in the big sculpture and mentioned that we'd bought the smaller replica. She asked what was inside that one. I said I didn't know, you and I'd never opened it. We left lunch right away and drove here." She reached into her pocket and held out a slip of paper.

Ian took it and smoothed out what looked to be a page torn from a sketch pad. He read the scribbled lines as best he could and realized three lines in that it was Katherine's testimony etched onto paper in the very moments following the bowing of her heart and the urgent plea for God to call her by her true name, whatever it may be. At the end there was a short set of directions to find the carving she'd been working on that evening. It would stand as her symbol to the power of a bowed heart.

"The praying woman?" Ian asked, looking up at Rebecca.

She nodded, almost shyly. "The house hadn't been sold yet, and we still had the key at the museum, so I grabbed a flashlight and headed over there. It was in the corner of her bedroom, under a loose floorboard."

Ian asked what had happened next.

"Next," she said, looking down at the table, her voice dropping, "next, I decided that I need to make some changes in my life. You've shown me, some of the people at church. And Katherine. This just sealed it for me. I've been missing it for a long time."

Ian's pulse thudded and his lips felt heavy. He hadn't felt this giddy, this nervous, in his wife's presence since that golden autumn day in Boston, throwing helicopter seeds into the Charles River, when he'd asked her to marry him. Just as then, he reached for her hand.

"Are you feeling all right?" she asked.

Ian tried to stop it, but he couldn't. He smiled. Soon after came a small laugh and then a larger one. They couldn't be stopped, and soon Rebecca was smiling along with him.

"What in the world is the matter?" she asked.

"You're my wife," he replied, and it made sense in a way it never had before.

Morning. Monday, August 26

Oakley phoned Monday morning before Rebecca had even stepped into the shower to let them know that his mother-in-law had died during the night. Complications from the pneumonia she'd contracted were the official explanation, but Oakley said they all knew what killed her was that night out alone.

"Even with the Alzheimer's," Oakley said, "she'd always pretended nothing was wrong. She'd smile through each and every time she forgot her own daughter's name. After that night, though, it was like she stopped pretending and finally owned up to how lost she was." There was a heavy relief in the man's voice, which he made no attempt to cover.

Rebecca nudged at Ian's elbow and whispered for him to ask how Anne was faring.

There was a pause before Oakley gave his answer.

"Worse than I expected. Worse than I think she ever expected."

Ian saw Rebecca watching him for an answer, so he simply closed his eyes and shook his head. It was the closest thing to what he was feeling — a growing understanding that the pain hadn't ended for the Oakleys but had simply gotten sharper and deeper.

"She never came back," the officer said in ending. "I think we expected one more chance — just a miracle or something. It never happened."

Ian said again how truly sorry he and Rebecca were, and on Rebecca's prompting asked if they needed anything taken care of with the house or meals. Oakley assured them that between the police wives and the doll shop staff they already had more offers for casseroles than they could ever eat. A small prayer for his wife and his father-in-law would be all they would need. And, if it was possible, it would mean a lot if they could make it to the funeral mass on Friday afternoon at St. Mary's. Ian said they would most certainly be there, gave more quick condolences, and then hung up and wrapped his arm around the waist of his wife. Rebecca leaned into his chest and together they stood in silence, consoling themselves with the unsatisfying assumption that a Monday beginning with death couldn't possibly get any worse.

Left alone in the house after his wife left for work, Ian found himself frustrated over the recent news. Why had the woman had such a predilection, such a drive, to find water? He'd asked Oakley if she had said anything before passing, but she'd died in silence. Ian recalled his first impression of her — standing outside of the doll store asking if he was a friend of the pool man. His novelist's heart rejected the idea of some thread not being knotted up in the end, and it gnawed at him throughout the day. This death did not make sense the way others had.

Howard Kepler had not been searching for heat but had been purposefully exploring the desert when he'd taken his fall. Trout had been standing guard at the top step of his rail car when the quick shove to the small of his back had sent him tumbling. His death, were it to happen, would make a bitter kind of sense. But this woman, leaving warmth and safety to follow some distant memory she kept hidden as a treasure left him anxious, even jittery. He wanted an answer.

What he got instead was a crew from the home-security company and a quick fix to his security problems. Ten minutes after arriving, they called Ian into the basement, pointed to the little changes they'd made.

"No more alarms, then, in the middle of the night?" Ian asked the foreman.

"That's right," the man assured him.

Satisfied, Ian motioned that the workers could head upstairs. Despite the warmth of summer, the basement was always a damp, clammy place, and already he could feel the chill begin to seek his bones. As they moved past stacks of boxes and around to the staircase, Ian saw one of the men nod his head off to the right and lean toward the fellow he was following.

"Do you think he uses that?" the man whispered, loudly enough that Ian could hear.

Ian turned his head and saw that what they were talking about was Katherine Jacoby's sculpture of the cross. It stood against the wall where they'd left it over a week ago, and Ian knew of no plans to move it anytime soon. He kept his eyes on it and the rib cage wind chime as he climbed the stairs until they were out of view. At the top he switched off the light and shut the door, the tiniest secondary click audible as the door locked from the inside. The alarm was fixed once more, and again his home was secure. Ian felt no immediate difference.

Rebecca swept through the door twenty minutes after the repair crew had pulled from the driveway. Normally she was one to walk through the door, perhaps even stumble into the house, after long hours of work, but this afternoon she practically floated.

"Good day at work?" Ian asked.

"Terrible," she answered. "But I'm not there anymore, I'm here. With you and that adorable dog of ours."

Cain looked up from her spot at the end of the couch as though she knew Rebecca was speaking about her and then joined the couple in the kitchen. For a few seconds Ian wondered if this was what it felt like with a real family — two-point-five kids, eager and bright — remembered he'd never know, and then got the treat of his life. Instead of the usual pang of regret — disappointment that biology would prevent them from being parents — Ian felt only a simple joy. He felt pleasure in his wife, amusement at this surrogate child who drooled too much, and sheer wonder that, in the end, this was family. The moment lasted but a second and then was gone.

He sat at the table. Rebecca unloaded her new leather bag and joined him. Cain stared at them as though wondering why she'd bothered to come over if all they were going to do was sit, before wandering back to the matted spot of carpet where she lay once more. Rebecca asked if Ian had heard anything more from the Oakleys and he said he hadn't. He inquired if anybody mentioned her new portfolio. She admitted grudgingly that nearly everyone who saw it exclaimed over it.

"You give a good gift," she said. She was all smiles again.

"Everything okay?" he asked.

Rebecca hesitated a moment before saying, "Actually, I have a surprise for you."

Ian had no idea what it could be.

"I made a phone call to the church this afternoon. I'm going to talk to the pastor about being baptized. Maybe even this Sunday."

Ian leaned forward, stunned. "That's . . . terrific."

"I wanted a moment," she said. "Like Katherine carving that figurine or your meeting with Howard."

"I understand," he said, and he did. He reached for her arm, and as he did, saw his fingers shaking with either great joy or great unworthiness. He knew that prayers he'd never put to words had been answered right before his eyes. He'd been so afraid of turning Rebecca off to the importance he'd found in God that he hadn't realized how close his wife had been to recognizing the same thing. Through no part of his own, she had come back to arms and hands he knew could never fail her.

Just before mounting the stairs for the night, Ian realized he hadn't heard about Trout in some time. He looked at the clock and wondered if it was too late to call the hospital, but realized instantly what a ridiculous thought that was. Ian tried to convince himself that he couldn't hear two sets of horrible news in one day and made the call.

"Mr. Respert was upgraded to stable

condition this afternoon," a nurse reported. Ian could actually hear a smile in her voice. Giving out good news was probably a treat for her. Ian asked when Trout would be released.

"Doctors are keeping him for observation until Thursday morning."

Ian thanked the woman and then clicked the phone off. A day that had started with death had ended with something different. Not quite life, of course, but certainly not death. The best word Ian could think of was recovery — and healing, in its own way, was a bit of life after all.

AFTERNOON. TUESDAY, AUGUST 27

The phone call from Kevin Contrade came at a little past eleven, and by half past the hour Ian was in downtown Titansburg, leaning against the front facade of DeCafé. He waited for the teacher to show up and tell him something he'd discovered about Norman Gruitt. Ian felt the warmth of the brick on his back and comforted himself with the aroma of brewing coffee that seeped through the café's screen door. There was no music inside, and outside was just as quiet. A few automobiles lazed their way down the street, and even though it was near the lunch hour the sidewalks and shops were surprisingly quiet. Summer's close was never more depressing or evident than on a late-August afternoon when the town was still dolled up for vacationers, but the people simply were not to be seen. A florist's van passed before Ian finally saw Kevin's brown car take the corner and head his way. Even from a distance, Ian could see he had a passenger, and as the car neared, the face of Cheryl Rose became plain to see. Kevin filled a space in the DeCafé parking lot, accompanied Cheryl to the sidewalk, and offered Ian a firm handshake.

"Things are afoot," he said, a frown knotting his brow.

"Norman Gruitt . . ." Ian prompted.

"Is gone," Kevin answered and winced at the sound of his own words. The two men regarded each other for a moment before Ian sighed and turned to Cheryl, who had stopped at a distance. Without her note pad to encourage her, the girl seemed her age. She smiled thinly when Ian waved, but mostly she looked shy and uncomfortable. Ian wondered if it was even her idea to be standing there.

"I've been to his apartment. It's cleaned out."

Ian sighed. Norman Gruitt was the least of his problems, and he wasn't sure why

Kevin kept bringing the blind artist up. Why bother with the poor fool if he wanted to skip the state and break parole?

"I think you should come see it," Kevin said, almost in answer.

The three crossed the street, took a right onto Holton, and made their way to the row of two-story lofts that housed Norman's blazing white studio. Kevin's limp seemed more noticeable this afternoon, and he seemed all nervous energy. Cheryl walked just to Ian's left, and he realized that the look he'd thought was shyness now seemed deeper, more important than that. It was concern — and not for Norman Gruitt, but for this strange man hobbling over the sidewalk.

Ian saw the apartment entrance ahead and recalled his last meeting with the man. The blank, egg-shell room certainly stuck in his mind as did the odd, unmentioned tension that seemed to fester between the artist and Kevin. Adding the sad story of Norman's incarceration and his progressing blindness to what Ian remembered simply twisted the memory and darkened its edges.

When they reached the door, Kevin neither took time to knock nor even stop and warn Cheryl and Ian of what to expect. Instead he threw the door open and stomped up the stairs, turning around only once to blink at Ian and Cheryl. Ian felt his pulse catch. Something loomed on the other side of the door, he was sure of it.

Kevin turned the knob and entered. Ian took one step and gasped.

The room was black. Windows, light bulbs, appliances, everything. Where once there had been glistening walls that enhanced shadows for the old man, there was now nothingness.

Cheryl, waiting by the door, said nothing. Ian watched her as she looked around and noticed she was blinking a lot. He realized the same thing about himself. Just as he had the first time in the room, he needed to blink. His eyes were so devoid of perception that they simply had to close, even for a millisecond, to regroup before opening again to nothingness.

"Why'd you bring me here?" Ian asked.

The teacher turned and stared at Ian, then pointed to a corner.

For the first time Ian could see the one thing in the room that wasn't painted over with the deepest shade of midnight. It looked like a scrap of grocery bag or a torn piece of tan construction paper.

Ian walked over, picked the scrap up, and read.

In pigeon-scratched letters that seemed barely to be from a known alphabet it read: *You're all that's left, Ian.* There was no signature, no revealing marks of any sort, and for a moment Ian thought that Norman Gruitt himself might have left it. But the words, the nearly unformed scrawl of a worried hand could never have belonged to the man who carved words into canvas with only the sharp point of his brush. This message had to have been left by someone else. Ian flipped the shred of paper over and could make out an address from a Lower East Manhattan grocer. Things made sense only if one person left this note. Though Ian tried to convince himself otherwise, he knew in his heart that it was true. Martin Hanover was around and was more intent than ever.

WEEK 8

MORNING. WEDNESDAY, AUGUST 28

First thing Wednesday morning Ian phoned the hospital again. The switchboard operator transferred his call to Jedidiah Respert's room. A woman's voice picked up, and Ian asked if it would be possible to speak with Mr. Respert.

"Who is this?" the woman asked warily.

"My name is Ian Merchant. I called last week to speak with your husband."

There was silence on the other end for a moment, and Ian could hear murmuring in the background. Soon the woman was back on the line saying that her husband didn't know an Ian Merchant.

"I was a passenger on the train," he said.

"My husband attends to many people, Mr. Merchant. I'm sorry —"

"Raspberry bush," Ian interrupted. "Tell him I got beat up by a raspberry bush."

There was another moment of murmuring followed by a new voice.

"Raspberry-bush man, sure I remember you." It was pale, weak, and breathless, but Ian knew it was Trout.

"I'm glad to hear you're improving, Trout. I was worried." He couldn't help but smile as he said it.

"Well now, that's something. I appreciate your wishes. Guys at work won't believe somebody actually called in to check up on me. The fellas at work haven't even called in." Ian heard the man half laugh, half cough at his joke. "Anything else, Mr. Merchant?"

Ian hesitated, unsure quite how to say what he was thinking. Finally he tried the simplest phrase he could. "I wanted to apologize, Trout."

"Apologize?" The word had taken him totally by surprise. "For what?"

Ian explained as best he could the circumstances that had lead to Martin Hanover making a mad rush to the platform, and when he finished Trout just whistled.

"Boy, you got worse problems than having to worry about me being mad at you. Now, I thank you for checking in, but I want you to know that I'm doing better and I have no blame for you at all. Don't be adding guilt to your problems."

"Thank you," Ian said.

"You're welcome. And I hope they catch the fellow soon. Gotta be terrible having that sort of nasty thing lingering around."

Ian nodded into the phone. They exchanged quick good-byes; Ian wished Trout a full recovery and then placed the phone back on the counter. He was still nodding, slowly, thinking that it was a nasty thing — nasty and terrible as could be.

That afternoon the nastiness gained yet another level of clarity.

"I apologize," Oakley said the moment Ian answered the phone. "We overlooked it before."

"What?" Ian asked, mind racing with all sorts of horrible inventions and circumstances that would force someone on the police force to apologize.

"It was there right in front of us, and we missed it. Martin Hanover knew Norman Gruitt."

"He did?"

"They were cell mates for two years right before Gruitt was released. I called the warden over at Manse Grove, and he confirmed it. The two were pretty close. Hanover was young, coming in on a larceny charge, and Gruitt became sort of a mentor for the guy. At least according to the warden."

"What's it mean?"

"Well, it explains Gruitt's disappearance and the note you found at the apartment. It might explain how your editor friend tracked down someone to hire for his scheme. Plus it'll give us two people to look for rather than one." He sighed, and in that second Ian realized that this phone call shouldn't even be taking place.

"What are you at work for, Mike? Why aren't you at home?"

"Had to get away for a little," he said. The authority in his voice was gone. This was the sound of a friend — a worn, grieving friend. "Anne's sleeping — she was up all night working on something for the funeral — and I figured I could come in and get some paper work done." There was a pause. "It's tough sitting around. Her dad is with us, and the poor guy just stares. It's not an easy place to be right now."

"Well, like I said yesterday, if there's any way Rebecca and I can help, let me know."

Oakley cleared his throat. "There are two things, actually. We just got word that one of Anne's brothers won't be able to make it in from Austin for the funeral. He was going to be the sixth pallbearer. I know it's awkward, but we were wondering if you'd be able to . . . lend a hand." He tried a laugh but it didn't sound too sincere.

"Without a doubt," Ian said.

Oakley sighed again, this time in relief. "Thanks, Ian. It means a lot to us."

"Anything to help," Ian said and realized how much he meant it. He heard the sorrow — that vacant monotone speaking of desperation and exhaustion — in Oakley's voice, and it pained him in a way surprising and almost energizing. He wanted to help. It was what he could give. "What's the second?"

"Just a small invitation. Rather than have a reception following the funeral, we'll be hosting one tomorrow evening. Anne wanted me to invite you and Rebecca. I can give you details about the funeral then."

Ian said that'd be fine and promised their attendance. Hanging up, Ian could only hope that at some point during the conversation his words had been a help to Mike. He was, he realized, beginning to learn from people like Pete and Trout the power of a well-spoken phrase.

The rest of the afternoon Ian spent running errands for the Labor Day party. Case after case of what seemed like every imaginable soda needed to be picked up, as did disposable cameras for candids, a guest book, and small candy favors in the shape of cacti being made by a woman two towns over.

Having completed his chores, Ian picked up his Bible. He hadn't read it too often since finding Trout's real first name, but in the quiet hour before his wife came home he began skimming Job. Not liking what he saw there, he moved to the Psalms, then Proverbs, picking portions and paragraphs to read. The utter existentialism of Ecclesiastes caught him off guard, and the wanton carnality of the Song of Solomon dropped his jaw. He glanced at Isaiah and Jeremiah and almost shut the book. Then he saw Ezekiel. In a flash he remembered Katherine's strange sculpture and figured the answer to her title would be found in the book. Weeks ago he had wondered what sense he'd make out of the proliferation of bones, and this seemed as fine a chance as any. He read until Rebecca came home, then set the book aside for dinner.

Afterward it felt strange to be headed out to DeCafé for writers group. Rebecca had always been at class, but tonight he worried about leaving her alone.

"Lock the doors," he insisted before leaving, and she promised she would. Besides, there was still an hour of light left, and the overnight police cruiser would arrive soon after. She'd be fine.

Heading into town he wasn't quite as confident, and twice he almost turned around. The only thing that pushed the worried thought aside was seeing Kevin, alone and waiting in the coffee shop. He looked ravaged.

"You okay, Kevin?"

"Police talked with me today. They think Norman's gone on the run." Ian nodded. It had been Oakley's theory. Kevin didn't appear to notice Ian agreeing. "He might even be helping your stalker." At this he scoffed, dry and almost mean. "And here I brought you into the middle of it."

Ian started to say he had no part in this at all, but Kevin cut him off, his voice thick.

"You ever feel sorry?"

He didn't look up as he said the words, and all Ian could see were the curls about his forehead and the slope of his nose. Still, Ian heard him, and he answered truthfully that yes, he often felt sorry.

"I've been feeling that way a lot, actually."

"Kevin, you don't need to apologize to me."

"I know . . . but Norman —" He stopped. "I think he's dying, maybe. I don't know why, but I just get this feeling. That's why he's taking all these risks. He knows it's the end."

Ian didn't know what to say, but Contrade kept on talking.

"He's like your Howard," he said, and it took Ian a second to understand.

"Kepler?"

"The guy from your book. Norman was to me what Howard was to you, I think. But I screwed up. Badly." Kevin looked down again, and Ian realized he wasn't going to say anything more that night, perhaps ever, about the topic. Someday the man's book would be written, and if it didn't find the flames this time Ian might be able to read the full story. If not, he might never know. Ian wondered how many others out there were putting words to paper for no reason other than to shout or scream things that would hurt too much to say aloud.

MORNING. THURSDAY, AUGUST 29

After a short walk with Cain through the morning's already fierce heat, Ian reclined in his den, waiting to cool enough in the air conditioning so he could enjoy his morning coffee. His computer sat silent, his phone still, and his printer motionless. It seemed like he'd been without them for a while now, even though he'd printed out his chapter for the group just last week. He sat there thinking about his writing, thinking about the group, when a draft of cool air lifted the smell of coffee to him. With it returned a memory, vivid and strong.

He saw himself sitting alone in DeCafé thinking that his world was collapsing. He remembered trying to pen out any combination of words onto his stupid pad and remembered staring at himself in the window as the setting sun left him with only a pale reflection. He also remembered for the first time in a while those two questions: *How will I ever write another horror novel? Who am I if I can't write anymore?*

The first had been answered. He wasn't going to write another horror novel. That was finished.

The second still lingered, only it didn't have the same daunting portentous feel to it now. The pieces were beginning to fall back into place.

First off, he knew he was Ian Merchant. Not *Bestselling Author Ian Merchant* or *The Scariest Man in America.* Just Ian Merchant.

Secondly, he knew he was a husband. Regardless of what happened in the future with work or play, he had Rebecca. She'd been missing from so many of his earlier thoughts, and he now saw how stupid that had been. They were together — through feast or famine.

Finally, he understood that small glimmer he'd thought of only as *life* before. That was all that had remained of a faith left unfulfilled. But then Pete and Jaret stumbled onto the scene, and Howard returned from the grave through his photos, and Ian had struggled through.

And now what?

The question surprised Ian with its simplicity. He'd been given answers to his two questions, and now what was he going to do with that knowledge? Would he write? Would he leave the business completely? Would he bury the past and start anew?

The memoir still presented itself as a possibility, but writing it and having it published were two very different things. Fans and the media were interested only in the macabre darkness behind the life of Ian Merchant, not the blinding transformation that left him seeking God in the wastelands of Utah.

He sighed a bit, finished the last swallow of coffee, and looked down at the chapter sitting on his desk. It was an economical fourteen pages from his first sentence to his last period, and yet managed to tell a good portion of his testimony. To finish it off he needed something more. More than just this stalking, which was frightening and terrible, but ultimately seemed to be without a lesson. He needed more than his wife's profession of faith and more than rediscovering who he was. He needed the final answer to that very simple question: What now? Perhaps the book itself was the answer, but Ian didn't think so. There was something he was still missing, even after all these weeks of change and worry and faith and fear. He felt it deep down, the way he'd first felt after finishing *Hunter,* as though some buried part of himself was clamoring with all its might to yell out. And right now he could only wait.

The answer didn't come that afternoon or evening, but it had managed to worry his stomach a bit, and when he and Rebecca stopped at the Oakleys' for their reception he found himself unable to eat. He left the crowded kitchen for the empty living room and was about to sit when a voice spoke from behind him. "Not hungry?"

Ian looked over his shoulder to see Anne. She was coming from the stairs and held what looked like poster board. She looked as though she'd just applied fresh lipstick, and Ian wondered in how short a time she'd worry it off again.

"Rebecca and I were sorry to hear the news, Anne," he said as the woman stepped past him. He now could see that the poster board was a collage of pictures and images with words and little drawings to decorate the empty spaces. Anne propped it on a high-back chair, and Ian moved to her side so that he could see it more clearly. When he'd finished he looked at the woman and asked if she had made it.

Anne nodded. She was looking down at the poster rather than at Ian, and her head was cocked to the side as though contemplating the thing she had just finished. When she spoke she didn't bother to look up.

"This helped me," she said, her voice almost a whisper. "I'd almost forgotten who she was." She began pointing and explaining all the pictures, telling the stories that made her remember her mother as she once was.

"This was Mother's first vacation ever," she said, motioning to a sepia image of a woman in front of a crashing wave. She moved her finger over a few inches and pointed to a photo of Lois, Charles, and little Anne standing in front of a serene pond. "Vermont," Anne said in way of explanation and made her way through the rest of the poster.

It was after the fourth picture — Lois standing ankle deep in a wading pool in a fifties-style bathing skirt with sixties-style bouffant hair — that Ian noticed the oddest thing: Each and every image included Lois Gavell and some type of water. There were lawn sprinklers and distant waterfalls, snowdrifts and ocean vistas, even a copy of the Poseidon fountain picture that Oakley had on the wall. Ian stopped listening to Anne and let his eyes track through the progression of photos until he could be absolutely sure, and when he was he simply brought his hand to his jaw and rubbed it in silent contemplation.

Lois Gavell had died — had, in fact, vanished a long time ago — leaving what Ian thought was a mystery that would go with her into the grave. Here, though, was an answer — she had searched, left safety and warmth, for the call of water. She died because of the piercing clarity of that one need through the interior fog of her otherwise murky life. Ian looked at the photos and wondered if it was so simple. Perhaps it was the place she remembered being happy, the lowest common denominator for a mind too confused to grasp anything but the obvious. It sought joy and peace, found only water, and looked no further.

Ian stopped stroking his jaw and looked at Anne, who seemed to be waiting for him to say something. "What was that last one?" he asked, looking toward the bottom of the poster where a black-and-white image of a young girl in white leggings, a frilly dress, and elbow-length gloves grinned at the camera as though she'd been caught making faces at a mirror.

"That was the day of her baptism," Anne answered. "It was against the times, but my grandparents always believed baptism was a decision to be made *by* you, not for you." She nodded and looked back at the image. "The only thing I know about it is that the water they dunked her in was cold. Mom always said you don't forget a shock like that."

Ian couldn't help it. The words came to his mouth before he considered them, and he spoke without pausing or listening to what he was saying. He knew he invited Anne and Mike and Jay to Rebecca's baptism on Sunday and that the explanation was tied somehow to the photo of the smiling girl in her church clothes. After Anne nodded, said they'd be there, he couldn't remember anything more than hearing the sound of rushing water as his own flailing baptism came back to him. His knees flexed gently as though expecting his feet to slip from under him, and in his mouth was the sharp taste of Utah clay, but when he blinked twice, nice and slow, he was back in the Oakley living room and Anne was still nodding, saying they'd be honored to be there for Rebecca.

EARLY MORNING. SATURDAY, AUGUST 31

Ian woke, confused and sweating. The T-shirt he was wearing felt damp, and the single cotton sheet still on his bed was twisted in knots at his feet. Rebecca slept soundly, the round of her back visible to him as he scanned his bedroom trying to gain his bearings. It seemed to Ian that it must be nearly time to rise, but looking to his alarm clock proved fruitless — no time glowed from its face. Ian realized the power had gone out, taking the air conditioning with it. Already the house had warmed to uncomfortable. Ian rolled from bed to get a drink of water and checked his watch as he passed the dresser. It was only a few minutes before six o'clock. Silver light began to creep through the blinds, and Ian decided trying to fall back to sleep would be futile.

Downstairs he ate a light breakfast and found the battery-operated radio they kept in the kitchen for emergencies. The brown-outs were the top story on all the news stations and would be used to conserve energy; power stations across the state had been overwhelmed by the late-summer heat. Brownouts would last as long as the outrageous temperatures. Perhaps through the weekend, hopefully not even that long.

Ian spent the rest of the morning reading through the morning paper. He'd made it to the sports section when Rebecca came downstairs. He explained the brownouts, and after she poured herself some juice she came to the kitchen table and collapsed beside him with a smile that said she didn't mind the heat.

They sat next to each other in silence, Ian reading an interview with Jay Miller, a Red Sox southpaw recently called up from Triple-A, and Rebecca taking slow, small sips from her glass. Ian had just reached the second-to-last paragraph when the house erupted into a violent shrieking that startled him so badly he ripped the paper. Rebecca screamed at the same time and jumped from her chair, and Cain, whom Ian hadn't seen that morning, bolted into the kitchen with wild fear in her eyes.

Eights blinked on the microwave, stove console, and coffeemaker, and the low groan of the refrigerator grumbling to life could be heard only in the momentary pauses of the deafening house alarm. Ian tossed both fragments of the newspaper onto the table, marched to the phone, and dialed the home-security office. As he waited on the line, the first cool breaths of air conditioning fluttered from a vent above him. Gaining cool air might just be worth the early-morning blare.

"This is driving us insane," Ian said when a service representative came on the line. "I thought your guys fixed it."

The voice on the line apologized, said nothing constructive, and suggested that the best option might be keeping everything offline for a little while. Ian was tempted, but the knowledge that Hanover was still out there forced his hand. He asked for the alarm to be reset.

"This might continue to happen, especially with the power outages," the technician hinted, and Ian answered that if five seconds of fright from a wailing alarm was all that he had to deal with, that would be quite all right with him.

into the driveway. He could tell the engine was small — Rebecca's coupe — and he grabbed the nozzle and pulled the hose after him while he ran around the house to soak his wife.

After a few steps he felt the ground grow hard and hot beneath his bare feet. He rounded the far end of the house, cocked the nozzle in front of him like a gun, and saw a teal sedan pull to a stop twelve feet in front of him. Ian took a few steps onto the pavement and felt the hot asphalt lick like flames at the soles of his feet. He jumped back to the grass. The car door opened and Kyle Turner, dressed in shirt and tie despite the heat, stepped onto the pavement. He looked at Ian, still holding the hose in front of him like a pistol, and raised his hands above his head in mock surrender.

"Turner . . ." Ian said and couldn't think what to say next.

"I knew I should have brought the video team," the reporter answered, dropping his hands to his side. He shook his head as if a soggy, disheveled Ian was exactly what he'd been expecting to find. Ian dropped the hose, smoothed his hair back as best he could, and asked the reporter to come inside. This kind of heat made people do crazy things.

Kyle began talking the moment they stepped inside — stopping only when Ian ran upstairs to change into some dry clothes — but nothing he said seemed to be making much sense so far as Ian could tell. There were brief mentions of Louis Kael and a break-in, but mostly it seemed to be about a man named Hugh and the wrongs he heaped upon a cub reporter named Kyle Turner many years ago.

What struck Ian was not the story, which was filled with precise and angry conversations, but the sheer energy that blazed in Kyle's eyes as he spoke. Ian had been so used to the bored, seen-it-all expression of the reporter that this new glint took him by surprise.

"When did this all take place?" he asked just to make sure he hadn't missed anything. Kyle said it had all gone down in the mid-eighties, *Miami Vice* time, before launching his attack once more on the man who had betrayed him over a scoop that the mayor of Lyme was having an affair with the treasurer from Mystic. It was small-town gossip, and yet the man had stabbed his young protégé in the back. Ian realized Kyle thought he'd met a compadre, one of the misused masses.

"Did you ever patch things up?" asked Ian, knowing the answer too well. The nervous tapping of the man's foot and the large gestures with his usually professionally choreographed hands told a story in themselves.

"He died," said Kyle and ended the story with those two words. Ian couldn't imagine a worse fine line in the world and tried to change the subject, tried to get Kyle back on focus.

"Did you need a response from me about something?" he prompted.

Kyle studied him without saying a word, so Ian looked back. The years since their on-stage scuffle had changed the man — deepened the grooved wrinkles about his Cheshire smile and thinned the otherwise exquisite hair — yet for the first time Ian was seeing things in Kyle he'd never noticed before. The missing ring that used to gleam from the man's left hand, the worried sores about the fingernails, and even the struggle it was for him to suck in the shallowest breath. Ian blinked, but the images wouldn't go away; he was seeing the man anew and only Kyle's words cleared his mind.

"Your editor's home was broken into. Police confirmed that it was an unrelated attack, but I wanted to know if you had any comment. Thought it might make a nice 'poetic justice' close to one of our shows."

Ian sighed and said he hadn't heard anything about it.

"The wife," Kyle said and glanced at a small note pad, "a Mrs. Kael, had to be admitted to the hospital because her blood pressure went through the roof. Apparently this, added to the strain of the past weeks, got to be too much."

Ian closed his eyes. He remembered the couple's cozy brownstone, a fire burning in the den fireplace during the winter. At once that image was shattered with a vision of Louis's wife gasping for air, the editor stabbing at the telephone trying to bring help.

The tiniest voice whispered that perhaps Louis had gotten what he deserved — a moment of pure terror to call his own.

"Comment?" Kyle asked again.

The little voice got louder, insistent. Telling Ian to say how Louis danced with the devil and had paid the price. How the editor had pulled the tiger's tail and been the first one eaten.

In the end the words wouldn't come. He knew Kyle wanted them, but he needed to say something else. He needed to show

Turner, show himself, that there was another way.

"I'm sorry for any danger that came to Louis and his wife," Ian began, and Kyle simply listened. Scribbling quotes or fumbling for microphones must be for hacks. Real journalists apparently got the gist and rewrote everything else. "I would never wish any harm for them, and I wish his wife a full recovery. I also expect that the authorities will exercise full diligence in apprehending the suspect."

"Noble," said Kyle in a voice that had been cynical so long it knew no other way. Even if the man meant what he said, his mouth wouldn't betray the fact. "You're a prince."

Ian walked Kyle out to his car listening to the arid gusts of air and the severe buzzing of summer insects. Turner's breath was ragged, and even after a few steps his brow was wet. Ian veered at the driveway toward the hose he'd left and turned to wait for Kyle to depart. The reporter didn't get in the car right away, though. Just stood there, sweating, hip resting on his door for a few seconds before speaking again.

"You've changed, Ian," he said, then coughed. "Gone soft or something."

Ian nodded; it was as good a phrase as any. The hardness he'd felt so long was going, almost gone even. He grinned then and said, "You should be glad. Means I won't have to beat you up anymore."

Kyle tried to keep from smiling. "I would have dropped you like an ugly first date."

It was the first time the men had even mentioned the incident. It felt good to Ian in a way to be talking about it, but he knew he shouldn't be making light. He shook his head as the smile left his face and said, "Seriously, though, Kyle, I'm sorry about that whole thing." He paused, "Just real sorry."

Kyle cracked his knuckles, raised an eyebrow, and said, "See, I told you you were going soft."

Ian shrugged and dropped his eyes. What more could be said? In that second, he saw his hose, water still dripping from the nozzle. Without thinking he dropped to a knee, grabbed, and came up pointing. They were back where they'd started, and Kyle raised his hands once more, broad swaths of sweat under his arms.

"Put me out of my misery," Turner said, and it sounded half serious to Ian.

For a second there was nothing. Then Ian squeezed, and there was mist and coolness and the shimmering of prisms in the afternoon light. Kyle closed his eyes against the water and let himself get drenched, saying nothing at all. After a few seconds Ian stopped, and the reporter blinked drops away from his face and opened his eyes.

"Just what I needed," he said, climbed in his car, and drove away.

Ian had a difficult time explaining fully the day's events when Rebecca returned from her meeting with the pastor, but she'd insisted on knowing why the side of the house was muddy and so he clarified as best he could. She narrowed her eyes a bit when he talked about shooting the reporter with the hose and suggested some latent bitterness behind the action, but Ian assured her it was all it good fun.

"It was like we crossed a bridge," he said. She patted his hand and said one less enemy was always a good thing.

Before she could ask even another question Ian forced her back onto the topic of her baptism. She seemed surprised by his interest.

"The discussion was very short, actually," she said. "He asked why I wanted to get baptized, I told him what I told you the other night, and he told me when to show up and what to wear. Then I went to the farmers' market."

Ian waited. There had to be more.

His wife offered nothing.

"So what did you tell him again?"

"Oh, you know," she said, unloading a brown bag of nectarines into a bowl by the microwave, "just how I wanted to make it my own decision. And how important it is for me to do it in front of other people." She sighed. "Nothing original, I guess."

The words struck Ian. Everything she had said up until that point had seemed to him to be completely new, completely personal. In a moment, though, she had changed all that, and he realized that it was true — the phrases were things he'd heard before. People had spoken them before dipping below the surface of the pool at the baptism service. A character or two had said things like them in Jaret's chapters. Ian even remembered saying something like it to Howard at the riverbed that early Sunday morning. The echoes seemed normal, a link to all those who had gone before, to all those who had heard God calling and given themselves over. Only the voice had changed, and that seemed to make all the difference.

■ ■ ■ ■

That night, Ian made his discovery.

His search through Ezekiel for some explanation of Katherine's sculpture was just becoming tiresome when he turned the page and found himself spirited away to a valley of bones. With a word, the prophet commanded the bones to live, and they began to tremble. All Ian could think about was the dry clicking sound the sculpture had made the first night they'd swept the sheet off of it.

Twice he read the portion of Scripture and found himself disappointed, realizing that some small part of him had hoped for the breath of the divine, the whisper of supernatural explanation. Instead, he was left with a sculpture and another question to add to his list — why this shuddering of bones?

EARLY MORNING. SUNDAY, SEPTEMBER 1

The room had the same gunmetal gray look that it had yesterday, and the air was just as thick when Ian awoke. The back of his neck felt damp from perspiration. He groaned twice and looked into the face of his wife, who was already awake. Today she would be baptized.

That thought was immediately interrupted by the growl of engines and the strain of gears as some early-morning driver labored up the hill outside. Within a minute it was clear that the vehicle was right outside; Rebecca parted the window blinds, glanced to the front lawn, and said that Ty Caller, builder of deserts, had arrived.

Rushing to make themselves semi-presentable, they dressed in shorts and T-shirts and headed downstairs. Caller was on the front stoop when they opened the door.

"You have no electricity," he stated as though Ian might not know.

"Brownouts. It'll be on at eight."

Ty looked at his watch and sighed deeply, with just the slightest roll to his eyes. Ian guessed that his New York clients rarely lost their electricity, and they could probably track down a spare power plant if necessary. Only here in the country . . . Without a word, Ty marched to the back of the truck and called for his driver to come assist him with some things. At least they could do the unloading.

Ian followed the pair, trying to gauge what access, if any, they would need to the house during the day, and what their estimated time for set-up would be. Ty explained that their late start would put them back a half hour, maybe more, but that Ian and Rebecca wouldn't need to be home for any of it. Tomorrow they would need to get into the house; today they would be working in the back and side yards and along the front entrance. Ty jumped up into the back of the trailer and shouted something that Ian didn't understand into its cluttered hold. From among the boxes and packing Ian heard a sound come in reply, but wouldn't pin it as human.

"You didn't bring the animals, did you?" he asked.

"Tomorrow, Mr. Merchant," Ty answered, staring down from his perch. "Today, I create the desert." He smiled a crooked little grin and added, "Even God took six days."

Two hours later Ian and Rebecca headed out for the morning. Ty and his workmen, submerged in their work, didn't even glance up as the Cherokee pulled from the driveway. Driving to church, Ian could only wonder what his lawn might look like the next time he saw it.

Pete Ray and his wife, Christine, greeted Ian and Rebecca at church and congratulated her for the baptism that would take place after the second service. They assured the Merchants they would stay for the occasion.

Rebecca thanked them, but her attention seemed elsewhere to Ian. Throughout the service he'd look over to make sure she was okay. Before he realized it the sermon was nearly over and the pastor was saying, "On the suggestion of a friend, I attended a wonderful exhibit this weekend. It was held down at the Historical Society, and it introduced me to a wonderful local artist."

Ian looked at Rebecca. His wife's back was straight, and on her face was a slim and happy smile. He wondered if she had been the one to recommend the museum.

"Her name was Katherine Jacoby, and she passed away recently. She apparently had an amazing gift in that she could carve wood to look like anything. If she carved a loaf of bread, you'd want to eat it. If a rose, you'd try to smell it." He paused.

"Apparently, at some point in her career she gave her life to the Lord and stopped" — he snapped his fingers — "these kinds of carvings. Now, I never knew the woman, but I wonder if it was because she discovered the truth behind the illusions she had been seeing.

"God knows the heart of all His people.

The men and women Hebrews talks about were the genuine article. We here are masters at image, at doing the right things, at the surface level. But God sees through that. If we're no more than a wooden sculpture dolled up to be a believer, well, that will get us nowhere." He shrugged as if saddened by the prospect and then lifted his hands above his head to give the benediction. Guitars chimed in and church concluded with the shaking of hands and called greetings from across the gym.

After agreeing to meet back with the Rays in an hour and a half for the baptism, Ian and Rebecca marched quickly to their car so that they could run to the store and pick up their supply of soft drinks.

Swinging out onto the main road, Ian asked Rebecca what she thought of the man's interpretation.

Rebecca laughed. "In her journals Katherine insisted that all her early works were just fun pieces, jokes almost." She paused. "But what he said made a lot of sense."

Ian didn't say anything, just kept his eyes on the road, mentally mapping the quickest way to the shop. The car's air conditioning finally overcame the heat that had gathered during the hour of church, and Ian could feel a spreading dampness under his arms.

Interrupting his thoughts, Rebecca spoke once more.

"Perhaps that's the key, though," she said. "Maybe after becoming a Christian she was able to look back and laugh."

"Laugh?" Ian asked. He wasn't sure what would be so funny.

"To think how you used to be? How hollow, how unreal?" She lifted an eyebrow. "You'd either have to laugh or cry."

She laughed, and soon Ian couldn't keep from joining her.

As the Merchants crossed the parking lot to the school doors, Ian recognized the Oakleys talking to Pete and Christine. Rebecca gave a small "Oh, good" to herself when she noticed them.

"There they are!" shouted Peter, a grin on his face. Ian wondered what the two couples had been chatting about. The connections that brought them to a stifling middle school on a Sunday morning, no doubt. The Oakleys turned around after Pete shouted, and Ian saw that they both looked rested and peaceful, if not happy.

The moment all three couples were together, Rebecca, Anne, and Christine split into a little group. Ian heard Anne thank

Rebecca for coming to the funeral yesterday and for all the help she and Ian had been. When he turned, Mike looked like he might echo the same thoughts, but the pastor motioned them all inside.

Before she could disappear, Ian gave Rebecca a kiss and watched as she followed Pastor Ron through the gym where he pointed her to the girls' locker room. Ian and the other couples made their way to the pool doors. A dozen or so members of the congregation, including the woman Rebecca knew from work as well as Jaret and his fiancée, were already seated in the bleachers. Jaret stood and waved, and Ian smiled and nodded in return before slipping into the first row of benches. Mike and Anne followed him, and the Rays took the row behind them.

"You went through this, right?" asked Mike after they were settled. Anne leaned in after hearing her husband's question, and Ian assented that he had. Just a few months ago.

"Of course, I was in a stream," he said. "In Utah."

The Oakleys nodded.

"And I almost drowned."

Mike raised an eyebrow as though trying to figure out if Ian was pulling his leg. When he decided the comment was serious, he just smiled and said, "Well, at least you would've gone straight to heaven."

Ian laughed — it was a good joke — but Pete just leaned in from the bleacher above them and said, "Well, that's not quite how it works."

Before he could explain, a door across the pool opened, and both Pastor Ron and Rebecca stepped through. She was in a long pair of mesh shorts and a black T-shirt with a Red Sox World Series logo on it, and as they crossed to the nearest ladder, Rebecca turned and gave Ian a wave. Soon they were both standing waist-deep in the pool, and the pastor began the ceremony.

"We are celebrating today. Celebrating with Rebecca Merchant as she stands before all of you and talks about what's important to her, what's made her new, what's compelling her to die and be raised again."

He looked at Rebecca and motioned to her. She immediately turned to face the bleachers and began to talk. Her voice, in those first few words, was so pure and strong and happy that Ian barely heard what she said because he was so focused on how she sounded. He remembered her speaking the same way as she repeated her vows during their wedding — strong, confident, joyous. It was something more than the voice she used during the auction, certainly different than when she related the medical news so many years ago. It was not a new voice, just one he hadn't heard much. He had to shake his head to focus on what she was saying.

". . . when I was a child. I credit my parents that they loved God, they told me about Him, and they showed their love for Him as well." Her eyes flickered to Ian's face, and she bit at her lip. Ian knew she was going to talk about him.

"Still, it wasn't until a month ago that things moved in my life. I saw my wonderful husband *wrestling* with this new faith that he found so perplexing. What amazed me wasn't this overwhelming godliness — sorry, honey — but how deep down, how individual, his struggle was. Every bit of my husband was affected.

"And I wondered if it was a fluke."

Her smile got a scattered laugh from the congregation.

"But then I met an artist, Katherine Jacoby. Well, not met, since she was dead. But I read her letters and her journal, and suddenly before me was another person, someone else who was just *wracked* by this determination and faith. And she was entangled with the same God, the same Savior my husband was. And I decided I needed that to be me."

Her head lowered for a moment; she then lifted her head and said, "I love God, I am overwhelmed that Jesus died for me, and I know that I have to tangle with this tremendous thing, make it part of me, make it me."

There was silence. Those in the bleachers waited for more, but Rebecca stood quietly. Pastor Ron splashed the water once and said the words Ian had heard him repeat during the baptism service.

"Because of your confession of faith and your obedience to Christ, I baptize you in the name of the Father, the Son, and the Holy Ghost. Be buried with your sins," he said, lowering Rebecca, "and be raised again into new life."

Dripping and smiling, Rebecca cleared water from her eyes and searched the stands to find her husband. Ian took in her beaming face, the tender body that her sopping T-shirt clung to, her quick hands as they smoothed her hair from her eyes, and he realized that there was not a part, not an inch of her that he didn't recognize, that he didn't love.

Three times as they drove back to the house Ian exclaimed how he felt almost newly married, and even as they pulled onto their road he couldn't shake the feeling that he was driving toward his honeymoon, new bride at his side and bright world ahead of him. He came close to saying the same thing for the fourth time when an unbelievable sight brought him up silent. Rebecca gasped, and Ian nearly drove the Cherokee off the road. Ty Caller, builder of deserts, had built one.

"Our yard . . ." Rebecca began but couldn't finish.

In fact, there was no yard. Stone, dust, and sand covered each square inch. Sage-colored shrubs and cacti as large as men stood in prickly bunches, and along the side of the house Ian swore he could see a stone arch.

He stopped the car at the top of the yard, well away from the semi, and killed the engine. The driveway was now fertile with small pale flowers and bunches of hairy plants that Ian had never seen before. Rebecca got out first and immediately began coughing as a quick wind snapped dust and sand into her hair. Ian followed quickly, and his mouth went dry. The arid rock and dust seemed to suck all the humidity straight from the air, and Ian felt as though he were back in Utah hiking with Howard.

"You can walk on it," a voice shouted, and Ian saw Ty emerge from the shadows of the arch. "We still have lots to do, so I will not talk to you unless there is a problem." He took two steps toward the backyard and disappeared once more. Ian and Rebecca shook their heads and began their walk to the front door, stopping every few feet to read the sign that identified another unique plant or flower.

The bushes were creosote and desert chicory. Dune evening primose was the pale flower and the hairy cactus was called an old man cactus. Yucca plants, barrel cacti, and a pair of saguaros needed no ID tag, but the desert paintbrush, the Mojave aster, the chain fruit cholla were all things Ian didn't recognize.

"Bet you're glad you didn't get caught in that bush," said Rebecca, pointing to a gnarled and leafless shrub that guarded the front door.

Ian looked closer and felt a knot tighten in his stomach. Bluish green with a tangle of thick branches, the plant had spines —

no, spikes — that were inches long and sharp enough to maim a person. Ian looked at the tag — *Corona de Cristo* — and needed no one to translate the Spanish. He shuddered at the ugly thought of touching one of those thorns and shuffled by it to his front door.

Cain stared up at them from the hall with what could only be called an incredulous look. Her yard, the luscious wealth of green and growth, had vanished, and all that remained were dried earth and a collection of plants you wouldn't want to make angry.

Rebecca took his hands, held them tight, and said, "It looks wonderful. Absolutely terrific."

Ian grinned a sly smile, one he hadn't used in years and said, "You're the one who looks wonderful." Suddenly all his feelings of being on a honeymoon rushed back to him. Surrounded by a growing desert, it was as though they weren't even in their own home. Ian stared into Rebecca's eyes, tried to cock a jaunty eyebrow at her, and then gave a small tug on her hand.

Rebecca broke into a fit of laughter.

"What if they need our help?" she asked.

"The dog can take care of it," Ian answered, jerking his thumb at Cain, who sat unamused on the tile floor and groaned for attention.

They ignored her and walked hand in hand to the staircase. Outside the sounds of men yelling to each other and the occasional curse filled the summer air. Inside, Ian tried to remember the first time he had led this bride to a bed. He knew he was far more nervous then than he was now, and he realized, in that instant, how his love had grown since those first days. They had buried friends, had swallowed the dream of family, and had put their hearts into a place to be home. They had been apart, put on weight and wrinkles, and searched for importance in jobs and money. Finally, they had separately come under the aegis of a living, loving God and found each other anew. And perhaps that was the importance of becoming new after all.

As his hand found the doorknob to their bedroom, Ian focused once more on Rebecca. She had her arm about his waist, and her eyes shone with a playful light that flashed through her grin.

Ian bent down to take off his shoes and socks and knew that he was fully blessed.

Just as Ian felt himself stirring from a restful nap, the doorbell rang. The bedroom was dim and shadowy, and Ian checked the clock to see how long they had been up here. It was nearly seven; Ty and his crew were probably ready to leave for the night.

The chime sounded again.

Ian untangled himself from the twisted sheets and apologized in a whisper to Rebecca, who rolled over with a sigh. Slipping into a pair of shorts and a T-shirt, Ian jogged from his room, through the hall, and down the stairs, straightening his hair as best he could. Cain lay at the base of the door, waiting, and Ian checked the peephole and saw the thinning hair on the top of Ty's head. He was a short man.

Ian apologized as he opened the door, but the designer said nothing in response. Instead the little man explained how early they would be arriving with animals tomorrow and the proper way for the caterer to enter the garage and handed Ian a piece of paper with a variety of telephone numbers in case something went wrong during the night.

"Wrong?"

Ty thought for a second. "Like an arch topples over, or a runaway car smashes into our cacti. We plan for the impossible."

Ian said that was usually a good plan. He added that the yard looked superb.

"I know," said Ty, and that was the end of conversation.

Ian looked at the numbers, repeated the instructions for the caterer to make sure he'd gotten them right. When everything was in order he said good night to the designer and said they'd see him at six-thirty in the morning.

When Ty slapped his hand against his thigh Ian was afraid he'd gotten something wrong.

"Forget to tell you," said the builder of deserts, "a man stopped by to see you. One of your neighbors, I think."

"My neighbor?" Ian said it aloud, but it was meant as a question for himself. He knew none of the neighbors well enough for them to stroll into his yard.

"He walked here, that's all I know. Anyway, he said it was important that he get in touch with you. Apparently he rang the bell but nobody answered." Ty looked at Ian disapprovingly, as though annoyed at having to relay the message.

"Did he leave a name?" Ian asked.

"I think," Ty said, "he said his name was Martin. I was busy with other things, so I'm not positive."

When the answer came, Ian had so little expected it that he swore straight into the face of the little designer. What peace, what respite they'd enjoyed from the past weeks' nightmare was shattered in that instant. When Ian shut the door he moved to the phone and dialed without hesitation the Titansburg police, a number he had memorized weeks ago.

A police search turned up nothing, and the cruiser arrived as usual to guard the front of the house. Ian swallowed his fear yet one more time and headed to bed. The worry gnawed at him, though, and he couldn't get Hanover — that ghoulish face — out of his mind.

The man seemed to be getting desperate. Why else would he approach the house in the middle of the day, especially with witnesses around? Would he return tomorrow during the party?

The Labor Day picnic sparked another thought — beverages. They'd left the soft drinks bought that afternoon in the back of the broiling Cherokee. Ian found himself staring at the ceiling. He knew it would bother him all night unless he did something, so he roused himself from bed and headed downstairs. As he hit the final step, the air conditioning coughed to a stop, and the small digital light from the kitchen appliances blinked out. The power was off.

Ian walked into the kitchen and grabbed a flashlight before moving across the living room. Stepping onto the front stoop, he realized the moon and stars were bright enough not to need the light, and he took a careful breath of night air. The expected crispness of September was nowhere to be had, and the air he tasted was like lukewarm soda. As he took his first step to the Cherokee, the dome light switched on in the police cruiser, and an officer stepped out.

"Everything all right?" the man called.

"Need to get something from my car. I would've turned on the lights, but we've got no electricity again."

The officer nodded and retreated to his car. Ian slipped past the crown-of-Christ bush and made his way to his Cherokee, where he retrieved the three cases of canned lemonade and iced tea. He tried to lift all three but found himself unable and was glad when the officer came to lend a hand. When the boxes had been delivered inside the hall, Ian shook the man's hand and wished him a good night.

"And watch the coyotes on your way back across the desert."

"Will do," said the officer, and Ian turned to his house.

Once inside, Ian brought each individual case to the top of his basement steps. He used one to prop the door open and carried the other two down the stairs and stowed them in the coolest, darkest corner he could find. He retreated back up the steps, made sure the door would reopen after he shut it, and carried the last case downstairs to tuck away in the same shadowed corner.

Behind him, something shuffled.

Ian whirled around, but the flashlight's anxious beam found nothing but a dusty gathering of old exercise equipment and a chalkboard he'd once used to diagram stories. Ian wondered if he'd heard a cricket or perhaps one of the toads that came out at night.

The moment he scanned the floor, the sound came again. This time from the other side of the basement steps.

Ian swung the light over the last few stairs and nearly screamed at what he saw.

It was a figure. Someone moving.

Ian's legs went numb, and his tongue stuck to the roof of his mouth. He wanted to shout but couldn't. He just stared as his unerring light rested on the swaying figure of a person.

The sound came once more.

A dry clacking in rhythm with the figure's

movement.

Ian bent over, dropping his hands to his knees, and sucked in a deep breath.

For a minute he stayed doubled over, calming his nerves and trying to figure why he hadn't remembered the sculptures, the cross and the rib cage that they'd stowed down here. Likely to scare you to death.

Again the noise came, this time louder. It was the bones of the sculpture chinking together.

Ian stood straight, aimed his flashlight once more, and crossed to the sculptures. The cross lay solid and heavy against the wall, a shadow almost cut into the white cinder block. The bones, however, swayed ever so slightly, brushing up against each other on occasion and rattling in the silent basement. Ian watched them for a moment before realizing something was wrong. The bones were moving but the air wasn't. There was neither wind, nor draft, nor breath of man — Ian was holding his — to stir the sculpture, and yet they swayed.

Ian took a step closer, lifted his light, and stared. The fear, the worry, drained from him and a warm sense of awe replaced it. He was aware of nothing in the moment but the movement of the sculpture and the sound of the pieces clacking against one another. He simply stared, a vague connection forming in his mind. He shut his eyes to concentrate, and the moment the bones sounded he had his answer.

Typewriter keys. The bones' clacking was the exact mimic of his old typewriter, the one on which he'd pounded out three novels. They trembled faster and Ian recognized a new sound, the memory of high heels clicking on a marble floor at his wedding. The bones shook with greater speed and he heard the thunder that rang down on the fairgrounds moments before the lightning came. The sound of a centrifuge in the fertility clinic where he and Rebecca had discovered they were never to be called Mom and Dad. The snapping of sticks as Ian and Howard tramped across the Utah desert. Finally came the image from a Bible passage he'd just finished.

In an instant he had his inspiration.

They remembered.

These terrible dry things had once been alive, once were bound by muscle and sinew. Blood fed them and they lived until death pared them clean and bleached them white. Still, somewhere deep inside, they remembered that life, remembered what it was to move, and when the Master's voice spoke they danced at the invitation to join him once more.

Ian swung his light from the bones to the cross and back again.

That had been his journey too. Just a bag of bones who'd thought he'd been living. It had taken the small intruding voice of God to point him in the right direction. Zion might seem like the worst of places to regain life, but there in the desert he had. He'd heard God's voice speak his true name, heard the echo of eternity in his heart, heard that invitation to live, and he'd shuddered.

So this is what it means to live. I remember.

EARLY MORNING. MONDAY, SEPTEMBER 2

Ian woke cool and dry for the first time in days and watched his wife sleep, her lips opened slightly and a faint wheeze accompanying each breath. He remembered how years ago the slightest stirring of one would awaken the other and they'd talk or make love or roll into each other's arms and fall back to sleep. Gradually their bodies had grown accustomed to each other, and now only the set sound of the radio switching on warranted waking. Indeed, once Rebecca's alarm sounded her eyes immediately fluttered, and after a few sleepy blinks she gave Ian a weak smile and asked why he had a shirt on.

"Aren't you hot?" she said.

Ian was about to say he'd slept great for the first time since Wednesday, when his trip outside and the odd experience in the basement came back to him. He remembered great chunks of vivid detail — the dome light in the police car switching on, bending down to make sure the boxes were aligned, the breeze-less dance of the wind chime — but out of sequence and tangled. He tried to relate it to Rebecca, but she thought he was talking about a dream.

"The bones moved," he insisted. "It's like they moved for me."

"A draft?" she asked.

Ian shrugged. Last night he could've sworn it had been still, but this morning he wasn't sure. "Maybe," he said. "I don't know. It was strange."

He started to say more but was interrupted, for the second straight day, by the sound of engines pulling up the road. Ty Caller, with his desert circus, had arrived.

They met the man outside, and Ian almost couldn't hide a smile. Caller was wearing wrap-around blade sunglasses, a safari hat, cargo shorts, and a linen shirt with a mesa scene printed on it. This circus might not have trains, but it certainly had managed a ringmaster. Without a word he motioned for Ian to follow him. As they tramped past the first of the vans, Ty began to whisper instructions about the animals.

"Your dog must stay inside at all times. Only the armadillo may be touched, the others are for show. No sudden movements around the jackrabbit, or he'll take off."

Ian half listened but was too busy staring at the glass cages as handlers began unloading the creatures. Each was labeled in bold letters, and Ian could see nine different kinds of lizards — including something called a Piebald Chuckwalla — a variety of snakes, some of which, like the sidewinder and the diamondback, looked meaner than devil's spit. There were wolf spiders, scorpions, and tarantulas, as well as cuter, furrier creatures like kangaroo rats, pack rats, a jackrabbit, and one prairie dog.

Ian followed the crew toward the house, opened the door for them, and got out of their way as they began to set up. Some animal stations would be in the shade of the house, while others would line the outside of the lawn. Guests should never have to crowd the animals.

Ty had just gone inside to complain again about the lack of electricity when the power switched on. Three lights blazed in the living room, and the security alarm began its wail. The problem, thought to be fixed, reared its ugly head yet again, and Ian jumped for the phone.

"I need my alarm shut off, *now!*" Ian said to the operator.

Without argument the voice on the line retreated, and in the few seconds Ian waited he could hear cries from the workers outside. Ty bolted into the backyard, and Ian had terrible visions of deadly desert snakes slithering across his lawn. When the woman came back on, she apologized for the inconvenience. Ian breathed deeply twice to keep from taking his frustrations out on her.

Instead he asked calmly for his entire system to be deactivated, at least until Tuesday or Wednesday. He received quick compliance and another apology. The house was quiet, and when Ian looked at the control box near the door to the garage he could see the LED lights fading to nothing. He thanked the woman and hung up.

Someone cleared his throat behind him.

Ian turned; it was Ty. The safari cap was missing and the man's face was a splotchy scarlet.

"I thought I told you no noises," he said. "Our jackrabbit is gone. He took off."

It was Ian's turn to apologize, but all he

could think about was the final bill from Ty Caller and whether the charge of one AWOL bunny would be compounded to the already sizable amount. It took all his will not to ask the going rate on a jackrabbit these days.

The caterer arrived at eleven o'clock and was bunkered in the kitchen by quarter of twelve, the smells of bubbling crocks of cheese, roasting chilies, and fresh cilantro knifing through the house. The birds of prey — two red-tailed hawks, an elf owl, and a barn owl missing one eye — arrived shortly thereafter and occupied the library, where one of the handlers recognized Howard's picture of the Great White Throne. Ty staked out the back patio as his command center, and whenever Ian looked outside he could see the little man making precise hand gestures in explaining where or how he wanted the illusion finished. Time fled. Guests would be arriving in another half hour.

Ian and Rebecca stayed out of the way, and the final touches were completed. All the animals, except for the missing rabbit, were in their cages, the food stood waiting to be placed on trays, and the weather was cooperating fully. Arcing to its zenith, the Connecticut sun blazed down on the Merchants' transformed lawn with an assaulting fury. Labor Day would be the hottest day of the week. Some said it might even reach three digits. A car door slammed, and Ian looked out through his living room window. The lawn was ashimmer, shards of halite sparkling in the fierce high light, and Ian could barely make out the first guests standing awestruck at the site of the Connecticut desert. Ian stood and took his wife's hand. The fun was about to begin.

The first guests were the chief of police and his wife, a sweet, rambunctious woman, who hugged Ian a few seconds longer than necessary. Still, Ian was glad to seem them, if only for the sake of having one more trained officer on duty.

Soon a line of cars could be seen stalled on the hill approaching the house, and rather than let the mob track inside, Ian met the guests at the curb, welcomed them with a handshake or hug, and sent them into the backyard. Most were too taken by surprise by the desert — "Sort of an anti-oasis," remarked a freelance journalist friend from Boston — to give Ian much of a proper greeting.

For more than an hour Ian and Rebecca stood and greeted the throng of invitees including Pete and his wife; the Oakleys, who looked worn; and Jaret. Not a single meaningful conversation could be had, and only after the line subsided were Ian and Rebecca able to join the party.

As expected, the conversations he did manage — especially with those who'd traveled from the city — tended to focus on the fallout with Louis, the identity of the stalker, and what lay ahead for Ian. He tried to stay away from the first two topics altogether and on the third he simply said that he was thinking about writing his memoirs. Completed chapters lay on his desk, and it was probably the only thing he could finish at this time with any honesty.

Finally, after taking in a falconer's demonstration with the barn owl, Ian turned and found himself face-to-face with Cheryl Rose and Kevin Contrade. He hadn't seen them arrive, but he was glad to be staring at two friendly faces. He welcomed them both with firm handshakes and even gave Kevin a swift slap on the back. The teacher grimaced but said nothing; it was Cheryl who started the conversation about Norman Gruitt, the missing artist.

"I was in DeCafé last night sitting in the back room when one of the staff came and started hanging some new words."

Cheryl paused for effect, and Ian looked

at Kevin, but apparently he'd heard the story and was now looking at his shoes.

She continued. "I asked the girl where she'd gotten the new words — said I heard the artist had moved. She assured me that she knew him, and it was definitely Norman Gruitt delivering those paintings. That's how the man survives."

Ian asked Kevin what he thought it meant. The teacher looked up from his shoes, took a deep breath, and released it with a sigh loud enough to turn heads. He assured Ian he had no idea what was happening anymore. Ian thought he looked as sad as a man could look without actually crying, and decided to change the subject.

"I sprayed down Kyle Turner with a hose the other day."

Even Kevin couldn't resist that. He and Cheryl urged Ian for the rest of the story, and Ian recounted it, acting both parts and adding sound effects where they seemed appropriate. By the time he and Kyle made it back to the driveway for the soaking, a crowd had gathered and was listening. Ian finished with flair and acknowledged that Kyle had taken the whole thing pretty well, considering.

A shrill whistle from Ty Caller focused the crowd's attention. He alerted everyone that the herpetologists would be doing a lizard and snake demonstration on the east side of the veranda. Kevin's eyes lit up at the mention of reptiles, and he practically pushed Ian out of the way to make it to the porch. Cheryl watched him go, rolled her eyes, and started after him. Ian watched the young woman weave her way through the crowd and he realized that Kevin, whether he knew it or not, had someone watching over his shoulder. Perhaps it was just in thanks for the help he'd given her, or perhaps she felt she owed him. Something about him just made you want to take him under a protective wing.

Ian was standing in the shade of what Ty had called a hoodoo — a rock column of bizarre shape formed by erosion — when he heard Jaret's unmistakable voice call his name. Jaret approached with his fiancée and the Rays. All four were dressed in white and looked as though they'd just stepped off the tennis courts somewhere.

"Hey there," Jaret said when he was close enough to chat. He took a pause to stuff a quesadilla in his mouth, swallowed it in what must have been one bite, and started a two-minute string of compliments that concluded with his description of a tarantula's legs as he'd just let one scramble up his arm.

Ian shuddered, said he was glad they were enjoying themselves, and asked how the food had been. Pete laughed and said Jaret would be the resident expert on that as well.

"Plus, he helped in the raptor demonstration and fed a cricket to one of the lizards."

"Chuckwalla," Jaret clarified.

Pete shrugged.

Jaret grinned, looking younger than usual, and Ian had to resist tousling his shaggy auburn hair. The man was in seminary, after all.

Pete asked if he had been able to enjoy any of the displays yet, but something caught Ian's attention before he could answer. First it was just a stirring in the bushes, but soon a rabbit hopped into view. Its ears were long, far longer than any eastern bunny, and Ian realized it had to be the missing jackrabbit. He pulled Jaret close and told him to go find Ty Caller, the little man dressed like he was about to shoot an elephant. As Jaret sprinted off, Pete leaned in and asked what the fuss was about. Ian pointed to the rabbit, which nibbled eagerly on some greenery at the outskirts of the desert. Pete whistled and said he hadn't seen one of those since tramping through

New Mexico twenty years ago.

"Uh-oh," Pete's wife murmured, just loud enough for Ian to hear.

Ian looked up in time to see something sleek and auburn and black blast from the bushes. Instantly the jackrabbit bolted, and in the slightest of seconds both animals crashed through the bushes and out of sight. Ian hadn't even managed a blink — it had happened just that fast.

Jaret reappeared a moment later with Ty Caller, both a little flushed, and asked what happened.

"Fox," Ian said.

Caller's mouth shut with a click, and Ian saw *jackrabbit* once more being added into his final invoice.

A half hour later, standing in the shadow of his house, Ian still felt bad for the poor, stupid animal. He didn't exactly know why, but the thing — all muscle and ears — reminded him just the slightest bit of Howard, and he was sorry the beast had come to just as bad an end.

Guests nodded and called to him, but most were content to give him his space, and he enjoyed his moment out of the sun. Finishing the last gulp of lemonade, he made a move back to the party when Mike Oakley hailed him with a wave and shook his hand when they were close enough.

"Having a good time?"

"Most certainly, quite a bash," Oakley said, but Ian could hear the exhaustion behind the man's voice. "Anne's wiped, though, and to tell you the truth so am I. We just wanted to drop by — everybody at the station talks about your parties."

"Get some sleep," Ian said and began walking the officer to the front of the house. As they passed the deck, Ian heard Ty Caller make an announcement that the mariachi band would be playing soon. It was the thing Rebecca was perhaps most excited about, and he hoped she'd heard.

"You guys have been great," said Oakley as they headed up the driveway. Anne stood at the end, watching them. "I was just telling him how great he and Rebecca have been," Oakley said to his wife. She nodded and leaned into her husband.

"Anything, anytime," Ian replied. "Just let us know."

Anne nodded, and together they disappeared down the hill. Ian guessed most couples looked that way when struggling through loss, leaning against each other as if there weren't strength enough for them individually. Ian knew he and Rebecca had done the same thing walking from the clinic those years ago and would do so again in the future. It was the leaning that mattered, and more than anything he wanted to be with his wife, his love, at this moment.

At a small jog, he headed back around the house. To his right the band members, decked out in sombreros and embroidered costumes, tuned their instruments. Ian smiled first to himself, then to a co-worker of Rebecca's who thought the greeting was for her. He walked past the woman a few steps, looked around for Rebecca without spotting her, and backed up.

"You haven't happened to see Rebecca, have you?"

The woman shook her head.

On stage one of the band members introduced their first song, a very old Mexican folk song. The guitars were strummed and the song began. Rebecca was still not in sight.

Ignoring the music for the moment, Ian slipped out of the crowd, moved toward the side yard, into the garage, and then into the kitchen. It was empty. Through the French doors Ian could see the caterer and her assistant moving to fill platters while the guests were occupied with the music. Ian turned to go out when he heard Cain bark upstairs. She obviously wasn't too happy about being locked up for the day with so much activity outside, but there wasn't anything to do about that at the moment. Ian exited through the garage and headed once more to the festivities.

Ty Caller stood outside the crowd, tapping one foot to the music. He smiled as Ian approached, the first pleasantry they'd exchanged all day, perhaps ever.

"Have you seen Rebecca?" Ian asked.

Ty looked over. "Not since she went to get some more beverages. That was maybe fifteen minutes ago, though."

A slender chill spiraled up Ian's spine. *Fifteen minutes ago.*

"Why?" Caller asked, and then his brow knotted in confusion. He no longer seemed to be staring at Ian but at something up in the air. "What in the world?" he said, almost to himself.

Ian turned and saw the smoke, gray and thick, rising in plumes from the far side of the house. For a second he could do nothing but stare. "Is that smoke?" he asked the desert builder, and the question seemed to energize them.

Caller burst through the crowd and began shouting to his assistants. Ian turned in a circle for a second before catching sight of two uniformed officers heading to the front of the house. A third trailed, and Ian shouted for him.

"My house!" he yelled, pointing.

The officer nodded and said the other two were already on their way to alert the fire department. He would get some men and make sure the house was empty and the guests safe.

Ian nodded. It was a plan. A good plan. He thanked the officer, who immediately moved away, when he realized he still didn't know where his wife was. The smoke had startled the thought from his mind, but now it hit him like a sledgehammer. He jogged in the direction where the officer had disappeared but found the yard vacated. He glanced to the garage and thought the men might already be inside the house. Making his way across the cement, he approached the stairs when he saw it — the house alarm lights were glowing. When had the security system been reactivated?

The basement.

Rebecca had gone to get drinks in the basement, and now the alarm was back on, automatically locking the basement door.

He rushed through the door, across the kitchen, and to the basement, barely aware of heavy sounds coming from upstairs. A foot of white haze hovered near the ceiling, and Ian felt the burn in his lungs. He took a deep breath, opened the basement door, and shouted his wife's name.

"Ian!" he heard her reply. He stepped down a few steps, making sure to hold the door open. There was the sound of footsteps across the basement floor, and he sighed in relief that she was safe. In a second she appeared, and he was about to wave her up when a shadow crossed her face and shoulder. From behind her another figure appeared, shaved head, sunken eyes, and no eyebrows. He was moving toward Ian's wife.

"Rebecca!" Ian yelled and scrambled down the stairs. He heard her shout something and thought she was in pain. Lowering his shoulder, he aimed at the only thing he saw, a shirt patterned with tiger stripes, and lunged off the stairs. His arm screamed against the impact of the floor and he could hear both himself and the other groan.

"Ian!" he heard almost instantly and tried to lift his head. Something pinned it against the floor, and only by twisting could he escape the heavy weight of the man's outstretched arm. Scrambling to his feet, he turned.

Rebecca stood with her hand to her mouth, frightened. She looked at him, then at the floor. Ian looked down too. Martin

Hanover, shaved bald and dressed in a Cincinnati Bengals shirt, lay crumpled on the floor, a thin line of blood already coming from his mouth.

"It's not what it seems," Rebecca said and reached for Ian's hand. "He tried to save me."

Ian blinked. Upstairs there were shouts and loud footsteps.

"I was watching," said a small voice, and Ian gasped. He looked down. Hanover had pulled himself to a sitting position and was leaning against the wall, dabbing at his mouth. "I saw the fire start and knew she hadn't come out of the house yet. Nobody seemed to know. I found her, but we didn't know about the door."

Ian glanced up the stairs. The steel door was heavy and imposing. He'd let it slam shut. He looked back to Rebecca. She nodded.

"Louis set him up, Ian." She tried to say more, but there was more shouting and thundering upstairs.

"Fire," Ian said and realized they had no more time for talk. He didn't understand a moment of what was happening, but right now they had to get out of the house. Taking the steps three at a time, he climbed to the door and began pounding. He shouted twice, but there was so much noise, including approaching sirens, that they'd never be heard.

"We need to make noise," he said, running back downstairs.

Instantly, all three began to search for anything loud enough to attract attention. Ian was reaching for a hammer when he saw something even better. Leaning against the wall, rugged and straight, rested Katherine Jacoby's rendering of Christ's final torture. Ian remembered seeing an iron plate on the foot of the cross, and he could only imagine the racket it would make if struck on the door.

"Rebecca!" he called. "And . . . you." It took a moment, but they managed to lift the sculpture, Ian at the back holding the crossarms, and, with screaming calves and great bursts of breath, began to carry it up the stairs.

On the fourth step they rested for a moment, but for the first time Ian saw small tendrils of smoke slipping through the ceiling into the basement. He shouted for them to move. Four more steps were climbed and then another small break. More smoke slithered in.

"Come on!" he urged, and they pushed toward the door.

Sweating now both with exertion and the gathering heat of the fire, Ian called for them to hoist the cross like a battering ram and slam it into the door. Rebecca and Hanover nodded. His bald head dripped with perspiration.

The cross went up. They rocked it forward and it gave a low moan as though a gong had been sounded.

"Again!" Ian shouted, and once more the cross swept forward. This time the sound was true and loud. Metal on metal.

"Once more!"

The cross struck and splintered in two, the crash tearing into Ian's hand and thundering in his ears. Holding what remained, Ian gasped for breath and sank to his knees. His eyes burned, and he could barely even see when the door was yanked open.

"People!" someone shouted, surprised, and all three of them piled up the stairs and out of the basement.

Someone shouted for Ian, but he only thought of one thing — getting Rebecca out of the house. Grabbing her arm, he steered her through the remains of their living room and out the front door. The blast of fresh air stunned them both, and they gasped.

"Ian," Rebecca said, pulling herself to him, and slowly they began to walk away

from the house. A small part of him realized that they were leaning on each other,
but most of his thoughts were taken by the
hoses that dripped water across his desert
lawn and the men and women struggling to
save his house. His lips burned and his back
ached and he could swear he tasted blood,
but at least he was out here, walking on his
own, holding his wife's hand.

They'd danced with heat and been saved.
They'd walked among flames.

EPILOGUE

A few days passing, as well as an evening of rain and a break in the heat, had restored the green to the Merchants' lawn, though the bitter smell of damp ash still hung over the grounds, thick and sour as an illness. As Ian rubbed sleep from his eyes, Oakley's cruiser pulled down the driveway for what Ian hoped would be the last time.

He met the officer near the garage and led him out back. A few chairs remained on the porch, and it would be better to talk there. For a few minutes neither said a word.

Finally Ian broke the silence. "Fire marshall get back to you?"

Oakley nodded. "You don't want to know."

"Arson?" Ian asked, hoping it wouldn't be.

"Faulty wiring in your security system."

"You're —" Ian began to say but gave it up and heard himself give a small laugh. He

580

noticed Oakley couldn't keep back a grin either. It was just so ridiculous in a lot of ways. He should have figured something was wrong, as many times as the thing had gone off.

"So Hanover's off the hook for that?"

Oakley nodded. "He'll go down for the train porter's injury, though. And whatever you and Rebecca want to throw at him."

Ian didn't respond for a moment. Then he said, "He saved Rebecca."

"That'll help. And to be honest, since we picked him up in the woods he's been cooperative. But somebody's got to pay." Then he waved his hand. "Later," he said. "You and Rebecca can talk it over. Decide if you believe him about Louis's double-cross."

Ian was realizing this thing wasn't over yet, when Oakley spoke again.

"We're going to try to find Norman Gruitt."

"Fine," Ian replied. He knew Kevin was worried about the old painter. And that with the prison connection established, Oakley thought the artist might have had a lot more to do with the stalking than first imagined.

"You want to know about the eyebrows?" Oakley asked, interrupting Ian's thoughts once more.

"Sure."

"He said they bother him when he wears stockings over his head."

Ian raised an eyebrow.

"Yeah, that was our reaction, too."

Another silence followed and Ian glanced to his house. That was his next big concern, figuring out what to do with the house. There was a lot of smoke damage but very little structural concern. It'd be possible to fix up, but perhaps not by winter. Part of Ian hoped that they could just sell and move into something smaller.

"So what now?" asked Oakley. His pad was put away, and he'd turned to Ian. The officer's eyes looked rested. Ian wondered if the same were true for Anne. "What will you do now?" the officer clarified.

Ian smiled. It was a question he'd answered for himself just yesterday after thinking back through the whole stack of weeks. Again and again he returned to the questions that had dogged his days and dreams and forced him to flee to the coffee house: *How will I ever write another horror novel? And who am I if I can't write anymore?*

And since the *how* had been answered in the negative, he'd been searching for an answer to the *who*. He thought he knew now. Knew ever since that night in the basement and those trembling bones.

"I'm going to write," he said. "It's what I do. I'm going to write the book I was writing about this whole mess and explain the one thing I've learned through it all."

"What's that?" Oakley asked.

Laughing, Ian said, "You'll have to wait for the book."

Oakley looked stunned.

"Just kidding. Mostly what I learned is that you're either living life as a dead man — just a walking skeleton — or you realize what it is you were always missing and live for that. I got so wrapped up in thinking about the skeleton underneath that I forgot for a time about living."

Oakley shook his head. "Maybe I will wait for the book." They both laughed, and then Oakley stood and stretched. A long shadow fell out behind him. He patted his pockets as if searching for his keys and said, "I guess this is it for a while, then."

Ian looked up, a little stunned. It would be it. There'd be no reason to see Oakley again. "Well," Ian said.

"Thanks again for helping Anne and me." He stuck out his hand.

"And thank you," Ian said, "well, for always being on duty."

They shook hands, and Oakley was about to say something, when his eyes narrowed just a little. "Huh," he said, perplexed. Ian turned around.

There, at the back of the yard, hopped the jackrabbit. Had to be. Its long ears were unmistakable, and it had a strange loping gait. The thing sat munching on grass for a moment and then hopped over to a low branch on the shrubs.

"Son of a gun," Ian said, mostly to himself. "He made it after all."

They watched for a moment, and then the detective moved toward his car. "Stay out of trouble, Merchant."

"Mike," Ian said, stopping the officer. "I do other things than get stalked, you know."

"Oh yeah?"

"Yeah. Get to a Sox game on occasion. Stuff like that."

"Ah."

"Got four tickets for next Sunday. You and Annie interested?"

Oakley paused, but just for a moment. "Sure," he said. "I know Anne would love to see Rebecca again."

"Well, then," said Ian. "After church we'll head out. Of course you're welcome to join us there, too."

"We'll see," said Oakley. He climbed into

his cruiser and headed up the driveway. At the top he stopped for a moment, waved, and took off.

Ian sat for just a moment longer. He glanced at his watch and realized he still had the whole day ahead of him. The hotel room and his laptop awaited. Endless minutes and hours, all stretching forward. Countless days to live — to live and remember living.

ACKNOWLEDGMENTS

This is the first real opportunity I've had to make a "public" statement of thanks to those who've been influential in my writing and to do so is a privilege. Recognition is due to a number of people who helped steer this from first word to last.

First, to my editors, David Horton and Julie Smith, because you helped me see the better book yet unwritten.

Second, to a good friend Craig McSparran, whose help was invaluable in shaping the history portions of this manuscript.

Third, to Jeremy, Dan, and Joe. I rely on you guys for fellowship rather than editorial advice, and you came through with both.

Finally, to my family — my mother, father, and sister, whom I love. And Sarah. Because.

ABOUT THE AUTHOR

David Ryan Long is a graduate of Penn State University with a degree in creative writing. *Ezekiel's Shadow* is his first novel. He, his wife, and their daughter make their home in Minneapolis, Minnesota.

The employees of Thorndike Press hope you have enjoyed this Large Print book. All our Thorndike and Wheeler Large Print titles are designed for easy reading, and all our books are made to last. Other Thorndike Press Large Print books are available at your library, through selected bookstores, or directly from us.

For information about titles, please call:
  (800) 223-1244

or visit our Web site at:
  www.gale.com/thorndike
  www.gale.com/wheeler

To share your comments, please write:
  Publisher
  Thorndike Press
  295 Kennedy Memorial Drive
  Waterville, ME 04901